PENGUIN ENGLISH LIBRARY

CRANFORD AND COUSIN PHILLIS
ELIZABETH GASKELL

Peter Keating is a lecturer in English
Literature at the University of Edinburgh. He is the author of *The Working Classes in Victorian Fiction* (1971)
and the editor of *Matthew Arnold:
Selected Prose*, which is published in the
Penguin English Library.

ELIZABETH GASKELL

Cranford and Cousin Phillis

❖

Edited by
PETER KEATING

PENGUIN BOOKS

Penguin Books Ltd, Harmondsworth, Middlesex, England
Penguin Books Inc., 7110 Ambassador Road, Baltimore, Maryland 21207, U.S.A.
Penguin Books Australia Ltd, Ringwood, Victoria, Australia
Penguin Books Canada Ltd, 41 Steelcase Road West, Markham, Ontario, Canada
Penguin Books (N.Z.) Ltd, 182–190 Wairau Road, Auckland 10, New Zealand

—

Published in Penguin English Library 1976
Introduction and Notes Copyright © Peter Keating, 1976

—

Made and printed in Great Britain
by Hazell Watson & Viney Ltd
Aylesbury, Bucks
Set in Linotype Juliana

Contents

Introduction

ON 31 January 1850 Charles Dickens wrote to Mrs Gaskell invit-
her to contribute to his new weekly journal *Household Words*.
His approach was extremely flattering: 'As I do honestly know
that there is no living English writer whose aid I would desire to
enlist in preference to the authoress of *Mary Barton* (a book that
most profoundly affected and impressed me), I venture to ask
whether you can give me any hope that you will write a short
tale, or any number of tales, for the projected pages.'* Mrs Gaskell
responded by sending 'Lizzie Leigh', a short story drawing on a
similar Manchester background to *Mary Barton*, and Dickens gave
it a prominent place in the first number of his journal. The relationship between the two writers was later to be severely
strained, but at this early stage it was one of respect and friendship on both sides : Dickens had captured the services of a novelist
he admired, and Mrs Gaskell had obtained a respectable, well-
paid outlet for almost anything she cared to write. Although she
was not bound contractually to Dickens, much of Mrs Gaskell's
best work over the next thirteen years appeared initially in the
periodicals he edited, at first *Household Words* and later *All The
Year Round*. Sketches, Christmas tales, historical studies, brief
anecdotal articles, and short stories were all accepted gratefully
by Dickens, as well as the serial version of *North and South*,
which infuriated him, and the eight sketches making up *Cranford*, which delighted him.

The first part of what was eventually to become *Cranford*,
consisting of the first two chapters of the present edition, appeared
in *Household Words* on 13 December 1851, after Dickens had
given it the title 'Our Society at Cranford' and diplomatically
changed the name of Captain Brown's favourite author from Boz
to Thomas Hood. It seems clear that Mrs Gaskell intended 'Our
Society at Cranford' to stand as a self-contained sketch. As she

* *The Letters of Charles Dickens*, Macmillan, 1893, pp. 212–13.

later explained to Ruskin: 'The beginning of *Cranford* was one paper in *Household Words*, and I never meant to write more, so killed Captain Brown very much against my will.'* The irregular way in which the remaining seven instalments were published suggests that although Mrs Gaskell soon changed her mind about writing further episodes, it was some time before she began to think of them as being sufficiently interrelated to make up a book: instalments 2 to 4 (Chapters III to VIII) appeared early in 1852, and the final four instalments (Chapters IX to XVI) between January and May 1853.

One reason for the delay is that Mrs Gaskell was busy writing *Ruth*, a three-volume novel which was published in January 1853. This marked a return to the social-problem fiction with which she had made her name, and as the new novel dealt with illegitimacy, a topic as controversial as the relationship between employers and employees which she had explored in *Mary Barton*, she fully expected, and in fact received, a good deal of hostile criticism. The strain imposed by this anticipated reception of *Ruth* was sufficient reason to take her mind off *Cranford*.

But it is also reasonable to assume that Mrs Gaskell was coming to realize the potential of the *Cranford* sketches, and was contemplating how they could be given a greater sense of unity than she originally intended. When she did return to the subject in January 1853 it was to introduce Signor Brunoni to Cranford Society, a deliberate echoing of Captain Brown, whose less exotic but equally disruptive appearance in the town Mrs Gaskell had regretfully terminated more than a year earlier. Signor Brunoni was the first of a number of comparisons and contrasts now introduced. They were to be used to blend together the two groups of sketches, and to give added depth of meaning to the book.

Another reason for continuing to write about Cranford was the enthusiasm the early sketches aroused in both Mrs Gaskell herself and the readers of *Household Words*. Writing to a friend about the cheapness of some dress material she had bought, Mrs Gaskell slipped naturally into Cranford terminology: ' "Elegant economy" as we say in Cranford – There now I dare say you

* J. A. V. Chapple and Arthur Pollard, eds., *The Letters of Mrs Gaskell*, Manchester University Press, 1966, p. 748.

think I've gone crazy but I'm not; but I've written a couple of tales about Cranford in *Household Words*, so you must allow me to quote from myself.'* Dickens described 'A Love Affair at Cranford' as 'delightful, and touched in the tenderest and most delicate manner'† and urged Mrs Gaskell to write more; while John Forster, Dickens's own closest friend and respected critic, wrote of the sketches: 'They positively grow better and better. I never saw so nice, so exquisite a touch. The little book which collects them will be a "hit" if there be any taste left for that kind of social painting.'‡ *Cranford* was published in book form in June 1853, followed by a second edition in the same year, and a cheap edition two years later. It was certainly much admired though not perhaps quite the 'hit' that Forster had prophesied, at least in terms of copies sold and money earned from it. By 1863 Mrs Gaskell could complain to her daughter that while *Cranford* was 'worth gold' it was out of print,§ and likely to remain so, because of a disagreement over copyright, but the quarrel between the publishers Chapman and Hall and Smith Elder was resolved almost immediately and an illustrated edition appeared in 1864.

The immense popularity of *Cranford* developed only after Mrs Gaskell's death in 1865. A. B. Hopkins estimated that by 1947 there had been about 170 editions and reprints, only nine of which appeared during Mrs Gaskell's lifetime. The peak years were 1899–1910 when 'the book was published seventy-five times; thirty-nine times in London; thirty-four in the United States, and twice in Leipzig in German translations.'¶ Impressive as these figures are in demonstrating the continuing popularity of *Cranford*, even more interesting is the consistency of the kind of praise given to the book. The terms used by Dickens and Forster – 'delightful', 'tender', 'delicate', 'exquisite,' 'social painting' – recur in *Cranford* criticism, and are usually linked to an acknowledgement of the lack of unity that one would expect from its original irregular publication in periodical form. A. W. Ward describes

* ibid., p. 174.

† *The Letters of Charles Dickens*, p. 262.

‡ Quoted in A. B. Hopkins, *Elizabeth Gaskell: Her Life and Work*, John Lehmann, 1952, p. 104.

§ *Letters*, p. 719.   ¶ *Elizabeth Gaskell*, p. 102.

Cranford as a 'brief series of sketches, strung together with easy grace like a wreath of flowers and ivy-leaves', and as 'an unpretentious but exquisite prose idyl.'* And A. B. Hopkins, author of the best biography of Mrs Gaskell, offers a similar description: '*Cranford* is practically structureless; this is part of its charm. The successive scenes pass before the reader as easily as if he were slipping different coloured beads along a string. From the architectural standpoint, the only unifying elements are furnished by the place and the people.'† Such views clearly represent the experience of many of the book's readers: no one can surely have failed to respond to its charm and 'exquisite social painting'. The problem is that these descriptions do not take us very far into the heart of the book; nor do they explain why it is that many adult readers (and it is emphatically a book for adults, not school-children) find *Cranford* an extraordinarily sensitive and at times painfully moving work.

It is a mistake to attribute the continuing popularity of *Cranford* simply to period charm, and to regard the book as a kind of literary pot-pourri, as though its importance lies in the sweetly innocent fragrance it is supposed to exhale. While it undeniably, and obviously, lacks the massive solidity of the great Victorian novels, it possesses a remarkable unity of tone and feeling which comes from Mrs Gaskell's rigorous exploration of a dying way of life. The social world of *Cranford* is sharply and precisely observed; its sentiment tightly controlled; and its analysis of an early Victorian country town, captured at a crucial moment of transition in English society, is penetrating. The famous 'charm', 'delicacy', and 'fragility' have their parts to play, but exclusive concentration on them can lead to a serious underestimation of the strength of *Cranford*, and it is, in reality, both as delicate and strong as that piece of 'fine old lace' which survived none the worse for being swallowed by Mrs Forrester's cat.

No one has done more to encourage this limited view than Hugh Thomson, whose illustrations for the 1891 edition established, during the period of the book's greatest popularity, the

* Introduction to *Cranford* (the Knutsford edition of the works of Mrs Gaskell, 8 vols., 1906), pp. ix, xi.

† *Elizabeth Gaskell*, p. 108.

image of the inhabitants of Cranford as being quaintly ridiculous. Mrs Gaskell does, of course, constantly draw attention to the odd or ridiculous nature of her characters' behaviour, but she is always careful to reveal, at such moments, the human or social reality which gives oddity a meaning beyond itself. Hugh Thomson's illustrations reflect little of this. They are curiously static, the men and women frozen, the human element obliterated by exaggerated period costumes and gestures. Nothing could be further from the true spirit of *Cranford*, which developed out of Mrs Gaskell's concern with the 'condition of England' question.

*

Mrs Gaskell was greatly upset by the criticism that in her first novel *Mary Barton* (1848) she had been guilty of class bias, favouring the workers against the employers. 'No one can feel more deeply than I', she wrote to a friend, 'how *wicked* it is to do anything to excite class against class; and the sin has been unconscious if I have done so . . . no praise could compensate me for the self-reproach I shall feel if I have written unjustly.'* The criticism was in one sense justified, as Mrs Gaskell soon came to realize, and when she returned to the theme of industrial relationships in *North and South* (1855), she was determined that the same charge would not be levelled at this novel. In *Mary Barton* the whole of Mrs Gaskell's sympathies are given to the workers, the employers being, in the main, portrayed as greedy, selfish, and indifferent to the men they employ. The symbolic reconciliation scene at the close of the novel between Carson and John Barton shows clearly enough that Mrs Gaskell was concerned to bring the warring classes together rather than do anything to divide them further, but her personal sympathies and understanding pulled her to one side, and her inexperience as a novelist, at this early stage in her career, did not at first allow her to see this was so. *North and South* is structured around the awakening consciousness of the heroine, Margaret Hale, to the need for deeper understanding between the classes. The social message is the same as that of *Mary Barton*, but its dramatization within the novel, as well as the variety of attitudes and values it encompasses,

* *Letters*, p. 67.

is far more profound. The central conflict between masters and men is just one strand in a complex web of contrasting attitudes and values (the North of England versus the South : culture versus lack of culture : past versus present : energy versus lethargy) so that the novel moves constantly beyond the industrial theme, by which it is usually placed, to become an exploration of the present state of English society, its connection with the past, and the need to prepare for its future. *North and South* is the most wide-ranging and balanced of that group of novels of the 1840s and 50s usually classified collectively as being about the 'Condition of England', and this sense of balance, a weighing up of all sides, was Mrs Gaskell's answer to the critics of *Mary Barton* as well as her final and deeply considered conclusion on the subject.

Edgar Wright has argued that Mrs Gaskell's determination to establish a balanced social viewpoint in *North and South* is the cause of one of the novel's weaknesses ('She tries to come to terms with the Manchester ethos but the resolution is artificial'),* and this is surely correct. The present interest, however, lies in the development of Mrs Gaskell's view between *Mary Barton* and *North and South*, and in this *Cranford* plays a crucial role.

In July 1849, nine months after the publication of *Mary Barton*, Mrs Gaskell published in *Sartain's Magazine* an article called 'The Last Generation in England'. Many of the incidents later to become so famous in *Cranford* appear here for the first time, but Mrs Gaskell speaks in her own voice, and attaches to her article a direct social purpose which was later to disappear :

This quarter of an hour's chance reading has created a wish in me to put upon record some of the details of country town life, either observed by myself, or handed down to me by older relations; for even in small towns, scarcely removed from villages, the phases of society are rapidly changing; and much will appear strange, which yet occurred only in the generation preceding ours.

The shift of consciousness was clearly from working-class Manchester, to which her marriage had introduced her, to the small country town of Knutsford in which she had grown up; it repre-

* *Mrs Gaskell: The Basis for Reassessment*, Oxford University Press, 1965, p. 140.

sented not an escape from sordid reality as it is so often presented, but rather a facing up to the extreme nature of the contrast of changing 'phases of society', which Mrs Gaskell now found forced upon her. In the works that followed 'The Last Generation in England', the small country town recurred, examined from different angles in *The Moorland Cottage*, *Ruth*, and, most interestingly, 'Mr Harrison's Confessions' which leads directly into *Cranford*.

'Mr Harrison's Confessions' is a slighter, much less impressive work than *Cranford*; tightly plotted to create a sense of farce and centred upon a conventional sentimentalized love story. But the basic situation of a small town dominated by women 'of a certain rank' who set the tone for their society and determine its values is already here, and there are other features which shortly after were to reappear in *Cranford*. Miss Tomkinson, who is described as being 'hard and masculine' and 'a perfect grenadier', and her younger, prettier sister Caroline, anticipate Miss Jenkyns and Matty, though the relationship between the sisters develops in a different way; there is the submerged sense of panic which is to be treated memorably in *Cranford* ('It was the custom of the ladies, when alarmed at night, to call an imaginary police, which had, they thought, an intimidating effect'); and even the name Hoggins is here to denote someone who is regarded as vulgar by the ladies of Duncombe, but who nonetheless marries into their circle. The similarities, however, are less interesting than the differences, for in the nine months which separate the first publication of the two works, Mrs Gaskell's technique developed remarkably.

The most striking change is in the use of a narrator. In both cases it is a young person who describes an older generation, but Mr Harrison is the hero of his own confessions; young, handsome, and single, he is pursued by the women of Duncombe almost regardless of their age, attractiveness, or eligibility, and survives to win Sophy, the vicar's beautiful daughter. Although Mr Harrison's adventures are alien to the tone of *Cranford*, he reappears in a brief vignette at the end of Chapter IX, transformed into Mr Hayter, the elderly rector who attends the entertainment at Cranford's Assembly Room surrounded by his National School boys who protect him from the Cranford ladies. Mary Smith notices this, as she notices everything that goes on in Cranford: 'To tell the truth, I always suspected Miss Pole of having given very rigorous chase to Mr Hayter when he first came to Cranford; and not the less, because now she appeared to share so vividly in his dread lest her name should ever be coupled with his.'

The impression often given by a first reading of *Cranford* is that the narrator is virtually anonymous, or simply a cover for Mrs Gaskell's own observations; certainly we learn of her name only late in the book when she begins to take a more active part in Cranford's affairs, and it would be foolish to try to argue that she is in any sense a fully developed character. But she is by no means anonymous. Her individuality is fixed from the beginning and plays an important part in establishing *Cranford*'s distinctive tone. By making her a woman Mrs Gaskell allowed her access to the inner lives of the Amazons – Mr Harrison's view was necessarily external – and by emphasizing both her youth and connections with industrial Drumble, it was possible to heighten the strangeness of Cranford's way of life by a subtle mixture of ironic distancing and affectionate concern. Mary Smith's early comments on fashion and manners neatly illustrates this: 'I will answer for it, the last gigot, the last tight and scanty petticoat in wear in England, was seen in Cranford – and seen without a smile.' The gentle smile is characteristic, as is the slightly slangy speech, of one generation regarding another. She has a strong sense of the ridiculous:

The card-table was an animated scene to watch; four ladies' heads, with niddle-noddling caps, all nearly meeting over the middle of the table, in their eagerness to whisper quick enough and loud enough: and every now and then came Miss Barker's 'Hush, ladies! if you please, hush! Mrs Jamieson is asleep.'

And at times her own view of what is important in life clashes briefly with those of the Cranford ladies:

'And how came Miss Matilda not to marry him?' asked I.
'Oh, I don't know. She was willing enough, I think; but you know Cousin Thomas would not have been enough of a gentleman for the rector and Miss Jenkyns.'

'Well! but they were not to marry him,' said I impatiently.

Her common-sense objection is brushed aside. Until Miss Matty's financial trouble Mary Smith is treated as a child by the Amazons, and she tells us herself that at home she is regarded as being 'indiscreet and incautious', characteristics which make her the ideal commentator on this world, for again and again it is her response which directs the reader's sympathy and prevents sentiment from running out of control. It is Mary Smith who bravely imitates Mr Holbrook's eating habits: 'I saw, I imitated, I survived!'; who sees through Miss Barker's attempt to ingratiate herself into the Cranford circle by serving an unusually lavish supper: 'Another tray! "Oh, gentility!" thought I, "can you endure this last shock?"'; and who is capable of describing as Miss Pole's morning costume, 'her being without teeth, and wearing a veil to conceal the deficiency.' This, and many similar comments, are directed at the reader: in the company of the Cranford ladies, Mary Smith's kindness of heart allows her to control her natural impetuosity: '"Did he look" – (unable to shape my question prudently, I put it in another form) – "How did he look?"'

It is not simply a matter of Mary Smith being two generations removed from Miss Matty and her friends, for, as has often been pointed out, she is like Mrs Gaskell in having 'vibrated all her life between Drumble and Cranford', and in this she anticipates Margaret Hale, the heroine of *North and South*, who must eventually decide between rural and industrial ways of life. Mary Smith is not called upon to make such a decision, but she is clearly the representative of a more vital and energetic world than that of Cranford. When Miss Matty loses her money invested in the Town and County Bank, her friends do all they can to help, but it is Mary Smith, drawing on both her Drumble experience and her sympathetic understanding of Cranford, who persuades Miss Matty that setting up a small shop could be the answer to her problems. It is Mary Smith's father, the Drumble businessman, who actually comes to the rescue of the Amazons, and his daughter who has, as usual, the last ironic word:

But to return to Miss Matty. It was really very pleasant to see how her unselfishness and simple sense of justice called out the same good qualities in others. She never never seemed to think any one would impose upon her, because she would be so grieved to do it to them. I have heard her put a stop to the asseverations of the man who brought her coals by quietly saying, 'I am sure you would be sorry to bring me wrong weight;' and if the coals were short measure that time, I don't believe they ever were again . . . my father says 'such simplicity might be very well in Cranford, but would never do in the world.' And I fancy the world must be very bad, for with all my father's suspicion of every one with whom he has dealings, and in spite of all his many precautions, he lost upwards of a thousand pounds by roguery only last year.

If the Amazons are helpless without Drumble, Drumble has by no means all the answers, as Mary Smith realizes.

It is this contrast between two seemingly separate worlds that Mrs Gaskell is exploring in *Cranford*. The small country town, gentle, kind, affectionate, and feminine (Mary Smith's use of the word 'Amazons' is, of course, an ironic reinforcement of the qualities not normally associated with the mythical Amazons), and Drumble, vital, energetic, forceful, and masculine, represent opposed values, and, respectively, a way of life that belongs essentially to the past and one that has taken control of the future. Mary Smith gradually comes to realize that in spite of the pettiness, snobbery, social and sexual frustration to be found in Cranford society, the Amazons are not simply quaint and old-fashioned, but live according to a code which puts a strong emphasis on humanity, loyalty, kindness, and good neighbourliness. And in spite of her father's reduction of these virtues to 'simplicity', she knows that they are precisely what the new bustling industrial world lacks. If it has no place for what Miss Matty represents, then the future is bleak: 'We all love Miss Matty, and I somehow think we are all of us better when she is near us.'

This central contrast between present and future, as seen by Mary Smith, is deepened by a similar contrast between past and present. Allowing for one or two unimportant inconsistencies, it is possible to date the action of *Cranford* with some precision. The references to the railways, the Catholic Emancipation Act, and the publication of Dickens's novels, fixes the main period as the

1830s and 40s. Miss Jenkyns dies in 1843, slightly older than her sister Matty who is in her fifties. The story of their parents' courtship and marriage told in Chapter V takes us back to the late eighteenth century, and there are several references to show that Miss Jenkyns and Matty grew up during the early years of the Napoleonic Wars : in 1805 Miss Jenkyns was old enough to visit friends in Newcastle.

These dates provide only the most obvious framework. Within it Mrs Gaskell builds up, with precision and subtlety, a structure of references and allusions which she employs partly to establish a sense of period, but more importantly, to indicate the nature of social change in the early nineteenth century, and her skill in this respect has received nothing like the acknowledgement it deserves. The specific details of furniture, fashions, eating habits, ways of speaking, and books or authors read or admired, act as social and historical indices filtered through the consciousness of Mary Smith. It is for this reason that while *Cranford* is a self-contained work, its true achievement can be better appreciated if it is placed carefully in Mrs Gaskell's development, and that means taking into account her growth as both an artist and a social thinker, for the two are inextricably blended in her best work.*

Mrs Gaskell's extensive use of social and historical detail is best made clear through the notes to this edition, but an illustration of how exactly the technique works within *Cranford* can be given by looking at the contrast drawn between Dr Johnson and Dickens. The clash between Captain Brown and Miss Jenkyns over the relative merits of Johnson and Dickens is one of the best-remembered parts of *Cranford*, as also is Captain Brown's death which Miss Jenkyns associated with his love of Dickens : 'Poor, dear, infatuated man', she sighs. As we have seen Mrs Gaskell later felt that she had killed Captain Brown a little too hastily, but she did not kill off the contrast between eighteenth-century and modern literature : this recurs in a variety

* The one really thorough attempt to trace Mrs Gaskell's artistic development is by Edgar Wright, who effectively rejects the traditional view that Mrs Gaskell simply wrote about different phases of her life without these being connected in any significant way in her work.

of ways throughout the book, reinforcing dominant themes and expanding the significance of central concerns.

In the 1830s the need to break completely with eighteenth-century literary models was felt by many writers. The balance and conciseness which exuded a sense of social confidence came to be seen as inappropriate and backward looking in the turbulent years after Waterloo. The writer who exerted the most influence in this respect, and who radically and consciously broke symbolically with the past was Carlyle. On 4 June 1835 he wrote to John Sterling:

> Do you reckon this really a time for Purism of Style . . .? I do not: with whole ragged battalions of Scott's-Novel Scotch, with Irish, German, French, and even Newspaper Cockney . . . storming in on us, and the whole structure of our Johnsonian English breaking up from its foundations, – revolution *there* as visible as anywhere else !*

Carlyle had already initiated this revolutionary overthrow of Johnsonian English with *Sartor Resartus* (1833–4) which had both shocked and delighted early Victorian readers. Dickens's background was very different from Carlyle's – he was in one sense a product of the 'Newspaper Cockney' which Carlyle lists as one of the forces making for stylistic change – but from the beginning of his career as a novelist there was fierce controversy among critics and readers about his strikingly individual style, or rather lack of style if the eighteenth-century model was called into use. And the controversy pursued Dickens throughout his life, with critics frequently making unfavourable comparisons between his style and that of Thackeray, especially, but later George Eliot as well. As Philip Collins has written: 'The comparison [between Dickens and Thackeray] became as much one of the set-pieces of Victorian journalism as, in the seventeenth century, had been the comparison between Shakespeare and Jonson.'†

* Alexander Carlyle, ed., *Letters of Thomas Carlyle to John Stuart Mill, John Sterling, and Robert Browning*, 1923, p. 192.

† *Dickens: The Critical Heritage*, Routledge, 1971, p. 3. See also on this topic, George H. Ford, *Dickens and his Readers*, Princeton University Press, 1955, chapter 6.

It is this controversy that underlies the clash between Captain Brown and Miss Jenkyns :

'Dr Johnson's style is a model for young beginners. My father recommended it to me when I began to write letters, – I have formed my own style upon it; I recommend it to your favourite.'

'I should be very sorry for him to exchange his style for any such pompous writing,' said Captain Brown.

Miss Jenkyns felt this as a personal affront, in a way of which the captain had not dreamed.

Captain Brown may not appreciate the full significance of the revolution he is advocating, but Mrs Gaskell certainly did. She makes it clear in this exchange and later that Miss Jenkyns is merely mouthing opinions handed down from her adored father, with very little understanding of what kind of writer Johnson was, and a mind closed to anything going on in the world around her. Captain Brown not only has more knowledge of Dr Johnson than Miss Jenkyns, he possesses the warmth and immediacy of character required to recognize the startling originality of a young writer, and to ignore the sneer about it being vulgar to publish in numbers – advice which Dickens himself received from his friends, and rejected : his connection with the railways (one of the most potent means of social change in Victorian Britain) gives added power to his disruptive influence.

Time and again Dr Johnson's name appears in *Cranford* doing much to evoke that 'spirit of the eighteenth century' which A. Stanton Whitfield noted as haunting the book,* and beyond this providing Mary Smith with a literary standard for everything she considers stiffly formal and out of touch with modern life. In Chapter V as she sits with Miss Matty by the fire burning the past, a characteristic distinction is drawn :

With my idea of the rector, derived from a picture in the dining-parlour, stiff and stately, in a huge full-bottomed wig, with gown, cassock, and bands, and his hand upon a copy of the only sermon he ever published, – it was strange to read these letters. They were full of eager, passionate ardour; short homely sentences, right fresh from the heart (very different from the grand Latinised, Johnsonian

* *Mrs Gaskell: Her Life and Work*, Routledge, p. 136.

style of the printed sermon, preached before some judge at assize time).

We are meant to pick up the description three chapters earlier of Miss Matty's letters as being, 'nice', 'kind' and 'rambling', and their human superiority over those of her sister: 'Everything in them was stately and grand like herself.' Miss Jenkyns inherits from her father the tradition of divorcing literary style from life, as well as the suppression of personal emotion in the name of respectability, and Miss Matty's happiness is unconsciously sacrificed in the process. Given the right occasion Miss Jenkyns can display spontaneous generosity, but her normal response to any emotional situation is to retreat to the safety of her jockey cap and Johnsonian English: 'as she put in each clove, she uttered a Johnsonian sentence. Indeed, she never could think of the Browns without talking Johnson; and, as they were seldom absent from her thoughts just then, I heard many a rolling three-piled sentence.'

On her deathbed Miss Jenkyns has Flora read to her from the *Rambler* while her mind wanders back to her childhood, confusing 'Boz' and 'Old Poz', and allowing Flora to ignore this 'improving reading' in favour of the *Christmas Carol* 'which Miss Matty had left on the table'. This clearly represents Dickens's victory over Johnson, though Miss Matty does try to persevere with her dead sister's favourite. When she visits her old lover Mr Holbrook she finds a man knowledgeable about the work of poets from 'Shakespeare and George Herbert to those of our own day', and with a particular passion for Tennyson (Victorian poetry's popular equivalent to the novelist Dickens). Yet when Miss Matty tries to enter the conversation by referring to, 'that beautiful poem of Dr Johnson's my sister used to read', Mr Holbrook has to confess that he knows little of Johnson's poetry, though one suspects not perhaps as little as Miss Matty. In one sense Holbrook is similar to Captain Brown, for here once again straightforward honesty and scorn for the meaningless trappings of Cranford gentility are associated with being alive to modern forces, both literary and non-literary; Mr Holbrook's admiration for France is even more disconcerting to the Amazons than Captain Brown's connection with the railway. His parting gift to Miss Matty is a book of Tennyson's poetry; with the improvement of Miss Matty's financial position on the return of Peter, she gives to Mary Smith, 'the handsomest-bound and best edition of Dr Johnson's works that could be procured'. Miss Matty's copy of Tennyson's poety is placed together with the Bible on her bedside table, but this acts solely as a personal consolation; her own rebellious spirit was crushed long ago and to the end she remains loyal to her sister as the true arbiter of taste.

The many references to Johnson and modern literature are not therefore simply local in their significance, but serve to create a wider framework which can encompass both the passage of time and the changing nature of fundamental attitudes and values, and the same is true of other kinds of historical and social reference throughout the book. Cranford is a town beseiged by forces it is incapable of understanding and ultimately of withstanding. There is no way in which it can adapt itself to the social transformation that will inevitably come. Cranford is the representative of those rapidly changing 'phases of society' described in 'The Last Generation in England', and it was to emphasize just this point that Mrs Gaskell peopled her town with spinsters and widows. The warrior imagery used to describe them – they are 'Spartans' as well as 'Amazons' – fixes with ironic precision their uncertain position. The few victories they enjoy (such as Miss Matty insisting on cashing the farm labourer's worthless five-pound note and the subsequent rallying of her friends to stave off financial disaster) are movingly humane gestures, but, as we have seen, they are regarded by the outside world merely as confirmation of Cranford's essential 'simplicity'. And it is difficult not to feel that this is part of the point being made by Mrs Gaskell herself, for much of the pathos of *Cranford* derives from the numerous defeats the Amazons suffer, and their gradual isolation from the mainstream of Victorian life. There is throughout the book a strong sense of modernity in a wide variety of forms encroaching upon the stability of Cranford : Dickens, the railways, an Irish beggarwoman, new and strange fashions, vulgar trade, financial crashes, news of gangs roaming the countryside, the widow of a peer (even if only a Scottish peer) who is so indifferent to the glories of the aristocracy that she marries a man called Hoggins.

Against such forces and shifting values, the Amazons are helpless. Sometimes they panic, at other times demonstrate total incomprehension (as when Mrs Forrester seems to believe that the Catholic Emancipation Bill will make it easier to get lace from the Continent); at an early stage they are dominated by Miss Jenkyns, who establishes a rigidly narrow and bullying exclusive code of conduct; and later they have the example of Mrs Jamieson, who on Mr and Mrs Hoggins's wedding day has her window blinds drawn down 'as if for a funeral'. The whole paraphernalia of 'elegant economy', while clearly necessary in some cases, becomes with them an obsessive substitute for involvement in the larger world of Cranford, and even their real attempts at controlling their own lives are ineffective. For all her aggressiveness Miss Jenkyns is shown to be a very poor businesswoman, and although Miss Matty believes she has adapted successfully to genteel trade, her little shop is a failure and she is supported by the kindness of her friends. When things really go wrong men must be brought in from the outside to correct them: Mr Smith from Drumble, Peter from India. And throughout the book Mary Smith maintains a superb balance of tone; observing, commenting, filling in details, dropping hints, bridging the old and new worlds, displaying the true humanity of Cranford together with its snobbery and stultifying narrowness, creating sympathy by her gradual focusing of attention on Miss Matty's inner life.

In a pioneering essay, written to counteract the critical tendency of regarding *Cranford* as 'a sympathetic record of a life of innocent triviality', Martin Dodsworth has argued that the psychological accuracy of the book lies in Mrs Gaskell's portrayal of the Amazons' sexual inadequacy in trying to live in a world without men.* The argument is a persuasive one, heightening as it does central aspects of the book which are normally glossed over – Miss Jenkyns's adoption of a substitute father role, her hostility to Captain Brown and sense of guilt at his death, and, most dis-

* 'Women without Men at Cranford', *Essays in Criticism*, April 1963.

turbingly, the pernicious influence she exercises over Miss Matty, whom, it seems impossible reasonably to deny, Mrs Gaskell treats as a study in repressed sexuality. At one moment Miss Jenkyns herself relaxes her normally rigid code and in doing so shocks her timid sister :

'Oh, goodness me!' she said. 'Deborah, there's a gentleman sitting in the drawing-room, with his arm round Miss Jessie's waist!' Miss Matty's eyes looked large with terror.
  Miss Jenkyns snubbed her down in an instant.
  'The most proper place in the world for his arm to be in. Go away, Matilda, and mind your own business.'

In temporarily departing from her public image as 'a model of feminine decorum', Miss Jenkyns is acknowledging that, in this particular case, a man is needed, for marriage alone can solve the problem of Jessie Brown's poverty and help her to avoid the sterility of life that spinsterhood in Cranford would represent. It is only later in one of Miss Matty's revealing moments of reminiscence that we see possibly deeper personal motives at work in Miss Jenkyns: 'Deborah said to me, the day of my mother's funeral, that if she had a hundred offers she never would marry and leave my father. It is not very likely she would have so many – I don't know that she had one; but it was not less to her credit to say so.' While Miss Jenkyns sacrifices her own possibility of marriage (or rationalizes her decision in this way) in order to look after her father, Miss Matty's love for Holbrook is frustrated so that class distinctions can be maintained.

  Mrs Gaskell's handling of Miss Matty's love for Holbrook provides a striking example of how *Cranford* gradually developed from the original sketches. 'A Love Affair at Cranford' (*Household Words*, 3 January 1852) consisted of what are now Chapters III and IV, and was clearly regarded as a self-contained episode. It begins with Mary Smith hearing for the first time of Holbrook, includes the visit to his farm, moves forward in time to include news of his death, and closes with Miss Matty allowing Martha to accept Jem Hearn as a 'follower': 'Though Miss Matty was startled, she submitted to Fate and Love.' She has, of course, many years earlier submitted to family pressures and the memory of her lost love, and it is by the accumulation of carefully chosen details that Mrs Gaskell reveals the pain this submission has brought her. It emerges through her young brother's admiration for Holbrook; the story Mrs Fitz-Adam tells, Chapter XIV, of the young Miss Matty and Holbrook walking together in a country lane; of Miss Matty's own naïvety about Martha's pregnancy, her deep love of babies and children, and most movingly, in the shivering fit that Peter's reminiscences provokes. It is also characteristic of Mrs Gaskell's method that she should introduce a further relationship which both compares and contrasts with that of Miss Matty and Holbrook. In choosing to marry Mr Hoggins, Lady Glenmire is rejecting any right of Cranford society to dictate the way she should behave: she does what many years earlier Miss Matty had been unable to do. At the news of the wedding Miss Matty's response is cryptically personal: 'Two people that we know going to be married. It's coming very near!' and it is left to Mrs Jamieson, who since Miss Jenkyns's death has taken upon herself the role of guardian of Cranford's social values, to make a stand. But no one follows her, and her own behaviour seems simply childish. Times are changing.

And it is precisely these changing times that *Cranford* is about. It is often claimed that Mrs Gaskell is looking back with sentimental affection on a way of life being destroyed by industrial society, but such an argument can stand hardly a moment's consideration. The humanity and simple goodness apparent in Cranford are admired by Mrs Gaskell and offered, as we have seen, for the reader's admiration also. But by placing the Amazons at the centre of her book, and gradually revealing the deep sadness of Miss Matty's life, we see a society which for all its charm is narrow, exclusive, indifferent to the world outside its own boundaries, and, because of this, often unconsciously cruel. Miss Jenkyns's masculine pose works only so long as no real men are present. When they do appear in the shapes of Captain Brown, Holbrook, Peter, and to a lesser extent Signor Brunoni, they bring with them by their very awareness of a wider world and larger values of life, a serious challenge to Cranford's existence. This challenge is not simply a matter of maturity or greater oppor-

tunity for experience: it is there in Peter from childhood, and he
provides one of the most astonishing indirect comments on the
sterile nature of Miss Jenkyns's snobbbery. In the prank which
results in his leaving home, he dresses as his elder sister and walks
in the garden pretending to nurse a baby, while a growing crowd
of people peer at him over the fence. 'It was only, as he told me
afterwards,' Miss Matty explains, 'to make something to talk
about in the town,' However conscious Peter's motives, his joke
would, as Martin Dodsworth has pointed out, have led to the town
gossips attributing an illegitimate child to the rector's daughter.
As a young boy he strikes instinctively at the repressive life
around him, and when punished leaves home altogether. He
returns, wealthy, experienced, and unrepentant, to bring 'peace'
to Cranford, and the final portrait of him is one of the successes of
the book. Gentle, tolerant, understanding, and by no means fooled
by the Amazons, he watches over and entertains them, fully aware
that he has become the patriarch of a dying society.

Mrs Gaskell always retained a special affection for *Cranford*.
'It is the only one of my own books', she told Ruskin, 'that I can
read again; – but whenever I am ailing or ill, I take *Cranford* and
– I was going to say, *enjoy* it! (but that would not be pretty!)
laugh over it afresh!'* The laughter must be part of our response
to *Cranford*; it comes from the lasting impression made upon Mrs
Gaskell by her childhood in Knutsford, in which affection and a
clear-sighted awareness of the ridiculous are blended: 'Shall I tell
you a Cranfordism,' she wrote to Forster, 'An old lady a Mrs
Frances Wright said to one of my cousins "I have never been able
to spell since I lost my teeth." '† But beyond this aspect of the
book, it remained especially important for Mrs Gaskell because it
was here that, at a crucial stage in her development as a novelist,
she confronted for the first time some of the contradictions she
felt in her own experiences of life, vibrating between industrial
Manchester and rural Knutsford. The tone of *Cranford* is unlike
that of any of her other works: it is the product of one very
special moment which was not to be repeated. This view is borne
out by the single occasion when Mrs Gaskell did return to the

* *Letters*, p. 747.   † *ibid.*, p. 290.

theme of Cranford. 'The Cage at Cranford' appeared in *All the Year Round* in November 1863, nearly ten years after the publication of *Cranford*. It is not entirely unsuccessful as an isolated sketch, but the controlled tone of the earlier work has gone, and is replaced by a selfconsciousness in handling the familiar characters which comes over as too great a striving to amuse. The old tone could not be recreated, and there was no real need even to try, for by this time Mrs Gaskell had reached a new and very successful stage in her growth as a writer.

*

Cousin Phillis was published originally as a four-part serial in the *Cornhill Magazine* from November 1863 to February 1864: it appeared in book form, first in America in 1864 and in England the following year, as *Cousin Phillis and Other Tales*. Together with the uncompleted novel *Wives and Daughters*, which was also serialized in the *Cornhill* in 1864–5, it represents Mrs Gaskell's maturest work as an imaginative writer. It is also characteristic of a type of fiction, falling between the novel and the short story ('the beautiful and blest *nouvelle*' as Henry James called it)* which is relatively rare in the mid-Victorian period, though it was to become far more popular with writers towards the end of the nineteenth century. It was a form that Mrs Gaskell had always found attractive, partly it would seem, because it did not impose upon her imagination the element of strain that is never entirely absent from her full-length novels, and, a purely practical consideration, because it could be fitted in more easily with the extremely busy life she led as a mother, wife, and hostess. But clearly what made her so successful in this form was her natural love of anecdotes, folk-tales, legends, reminiscences, and the revealing details of social history. Most of her novels contain interpolated stories of this kind, as also do her letters, and, as we have seen, *Cranford* can be regarded as being built upon a whole series of reminiscences and anecdotes. *Cousin Phillis* is presented as a remembered episode, a fleeting, unfulfilled, love affair: it is a dramatization of the situation described but not elaborated by Wordsworth in his 'Lucy' poems:

* *The Art of the Novel*, New York, Scribner, 1962, p. 220.

She dwelt among the untrodden ways
  Beside the springs of Dove,
A Maid whom there were none to praise
  And very few to love.

The lines are quoted by Paul Manning as reminding him of Phillis, and although he adds, 'yet they were not true of her either', his is a limited viewpoint in the story, and subsequent references to Lucy would seem to suggest that Mrs Gaskell had the mood as well as the hinted situation of these poems very much in mind when writing *Cousin Phillis*.

After *North and South* the conscious exploration of contrasting phases of English life, with Manchester providing the modern industrialized world which needs to be incorporated somehow into the final vision of the novels, does, as Edgar Wright has argued, largely disappear from Mrs Gaskell's work.* But, in the case of *Cousin Phillis* especially, this is not so much a turning away from social issues as the development of new techniques by which those same issues can be re-examined. In spite of the differences of tone and mood in *Cranford* and *Cousin Phillis* they do have much in common. The opening description of Paul's arrival in Eltham fleetingly reintroduces the world of Cranford before narrowing on to Heathbridge and the Hope Farm. Once again Mrs Gaskell is taking as her social model a small community, relatively isolated from the wider world, and examining the impact upon it of external forces and values. The action of the story, like that of *Cranford*, is set in the 1840s; Paul and Holdsworth follow Captain Brown in being brought into contact with this community by the new railways; and the arrival of Paul's father in Heathbridge is similar to Mr Smith's descent on Cranford in that both are successful representatives of the new order. The differences in the encounter between Mr Manning and Minister Holman are, however, significant. For this is not the harsh, mean, superstitious rural world of *North and South*, or the fading shabby-genteel society of Cranford, both of which are seen as requiring some sort of deliverance. In *Cousin Phillis* the two men meet as equals, each finding much to respect in the other; they both belong to

* *Mrs Gaskell: The Basis for Reassessment*, p. 118.

living communities, and practicality and creative energy are now regarded as innate in certain kinds of men rather than produced more readily by one part of English society. The confrontation between old and new is presented here with greater subtlety and understanding than in any of Mrs Gaskell's earlier novels.

The story is told by Paul and his voice is, once again, that of the younger generation, but whereas Mary Smith had embodied Mrs Gaskell's own perceptions of Cranford, he lacks any truly sympathetic understanding of the lives and events he describes. Phillis recognizes immediately his youthfulness; his father acknowledges in him little imagination ('Thou'rt not great shakes, I know, in th'inventing line; but many a one gets on better without having fancies for something he does not see and never has seen'); Holdsworth chides him gently for his undeveloped sexuality; and old Betty, after some fierce abuse, decides: 'Poor lad! you're but a big child, after all.' It is Paul's error of judgement that precipitates Phillis's illness, but as Holman makes clear, this is the result of inexperience of life rather than any fundamental flaw in his character: 'Paul! I was unjust to you. You deserved blame, but not all that I said.' Much the same judgement can be passed on most of the major characters in *Cousin Phillis*. Holman carries some of the blame for refusing to recognize that Phillis is no longer a child and for restricting his wife's influence on their daughter's upbringing. And if Holdsworth is shown eventually as flirtatious and shallow, he is by no means a conventional seducer of innocence. He refrains from telling Phillis of his love for her, and in flirting with her seems merely to be acting out the natural, if irresponsible, side of his personality. Once the prejudice against his foreignness is overcome, Paul, Mr Manning, Holman and his wife, as well as Phillis, all find him attractive; only Betty really stands aside and distrusts him. Holman, Paul, and Holdsworth, all suffer from an inability to foresee the probable results of their actions, and share the blame for what happens to Phillis.

It is this, together with the passivity of Phillis and the way she is associated with natural forces and the movement of the seasons that gives a mood of inevitability to her sufferings. If she too has little experience of life and therefore nothing with which to combat the human weaknesses of those around her, she does have as great a feeling *for* life as anyone. Old Betty's blunt warning at the close emphasizes that life must be faced and learnt from, that it is impossible to remain simply a child of nature. Phillis's reported response shows a willingness to acknowledge the truth of this, though we are left with a final irony, for if the lesson has been truly learnt then there can never be a return to 'the peace of the old days'.

That the 'peace of the old days' was in one sense illusory is a conclusion that must be balanced against the wider implications of the rural community as it is portrayed in *Cousin Phillis*. Heathbridge is another of those 'phases of society' which could disappear with the growth of industrialism, but unlike Cranford there is little about it that is ridiculous. Life at Hope Farm is dominated by the demands of the land and regulated by seasonal change; a place where work is inspired by a deep religious faith which finds expression in a practical concern with living rather than tired doctrinal issues. It can also encompass Holman's wideranging intellectual curiosity and an aesthetic sense which appreciates Virgil's *Georgics* for their beauty as well as their knowledge of agriculture.

Yet it is characteristic of Mrs Gaskell that her profound understanding of the nature of social change in the nineteenth century should finally have held her back from offering the Hope Farm community as an ideal. Paul has little of the faith in nonconformity that has worked so powerfully in his father and Holman, while Holdsworth has no appreciation of it at all. These attitudes of the younger generation, together with the satirical glimpses we get of Brother Robinson, serve to heighten the unusual nature of Holman's way of life, and reflect upon his failure fully to understand the needs of his own daughter. In *Cousin Phillis*, as in *Cranford* and *North and South*, Mrs Gaskell is concerned to delineate the qualities which the process of change must not be allowed to obliterate, without taking a stand against change itself. However different the approach, we still find in *Cousin Phillis* that need to arbitrate between contrasting phases of society, to test and evaluate them, which seems to have been one of Mrs Gaskell's deepest motivating forces as a writer. In *Cranford* the accumulation of historical and social detail provided a means for Mrs

Gaskell to clarify her feelings about the past and present: in *Cousin Phillis* these details are still employed, and the concern with past and present remains, but they are absorbed within the frame of the *nouvelle* and skilfully dramatized as a tale of lost innocence.

A Note on the Text

Cranford was published originally as an eight-part serial in *Household Words*. The dates and titles of the parts, together with the subsequent chapter division for the first book edition of 1853, are: 'Our Society at Cranford', 13 December 1851 (Chapters I to II, Our Society, The Captain); 'A Love Affair at Cranford', 3 January 1852 (Chapters III to IV, A Love Affair of Long Ago, A Visit to an Old Bachelor); 'Memory at Cranford', 13 March 1852 (Chapters V to VI, Old Letters, Poor Peter); 'Visiting at Cranford', 3 April 1852 (Chapters VII to VIII, Visiting, 'Your Ladyship'); 'The Great Cranford Panic', published in two instalments, 8 and 15 January 1853 (chapters IX to XI, Signor Brunoni, The Panic, Samuel Brown); 'Stopped Payment at Cranford', 2 April 1853 (Chapters XII to XIII, Engaged to be Married, Stopped Payment); 'Friends in Need, at Cranford', 7 May 1853 (Chapter XIV, Friends in Need); 'A Happy Return to Cranford', 21 May 1853 (Chapters XV to XVI, A Happy Return, Peace to Cranford).

Mrs Gaskell revised the *Household Words* text for the 1853 edition, changing some of the names of characters (Miss Matey to Miss Matty being the most significant), reintroducing the references to Dickens, dividing the original instalments into chapters as given above, and making a number of minor stylistic changes. These are detailed by Elizabeth Porges Watson in her edition of *Cranford* published in 1972 in the 'Oxford English Novels' series. A few errors and inconsistencies remained in the 1853 and later editions, and where I have followed Miss Watson in finding the *Household Words* reading obviously correct or superior this has been indicated in the Notes. Otherwise the present text is substantially that of the 1864 edition, the last revised by Mrs Gaskell before her death the following year.

Cousin Phillis was published originally as a four-part serial (corresponding to the present division of the tale) in the *Cornhill Magazine*, appearing monthly from November 1863 to February

1864. The present text is that of the first English book edition, *Cousin Phillis and Other Tales* (1865).

'The Cage at Cranford' appeared as a separate sketch in *All the Year Round*, November 1863, and was not collected in volume form in Mrs Gaskell's lifetime though it has been reprinted many times since. 'The Last Generation in England' was first published in the American periodical *Sartain's Union Magazine*, July 1849, and remained uncollected until E. P. Watson included it in her edition of *Cranford*.

Select Bibliography

J. A. V. Chapple and Arthur Pollard, eds., *The Letters of Mrs Gaskell*, Manchester University Press, 1966.

Martin Dodsworth, 'Women without Men at Cranford', *Essays in Criticism*, vol. 13, 1963.

Margaret Ganz, *Elizabeth Gaskell: the Artist in Conflict*, Twayne Publishers, New York, 1969.

A. B. Hopkins, *Elizabeth Gaskell: Her Life and Work*, John Lehmann, 1952.

John Lucas, 'Mrs Gaskell and Brotherhood', *Tradition and Tolerance in Nineteenth-Century Fiction*, Routledge, 1966.

Arthur Pollard, *Mrs Gaskell: Novelist and Biographer*, Manchester University Press, 1965.

Aina Rubenius, *The Woman Question in Mrs Gaskell's Life and Works*, Copenhagen and Cambridge, Mass., 1950.

J. G. Sharps, *Mrs Gaskell's Observation and Invention*, (Sussex), Linden Press, Fontwell, 1970.

Margaret Tarratt, 'Cranford and "the Strict Code of Gentility"', *Essays in Criticism*, vol. 18, 1968.

A. S. Whitfield, *Mrs Gaskell: Her Life and Work*, Routledge, 1929.

Patricia A. Wolfe, 'Structure and Movement in Cranford', *Nineteenth-Century Fiction*, vol. 23, 1968.

Edgar Wright, *Mrs Gaskell: The Basis for Reassessment*, Oxford University Press, 1965.

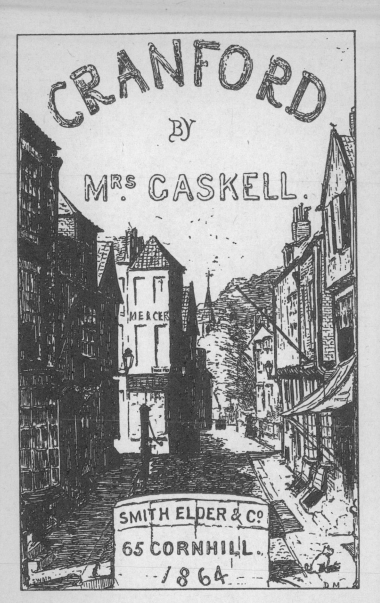

CRANFORD

BY

MRS GASKELL.

MERCER

SMITH ELDER & Cº
65 CORNHILL.
1864

Contents

CRANFORD

CHAPTER I

Our Society

IN the first place, Cranford is in possession of the Amazons;[1] all
the holders of houses, above a certain rent, are women. If a married
couple come to settle in the town, somehow the gentleman dis-
appears; he is either fairly frightened to death by being the only
man in the Cranford evening parties, or he is accounted for by being with his regiment, his ship, or closely engaged in business all
the week in the great neighbouring commercial town of Drumble,[2]
distant only twenty miles on a railroad. In short, whatever does
become of the gentlemen, they are not at Cranford. What could
they do if they were there? The surgeon has his round of thirty
miles, and sleeps at Cranford; but every man cannot be a surgeon.
For keeping the trim gardens full of choice flowers without a weed
to speck them; for frightening away little boys who look wistfully
at the said flowers through the railings; for rushing out at the
geese that occasionally venture into the gardens if the gates are left
open; for deciding all questions of literature and politics without
troubling themselves with unnecessary reasons or arguments; for
obtaining clear and correct knowledge of everybody's affairs in the
parish; for keeping their neat maid-servants in admirable order;
for kindness (somewhat dictatorial) to the poor, and real tender
good offices to each other whenever they are in distress, the ladies
of Cranford are quite sufficient. 'A man,' as one of them observed
to me once, 'is so in the way in the house!' Although the ladies of
Cranford know all each other's proceedings; they are exceedingly
indifferent to each other's opinions. Indeed, as each has her own
individuality, not to say eccentricity, pretty strongly developed,

nothing is so easy as verbal retaliation; but somehow good-will reigns among them to a considerable degree.

The Cranford ladies have only an occasional little quarrel, spirted out in a few peppery words and angry jerks of the head; just enough to prevent the even tenor of their lives from becoming too flat. Their dress is very independent of fashion; as they observe, 'What does it signify how we dress here at Cranford, where everybody knows us?' And if they go from home, their reason is equally cogent: 'What does it signify how we dress here, where nobody knows us?' The materials of their clothes are, in general, good and plain, and most of them are nearly as scrupulous as Miss Tyler, of cleanly memory;[3] but I will answer for it, the last gigot, the last tight and scanty petticoat [4] in wear in England, was seen in Cranford – and seen without a smile.

I can testify to a magnificent family red silk umbrella, under which a gentle little spinster, left alone of many brothers and sisters, used to patter to church on rainy days. Have you any red silk umbrellas in London? We had a tradition of the first that had ever been seen in Cranford; and the little boys mobbed it, and called it 'a stick in petticoats.' It might have been the very red silk one I have described, held by a strong father over a troop of little ones; the poor little lady – the survivor of all – could scarcely carry it.

Then there were rules and regulations for visiting and calls; and they were announced to any young people, who might be staying in the town, with all the solemnity with which the old Manx laws were read once a year on the Tinwald Mount.[5]

'Our friends have sent to inquire how you are after your journey to-night, my dear' (fifteen miles, in a gentlemen's carriage); 'they will give you some rest to-morrow, but the next day, I have no doubt, they will call; so be at liberty after twelve; – from twelve to three are our calling-hours.'

Then, after they had called,

'It is the third day; I dare say your mamma has told you, my dear, never to let more than three days elapse between receiving a call and returning it; and also, that you are never to stay longer than a quarter of an hour.'

'But am I to look at my watch? How am I to find out when a quarter of an hour has passed?'

'You must keep thinking about the time, my dear, and not allow yourself to forget it in conversation.'

As everybody had this rule in their minds, whether they received or paid a call, of course no absorbing subject was ever spoken about. We kept ourselves to short sentences of small talk, and were punctual to our time.

I imagine that a few of the gentlefolks of Cranford were poor, and had some difficulty in making both ends meet; but they were like the Spartans, and concealed their smart under a smiling face. We none of us spoke of money, because that subject savoured of commerce and trade, and though some might be poor, we were all aristocratic. The Cranfordians had that kindly *esprit de corps* which made them overlook all deficiencies in success when some among them tried to conceal their poverty. When Mrs Forrester, for instance, gave a party in her baby-house of a dwelling, and the little maiden disturbed the ladies on the sofa by a request that she might get the tea-tray out from underneath, every one took this novel proceeding as the most natural thing in the world; and talked on about household forms and ceremonies, as if we all believed that our hostess had a regular servants' hall, second table, with housekeeper and steward, instead of the one little charity-school maiden,[6] whose short ruddy arms could never have been strong enough to carry the tray up-stairs, if she had not been assisted in private by her mistress, who now sat in state, pretending not to know what cakes were sent up, though she knew, and we knew, and she knew that we knew, and we knew that she knew we knew, she had been busy all the morning making tea-bread [7] and sponge cakes.

There were one or two consequences arising from this general but unacknowledged poverty, and this very much acknowledged gentility, which were not amiss, and which might be introduced into many circles of society to their great improvement. For instance, the inhabitants of Cranford kept early hours, and clattered home in their pattens,[8] under the guidance of a lantern-bearer, about nine o'clock at night; and the whole town was abed and asleep by half-past ten. Moreover, it was considered 'vulgar' (a tremendous word in Cranford) to give anything expensive, in the way of eatable or drinkable, at the evening entertainments. Wafer bread-and-butter and sponge-biscuits were all that the Honourable Mrs Jamieson gave; and she was sister-in-law to the late Earl of Glenmire, although she did practise such 'elegant economy.'

'Elegant economy!' How naturally one falls back into the phraseology of Cranford! There, economy was always 'elegant,' and money-spending always 'vulgar and ostentatious;' a sort of sour grapeism, which made us very peaceful and satisfied. I never shall forget the dismay felt when a certain Captain Brown came to live at Cranford, and openly spoke about his being poor – not in a whisper to an intimate friend, the doors and windows being previously closed; but, in the public street! in a loud military voice! alleging his poverty as a reason for not taking a particular house. The ladies of Cranford were already rather moaning over the invasion of their territories by a man and a gentleman. He was a half-pay captain,[9] and had obtained some situation on a neighbouring railroad,[10] which had been vehemently petitioned against by the little town; and if, in addition to his masculine gender, and his connexion with the obnoxious railroad, he was so brazen as to talk of being poor – why! then, indeed, he must be sent to Coventry. Death was as true and as common as poverty; yet people never spoke about that, loud out in the streets. It was a word not to be mentioned to ears polite. We had tacitly agreed to ignore that any with whom we associated on terms of visiting equality could ever be prevented by poverty from doing anything that they wished. If we walked to or from a party, it was because the night was so fine, or the air so refreshing; not because sedan-chairs were expensive.[11] If we wore prints, instead of summer silks, it was because we preferred a washing material; and so on, till we blinded ourselves to the vulgar fact, that we were, all of us, people of very moderate means. Of course, then, we did not know what to make of a man who could speak of poverty as if it was not a disgrace. Yet, somehow, Captain Brown made himself respected in Cranford, and was called upon in spite of all resolutions to the contrary. I was surprised to hear his opinions quoted as authority, at a visit which I paid to Cranford, about a year after he had settled in the

Our Society

town. My own friends had been among the bitterest opponents of
any proposal to visit the captain and his daughters, only twelve
months before; and now he was even admitted in the tabooed
hours before twelve. True, it was to discover the cause of a smoking chimney, before the fire was lighted; but still Captain Brown
walked up-stairs, nothing daunted, spoke in a voice too large for
the room, and joked quite in the way of a tame man, about the
house. He had been blind to all the small slights, and omissions of
trivial ceremonies, with which he had been received. He had been
friendly, though the Cranford ladies had been cool; he had
answered small sarcastic compliments in good faith; and with his
manly frankness had overpowered all the shrinking which met
him as a man who was not ashamed to be poor. And, at last, his
excellent masculine common sense, and his facility in devising ex-
pedients to overcome domestic dilemmas, had gained him an extraordinary place as authority among the Cranford ladies. He, himself, went on in his course, as unaware of his popularity as he had
been of the reverse; and I am sure he was startled one day, when
he found his advice so highly esteemed, as to make some counsel
which he had given in jest, to be taken in sober, serious earnest.

It was on this subject; – an old lady had an Alderney cow,
which she looked upon as a daughter. You could not pay the short
quarter of an hour call, without being told of the wonderful milk
or wonderful intelligence of his animal. The whole town knew
and kindly regarded Miss Betty[12] Barker's Alderney; therefore
great was the sympathy and regret when, in an unguarded moment, the poor cow tumbled into a lime-pit. She moaned so loudly
that she was soon heard, and rescued; but meanwhile the poor
beast had lost most of her hair and came out looking naked, cold,
and miserable, in a bare skin. Everybody pitied the animal, though
a few could not restrain their smiles at her droll appearance. Miss
Betty Barker absolutely cried with sorrow and dismay; and it was
said she thought of trying a bath of oil. This remedy, perhaps, was
recommended by some one of the number whose advice she asked;
but the proposal, if ever it was made, was knocked on the head by
Captain Brown's decided 'Get her a flannel waistcoat and flannel
drawers, ma'am, if you wish to keep her alive. But my advice is,
kill the poor creature at once.'

Miss Betty Barker dried her eyes and thanked the captain heartily; she set to work, and by-and-by all the town turned out to see the Alderney meekly going to her pasture, clad in dark grey flannel. I have watched her myself many a time. Do you ever see cows dressed in grey flannel in London?

Captain Brown had taken a small house on the outskirts of the town, where he lived with his two daughters. He must have been upwards of sixty at the time of the first visit I paid to Cranford, after I had left it as a residence. But he had a wiry, well-trained, elastic figure; a stiff military throw-back of his head, and a springing step, which made him appear much younger than he was. His eldest daughter looked almost as old as himself, and betrayed the fact that his real, was more than his apparent, age. Miss Brown must have been forty; she had a sickly, pained, careworn expression on her face, and looked as if the gaiety of youth had long faded out of sight. Even when young she must have been plain and hard featured. Miss Jessie Brown was ten years younger than her sister, and twenty shades prettier. Her face was round and dimpled. Miss Jenkyns once said, in a passion against Captain Brown (the cause of which I will tell you presently), 'that she thought it was time for Miss Jessie to leave off her dimples, and not always to be trying to look like a child.' It was true there was something child-like in her face; and there will be, I think, till she dies, though she should live to a hundred. Her eyes were large blue wondering eyes, looking straight at you; her nose was unformed and snub, and her lips were red and dewy; she wore her hair, too, in little rows of curls, which heightened this appearance. I do not know whether she was pretty or not; but I liked her face, and so did everybody, and I do not think she could help her dimples. She had something of her father's jauntiness of gait and manner; and any female observer might detect a slight difference in the attire of the two sisters – that of Miss Jessie being about two pounds per annum more expensive than Miss Brown's. Two pounds was a large sum in Captain Brown's annual disbursements.

Such was the impression made upon me by the Brown family, when I first saw them all together in Cranford church. The captain I had met before – on the occasion of the smoky chimney, which he had cured by some simple alteration in the flue. In church, he held his double eye-glass to his eyes during the Morning Hymn, and then lifted up his head erect and sang out loud and joyfully. He made the responses louder than the clerk[13] – an old man with a piping feeble voice, who, I think, felt aggrieved at the captain's sonorous bass, and quavered higher and higher in consequence.

On coming out of church, the brisk captain paid the most gallant attention to his two daughters. He nodded and smiled to his acquaintances; but he shook hands with none until he had helped Miss Brown to unfurl her umbrella, had relieved her of her prayer-book, and had waited patiently till she, with trembling nervous hands, had taken up her gown to walk through the wet roads.

I wondered what the Cranford ladies did with Captain Brown at their parties. We had often rejoiced, in former days, that there was no gentleman to be attended to, and to find conversation for, at the card-parties. We had congratulated ourselves upon the snugness of the evenings; and, in our love for gentility, and distaste of mankind, we had almost persuaded ourselves that to be a man was to be 'vulgar;' so that when I found my friend and hostess, Miss Jenkyns, was going to have a party in my honour, and that Captain and the Miss Browns were invited, I wondered much what would be the course of the evening. Card-tables, with green-baize tops, were set out by daylight, just as usual; it was the third week in November, so the evenings closed in about four. Candles, and clean packs of cards were arranged on each table. The fire was made up; the neat maid-servant had received her last directions; and there we stood dressed in our best, each with a candle-lighter in our hands, ready to dart at the candles as soon as the first knock came. Parties in Cranford were solemn festivities, making the ladies feel gravely elated, as they sat together in their best dresses. As soon as three had arrived, we sat down to 'Preference',[14] I being the unlucky fourth. The next four comers were put down immediately to another table; and presently the tea-trays, which I had seen set out in the store-room as I passed in the morning, were placed each on the middle of a card-table. The china was delicate egg-shell; the old-fashioned silver glittered with polishing; but the eatables were of the slightest description. While the trays were yet on the tables, Captain and the Miss Browns came in; and I could see, that somehow or other the captain was a favourite with all the ladies present. Ruffled brows were smoothed, sharp voices lowered at his approach. Miss Brown looked ill, and depressed almost to gloom. Miss Jessie smiled as usual, and seemed nearly as popular as her father. He immediately and quietly assumed the man's place in the room; attended to every one's wants, lessened the pretty maid-servant's labour by waiting on empty cups, and bread-and-butter-less ladies; and yet did it all in so easy and dignified a manner, and so much as if it were a matter of course for the strong to attend to the weak, that he was a true man throughout. He played for three-penny points with as grave an interest as if they had been pounds; and yet, in all his attention to strangers, he had an eye on his suffering daughter; for suffering I was sure she was, though to many eyes she might only appear to be irritable. Miss Jessie could not play cards; but she talked to the sitters-out, who, before her coming, had been rather inclined to be cross. She sang, too, to an old cracked piano, which I think had been a spinnet in its youth. Miss Jessie sang 'Jock of Hazeldean'[15] a little out of tune; but we were none of us musical, though Miss Jenkyns beat time, out of time, by way of appearing to be so.

It was very good of Miss Jenkyns to do this; for I had seen that, a little before, she had been a good deal annoyed by Miss Jessie Brown's unguarded admission (*à propos* of Shetland wool) that she had an uncle, her mother's brother, who was a shopkeeper in Edinburgh. Miss Jenkyns tried to drown this confession by a terrible cough – for the Honourable Mrs Jamieson was sitting at the card-table nearest Miss Jessie, and what would she say or think, if she found out she was in the same room with a shopkeeper's niece! But Miss Jessie Brown (who had no tact, as we all agreed, the next morning) *would* repeat the information, and assure Miss Pole she could easily get her the identical Shetland wool required, 'through my uncle, who has the best assortment of Shetland goods of any one in Edinbro'.' It was to take the taste of this out of our mouths, and the sound of this out of our ears, that Miss Jenkyns proposed music; so I say again, it was very good of her to beat time to the song.

When the trays reappeared with biscuits and wine, punctually at a quarter to nine, there was conversation; comparing of cards, and talking over tricks; but by-and-by, Captain Brown sported a bit of literature.

'Have you seen any numbers of "The Pickwick Papers?" '[16] said he. (They were then publishing in parts.) 'Capital thing !'

Now, Miss Jenkyns was daughter of a deceased rector of Cranford; and, on the strength of a number of manuscript sermons, and a pretty good library of divinity, considered herself literary, and looked upon any conversation about books as a challenge to her. So she answered and said, 'Yes, she had seen them; indeed, she might say she had read them.'

'And what do you think of them?' exclaimed Captain Brown. 'Aren't they famously good?'

So urged, Miss Jenkyns could not but speak.

'I must say, I don't think they are by any means equal to Dr Johnson. Still, perhaps, the author is young. Let him persevere, and who knows what he may become if he will take the great Doctor for his model.' This was evidently too much for Captain Brown to take placidly; and I saw the words on the tip of his tongue before Miss Jenkyns had finished her sentence.

'It is quite a different sort of thing, my dear madam,' he began.

'I am quite aware of that,' returned she. 'And I make allowances, Captain Brown.'

'Just allow me to read you a scene out of this month's number,' pleaded he. 'I had it only this morning, and I don't think the company can have read it yet.'

'As you please,' said she, settling herself with an air of resignation. He read the account of the 'swarry' which Sam Weller gave at Bath.[17] Some of us laughed heartily. I did not dare, because I was staying in the house. Miss Jenkyns sat in patient gravity. When it was ended, she turned to me, and said with mild dignity :

'Fetch me *Rasselas*,[18] my dear, out of the bookroom.'

When I brought it to her, she turned to Captain Brown :

'Now allow me to read you a scene, and then the present company can judge between your favourite, Mr Boz, and Dr Johnson.'

She read one of the conversations between Rasselas and Imlac, in a high-pitched majestic voice; and when she had ended, she said, 'I imagine I am now justified in my preference of Dr Johnson as a writer of fiction.' The captain screwed his lips up, and drummed on the table, but he did not speak. She thought she would give a finishing blow or two.

'I consider it vulgar, and below the dignity of literature, to publish in numbers.'

'How was the *Rambler* published, ma'am?'[19] asked Captain Brown in a low voice; which I think Miss Jenkyns could not have heard.

'Dr Johnson's style is a model for young beginners. My father recommended it to me when I began to write letters, – I have formed my own style upon it; I recommend it to your favourite.'

'I should be very sorry for him to exchange his style for any such pompous writing,' said Captain Brown.

Miss Jenkyns felt this as a personal affront, in a way of which the captain had not dreamed. Epistolary writing, she and her friends considered as her *forte*. Many a copy of many a letter have I seen written and corrected on the slate, before she 'seized the half-hour just previous to post-time to assure' her friends of this or of that; and Dr Johnson was, as she said, her model in these compositions. She drew herself up with dignity and only replied to Captain Brown's last remark by saying, with marked emphasis on every syllable, 'I prefer Dr Johnson to Mr Boz.'

It is said – I won't vouch for the fact – that Captain Brown was heard to say *sotto voce*,[20] 'D—n Dr Johnson !' If he did, he was penitent afterwards, as he showed by going to stand near Miss Jenkyns's arm-chair, and endeavouring to beguile her into conversation on some more pleasing subject. But she was inexorable. The next day, she made the remark I have mentioned, about Miss Jessie's dimples.

CHAPTER II

The Captain

I T was impossible to live a month at Cranford, and not know the daily habits of each resident; and long before my visit was ended, I knew much concerning the whole Brown trio. There was nothing new to be discovered respecting their poverty; for they had spoken simply and openly about that from the very first. They made no mystery of the necessity for their being economical. All that remained to be discovered was the captain's infinite kindness of heart, and the various modes in which, unconsciously to himself, he manifested it. Some little anecdotes were talked about for some time after they occurred. As we did not read much, and as all the ladies were pretty well suited with servants, there was a dearth of subjects for conversation. We therefore discussed the circumstance of the captain taking a poor old woman's dinner out of her hands, one very slippery Sunday. He had met her returning from the bakehouse[1] as he came from church, and noticed her precarious footing; and, with the grave dignity with which he did everything, he relieved her of her burden, and steered along the street by her side, carrying her baked mutton and potatoes safely home. This was thought very eccentric; and it was rather expected that he would pay a round of calls, on the Monday morning, to explain and apologize to the Cranford sense of propriety : but he did no such thing; and then it was decided that he was ashamed, and was keeping out of sight. In a kindly pity for him, we began to say – 'After all, the Sunday morning's occurrence showed great goodness of heart;' and it was resolved that he should be comforted on his next appearance amongst us; but, lo ! he came down upon us, untouched by any sense of shame, speaking loud and bass as ever, his head thrown back, his wig as jaunty and well-curled as usual, and we were obliged to conclude he had forgotten all about Sunday.

Miss Pole and Miss Jessie Brown had set up a kind of intimacy, on the strength of the Shetland wool and the new knitting stitches; so it happened that when I went to visit Miss Pole, I saw more of the Browns than I had done while staying with Miss Jenkyns; who had never got over what she called Captain Brown's disparaging remarks upon Dr Johnson, as a writer of light and agreeable fiction. I found that Miss Brown was seriously ill of some lingering, incurable complaint, the pain occasioned by which gave the uneasy expression to her face that I had taken for unmitigated crossness. Cross, too, she was at times, when the nervous irritability occasioned by her disease became past endurance. Miss Jessie bore with her at these times even more patiently than she did with the bitter self-upbraidings by which they were invariably succeeded. Miss Brown used to accuse herself, not merely of hasty and irritable temper; but also of being the cause why her father and sister were obliged to pinch, in order to allow her the small luxuries which were necessaries in her condition. She would so fain have made sacrifices for them and have lightened their cares, that the original generosity of her disposition added acerbity to her temper. All this was borne by Miss Jessie and her father with more than placidity – with absolute tenderness. I forgave Miss Jessie her singing out of tune, and her juvenility of dress, when I saw her at home. I came to perceive that Captain Brown's dark Brutus wig[2] and padded coat (alas ! too often threadbare) were remnants of the military smartness of his youth, which he now wore unconsciously. He was a man of infinite resources, gained in his barrack experience. As he confessed, no one could black his boots to please him, except himself : but, indeed, he was not above saving the little maid-servant's labours in every way, – knowing, most likely, that his daughter's illness made the place a hard one.

He endeavoured to make peace with Miss Jenkyns soon after the memorable dispute I have named, by a present of a wooden fire-shovel (his own making), having heard her say how much the grating of an iron one annoyed her. She received the present with cool gratitude, and thanked him formally. When he was gone, she bade me put it away in the lumber-room; feeling, probably, that no present from a man who preferred Mr Boz to Dr Johnson could be less jarring than an iron fire-shovel.

Such was the state of things when I left Cranford and went to Drumble. I had, however, several correspondents who kept me *au fait* as to the proceedings of the dear little town. There was Miss Pole, who was becoming as much absorbed in crochet as she had been once in knitting; and the burden of whose letter was something like, 'But don't you forget the white worsted at Flint's,'[3] of the old song; for, at the end of every sentence of news, came a fresh direction as to some crochet commission which I was to execute for her. Miss Matilda Jenkyns (who did not mind being called Miss Matty, when Miss Jenkyns was not by) wrote nice, kind, rambling letters; now and then venturing into an opinion of her own; but suddenly pulling herself up, and either begging me not to name what she had said, as Deborah thought differently, and *she* knew; or else putting in a postscript to the effect that, since writing the above, she had been talking over the subject with Deborah, and was quite convinced that, &c. – (here, probably followed a recantation of every opinion she had given in the letter). Then came Miss Jenkyns – Deborah,[4] as she liked Miss Matty to call her; her father having once said that the Hebrew name ought to be so pronounced. I secretly think she took the Hebrew prophetess for a model in character; and, indeed, she was not unlike the stern prophetess in some ways; making allowance, of course, for modern customs and difference in dress. Miss Jenkyns wore a cravat, and a little bonnet like a jockey-cap,[5] and altogether had the appearance of a strong-minded woman; although she would have despised the modern idea of women being equal to men. Equal, indeed! she knew they were superior. – But to return to her letters. Everything in them was stately and grand, like herself. I have been looking them over (dear Miss Jenkyns, how I honoured her!), and I will give an extract, more especially because it relates to our friend Captain Brown:

'The Honourable Mrs. Jamieson has only just quitted me; and, in the course of conversation, she communicated to me the intelligence, that she had yesterday received a call from her revered husband's quondam friend, Lord Mauleverer. You will not easily conjecture what brought his lordship within the precincts of our little town. It was to see Captain Brown, with whom, it appears, his lordship was acquainted in the "plumed wars,"[6] and who had the privilege of averting destruction from his lordship's head, when some great peril was impending over it, off the misnomered Cape of Good Hope. You know our friend the Honourable Mrs Jamieson's deficiency in the spirit of innocent curiosity; and you will therefore not be so much surprised when I tell you she was quite unable to disclose to me the exact nature of the peril in question. I was anxious, I confess, to ascertain in what manner Captain Brown, with his limited establishment, could receive so distinguished a guest; and I discovered that his lordship retired to rest, and, let us hope to refreshing slumbers, at the Angel Hotel; but shared the Brunonian[7] meals during the two days that he honoured Cranford with his august presence. Mrs Johnson, our civil butcher's wife, informs me that Miss Jessie purchased a leg of lamb; but, besides this, I can hear of no preparation whatever to give a suitable reception to so distinguished a visitor. Perhaps they entertained him with "the feast of reason and the flow of soul;"[8] and to us, who are acquainted with Captain Brown's sad want of relish for "the pure wells of English undefiled,"[9] it may be matter for congratulation, that he has had the opportunity of improving his taste by holding converse with an elegant and refined member of the British aristocracy. But from some mundane failings who is altogether free?'

Miss Pole and Miss Matty wrote to me by the same post. Such a piece of news as Lord Mauleverer's visit was not to be lost on the Cranford letter-writers: they made the most of it. Miss Matty humbly apologized for writing at the same time as her sister, who was so much more capable than she to describe the honour done to Cranford; but, in spite of a little bad spelling, Miss Matty's account gave me the best idea of the commotion occasioned by his lordship's visit, after it had occurred; for, except the people at the Angel, the Browns, Mrs Jamieson, and a little lad his lordship had sworn at for driving a dirty hoop against the aristocratic legs, I could not hear of any one with whom his lordship had held conversation.

My next visit to Cranford was in the summer. There had been neither births, deaths, nor marriages since I was there last. Everybody lived in the same house, and wore pretty nearly the same well-preserved, old-fashioned clothes. The greatest event was, that Miss Jenkynses had purchased a new carpet for the drawing-room. Oh the busy work Miss Matty and I had in chasing the sunbeams, as they fell in an afternoon right down on this carpet through the blindness window! We spread newspapers over the places, and sat down to our book or our work; and, lo! in a quarter of an hour the sun had moved, and was blazing away on a fresh spot; and down again we went on our knees to alter the position of the newspapers. We were very busy, too, one whole morning, before Miss Jenkyns gave her party, in following her directions, and in cutting out and stitching together pieces of newspaper, so as to form little paths to every chair, set for the expected visitors, lest their shoes might dirty or defile the purity of the carpet. Do you make paper paths for every guest to walk upon in London?

Captain Brown and Miss Jenkyns were not very cordial to each other. The literary dispute, of which I had seen the beginning, was a 'raw,' the slightest touch on which made them wince. It was the only difference of opinion they had ever had; but that difference was enough. Miss Jenkyns could not refrain from talking *at* Captain Brown; and though he did not reply, he drummed with his fingers; which action she felt and resented as very disparaging to Dr Johnson. He was rather ostentatious in his preference of the writings of Mr Boz; would walk through the streets so absorbed in them, that he all but ran against Miss Jenkyns; and though his apologies were earnest and sincere, and though he did not, in fact, do more than startle her and himself, she owned to me she had rather he had knocked her down, if he had only been reading a higher style of literature. The poor, brave captain! he looked older, and more worn, and his clothes were very threadbare. But he seemed as bright and cheerful as ever, unless he was asked about his daughter's health.

'She suffers a great deal, and she must suffer more; we do what we can to alleviate her pain; – God's will be done!' He took off his hat at these last words. I found, from Miss Matty, that everything had been done, in fact. A medical man, of high repute in that country neighbourhood, had been sent for, and every injunction he had given was attended to, regardless of expense. Miss Matty was sure they denied themselves many things in order to make the invalid comfortable; but they never spoke about it; and as for Miss Jessie! 'I really think she's an angel,' said poor Miss Matty, quite overcome. 'To see her way of bearing with Miss Brown's crossness, and the bright face she puts on after she's been sitting up a whole night and scolded above half of it, is quite beautiful. Yet she looks as neat and as ready to welcome the captain at breakfast-time, as if she had been asleep in the Queen's bed all night. My dear! you could never laugh at her prim little curls or her pink bows again, if you saw her as I have done.' I could only feel very penitent, and greet Miss Jessie with double respect when I met her next. She looked faded and pinched; and her lips began to quiver, as if she was very weak, when she spoke of her sister. But she brightened, and sent back the tears that were glittering in her pretty eyes, as she said:

'But, to be sure, what a town Cranford is for kindness! I don't suppose any one has a better dinner than usual cooked, but the best part of all comes in a little covered basin for my sister. The poor people will leave their earliest vegetables at our door for her. They speak short and gruff, as if they were ashamed of it; but I am sure it often goes to my heart to see their thoughtfulness.' The tears now came back and overflowed; but after a minute or two, she began to scold herself, and ended by going away, the same cheerful Miss Jessie as ever.

'But why does not this Lord Mauleverer do something for the man who saved his life?' said I.

'Why, you see, unless Captain Brown has some reason for it, he never speaks about being poor; and he walked along by his lordship, looking as happy and cheerful as a prince; and as they never called attention to their dinner by apologies, and as Miss Brown was better that day, and all seemed bright, I dare say his lordship never knew how much care there was in the background. He did send game in the winter pretty often, but now he is gone abroad.'

I had often occasion to notice the use that was made of fragments and small opportunities in Cranford; the rose-leaves that were gathered ere they fell, to make into a pot-pourri[10] for some one who had no garden; the little bundles of lavender-flowers sent to strew the drawers of some town-dweller, or to burn in the chamber of some invalid. Things that many would despise, and actions which it seemed scarcely worth while to perform, were all attended to in Cranford. Miss Jenkyns stuck an apple full of cloves, to be heated and smell pleasantly in Miss Brown's room; and as she put in each clove, she uttered a Johnsonian sentence. Indeed, she never could think of the Browns without talking Johnson; and, as they were seldom absent from her thoughts just then, I heard many a rolling three-piled sentence.[11]

Captain Brown called one day to thank Miss Jenkyns for many little kindnesses, which I did not know until then that she had rendered. He had suddenly become like an old man; his deep bass voice had a quavering in it; his eyes looked dim, and the lines on his face were deep. He did not – could not – speak cheerfully of his daughter's state, but he talked with manly pious resignation, and not much. Twice over he said, 'What Jessie has been to us, God only knows!' and after the second time, he got up hastily, shook hands all round without speaking, and left the room.

That afternoon we perceived little groups in the street, all listening with faces aghast to some tale or other. Miss Jenkyns wondered what could be the matter, for some time before she took the undignified step of sending Jenny out to inquire.

Jenny came back with a white face of terror. 'Oh, ma'am! oh, Miss Jenkyns, ma'am! Captain Brown is killed by them nasty cruel railroads!' and she burst into tears. She, along with many others, had experienced the poor Captain's kindness.

'How? – where – where? Good God! Jenny, don't waste time in crying, but tell us something.' Miss Matty rushed out into the street at once, and collared the man who was telling the tale.

'Come in – come to my sister at once, – Miss Jenkyns, the rector's daughter. Oh, man, man! say it is not true,' – she cried, as she brought the affrighted carter, sleeking down his hair, into the drawing-room, where he stood with his wet boots on the new carpet, and no one regarded it.

'Please mum, it is true. I seed it myself,' and he shuddered at the recollection. 'The Captain was a-reading some new book as he was deep in, a-waiting for the down train; and there was a little lass as wanted to come to it's mammy, and gave it's sister the slip, and came toddling across the line. And he looked up sudden, at the sound of the train coming, and seed the child, and he darted on the line and cotched it up, and his foot slipped, and the train came over him in no time. Oh Lord, Lord! Mum, it's quite true – and they've come over to tell his daughters. The child's safe, though, with only a bang on it's shoulder, as he threw it to its mammy. Poor Captain would be glad of that, mum, wouldn't he? God bless him!' The great rough carter puckered up his manly face, and turned away to hide his tears. I turned to Miss Jenkyns. She looked very ill, as if she were going to faint, and signed to me to open the window.

'Matilda, bring me my bonnet. I must go to those girls. God pardon me, if ever I have spoken contemptuously to the Captain!'

Miss Jenkyns arrayed herself to go out, telling Miss Matilda to give the man a glass of wine. While she was away, Miss Matty and I huddled over the fire, talking in a low and awestruck voice. I know we cried quietly all the time.

Miss Jenkyns came home in a silent mood, and we durst not ask her many questions. She told us that Miss Jessie had fainted, and that she and Miss Pole had had some difficulty in bringing her round : but that, as soon as she recovered, she begged one of them to go and sit with her sister.

'Mr Hoggins says she cannot live many days, and she shall be spared this shock,' said Miss Jessie, shivering with feelings to which she dared not give way.

'But how can you manage, my dear?' asked Miss Jenkyns; 'you cannot bear up, she must see your tears.'

'God will help me – I will not give way – she was asleep when the news came; she may be asleep yet. She would be so utterly miserable, not merely at my father's death, but to think of what would become of me; she is so good to me.' She looked up earnestly in their faces with her soft true eyes, and Miss Pole told Miss Jenkyns afterwards she could hardly bear it, knowing, as she did, how Miss Brown treated her sister.

However, it was settled according to Miss Jessie's wish. Miss Brown was to be told her father had been summoned to take a short journey on railway business. They had managed it in some way – Miss Jenkyns could not exactly say how. Miss Pole was to stop with Miss Jessie. Mrs Jamieson had sent to inquire. And this was all we heard that night; and a sorrowful night it was. The next day a full account of the fatal accident was in the county paper, which Miss Jenkyns took in. Her eyes were very weak, she said, and she asked me to read it. When I came to the 'gallant gentleman was deeply engaged in the perusal of a number of *Pickwick*, which he had just received,' Miss Jenkyns shook her head long and solemnly, and then sighed out, 'Poor, dear, infatuated man!'"

The corpse was to be taken from the station to the parish church, there to be interred. Miss Jessie had set her heart on following it to the grave; and no dissuasives could alter her resolve. Her restraint upon herself made her almost obstinate; she resisted all Miss Pole's entreaties, and Miss Jenkyns's advice. At last Miss Jenkyns gave up the point; and after a silence, which I feared portended some deep displeasure against Miss Jessie, Miss Jenkyns said she should accompany the latter to the funeral.

'It is not fit for you to go alone. It would be against both propriety and humanity were I to allow it.'

Miss Jessie seemed as if she did not half like this arrangement; but her obstinacy if she had any, had been exhausted in her determination to go to the interment. She longed, poor thing! I have no doubt, to cry alone over the grave of the dear father to whom she had been all in all: and to give way, for one little half-hour, uninterrupted by sympathy, and unobserved by friendship. But it was not to be. That afternoon Miss Jenkyns sent out for a yard of black crape, and employed herself busily in trimming the little black silk bonnet I have spoken about. When it was finished she put it on and looked at us for approbation – admiration she despised. I was full of sorrow, but, by one of those whimsical thoughts which come unbidden into our heads, in times of deepest grief, I no sooner saw the bonnet than I was reminded of a helmet; and in that hybrid bonnet, half-helmet, half-jockey cap, did Miss Jenkyns attend Captain Brown's funeral; and, I believe, supported Miss Jessie with a tender indulgent firmness which was invaluable, allowing her to weep her passionate fill before they left.

Miss Pole, Miss Matty, and I, meanwhile, attended to Miss Brown: and hard work we found it to relieve her querulous and never-ending complaints. But if we were so weary and dispirited, what must Miss Jessie have been! Yet she came back almost calm, as if she had gained a new strength. She put off her mourning dress, and came in, looking pale and gentle; thanking us each with a soft pressure of the hand. She could even smile – a faint, sweet, wintry smile – as if to reassure us of her power to endure; but her look made our eyes fill suddenly with tears, more than if she had cried outright.

It was settled that Miss Pole was to remain with her all the watching livelong night; and that Miss Matty and I were to return in the morning to relieve them and give Miss Jessie the opportunity for a few hours of sleep. But when the morning came, Miss Jenkyns appeared at the breakfast table, equipped in her helmet bonnet, and ordered Miss Matty to stay at home, as she meant to go and help to nurse. She was evidently in a state of great friendly excitement, which she showed by eating her breakfast standing, and scolding the household all round.

No nursing – no energetic strong-minded woman could help Miss Brown now. There was that in the room as we entered, which was stronger than us all, and made us shrink into solemn awe-struck helplessness. Miss Brown was dying. We hardly knew her voice, it was so devoid of the complaining tone we had always associated with it. Miss Jessie told me afterwards that it, and her face too, were just what they had been formerly, when her mother's death left her the young anxious head of the family, of whom only Miss Jessie survived.

She was conscious of her sister's presence, though not, I think, of ours. We stood a little behind the curtain: Miss Jessie knelt with her face near her sister's, in order to catch the last soft awful whispers.

'Oh, Jessie! Jessie! How selfish I have been! God forgive me for letting you sacrifice yourself for me as you did. I have so loved you – and yet I have thought only of myself. God forgive me!'

'Hush, love! hush!' said Miss Jessie, sobbing.

'And my father! my dear, dear father! I will not complain now, if God will give me strength to be patient. But, oh, Jessie! tell my father how I longed and yearned to see him at last, and to ask his forgiveness. He can never know how I loved him – oh! if I might but tell him, before I die! What a life of sorrow his has been, and I have done so little to cheer him!'

A light came into Miss Jessie's face. 'Would it comfort you, dearest, to think that he does know – would it comfort you, love, to know that his cares, his sorrows –' Her voice quivered, but she steadied it into calmness, – 'Mary! he has gone before you to the place where the weary are at rest.[12] He knows now how you loved him.'

A strange look, which was not distress, came over Miss Brown's face. She did not speak for some time, but then we saw her lips form the words, rather than heard the sound – 'Father, mother, Harry, Archy;' – then, as if it was a new idea throwing a filmy shadow over her darkened mind – 'But you will be alone – Jessie!'

Miss Jessie had been feeling this all during the silence, I think; for the tears rolled down her cheeks like rain, at these words; and she could not answer at first. Then she put her hands together tight, and lifted them up, and said, – but not to us –

'Though He slay me, yet will I trust in Him.'[13]

In a few moments more, Miss Brown lay calm and still; never to sorrow or murmur more.

After this second funeral, Miss Jenkyns insisted that Miss Jessie should come to stay with her, rather than go back to the desolate house; which, in fact, we learned from Miss Jessie, must now be given up, as she had not wherewithal to maintain it. She had something above twenty pounds a-year, besides the interest of the money for which the furniture would sell; but she could not live upon that: and so we talked over her qualifications for earning money.

'I can sew neatly,' said she, 'and I like nursing. I think, too, I could manage a house, if any one would try me as housekeper; or I would go into a shop, as saleswoman, if they would have patience with me at first.'

Miss Jenkyns declared, in an angry voice, that she should do no such thing; and talked to herself about 'some people having no idea of their rank as a captain's daughter,' nearly an hour afterwards, when she brought Miss Jessie up a basin of delicately-made arrowroot,[14] and stood over her like a dragoon until the last spoonful was finished: then she disappeared. Miss Jessie began to tell me some more of the plans which had suggested themselves to her, and insensibly fell into talking of the days that were past and gone, and interested me so much, I neither knew nor heeded how time passed. We were both startled when Miss Jenkyns reappeared, and caught us crying. I was afraid lest she would be displeased, as she often said that crying hindered digestion, and I knew she wanted Miss Jessie to get strong; but, instead, she looked queer and excited, and fidgeted round us without saying anything. At last she spoke.

'I have been so much startled – no, I've not been at all startled – don't mind me, my dear Miss Jessie – I've been very much surprised – in fact, I've had a caller, whom you knew once, my dear Miss Jessie –'

Miss Jessie went very white, then flushed scarlet, and looked eagerly at Miss Jenkyns.

'A gentleman, my dear, who wants to know if you would see him.'

'Is it? – it is not –' stammered out Miss Jessie – and got no farther.

'This is his card,' said Miss Jenkyns, giving it to Miss Jessie; and while her head was bent over it, Miss Jenkyns went through a series of winks and odd faces to me, and formed her lips into a long sentence, of which, of course, I could not understand a word.

'May he come up?' asked Miss Jenkyns at last.

'Oh, yes! certainly!' said Miss Jessie, as much as to say, this is your house, you may show any visitor where you like. She took up some knitting of Miss Matty's and began to be very busy, though I could see how she trembled all over.

Miss Jenkyns rang the bell and told the servant who answered it to show Major Gordon up-stairs; and presently in walked a tall, fine, frank-looking man of forty, or upwards. He shook hands with Miss Jessie; but he could not see her eyes, she kept them so fixed on the ground. Miss Jenkyns asked me if I would come and help her to tie up the preserves in the store-room; and, though Miss Jessie plucked at my gown, and even looked up at me with begging eye, I durst not refuse to go where Miss Jenkyns asked. Instead of tying up preserves in the store-room, however, we went to talk in the dining-room; and there Miss Jenkyns told me what Major Gordon had told her; – how he had served in the same regiment with Captain Brown, and had become acquainted with Miss Jessie, then a sweet-looking, blooming girl of eighteen; how the acquaintance had grown into love, on his part, though it had been some years before he had spoken; how, on becoming possessed through the will of an uncle, of a good estate in Scotland, he had offered, and been refused, though with so much agitation, and evident distress, that he was sure she was not indifferent to him; and how he had discovered that the obstacle was the fell disease which was even then, too surely threatening her sister. She had mentioned that the surgeons foretold intense suffering; and there was no one but herself to nurse her poor Mary, or cheer and comfort her father during the time of illness. They had had long discussions; and, on her refusal to pledge herself to him as his wife, when all should be over, he had grown angry, and broken off entirely, and gone abroad, believing that she was a cold-hearted person, whom he would do well to forget. He had been travelling in the East, and was on his return home when, at Rome, he saw the account of Captain Brown's death in *Galignani*.[15]

Just then Miss Matty, who had been out all the morning, and had only lately returned to the house, burst in with a face of dismay and outraged propriety:

'Oh, goodness me!' she said. 'Deborah, there's a gentleman sitting in the drawing-room, with his arm round Miss Jessie's waist!' Miss Matty's eyes looked large with terror.

Miss Jenkyns snubbed her down in an instant:

"The most proper place in the world for his arm to be in. Go away, Matilda, and mind your own business.' This from her sister, who had hitherto been a model of feminine decorum, was a blow for poor Miss Matty, and with a double shock she left the room.

The last time I ever saw poor Miss Jenkyns was many years after this. Mrs Gordon had kept up a warm and affectionate intercourse with all at Cranford. Miss Jenkyns, Miss Matty, and Miss Pole had all been to visit her, and returned with wonderful accounts of her house, her husband, her dress, and her looks. For, with happiness, something of her early bloom returned; she had been a year or two younger than we had taken her for. Her eyes were always lovely, and, as Mrs Gordon, her dimples were not out of place. At the time to which I have referred, when I last saw Miss Jenkyns, that lady was old and feeble, and had lost something of her strong mind. Little Flora Gordon was staying with the Misses Jenkyns, and when I came in she was reading aloud to Miss Jenkyns, who lay feeble and changed on the sofa. Flora put down the *Rambler* when I came in.

'Ah !' said Miss Jenkyns, 'you find me changed, my dear. I can't see as I used to do. If Flora were not here to read to me, I hardly know how I should get through the day. Did you ever read the *Rambler*? It's a wonderful book – wonderful ! and the most improving reading for Flora' – (which I dare say it would have been, if she could have read half the words without spelling, and could have understood the meaning of a third) – 'better than that strange old book, with the queer name, poor Captain Brown was killed for reading – that book by Mr Boz, you know – "Old Poz;" [16] when I was a girl – but that's a long time ago – I acted Lucy in "Old Poz." ' – She babbled on long enough for Flora to get a good long spell at the *Christmas Carol*,[17] which Miss Matty had left on the table.

CHAPTER III

A Love Affair of Long Ago

I thought that probably my connexion with Cranford would cease after Miss Jenkyns's death; at least, that it would have to be kept up by correspondence, which bears much the same relationship to personal intercourse that the books of dried plants I sometimes see ('Hortus Siccus,'[1] I think they call the thing) do to the living and fresh flowers in the lanes and meadows. I was pleasantly surprised, therefore, by receiving a letter from Miss Pole (who had always come in for a supplementary week, after my annual visit to Miss Jenkyns) proposing that I should go and stay with her; and then, in a couple of days after my acceptance, came a note from Miss Matty, in which, in a rather circuitous and very humble manner, she told me how much pleasure I should confer, if I could spend a week or two with her, either before or after I had been at Miss Pole's; 'for,' she said, 'since my dear sister's death, I am well aware I have no attractions to offer; it is only to the kindness of my friends that I can owe their company.'

Of course, I promised to come to dear Miss Matty, as soon as I had ended my visit to Miss Pole; and the day after my arrival at Cranford, I went to see her, much wondering what the house would be like without Miss Jenkyns, and rather dreading the changed aspect of things. Miss Matty began to cry as soon as she saw me. She was evidently nervous from having anticipated my call. I comforted her as well as I could; and I found the best consolation I could give was the honest praise that came from my heart as I spoke of the deceased. Miss Matty slowly shook her head over each virtue as it was named and attributed to her sister; and at last she could not restrain the tears which had long been silently flowing, but hid her face behind her handkerchief, and sobbed aloud.

'Dear Miss Matty!' said I, taking her hand – for indeed I did not know in what way to tell her how sorry I was for her, left deserted in the world. She put down her handkerchief, and said:

'My dear, I'd rather you did not call me Matty. *She* did not like it; but I did many a thing she did not like, I'm afraid – and now she's gone ! If you please, my love, will you call me Matilda?'

I promised faithfully, and began to practise the new name with Miss Pole that very day; and, by degrees, Miss Matilda's feelings on the subject was known through Cranford, and we all tried to drop the more familiar name, but with so little success that by-and-by we gave up the attempt.

My visit to Miss Pole was very quiet. Miss Jenkyns had so long taken the lead in Cranford, that, now she was gone, they hardly knew how to give a party. The Honourable Mrs Jamieson, to whom Miss Jenkyns herself had always yielded the post of honour, was fat and inert, and very much at the mercy of her old servants. If they chose that she should give a party, they reminded her of the necessity for so doing; if not, she let it alone. There was all the more time for me to hear old-world stories from Miss Pole, while she sat knitting, and I making my father's shirts. I always took a quantity of plain sewing to Cranford; for, as we did not read much, or walk much, I found it a capital time to get through my work. One of Miss Pole's stories related to a shadow of a love affair that was dimly perceived or suspected long years before.

Presently, the time arrived when I was to remove to Miss Matilda's house. I found her timid and anxious about the arrangements for my comfort. Many a time, while I was unpacking, did she come backwards and forwards to stir the fire, which burned all the worse for being so frequently poked.

'Have you drawers enough, dear?' asked she. 'I don't know exactly how my sister used to arrange them. She had capital methods. I am sure she would have trained a servant in a week to make a better fire than this, and Fanny has been with me four months.'

This subject of servants was a standing grievance, and I could not wonder much at it; for if gentlemen were scarce, and almost unheard of in the 'genteel society' of Cranford, they or their counterparts – handsome young men – abounded in the lower classes. The pretty neat servant-maids had their choice of desirable 'followers', and their mistresses, without having the sort of mysterious dread of men and matrimony that Miss Matilda had, might well feel a little anxious, lest the heads of their comely maids should be turned by the joiner, or the butcher, or the gardener; who were obliged, by their callings, to come to the house; and who, as ill-luck would have it, were generally handsome and unmarried. Fanny's lovers, if she had any – and Miss Matilda suspected her of so many flirtations, that, if she had not been very pretty, I should have doubted her having one – were a constant anxiety to her mistress. She was forbidden, by the articles of her engagement, to have 'followers;'[2] and though she had answered innocently enough, doubling up the hem of her apron as she spoke, 'Please, ma'am, I never had more than one at a time,' Miss Matty prohibited that one. But a vision of a man seemed to haunt the kitchen. Fanny assured me that it was all fancy; or else I should have said myself that I had seen a man's coat-tails whisk into the scullery once, when I went on an errand into the store-room at night; and another evening, when, our watches having stopped, I went to look at the clock, there was a very odd appearance, singularly like a young man squeezed up between the clock and the back of the open kitchen-door : and I thought Fanny snatched up the candle very hastily, so as to throw the shadow on the clock-face, while she very positively told me the time half an hour too early, as we found out afterwards by the church-clock. But I did not add to Miss Matty's anxieties by naming my suspicions, especially as Fanny said to me, the next day, that it was such a queer kitchen for having odd shadows about it, she really was almost afraid to stay; 'for you know, miss,' she added, 'I don't see a creature from six o'clock tea, till Missus rings the bell for prayers at ten.'[3]

However, it so fell out that Fanny had to leave; and Miss Matilda begged me to stay and 'settle her' with the new maid; to which I consented, after I had heard from my father that he did not want me at home. The new servant was a rough, honest-looking country-girl, who had only lived in a farm place before; but I liked her looks when she came to be hired; and I promised Miss Matilda to put her in the ways of the house. The said ways were religiously such as Miss Matilda thought her sister would approve. Many a domestic rule and regulation had been a subject of plaintive whispered murmur to me, during Miss Jenkyns's life; but now that she was gone, I do not think that even I, who was a favourite, durst have suggested an alteration. To give an instance: we constantly adhered to the forms which were observed, at meal times, in 'my father, the rector's house.' Accordingly, we had always wine and dessert; but the decanters were only filled when there was a party; and what remained was seldom touched, though we had two wine glasses apiece every day after dinner, until the next festive occasion arrived; when the state of the remainder wine was examined into, in a family council. The dregs were often given to the poor; but occasionally, when a good deal had been left at the last party (five months ago, it might be), it was added to some of a fresh bottle, brought up from the cellar. I fancy poor Captain Brown did not much like wine; for I noticed he never finished his first glass, and most military men take several. Then, as to our dessert, Miss Jenkyns used to gather currants and gooseberries for it herself, which I sometimes thought would have tasted better fresh from the trees; but then, as Miss Jenkyns observed, there would have been nothing for dessert in summer-time. As it was, we felt very genteel with our two glasses apiece, and a dish of gooseberries at the top, of currants and biscuits at the sides, and two decanters at the bottom. When oranges came in, a curious proceeding was gone through. Miss Jenkyns did not like to cut the fruit; for, as she observed, the juice all ran out nobody knew where; sucking (only I think she used some more recondite word) was in fact the only way of enjoying oranges; but then there was the unpleasant association with a ceremony frequently gone through by little babies; and so, after dessert, in orange season, Miss Jenkyns and Miss Matty used to rise up, possess themselves each of an orange in silence, and withdraw to the privacy of their own rooms, to indulge in sucking oranges.

I had once or twice tried, on such occasions, to prevail on Miss Matty to stay; and had succeeded in her sister's lifetime. I held up a screen,[4] and did not look, and, as she said, she tried not to make the noise very offensive; but now that she was left alone, she seemed quite horrified when I begged her to remain with me in the warm dining-parlour, and enjoy her orange as she liked best. And so it was in everything. Miss Jenkyns's rules were made more stringent than ever, because the framer of them was gone where there could be no appeal. In all things else Miss Maltida was meek and undecided to a fault. I have heard Fanny turn her round twenty times in a morning about dinner, just as the little hussy chose; and I sometimes fancied she worked on Miss Matilda's weakness in order to bewilder her, and to make her feel more in the power of her clever servant. I determined that I would not leave her till I had seen what sort of a person Martha was; and, if I found her trustworthy, I would tell her not to trouble her mistress with every little decision.

Martha was blunt and plain-spoken to a fault; otherwise she was a brisk, well-meaning, but very ignorant girl. She had not been with us a week before Miss Matilda and I were astounded one morning by the receipt of a letter from a cousin of hers, who had been twenty or thirty years in India, and who had lately, as we had seen by the 'Army List,' returned to England, bringing with him an invalid wife who had never been introduced to her English relations. Major Jenkyns wrote to propose that he and his wife should spend a night at Cranford, on his way to Scotland – at the inn, if it did not suit Miss Matilda to receive them into her house; in which case they should hope to be with her as much as possible during the day. Of course, it *must* suit her, as she said; for all Cranford knew that she had her sister's bedroom at liberty; but I am sure she wished the Major had stopped in India and forgotten his cousins out and out.

'Oh! how must I manage?' asked she, helplessly. 'If Deborah had been alive, she would have known what to do with a gentleman-visitor. Must I put razors in his dressing-room? Dear! dear! and I've got none. Deborah would have had them. And slippers, and coat-brushes?' I suggested that probably he would bring all these things with him. 'And after dinner, how am I to know when to get up, and leave him to his wine? Deborah would have done it so well; she would have been quite in her element. Will he want coffee, do you think?' I undertook the management of the coffee, and told her I would instruct Martha in the art of waiting, in which it must be owned she was terribly deficient; and that I had no doubt Major and Mrs Jenkyns would understand the quiet mode in which a lady lived by herself in a country town. But she was sadly fluttered. I made her empty her decanters, and bring up two fresh bottles of wine. I wished I could have prevented her from being present at my instructions to Martha; for she frequently cut in with some fresh direction, muddling the poor girl's mind, as she stood open-mouthed, listening to us both.

'Hand the vegetables round,' said I (foolishly, I see now – for it was aiming at more than we could accomplish with quietness and simplicity): and then, seeing her look bewildered, I added, 'Take the vegetables round to people, and let them help themselves.'

'And mind you go first to the ladies,' put in Miss Matilda. 'Always go to the ladies before gentlemen, when you are waiting.'

'I'll do it as you tell me, ma'am,' said Martha; 'but I like lads best.'

We felt very uncomfortable and shocked at this speech of Martha's; yet I don't think she meant any harm; and, on the whole, she attended very well to our directions, except that she 'nudged' the major, when he did not help himself as soon as she expected, to the potatoes, while she was handing them round.

The major and his wife were quiet, unpretending people enough when they did come; languid, as all East Indians are, I suppose. We were rather dismayed at their bringing two servants with them, a Hindoo body-servant for the major, and a steady elderly maid for his wife; but they slept at the inn, and took off a good deal of the responsibility by attending carefully to their master's and mistress's comfort. Martha, to be sure, had never ended her staring at the East Indian's white turban and brown complexion, and I saw that Miss Matilda shrunk away from him a little as he waited at dinner. Indeed, she asked me, when they were gone, if he did not remind me of Blue Beard?[5] On the whole, the visit was most satisfactory, and is a subject of conversation even now with Miss Matilda; at the time, it greatly excited Cranford, and even stirred up the apathetic and Honourable Mrs Jamieson to some expression of interest, when I went to call and thank her for the kind answers she had vouchsafed to Miss Matilda's inquiries as to the arrangement of a gentleman's dressing-room – answers which I must confess she had given in the wearied manner of the Scandinavian prophetess,[6] –

Leave me, leave me to repose.

And *now* I come to the love affair.

It seems that Miss Pole had a cousin, once or twice removed, who had offered to Miss Matty long ago. Now, this cousin lived four or five miles from Cranford on his own estate; but his property was not large enough to entitle him to rank higher than a yeoman; or rather, with something of the 'pride which apes humility,'[7] he had refused to push himself on, as so many of his class had done, into the ranks of the squires. He would not allow himself to be called Thomas Holbrook, *Esq.*; he even sent back letters with his address, telling the postmistress at Cranford that his name was Mr Thomas Holbrook, yeoman.[8] He rejected all domestic innovations; he would have the house door stand open in summer, and shut in winter, without knocker or bell to summon a servant. The closed fist or the knob of the stick did this office for him, if he found the door locked. He despised every refinement which had not its root deep down in humanity. If people were not ill, he saw no necessity for moderating his voice. He spoke the dialect of the country in perfection, and constantly used it in conversation; although Miss Pole (who gave me these particulars) added, that he read aloud more beautifully and with more feeling than any one she had ever heard, except the late rector.

'And how came Miss Matilda not to marry him?' asked I.

'Oh, I don't know. She was willing enough, I think; but you know cousin Thomas would not have been enough of a gentleman for the rector and Miss Jenkyns.'

'Well! but they were not to marry him,' said I, impatiently,

'No; but they did not like Miss Matty to marry below her rank. You know she was the rector's daughter, and somehow they are related to Sir Peter Arley: Miss Jenkyns thought a deal of that.'

'Poor Miss Matty!' said I.

'Nay, now, I don't know anything more than that he offered and was refused. Miss Matty might not like him – and Miss Jenkyns might never have said a word – it is only a guess of mine.'

'Has she never seen him since?' I inquired.

'No, I think not. You see, Woodley, cousin Thomas's house,

lies half-way between Cranford and Misselton; and I know he
made Misselton his market-town very soon after he had offered to
Miss Matty; and I don't think he has been into Cranford above
once or twice since – once, when I was walking with Miss Matty,
in High-street; and suddenly she darted from me, and went up
Shire-lane. A few minutes after, I was startled by meeting cousin
Thomas.'

'How old is he?' I asked, after a pause of castle-building.

'He must be about seventy, I think, my dear,' said Miss Pole,
blowing up my castle, as if by gunpowder, into small fragments.

Very soon after – at least during my long visit to Miss Matilda
– I had the opportunity of seeing Mr Holbrook; seeing, too, his
first encounter with his former love, after thirty or forty years'
separation. I was helping to decide whether any of the new assortment of coloured silks which they had just received at the shop,
would do to match a grey and black mousseline-de-laine⁹ that
wanted a new breadth, when a tall, thin, Don Quixote-looking
old man came into the shop for some woollen gloves. I had never
seen the person (who was rather striking) before, and I watched
him rather attentively, while Miss Matty listened to the shopman. The stranger wore a blue coat with brass buttons, drab
breeches, and gaiters, and drummed with his fingers on the counter until he was attended to. When he answered the shop-boy's
question, 'What can I have the pleasure of showing you to-day,
sir?' I saw Miss Matilda start, and then suddenly sit down; and
instantly I guessed who it was. She had made some inquiry which
had to be carried round to the other shopman.

'Miss Jenkyns wants the black sarsenet¹⁰ two-and-twopence
the yard;' and Mr Holbrook had caught the name, and was across
the shop in two strides.

'Matty – Miss Matilda – Miss Jenkyns! God bless my soul! I
should not have known you. How are you? how are you?' He
kept shaking her hand in a way which proved the warmth of his
friendship; but he repeated so often, as if to himself, 'I should not
have known you!' that any sentimental romance which I might
be inclined to build, was quite done away with by his manner.

However, he kept talking to us all the time we were in the
shop; and then waving the shopman with the unpurchased gloves

on one side, with 'Another time, sir! another time!' he walked home with us. I am happy to say my client, Miss Matilda, also left the shop in an equally bewildered state, not having purchased either green or red silk. Mr Holbrook was evidently full with honest, loud-spoken joy at meeting his old love again; he touched on the changes that had taken place; he even spoke of Miss Jenkyns as 'Your poor sister! Well, well! we have all our faults;' and bade us good-by with many a hope that he should soon see Miss Matty again. She went straight to her room; and never came back till our early tea-time, when I thought she looked as if she had been crying.

CHAPTER IV

A Visit to an Old Bachelor

A FEW days after, a note came from Mr Holbrook, asking us – impartially asking both of us – in a formal, old-fashioned style, to spend a day at his house – a long June day – for it was June now. He named that he had also invited his cousin, Miss Pole; so that we might join in a fly,[1] which could be put up at his house.

I expected Miss Matty to jump at this invitation; but no! Miss Pole and I had the greatest difficulty in persuading her to go. She thought it was improper; and was even half annoyed when we utterly ignored the idea of any impropriety in her going with two other ladies to see her old lover. Then came a more serious difficulty. She did not think Deborah would have liked her to go. This took us half a day's good hard talking to get over; but, at the first sentence of relenting, I seized the opportunity, and wrote and despatched an acceptance in her name – fixing day and hour, that all might be decided and done with.

The next morning she asked me if I would go down to the shop with her; and there, after much hesitation, we chose out three caps to be sent home and tried on, that the most becoming might be selected to take with us on Thursday.

She was in a state of silent agitation all the way to Woodley. She had evidently never been there before; and, although she little dreamt I knew anything of her early story, I could perceive she was in a tremor at the thought of seeing the place which might have been her home, and round which it is probable that many of her innocent girlish imaginations had clustered. It was a long drive there, through paved jolting lanes. Miss Matilda sat bolt upright, and looked wistfully out of the windows, as we drew near the end of our journey. The aspect of the country was quiet and pastoral. Woodley stood among fields; and there was an old-fashioned garden, where roses and currant-bushes touched each other, and where the feathery asparagus formed a pretty background to the pinks and gilly-flowers;[2] there was no drive up to the door: we got out at a little gate, and walked up a straight box-edged path.

'My cousin might make a drive, I think,' said Miss Pole, who was afraid of ear-ache, and had only her cap on.

'I think it is very pretty,' said Miss Matty, with a soft plaintiveness in her voice, and almost in a whisper; for just then Mr Holbrook appeared at the door, rubbing his hands in very effervescence of hospitality. He looked more like my idea of Don Quixote than ever, and yet the likeness was only external. His respectable housekeeper stood modestly at the door to bid us welcome; and, while she led the elder ladies up-stairs to a bed-room, I begged to look about the garden. My request evidently pleased the old gentleman; who took me all round the place, and showed me his six-and-twenty cows, named after the different letters of the alphabet. As we went along, he surprised me occasionally by repeating apt and beautiful quotations from the poets, ranging easily from Shakespeare and George Herbert to those of our own day. He did this as naturally as if he were thinking aloud, and their true and beautiful words were the best expression he could find for what he was thinking or feeling. To be sure, he called Byron 'my Lord Byrron,' and pronounced the name of Goethe strictly in accordance with the English sound of the letters – 'As Goëthe says, "Ye ever-verdant palaces,"' &c.[3] Altogether, I never met·with a man, before or since, who had spent so long a life in a secluded and not impressive country with ever-increasing delight in the daily and yearly change of season and beauty.

When he and I went in, we found that dinner was nearly ready in the kitchen, – for so I suppose the room ought to be called, as there were oak dressers and cupboards all round, all over by the side of the fireplace, and only a small Turkey carpet in the middle of the flag-floor. The room might have been easily made into a handsome dark-oak dining-parlour, by removing the oven, and a few other appurtenances of a kitchen, which were evidently never used; the real cooking place being at some distance. The room in which we were expected to sit was a stiffly furnished, ugly apartment; but that in which we did sit was what Mr Holbrook called the counting-house, when he paid his labourers their weekly wages, at a great desk near the door. The rest of the pretty sitting-room – looking into the orchard, and all covered over with dancing tree-shadows – was filled with books. They lay on the ground, they covered the walls, they strewed the table. He was evidently half ashamed and half proud of his extravagance in this respect. They were of all kinds, – poetry, and wild weird tales prevailing. He evidently chose his books in accordance with his own tastes, not because such and such were classical, or established favourites.

'Ah!' he said, 'we farmers ought not to have much time for reading; yet somehow one can't help it.'

'What a pretty room!' said Miss Matty, *sotto voce*.

'What a pleasant place!' said I, aloud, almost simultaneously.

'Nay! if you like it,' – replied he; 'but you can sit on these great black leather three-cornered chairs? I like it better than the best parlour; but I thought ladies would take that for the smarter place.'

It was the smarter place; but, like most smart things, not at all pretty, or pleasant, or home-like; so, while we were at dinner, the servant-girl dusted and scrubbed the counting-house chairs, and we sat there all the rest of the day.

We had pudding before meat; and I thought Mr Holbrook was going to make some apology for his old-fashioned ways, for he began, –

'I don't know whether you like new-fangled ways.'

'Oh! not at all!' said Miss Matty.

'No more do I,' said he. 'My housekeeper *will* have these in her new fashion; or else I tell her, that when I was a young man, we used to keep strictly to my father's rule, "No broth, no ball; no ball, no beef;"[4] and always began dinner with broth. Then we had suet puddings, boiled in the broth with the beef; and then the meat itself. If we did not sup our broth, we had no ball, which we liked a deal better; and the beef came last of all, and only those had it who had done justice to the broth and the ball. Now folks begin with sweet things, and turn their dinners topsy-turvy.'

When the ducks and green peas came, we looked at each other in dismay; we had only two-pronged, black-handled forks. It is true, the steel was as bright as silver; but what were we to do?

Miss Matty picked up her peas, one by one, on the point of the prongs, much as Aminé ate her grains of rice after her previous feast with the Ghoul.[5] Miss Pole sighed over her delicate young peas as she left them on one side of her plate untasted; for they would drop between the prongs. I looked at my host: the peas were going wholesale into his capacious mouth, shovelled up by his large round-ended knife. I saw, I imitated, I survived! My friends, in spite of my precedent, could not muster up courage enough to do an ungenteel thing; and, if Mr Holbrook had not been so heartily hungry, he would probably have seen that the good peas went away almost untouched.

After dinner, a clay pipe was brought in, and a spittoon; and, asking us to retire to another room, where he would soon join us, if we disliked tobacco-smoke, he presented his pipe to Miss Matty, and requested her to fill the bowl. This was a compliment to a lady in his youth; but it was rather inappropriate to propose it as an honour to Miss Matty, who had been trained by her sister to hold smoking of every kind in utter abhorrence. But if it was a shock to her refinement, it was also a gratification to her feelings to be thus selected; so she daintily stuffed the strong tobacco into the pipe; and then we withdrew.

'It is very pleasant dining with a bachelor,' said Miss Matty, softly, as we settled ourselves in the counting-house. 'I only hope it is not improper; so many pleasant things are!'

'What a number of books he has!' said Miss Pole, looking round the room. 'And how dusty they are!'

'I think it must be like one of the great Dr Johnson's rooms,' said Miss Matty. 'What a superior man your cousin must be!'

'Yes!' said Miss Pole; 'he's a great reader; but I am afraid he has got into very uncouth habits with living alone.'

'Oh! uncouth is too hard a word. I should call him eccentric; very clever people always are!' replied Miss Matty.

When Mr Holbrook returned, he proposed a walk in the fields; but the two elder ladies were afraid of damp, and dirt; and had only very unbecoming calashes[6] to put on over their caps; so they declined; and I was again his companion in a turn which he said he was obliged to take, to see after his men. He strode along, either

wholly forgetting my existence, or soothed into silence by his pipe
– and yet it was not silence exactly. He walked before me, with a
stooping gait, his hands clasped behind him; and, as some tree or
cloud, or glimpse of distant upland pastures, struck him, he quoted
poetry to himself; saying it out loud in a grand sonorous voice,
with just the emphasis that true feeling and appreciation give. We
came upon an old cedar-tree, which stood at one end of the
house: –

The cedar spreads his dark-green layers of shade.[7]

'Captial term – "layers!" Wonderful man!' I did not know
whether he was speaking to me or not; but I put in an assenting
'wonderful,' although I knew nothing about it; just because I was
tired of being forgotten, and of being consequently silent.

He turned sharp round. 'Ay! you may say "wonderful." Why,
when I saw the review of his poems in *Blackwood*,[8] I set off within
an hour, and walked seven miles to Misselton (for the horses were
not in the way) and ordered them. Now, what colour are ash-
buds in March?'

Is the man going mad? thought I. He is very like Don Quixote.

'What colour are they, I say?' repeated he, vehemently.

'I am sure I don't know, sir,' said I, with the meekness of ignorance.

'I knew you didn't. No more did I – an old fool that I am! –
till this young man comes and tells me. Black as ash-buds in
March.[9] And I've lived all my life in the country; more shame
for me not to know. Black: they are jet-black, madam.' And he
went off again, swinging along to the music of some rhyme he
had got hold of.

When we came back, nothing would serve him but he must
read us the poems he had been speaking of; and Miss Pole encouraged him in his proposal, I thought, because she wished me to
hear his beautiful reading, of which she had boasted; but she
afterwards said it was because she had got to a difficult part of her
crochet, and wanted to count her stitches without having to talk.
Whatever he had proposed would have been right to Miss Matty;
although she did fall asleep within five minutes after he had
begun a long poem, called *Locksley Hall*,[10] and had a comfortable

nap, unobserved, till he ended; when the cessation of his voice wakened her up, and she said, feeling that something was expected, and that Miss Pole was counting, –

'What a pretty book!'

'Pretty! madam! it's beautiful! Pretty, indeed!'

'Oh yes I meant beautiful!' said she, fluttered at his disapproval of her word. 'It is so like that beautiful poem of Dr Johnson's my sister used to read – I forget the name of it; what was it, my dear?' turning to me.

'Which do you mean, ma'am? What was it about?'

'I don't remember what it was about, and I've quite forgotten what the name of it was; but it was written by Dr Johnson, and was very beautiful, and very like what Mr Holbrook has just been reading.'

'I don't remember it,' said he, reflectively. 'But I don't know Dr Johnson's poems well. I must read them.'

As we were getting into the fly to return, I heard Mr Holbrook say he should call on the ladies soon, and inquire how they got home;[11] and this evidently pleased and fluttered Miss Matty at the time he said it; but after we had lost sight of the old house among the trees her sentiments towards the master of it were gradually absorbed into a distressing wonder as to whether Martha had broken her word, and seized on the opportunity of her mistress's absence to have a 'follower.' Martha looked good, and steady, and composed enough, as she came to help us out; she was always careful of Miss Matty, and to-night she made use of this unlucky speech:

'Eh! dear ma'am, to think of your going out in an evening in such a thin shawl! It's no better than muslin. At your age, ma'am, you should be careful.'

'My age!' said Miss Matty, almost speaking crossly, for her; for she was usually gentle. 'My age! Why, how old do you think I am, that you talk about my age?'

'Well, ma'am, I should say you were not far short of sixty: but folks' looks is often against them – and I'm sure I meant no harm.'

'Martha, I'm not yet fifty-two!' said Miss Matty, with grave emphasis; for probably the remembrance of her youth had come very vividly before her this day, and she was annoyed at finding that golden time so far away in the past.

But she never spoke of any former and more intimate acquaintance with Mr Holbrook. She had probably met with so little sympathy in her early love, that she had shut it up close in her heart; and it was only by a sort of watching, which I could hardly avoid since Miss Pole's confidence, that I saw how faithful her poor heart had been in its sorrow and its silence.

She gave me some good reason for wearing her best cap every day, and sat near the window, in spite of her rheumatism, in order to see, without being seen, down into the street.

He came. He put his open palms upon his knees, which were far apart, as he sat with his head bent down, whistling, after we had replied to his inquiries about our safe return. Suddenly, he jumped up:

'Well, madam! have you any commands for Paris? I am going there in a week or two.'

'To Paris!' [12] we both exclaimed.

'Yes, madam! I've never been there, and always had a wish to go; and I think if I don't go soon, I mayn't go at all; so as soon as the hay is got in I shall go, before harvest time.'

We were so much astonished, that we had no commissions.

Just as he was going out of the room, he turned back, with his favourite exclamation:

'God bless my soul, madam! but I nearly forgot half my errand. Here are the poems for you, you admired so much the other evening at my house.' He tugged away at a parcel in his coat-pocket. 'Good-by, miss,' said he; 'good-by, Matty! take care of yourself.' And he was gone. But he had given her a book, and he had called her Matty, just as he used to do thirty years ago.

'I wish he would not go to Paris,' said Miss Matilda, anxiously. 'I don't believe frogs will agree with him; he used to have to be very careful what he ate, which was curious in so strong-looking a young man.'

Soon after this I took my leave, giving many an injunction to Martha to look after her mistress, and to let me know if she thought that Miss Matilda was not so well; in which case I would volunteer a visit to my old friend, without noticing Martha's intelligence to her.

Accordingly I received a line or two from Martha every now and then; and, about November, I had a note to say her mistress was 'very low and sadly off her food;' and the account made me so uneasy that, although Martha did not decidedly summon me, I packed up my things and went.

I received a warm welcome, in spite of the little flurry produced by my impromptu visit, for I had only been able to give a day's notice. Miss Matilda looked miserably ill; and I prepared to comfort and cosset her.

I went down to have a private talk with Martha.

'How long has your mistress been so poorly?' I asked, as I stood by the kitchen fire.

'Well! I think it's better than a fortnight; it is, I know; it was one Tuesday, after Miss Pole had been, that she went into this moping way. I thought she was tired, and it would go off with a night's rest; but no! she has gone on and on ever since, till I thought it my duty to write to you, ma'am.'

'You did quite right, Martha. It is a comfort to think she has so faithful a servant about her. And I hope you find your place comfortable?'

'Well, ma'am, missus is very kind, and there's plenty to eat and drink, and no more work but what I can do easily, – but—' Martha hesitated.

'But what, Martha?'

'Why, it seems so hard of missus not to let me have any followers; there's such lots of young fellows in the town; and many a one has as much as offered to keep company with me; and I may never be in such a likely place again, and it's like wasting an opportunity. Many a girl as I know would have 'em unbeknownst to missus; but I've given my word, and I'll stick to it; or else this is just the house for missus never to be the wiser if they did come: and it's such a capable [13] kitchen – there's such good dark corners in it – I'd be bound to hide any one. I counted up last Sunday night – for I'll not deny I was crying because I had to shut the door in Jem Hearn's face; and he's a steady young man,

79

fit for any girl; only I had given missus my word.' Martha was all but crying again; and I had little comfort to give her, for I knew, from old experience, of the horror with which both the Miss Jenkynses looked upon 'followers;' and in Miss Matty's present nervous state this dread was not likely to be lessened.

I went to see Miss Pole the next day, and took her completely by surprise; for she had not been to see Miss Matilda for two days.

'And now I must go back with you, my dear, for I promised to let her know how Thomas Holbrook went on; and, I'm sorry to say, his housekeeper has sent me word to-day that he hasn't long to live. Poor Thomas! That journey to Paris was quite too much for him. His housekeeper says he has hardly ever been round his fields since; but just sits with his hands on his knees in the counting-house, not reading or anything, but only saying, what a wonderful city Paris was! Paris has much to answer for, if it's killed my cousin Thomas, for a better man never lived.'

'Does Miss Matilda know of his illness?' asked I; – a new light as to the cause of her indisposition dawning upon me.

'Dear! to be sure, yes! Has not she told you? I let her know a fortnight ago, or more, when I first heard of it. How odd she shouldn't have told you!'

Not at all, I thought; but I did not say anything. I felt almost guilty of having spied too curiously into that tender heart, and I was not going to speak of its secrets, – hidden, Miss Matty believed, from all the world. I ushered Miss Pole into Miss Matilda's little drawing-room; and then left them alone. But I was not surprised when Martha came to my bedroom door, to ask me to go down to dinner alone, for that missus had one of her bad headaches. She came into the drawing-room at tea-time; but it was evidently an effort to her; and, as if to make up for some reproachful feeling against her late sister, Miss Jenkyns, which had been troubling her all the afternoon, and for which she now felt penitent, she kept telling me how good and how clever Deborah was in her youth; how she used to settle what gowns they were to wear at all the parties (faint, ghostly ideas of grim parties, far away in the distance, when Miss Matty and Miss Pole were young!); and how Deborah and her mother had started the benefit society for the poor, and taught girls cooking and plain sewing; and how Deborah had once danced with a lord; and how she used to visit at Sir Peter Arley's, and try to remodel the quiet rectory establishment on the plans of Arley Hall, where they kept thirty servants; and how she had nursed Miss Matty through a long, long illness, of which I had never heard before, but which I now dated in my own mind as following the dismissal of the suit of Mr Holbrook. So we talked softly and quietly of old times, through the long November evening.

The next day Miss Pole brought us word that Mr Holbrook was dead. Miss Matty heard the news in silence; in fact, from the account of the previous day, it was only what we had to expect. Miss Pole kept calling upon us for some expression of regret, by asking if it was not sad that he was gone, and saying:

'To think of that pleasant day last June, when he seemed so well! And he might have lived this dozen years if he had not gone to that wicked Paris, where they are always having revolutions.'

She paused for some demonstration on our part. I saw Miss Matty could not speak, she was trembling so nervously; so I said what I really felt: and after a call of some duration – all the time of which I have no doubt Miss Pole thought Miss Matty received the news very calmly – our visitor took her leave.

Miss Matty made a strong effort to conceal her feelings – a concealment she practised even with me, for she has never alluded to Mr Holbrook again, although the book he gave her lies with her Bible on the little table by her bedside. She did not think I heard her when she asked the little milliner of Cranford to make her caps something like the Honourable Mrs Jamieson's, or that I noticed the reply –

'But she wears widows' caps, ma'am?'

'Oh! I only meant something in that style; not widows', of course, but rather like Mrs Jamieson's.'

This effort at concealment was the beginning of the tremulous motion of head and hands which I have seen ever since in Miss Matty.

The evening of the day on which we heard of Mr Holbrook's death, Miss Matilda was very silent and thoughtful; after prayers she called Martha back, and then she stood uncertain what to say.

'Martha!' she said at last; 'you are young,' – and then she made so long a pause that Martha, to remind her of her half-finished sentence, dropped a courtesy, and said –

'Yes, please, ma'am; two-and-twenty last third of October, please, ma'am.'

'And perhaps, Martha, you may some time meet with a young man you like, and who likes you. I did say you were not to have followers; but if you meet with such a young man, and tell me, and I find he is respectable, I have no objection to his coming to see you once a week. God forbid!' said she, in a low voice, 'that I should grieve any young hearts.' She spoke as if she were providing for some distant contingency, and was rather startled when Martha made her ready eager answer.

'Please, ma'am, there's Jem Hearn, and he's a joiner making three-and-sixpence a-day, and six foot one in his stocking-feet, please, ma'am; and if you'll ask about him to-morrow morning, every one will give him a character for steadiness; and he'll be glad enough to come to-morrow night, I'll be bound.'

Though Miss Matty was startled, she submitted to Fate and Love.

CHAPTER V

Old Letters

I HAVE often noticed that almost every one has his own individual small economies – careful habits of saving fractions of pennies in some one peculiar direction – any disturbance of which annoys him more than spending shillings or pounds on some real extravagance. An old gentleman of my acquaintance, who took the intelligence of the failure of a Joint-Stock Bank,[1] in which some of his money was invested, with stoical mildness, worried his family all through a long summer's day, because one of them had torn (instead of cutting) out the written leaves of his now useless bank-book; of course, the corresponding pages at the other end came out as well; and this little unnecessary waste of paper (his private economy) chafed him more than all the loss of his money. Envelopes fretted his soul terribly when they first came in;[2] the only way in which he could reconcile himself to such waste of his cherished article, was by patiently turning inside out all that were sent to him, and so making them serve again. Even now, though tamed by age, I see him casting wistful glances at his daughters when they send a whole inside of a half sheet of note-paper, with the three lines of acceptance to an invitation, written on only one of the sides. I am not above owning that I have this human weakness myself. String is my foible. My pockets get full of little hanks of it, picked up and twisted together, ready for uses that never come. I am seriously annoyed if any one cuts the string of a parcel, instead of patiently and faithfully undoing it fold by fold. How people can bring themselves to use India-rubber rings, which are a sort of deification of string, as lightly as they do, I cannot imagine. To me an India-rubber ring is a precious treasure. I have one which is not new; one that I picked up off the floor, nearly six years ago. I have really tried to use it; but my heart failed me, and I could not commit the extravagance.

Small pieces of butter grieve others. They cannot attend to conversation, because of the annoyance occasioned by the habit which some people have of invariably taking more butter than they want. Have you not seen the anxious look (almost mesmeric) which such persons fix on the article? They would feel it a relief if they might bury it out of their sight by popping it into their own mouths, and swallowing it down: and they are really made happy if the person on whose plate it lies unused, suddenly breaks off a piece of toast (which he does not want at all) and eats up his butter. They think that this is not waste.

Now Miss Matty Jenkyns was chary of candles. We had many devices to use as few as possible. In the winter afternoons she would sit knitting for two or three hours; she could do this in the dark, or by fire-light; and when I asked if I might not ring for candles to finish stitching my wristbands, she told me to 'keep blind man's holiday.'[3] They were usually brought in with tea; but we only burnt one at a time. As we lived in constant preparation for a friend who might come in any evening (but who never did), it required some contrivance to keep our two candles of the same length, ready to be lighted, and to look as if we burnt two always. The candles took it in turns; and, whatever we might be talking about or doing, Miss Matty's eyes were habitually fixed upon the candle, ready to jump up and extinguish it, and to light the other before they had become too uneven in length to be restored to equality in the course of the evening.

One night, I remember this candle economy particularly annoyed me. I had been very much tired of my compulsory 'blind man's holiday,' especially as Miss Matty had fallen asleep, and I did not like to stir the fire, and run the risk of awakening her; so I could not even sit on the rug, and scorch myself with sewing by fire-light, according to my usual custom. I fancied Miss Matty must be dreaming of her early life; for she spoke one or two words in her uneasy sleep, bearing reference to persons who were dead long before. When Martha brought in the lighted candle and tea, Miss Matty started into wakefulness, with a strange, bewildered look around, as if we were not the people she expected to see about her. There was a little sad expression that shadowed her face as she recognised me; but immediately afterwards she tried to give me her usual smile. All through tea-time, her talk ran upon the days of her childhood and youth. Perhaps this reminded her of the desirableness of looking over all the old family letters, and destroying such as ought not to be allowed to fall into the hands of strangers; for she had often spoken of the necessity of this task, but had always shrunk from it, with a timid dread of something painful. To-night, however, she rose up after tea, and went for them – in the dark; for she piqued herself on the precise neatness of all her chamber arrangements, and used to look uneasily at me, when I lighted a bed candle to go to another room for anything. When she returned, there was a faint pleasant smell of Tonquin beans[4] in the room. I had always noticed this scent about any of the things which had belonged to her mother; and many of the letters were addressed to her – yellow bundles of love-letters, sixty or seventy years old.

Miss Matty undid the packet with a sigh; but she stifled it directly, as if it were hardly right to regret the flight of time, or of life either. We agreed to look them over separately, each taking a different letter out of the same bundle, and describing its contents to the other, before destroying it. I never knew what sad work the reading of old letters was before that evening, though I could hardly tell why. The letters were as happy as letters could be – at least those early letters were. There was in them a vivid and intense sense of the present time, which seemed so strong and full, as if it could never pass away, and as if the warm, living hearts that so expressed themselves could never die, and be as nothing to the sunny earth. I should have felt less melancholy, I believe, if the letters had been more so. I saw the tears stealing down the well-worn furrows of Miss Matty's cheeks, and her spectacles often wanted wiping. I trusted at last that she would light the other candle, for my own eyes were rather dim, and I wanted more light to see the pale, faded ink; but no – even through her tears, she saw and remembered her little economical ways.

The earliest set of letters were two bundles tied together, and ticketed (in Miss Jenkyns's handwriting), 'Letters interchanged between my ever-honoured father and my dearly-beloved mother, prior to their marriage, in July, 1774.' I should guess that the rector of Cranford was about twenty-seven years of age when he wrote those letters; and Miss Matty told me that her mother was just eighteen at the time of her wedding. With my idea of the rector, derived from a picture in the dining-parlour, stiff and stately, in a huge full-bottomed wig,[5] with gown, cassock, and bands, and his hand upon a copy of the only sermon he ever published, – it was strange to read these letters. They were full of eager, passionate ardour; short homely sentences, right fresh from the heart – (very different from the grand Latinised, Johnsonian style of the printed sermon, preached before some judge at assize time). His letters were a curious contrast to those of his girl-bride. She was evidently rather annoyed at his demands upon her for expressions of love, and could not quite understand what he meant by repeating the same thing over in so many different ways; but what she was quite clear about was her longing for a white 'Padua-soy,'[6] – whatever that might be; and six or seven letters were principally occupied in asking her lover to use his influence with her parents (who evidently kept her in good order) to obtain this or that article of dress, more especially the white 'Paduasoy.' He cared nothing how she was dressed; she was always lovely enough for him, as he took pains to assure her, when she begged him to express in his answers a predilection for particular pieces of finery, in order that she might show what he said to her parents. But at length he seemed to find out that she would not be married till she had a 'trousseau' to her mind; and then he sent her a letter, which had evidently accompanied a whole box full of finery, and in which he requested that she might be dressed in everything her heart desired. This was the first letter, ticketed in a frail, delicate hand, 'From my dearest John.' Shortly afterwards they were married, – I suppose, from the intermission in their correspondence.

'We must burn them, I think,' said Miss Matty, looking doubt-fully at me. 'No one will care for them when I am gone.' And one by one she dropped them into the middle of the fire; watching each blaze up, die out, and rise away, in faint, white, ghostly semblance, up the chimney, before she gave another to the same fate. The room was light enough now; but I, like her, was fas-cinated into watching the destruction of those letters, into which the honest warmth of a manly heart had been poured forth.

The next letter, likewise docketed by Miss Jenkyns, was en-dorsed, 'Letter of pious congratulation and exhortation from my venerable grandfather to my beloved mother, on occasion of my own birth. Also some practical remarks on the desirability of keeping warm the extremities of infants, from my excellent grandmother.'

The first part was, indeed, a severe and forcible picture of the responsibilities of mothers, and a warning against the evils that were in the world, and lying in ghastly wait for the little baby of two days old. His wife did not write, said the old gentleman, because he had forbidden it, she being indisposed with a sprained ankle, which (he said) quite incapacitated her from holding a pen. However, at the foot of the page was a small 'T.O.,' and on turning it over, sure enough, there was a letter to 'my dear, dearest Molly,' begging her, when she left her room, whatever she did to go *up* stairs before going *down* : and telling her to wrap her baby's feet up in flannel, and keep it warm by the fire, although it was summer, for babies were so tender.

It was pretty to see from the letters, which were evidently exchanged with some frequency, between the young mother and the grandmother, how the girlish vanity was being weeded out of her heart by love for her baby. The white 'Paduasoy' figured again in the letters, with almost as much vigour as before. In one, it was being made into a christening cloak for the baby. It decked it when it went with its parents to spend a day or two at Arley Hall. It added to its charms when it was 'the prettiest little baby that ever was seen. Dear mother, I wish you could see her ! Without any parshality, I do think she will grow up a regular bewty !' [7] I thought of Miss Jenkyns, grey, withered, and wrinkled; and I wondered if her mother had known her in the courts of heaven; and then I knew that she had, and that they stood there in angelic guise.

There was a great gap before any of the rector's letters appeared. And then his wife changed her mode of endorsement. It was no longer from 'My dearest John;' it was from 'My honoured Husband.' The letters were written on occasion of the publication of the same Sermon which was represented in the picture. The preaching before 'My Lord Judge,' and the 'publishing by request,' was evidently the culminating point – the event of his life. It had been necessary for him to go up to London to superintend it

through the press. Many friends had to be called upon, and consulted, before he could decide on any printer fit for so onerous a
task; and at length it was arranged that J. and J. Rivingtons[8] were
to have the honourable responsibility. The worthy rector seemed
to be strung up by the occasion to a high literary pitch, for he
could hardly write a letter to his wife without cropping out into
Latin. I remember the end of one of his letters ran thus: – 'I shall
ever hold the virtuous qualities of my Molly in remembrance, *dum
memor ipse mei, dum spiritus regit artus,*'[9] which, considering
that the English of his correspondent was sometimes at fault in
grammar, and often in spelling, might be taken as a proof of how
much he 'idealised his Molly:' and, as Miss Jenkyns used to say,
'People talk a great deal about idealising now-a-days, whatever that
may mean.' But this was nothing to a fit of writing classical
poetry, which soon seized him; in which his Molly figured away
as 'Maria.' The letter containing the *carmen* [10] was endorsed by
her, 'Hebrew verses sent me by my honoured husband. I thowt to
have had a letter about killing the pig, but must wait. Mem., to
send the poetry to Sir Peter Arley, as my husband desires.' And in
a post-scriptum note in his hand-writing it was stated that the
Ode had appeared in the *Gentleman's Magazine*,[11] December,
1782.

Her letters back to her husband (treasured as fondly by him
as if they had been M. T. *Ciceronis Epistolae*) [12] were more satisfactory to an absent husband and father than his could ever have
been to her. She told him how Deborah sewed her seam very neatly
every day, and read in the books he had set her; how she was a
very 'forrard,' good child, but *would* ask questions her mother
could not answer, but how she did not let herself down by saying
she did not know, but took to stirring the fire, or sending the
'forrard' child on an errand. Matty was now the mother's darling,
and promised (like her sister at her age) to be a great beauty. I
was reading this aloud to Miss Matty, who smiled and sighed a
little at the hope, so fondly expressed, that 'little Matty might not
be vain, even if she were a bewty.'

'I had very pretty hair, my dear,' said Miss Matilda; 'and not a
bad mouth.' And I saw her soon afterwards adjust her cap and
draw herself up.

But to return to Mrs Jenkyns's letters. She told her husband about the poor in the parish; what homely domestic medicines she had administered; what kitchen physic she had sent. She had evidently held his displeasure as a rod in pickle [13] over the heads of all the ne'er-do-wells. She asked for his directions about the cows and pigs; and did not always obtain them, as I have shown before.

The kind old grandmother was dead, when a little boy was born, soon after the publication of the Sermon; but there was another letter of exhortation from the grandfather, more stringent and admonitory than ever, now that there was a boy to be guarded from the snares of the world. He described all the various sins into which men might fall, until I wondered how any man ever came to a natural death. The gallows seemed as if it must have the termination of the lives of most of the grandfather's friends and acquaintance; and I was not surprised at the way in which he spoke of this life being 'a vale of tears.'

It seemed curious that I should never have heard of this brother before; but I concluded that he had died young; or else surely his name would have been alluded to by his sisters.

By-and-by we came to packets of Miss Jenkyns's letters. These, Miss Matty did regret to burn. She said all the others had been only interesting to those who loved the writers; and that it seemed as if it would have hurt her to allow them to fall into the hands of strangers, who had not known her dear mother, and how good she was, although she did not always spell quite in the modern fashion; but Deborah's letters were so very superior! Any one might profit by reading them. It was a long time since she had read Mrs Chapone, [14] but she knew she used to think that Deborah could have said the same things quite as well; and as for Mrs Carter! [15] people thought a deal of her letters, just because she had written *Epictetus*, but she was quite sure Deborah would never have made use of such a common expression as 'I canna be fashed!' [16]

Miss Matty did grudge burning these letters, it was evident. She would not let them be carelessly passed over with any quiet reading, and skipping, to myself. She took them from me, and even lighted the second candle, in order to read them aloud with a proper emphasis, and without stumbling over the big words. Oh dear ! how I wanted facts instead of reflections, before those letters were concluded ! They lasted us two nights; and I won't deny that I made use of the time to think of many other things, and yet I was always at my post at the end of each sentence.

The Rector's letters, and those of his wife and mother-in-law, had all been tolerably short and pithy, written in a straight hand, with the lines very close together. Sometimes the whole letter was contained on a mere scrap of paper. The paper was very yellow, and the ink very brown; some of the sheets were (as Miss Matty made me observe) the old original post,[17] with the stamp in the corner, representing a post-boy riding for life and twanging his horn. The letters of Mrs Jenkyns and her mother were fastened with a great round red wafer; for it was before Miss Edgeworth's *Patronage* had banished wafers from polite society.[18] It was evident, from the tenor of what was said, that franks were in great request, and were even used as a means of paying debts by needy members of parliament.[19] The rector sealed his epistles with an immense coat of arms, and showed by the care with which he had performed this ceremony, that he expected they should be cut open, not broken by any thoughtless or impatient hand. Now, Miss Jenkyns's letters were of a later date in form and writing. She wrote on the square sheet, which we have learned to call old-fashioned. Her hand was admirably calculated, together with her use of many-syllabled words, to fill up a sheet, and then came the pride and delight of crossing. Poor Miss Matty got sadly puzzled with this, for the words gathered size like snowballs, and towards the end of her letter, Miss Jenkyns used to become quite sesquipedalian.[20] In one to her father, slightly theological and controversial in its tone, she had spoken of Herod, Tetrarch of Idumea. Miss Matty read it 'Herod Petrarch of Etruria',[21] and was just as well pleased as if she had been right.

I can't quite remember the date, but I think it was in 1805 that Miss Jenkyns wrote the longest series of letters; on occasion of her absence on a visit to some friends near Newcastle-upon-Tyne. These friends were intimate with the commandant of the garrison there, and heard from him of all the preparations that were being made to repel the invasion of Buonaparte, which some people imagined might take place at the mouth of the Tyne. Miss

Jenkyns was evidently very much alarmed; and the first part of her letters was often written in pretty intelligible English, conveying particulars of the preparations which were made in the family with whom she was residing against the dreaded event; the bundles of clothes that were packed up ready for a flight to Alston Moor (a wild hilly piece of ground between Northumberland and Cumberland); the signal that was to be given for this flight, and for the simultaneous turning out of the volunteers under arms; which said signal was to consist (if I remember right) in ringing the church bells in a particular and ominous manner. One day, when Miss Jenkyns and her hosts were at a dinner-party in New-castle, this warning summons was actually given (not a very wise proceeding, if there be any truth in the moral attached to the fable of the Boy and the Wolf; [22] but so it was), and Miss Jenkyns, hardly recovered from her fright, wrote the next day to describe the sound, the breathless shock, the hurry and alarm; and then, taking breath, she added, 'How trivial, my dear father, do all our apprehensions of the last evening appear, at the present moment, to calm and inquiring minds!' And here Miss Matty broke in with –

'But, indeed, my dear, they were not at all trivial or trifling at the time. I know I used to wake up in the night many a time, and think I heard the tramp of the French entering Cranford. Many people talked of hiding themselves in the salt-mines; – and meat would have kept capitally down there, only perhaps we should have been thirsty. And my father preached a whole set of sermons on the occasion; one set in the mornings, all about David and Goliath,[23] to spirit up the people to fighting with spades or bricks, if need were; and the other set in the afternoons, proving that Napoleon (that was another name for Bony, as we used to call him) was all the same as an Apollyon and Abaddon.[24] I remember my father rather thought he should be asked to print this last set; but the parish had, perhaps, had enough of them with hearing.'

Peter Marmaduke Arley Jenkyns ('poor Peter!' as Miss Matty began to call him) was at school at Shrewsbury by this time. The Rector took up his pen, and rubbed up his Latin, once more, to correspond with his boy. It was very clear that the lad's were what are called show-letters. They were of a highly mental description, giving an account of his studies, and his intellectual hopes of various kinds, with an occasional quotation from the classics; but, now and then, the animal nature broke out in such a little sentence as this, evidently written in a trembling hurry, after the letter had been inspected; 'Mother dear, do send me a cake, and put plenty of citron in.' The 'mother dear' probably answered her boy in the form of cakes and 'goody,' for there were none of her letters among this set; but a whole collection of the rector's, to whom the Latin in his boy's letters was like a trumpet to the old war-horse. I do not know much about Latin, certainly, and it is, perhaps, an ornamental language; but not very useful, I think – at least to judge from the bits I remember out of the rector's letters. One was : 'You have not got that town in your map of Ireland; but *Bonus Bernardus non videt omnia,*[25] as the Proverbia say.' Presently it became very evident that 'poor Peter' got himself into many scrapes. There were letters of stilted penitence to his father, for some wrong-doing; and, among them all, was a badly-written, badly-sealed, badly-directed, blotted note – 'My dear, dear, dear, dearest mother, I will be a better boy – I will, indeed; but don't, please, be ill for me; I am not worth it; but I will be good, darling mother.'

Miss Matty could not speak for crying, after she had read this note. She gave it to me in silence, and then got up and took it to her sacred recesses in her own room, for fear, by any chance, it might get burnt. 'Poor Peter !' she said; 'he was always in scrapes; he was too easy. They led him wrong, and then left him in the lurch. But he was too found of mischief. He could never resist a joke. Poor Peter !'

CHAPTER VI

Poor Peter

POOR Peter's career lay before him rather pleasantly mapped out by kind friends, but *Bonus Bernardus non videt omnia*, in this map too. He was to win honours at Shrewsbury school, and carry them thick to Cambridge, and after that, a living awaited him, the gift of his godfather, Sir Peter Arley. Poor Peter! his lot in life was very different to what his friends had hoped and planned. Miss Matty told me all about it, and I think it was a relief to her when she had done so.

He was the darling of his mother, who seemed to dote on all her children, though she was, perhaps, a little afraid of Deborah's superior acquirements. Deborah was the favourite of her father, and when Peter disappointed him, she became his pride. The sole honour Peter brought away from Shrewsbury, was the reputation of being the best good fellow that ever was, and of being the captain of the school in the art of practical joking. His father was disappointed, but set about remedying the matter in a manly way. He could not afford to send Peter to read with any tutor, but he could read with him himself; and Miss Matty told me much of the awful preparations in the way of dictionaries and lexicons that were made in her father's study the morning Peter began.

'My poor mother!' said she. 'I remember how she used to stand in the hall, just near enough the study-door to catch the tone of my father's voice. I could tell in a moment if all was going right, by her face. And it did go right for a long time."

'What went wrong at last?' said I. 'That tiresome Latin, I dare say.'

'No! it was not the Latin. Peter was in high favour with my father, for he worked up well for him. But he seemed to think that the Cranford people might be joked about, and made fun of, and they did not like it; nobody does. He was always hoaxing them; "hoaxing" is not a pretty word, my dear, and I hope you won't tell your father I used it, for I should not like him to think that I was not choice in my language, after living with such a woman as Deborah. And be sure you never use it yourself. I don't know how it slipped out of my mouth, except it was that I was thinking of poor Peter, and it was always his expression. But he was a very gentlemanly boy in many things. He was like dear Captain Brown in always being ready to help any old person or a child. Still, he did like joking and making fun; and he seemed to think the old ladies in Cranford would believe anything. There were many old ladies living here then; we are principally ladies now, I know; but we are not so old as the ladies used to be when I was a girl. I could laugh to think of some of Peter's jokes. No! my dear, I won't tell you of them, because they might not shock you as they ought to do; and they were very shocking. He even took in my father once, by dressing himself up as a lady that was passing through the town and wished to see the Rector of Cranford, "who had published that admirable Assize Sermon." Peter said, he was awfully frightened himself when he saw how my father took it all in, and even offered to copy out all his Napoleon Buonaparte sermons for her – him, I mean – no, her, for Peter was a lady then. He told me he was more terrified than he ever was before, all the time my father was speaking. He did not think my father would have believed him; and yet if he had not, it would have been a sad thing for Peter. As it was, he was none so glad of it, for my father kept him hard at work copying out all those twelve Buonaparte sermons for the lady – that was for Peter himself, you know. He was the lady. And once when he wanted to go fishing, Peter said, "Confound the woman!" – very bad language, my dear; but Peter was not always so guarded as he should have been; my father was so angry with him, it nearly frightened me out of my wits: and yet I could hardly keep from laughing at the little curtseys Peter kept making, quite slyly, whenever my father spoke of the lady's excellent taste and sound discrimination.'

'Did Miss Jenkyns know of these tricks?' said I.

'Oh, no! Deborah would have been too much shocked. No! no one knew but me. I wish I had always known of Peter's plans; but sometimes he did not tell me. He used to say, the old ladies in the town wanted something to talk about; but I don't think they did. They had the *St James's Chronicle*[1] three times a-week, just as we have now, and we have plenty to say; and I remember the clacking noise there always was when some of the ladies got together. But, probably, school-boys talk more than ladies. At last there was a terrible sad thing happened.' Miss Matty got up, went to the door, and opened it; no one was there. She rang the bell for Martha; and when Martha came, her mistress told her to go for eggs to a farm at the other end of the town.

'I will lock the door after you, Martha. You are not afraid to go, are you?'

'No, ma'am, not at all; Jem Hearn will be only too proud to go with me.'

Miss Matty drew herself up, and as soon as we were alone, she wished that Martha had more maidenly reserve.

'We'll put out the candle, my dear. We can talk just as well by firelight, you know. There! well! you see, Deborah had gone from home for a fortnight or so; it was a very still, quiet day, I remember, overhead and the lilacs were all in flower, so I suppose it was spring. My father had gone out to see some sick people in the parish; I recollect seeing him leave the house, with his wig and shovel-hat,[2] and cane. What possessed our poor Peter I don't know; he had the sweetest temper, and yet he always seemed to like to plague Deborah. She never laughed at his jokes, and thought him ungenteel, and not careful enough about improving his mind; and that vexed him.

'Well! he went to her room, it seems, and dressed himself in her old gown, and shawl, and bonnet; just the things she used to wear in Cranford, and was known by everywhere; and he made the pillow into a little – you are sure you locked the door, my dear, for I should not like any one to hear – into – into – a little baby, with white long clothes. It was only, as he told me afterwards, to make something to talk about in the town; he never thought of it as affecting Deborah. And he went and walked up and down in the Filbert walk – just half hidden by the rails, and half seen; and he cuddled his pillow, just like a baby; and talked to it all the nonsense people do. Oh dear! and my father came stepping stately up the street, as he always did; and what should he see but a little black crowd of people – I dare say as many as

twenty – all peeping through his garden rails. So he thought, at
first, they were only looking at a new rhododendron [3] that was in
full bloom, and that he was very proud of; and he walked slower,
that they might have more time to admire. And he wondered if
he could make out a sermon from the occasion, and thought, perhaps, there was some relation between the rhododendrons and the
lilies of the field. My poor father! When he came nearer, he
began to wonder that they did not see him; but their heads were
all so close together, peeping and peeping! My father was
amongst them, meaning, he said, to ask them to walk into the
garden with him, and admire the beautiful vegetable production,
when – oh, my dear! I tremble to think of it – he looked through
the rails himself, and saw – I don't know what he thought he
saw, but old Clare told me his face went quite grey-white with
anger, and his eyes blazed out under his frowning black brows;
and he spoke out – oh, so terribly! – and bade them all stop
where they were – not one of them to go, not one to stir a step;
and, swift as light, he was in at the garden door, and down the
Filbert walk, and seized hold of poor Peter, and tore his clothes
off his back – bonnet, shawl, gown, and all – and threw the pillow
among the people over the railings: and then he was very, very
angry indeed; and before all the people he lifted up his cane, and
flogged Peter!

'My dear! that boy's trick, on that sunny day, when all
seemed going straight and well, broke my mother's heart, and
changed my father for life. It did, indeed. Old Clare said, Peter
looked as white as my father; and stood as still as a statue to be
flogged; and my father struck hard! When my father stopped to
take breath, Peter said, "Have you done enough, sir?" quite
hoarsely, and still standing quite quiet. I don't know what my
father said – or if he said anything. But old Clare said, Peter
turned to where the people outside the railing were, and made
them a low bow, as grand and as grave as any gentleman; and
then walked slowly into the house. I was in the store-room helping my mother to make cowslip-wine. I cannot abide the wine
now, nor the scent of the flowers; they turn me sick and faint, as
they did that day, when Peter came in, looking as haughty as any
man – indeed, looking like a man, not like a boy. 'Mother!' he

said, "I am come to say, God bless you for ever." I saw his lips quiver as he spoke and I think he durst not say anything more loving, for the purpose that was in his heart. She looked at him rather frightened, and wondering, and asked him what was to do? He did not smile or speak, but put his arms round her, and kissed her as if he did not know how to leave off; and before she could speak again, he was gone. We talked it over, and could not understand it, and she bade me go and seek my father, and ask what it was all about. I found him walking up and down, looking very highly displeased.

' "Tell your mother I have flogged Peter, and that he richly deserved it."

'I durst not ask any more questions. When I told my mother, she sat down, quite faint, for a minute. I remember, a few days after, I saw the poor, withered cowslip-flowers thrown out to the leaf heap, to decay and die there. There was no making of cowslip-wine that year at the rectory – nor, indeed, ever after.

'Presently, my mother went to my father. I know I thought of Queen Esther and King Ahasuerus;[4] for my mother was very pretty and delicate-looking, and my father looked as terrible as King Ahasuerus. Some time after, they came out together; and then my mother told me what had happened, and that she was going up to Peter's room, at my father's desire – though she was not to tell Peter this – to talk the matter over with him. But no Peter was there. We looked over the house; no Peter was there! Even my father, who had not liked to join in the search at first, helped us before long. The rectory was a very old house: steps up into a room, steps down into a room, all through. At first, my mother went calling low and soft – as if to reassure the poor boy – "Peter! Peter, dear! it's only me;" but, by-and-by, as the servants came back from the errands my father had sent them, in different directions, to find where Peter was – as we found he was not in the garden, nor the hayloft, nor anywhere about – my mother's cry grew louder and wilder – "Peter! Peter, my darling! where are you?" for then she felt and understood that that long kiss meant some sad kind of "good-by." The afternoon went on – my mother never resting, but seeking again and again in every possible place that had been looked into twenty times before;

nay, that she had looked into over and over again herself. My father sat with his head in his hands, not speaking, except when his messengers came in, bringing no tidings; then he lifted up his face so strong and sad, and told them to go again in some new direction. My mother kept passing from room to room, in and out of the house, moving noiselessly, but never ceasing. Neither she nor my father durst leave the house, which was the meeting-place for all the messengers. At last (and it was nearly dark), my father rose up. He took hold of my mother's arm, as she came with wild, sad pace, through one door, and quickly towards another. She started at the touch of his hand, for she had forgotten all in the world but Peter.

' "Molly!" said he, "I did not think all this would happen." He looked into her face for comfort – her poor face, all wild and white; for neither she nor my father had dared to acknowledge – much less act upon – the terror that was in their hearts, lest Peter should have made away with himself. My father saw no conscious look in his wife's hot, dreary eyes, and he missed the sympathy that she had always been ready to give him – strong man as he was: and at the dumb despair in her face, his tears began to flow. But when she saw this, a gentle sorrow came over her countenance, and she said, "Dearest John! don't cry; come with me, and we'll find him," almost as cheerfully as if she knew where he was. And she took my father's great hand in her little soft one, and led him along, the tears dropping, as he walked on that same unceasing, weary walk, from room to room, through house and garden.

'Oh, how I wished for Deborah! I had no time for crying, for now all seemed to depend on me. I wrote for Deborah to come home. I sent a message privately to that same Mr Holbrook's house – poor Mr Holbrook! – you know who I mean. I don't mean I sent a message to him, but I sent one that I could trust, to know if Peter was at his house. For at one time Mr Holbrook was an occasional visitor at the rectory – you know he was Miss Pole's cousin – and he had been very kind to Peter, and taught him how to fish – he was very kind to everybody, and I thought Peter might have gone there. But Mr Holbrook was from home, and Peter had never been seen. It was night now; but the doors were all wide open, and my father walked on and on; it was more than an hour since he had joined her, and I don't believe they had ever spoken all that time. I was getting the parlour fire lighted, and one of the servants was preparing tea, for I wanted them to have something to eat and drink and warm them, when old Clare asked to speak to me.

' "I have borrowed the nets from the weir, Miss Matty. Shall we drag the ponds to-night, or wait for the morning?'

'I remember staring in his face to gather his meaning; and when I did, I laughed out loud. The horror of that new thought – our bright, darling Peter, cold, and stark, and dead! I remember the ring of my own laugh now.

'The next day Deborah was at home before I was myself again. She would not have been so weak as to give way as I had done; but my screams (my horrible laughter had ended in crying) had roused my sweet dear mother, whose poor wandering wits were called back and collected, as soon as a child needed her care. She and Deborah sat by my bedside; I knew by the looks of each that there had been no news of Peter – no awful, ghastly news, which was what I had dreaded in my dull state between sleeping and waking.

'The same result of all the searching had brought something of the same relief to my mother, to whom, I am sure, the thought that Peter might even then be hanging dead in some of the familiar home places had caused that never-ending walk of yesterday. Her soft eyes never were the same again after that; they had always a restless craving look, as if seeking for what they could not find. Oh! it was an awful time; coming down like a thunderbolt on the still sunny day, when the lilacs were all in bloom.'

'Where was Mr Peter?' said I.

'He had made his way to Liverpool; and there was war then; and some of the king's ships lay off the mouth of the Mersey; and they were only too glad to have a fine likely boy such as him (five foot nine he was) come to offer himself. The captain wrote to my father, and Peter wrote to my mother. Stay! those letters will be somewhere here.'

We lighted the candle, and found the captain's letter and Peter's too. And we also found a little simple begging letter from

Mrs Jenkyns to Peter, addressed to him at the house of an old schoolfellow, whither she fancied he might have gone. They had returned it unopened; and unopened it had remained ever since, having been inadvertently put by among the other letters of that time. This is it:

'MY DEAREST PETER,

'You did not think we should be so sorry as we are, I know, or you would never have gone away. You are too good. Your father sits and sighs till my heart aches to hear him. He cannot hold up his head for grief; and yet he only did what he thought was right. Perhaps he has been too severe, and perhaps I have not been kind enough; but God knows how we love you, my dear only boy. Dor⁵ looks so sorry you are gone. Come back, and make us happy, who love you so much. I *know* you will come back.'

But Peter did not come back. That spring day was the last time he ever saw his mother's face. The writer of the letter – the last – the only person who had ever seen what was written in it, was dead long ago – and I, a stranger, not born at the time when this occurrence took place, was the one to open it.

The captain's letter summoned the father and mother to Liverpool instantly, if they wished to see their boy; and by some of the wild chances of life, the captain's letter had been detained somewhere, somehow.

Miss Matty went on: 'And it was race-time, and all the post-horses at Cranford were gone to the races; but my father and mother set off in our own gig,⁶ – and oh! my dear, they were too late – the ship was gone! And now, read Peter's letter to my mother!'

It was full of love, and sorrow, and pride in his new profession, and a sore sense of his disgrace in the eyes of the people at Cranford; but ending with a passionate entreaty that she would come and see him before he left the Mersey: 'Mother! we may go into battle. I hope we shall, and lick those French; but I must see you again before that time.'

'And she was too late,' said Miss Matty; 'too late!'

We sat in silence, pondering on the full meaning of those sad,

sad words. At length I asked Miss Matty to tell me how her mother bore it.

'Oh!' she said, 'she was patience itself. She had never been strong, and this weakened her terribly. My father used to sit looking at her: far more sad than she was. He seemed as if he could look at nothing else when she was by; and he was so humble, – so very gentle now. He would, perhaps, speak in his old way – laying down the law, as it were – and then, in a minute or two he would come round and put his hand on our shoulders, and ask us in a low voice if he had said anything to hurt us? I did not wonder at his speaking so to Deborah, for she was so clever; but I could not bear to hear him talking so to me.

'But, you see, he saw what we did not – that it was killing my mother. Yes! killing her – (put out the candle, my dear; I can talk better in the dark) – for she was but a frail woman, and ill-fitted to stand the fright and shock she had gone through; and she would smile at him and comfort him, not in words but in her looks and tones, which were always cheerful when he was there. And she would speak of how she thought Peter stood a good chance of being admiral very soon – he was so brave and clever; and how she thought of seeing him in his navy uniform, and what sort of hats admirals wore; and how much more fit he was to be a sailor than a clergyman; and all in that way, just to make my father think she was quite glad of what came of that unlucky morning's work, and the flogging which was always in his mind, as we all knew. But oh, my dear! the bitter, bitter crying she had when she was alone; – and at last, as she grew weaker, she could not keep her tears in when Deborah or me was by, and would give us message after message for Peter – (his ship had gone to the Mediterranean, or somewhere down there, and then he was ordered off to India, and there was no overland route then);[7] – but she still said that no one knew where their death lay in wait, and that we were not to think hers was near. We did not think it, but we knew it, as we saw her fading away.

'Well, my dear, it's very foolish of me, I know, when in all likelihood I am so near to seeing her again.

'And only think, love! the very day after her death – for she did not live quite a twelvemonth after Peter went away – the very day after – came a parcel for her from India – from her poor boy. It was a large, soft, white Indian shawl, with just a little narrow border all round; just what my mother would have liked.

'We thought it might arouse my father, for he had sat with her hand in his all night long; so Deborah took it in to him, and Peter's letter to her, and all. At first, he took no notice; and we tried to make a kind of light careless talk about the shawl, opening it out and admiring it. Then, suddenly, he got up and spoke : – "She shall be buried in it," he said; "Peter shall have that comfort; and she would have liked it."

'Well ! perhaps it was not reasonable, but what could we do or say? One gives people in grief their own way. He took it up and felt it – "It is just such a shawl as she wished for when she was married, and her mother did not give it her. I did not know of it till after, or she should have had it – she should; but she shall have it now."

'My mother looked so lovely in her death ! She was always pretty, and now she looked fair, and waxen, and young – younger than Deborah, as she stood trembling and shivering by her. We decked her in the long soft fold; she lay, smiling as if pleased; the people came – all Cranford came – to beg to see her, for they had loved her dearly – as well they might; and the country-women brought posies; old Clare's wife brought some white violets, and begged they might lie on her breast.

'Deborah said to me, the day of my mother's funeral, that if she had a hundred offers, she never would marry and leave my father. It was not very likely she would have so many – I don't know that she had one; but it was not less to her credit to say so. She was such a daughter to my father, as I think there never was before, or since. His eyes failed him, and she read book after book, and wrote, and copied, and was always at his service in any parish business. She could do many more things than my poor mother could; she even once wrote a letter to the bishop for my father. But he missed my mother sorely; the whole parish noticed it. Not that he was less active; I think he was more so, and more patient in helping every one. I did all I could to set

Deborah at liberty to be with him; for I knew I was good for little, and that my best work in the world was to do odd jobs quietly, and set others at liberty. But my father was a changed man.'

'Did Mr Peter ever come home?'

'Yes, once. He came home a Lieutenant; he did not get to be Admiral. And he and my father were such friends! My father took him into every house in the parish, he was so proud of him. He never walked out without Peter's arm to lean upon. Deborah used to smile (I don't think we ever laughed again after my mother's death), and say she was quite put in a corner. Not but what my father always wanted her when there was letter-writing, or reading to be done, or anything to be settled.'

'And then?' said I, after a pause.

'Then Peter went to sea again; and, by-and-by, my father died, blessing us both, and thanking Deborah for all she had been to him; and, of course, our circumstances were changed; and, in-stead of living at the rectory, and keeping three maids and a man, we had to come to this small house, and be content with a servant-of-all-work; but, as Deborah used to say, we have always lived genteelly, even if circumstances have compelled us to simplicity. – Poor Deborah!'

'And Mr Peter?' asked I.

'Oh, there was some great war in India[8] – I forget what they call it – and we have never heard of Peter since then. I believe he is dead myself; and it sometimes fidgets me that we have never put on mourning for him. And then, again, when I sit by myself, and all the house is still, I think I hear his step coming up the street, and my heart begins to flutter and beat; but the sound always goes past – and Peter never comes.'

'That's Martha back? No! I'll go, my dear; I can always find my way in the dark, you know. And a blow of fresh air at the door will do my head good, and it's rather got a trick of aching.'

So she pattered off. I had lighted the candle, to give the room a cheerful appearance against her return.

'Was it Martha?' asked I.

'Yes. And I am rather uncomfortable, for I heard such a strange noise just as I was opening the door.'

'Where?' I asked, for her eyes were round with affright.

'In the street – just outside – it sounded like –'

'Talking?' I put in, as she hesitated a little.

'No! kissing –'

CHAPTER VII

Visiting

ONE morning, as Miss Matty and I sat at our work – it was before twelve o'clock, and Miss Matty had not changed the cap with yellow ribbons, that had been Miss Jenkyns's best, and which Miss Matty was now wearing out in private, putting on the one made in imitation of Mrs Jamieson's at all times when she expected to be seen – Martha came up, and asked if Miss Betty Barker might speak to her mistress. Miss Matty assented, and quickly disappeared to change the yellow ribbons, while Miss Barker came up-stairs; but, as she had forgotten her spectacles, and was rather flurried by the unusual time of the visit, I was not surprised to see her return with one cap on top of the other. She was quite unconscious of it herself, and looked at us with bland satisfaction. Nor do I think Miss Barker perceived it; for, putting aside the little circumstance that she was not so young as she had been, she was very much absorbed in her errand; which she delivered herself of, with an oppressive modesty that found vent in endless apologies.

Miss Betty Barker was the daughter of the old clerk at Cranford, who had officiated in Mr Jenkyns's time. She and her sister had had pretty good situations as ladies' maids, and had saved money enough to set up a milliner's shop, which had been patronized by the ladies in the neighbourhood. Lady Arley, for instance, would occasionally give Miss Barkers the pattern of an old cap of hers, which they immediately copied and circulated among the *élite* of Cranford. I say the *élite*, for Miss Barkers had caught the trick of the place, and piqued themselves upon their 'aristocratic connexion.' They would not sell their caps and ribbons to any one without a pedigree. Many a farmer's wife or daughter turned away huffed from Miss Barkers' select millinery, and went rather to the universal shop, where the profits of brown soap and moist sugar enabled the proprietor to go straight to (Paris, he said, until he found his customers too patriotic and John Bullish to wear what the Mounseers wore)[1] London; where, as he often told his customers, Queen Adelaide[2] had appeared, only the very week before, in a cap exactly like the one he showed them, trimmed with yellow and blue ribbons, and had been complimented by King William on the becoming nature of her head-dress.

Miss Barkers, who confined themselves to truth, and did not approve of miscellaneous customers, throve notwithstanding. They were self-denying, good people. Many a time I have seen the eldest of them (she that had been maid to Mrs Jamieson) carrying out some delicate mess[3] to a poor person. They only aped their betters in having 'nothing to do' with the class immediately below theirs. And when Miss Barker died, their profits and income were found to be such that Miss Betty was justified in shutting up shop, and retiring from business. She also (as I think I have before said) set up her cow; a mark of respectability in Cranford almost as decided as setting up a gig is among some people. She dressed finer than any lady in Cranford; and we did not wonder at it; for it was understood that she was wearing out all the bonnets and caps, and outrageous ribbons, which had once formed her stock in trade. It was five or six years since she had given up shop: so in any other place than Cranford her dress might have been considered *passée*.[4]

And now, Miss Betty Barker had called to invite Miss Matty to tea at her house on the following Tuesday. She gave me also an impromptu invitation, as I happened to be a visitor; though I could see she had a little fear lest, since my father had gone to live in Drumble, he might have engaged in that 'horrid cotton trade,' and so dragged his family down out of 'aristocratic society.' She prefaced this invitation with so many apologies, that she quite excited my curiosity. 'Her presumption' was to be excused. What had she been doing? She seemed so overpowered by it, I could only think that she had been writing to Queen Adelaide, to ask for a receipt for washing lace; but the act which she so characterized was only an invitation she had carried to her sister's former mistress, Mrs Jamieson. 'Her former occupation considered, could Miss Matty excuse the liberty?' Ah! thought I, she has found out that double cap, and is going to rectify Miss Matty's head-dress. No! It was simply to extend her invitation to Miss Matty and to me. Miss Matty bowed acceptance; and I wondered that, in the graceful action, she did not feel the unusual weight and extraordinary height of her head-dress. But I do not think she did; for she recovered her balance, and went on talking to Miss Betty in a kind, condescending manner, very different from the fidgety way she would have had, if she had suspected how singular her appearance was.

'Mrs Jamieson is coming, I think you said?' asked Miss Matty.

'Yes. Mrs Jamieson most kindly and condescendingly said she would be happy to come. One little stipulation she made, that she should bring Carlo. I told her that if I had a weakness, it was for dogs.'

'And Miss Pole?' questioned Miss Matty, who was thinking of her pool at Preference,[5] in which Carlo would not be available as a partner.

'I am going to ask Miss Pole. Of course, I could not think of asking her until I had asked you, madam – the rector's daughter, madam. Believe me, I do not forget the situation my father held under yours.'

'And Mrs Forrester, of course?'

'And Mrs Forrester. I thought, in fact, of going to her before I went to Miss Pole. Although her circumstances are changed, madam, she was born a Tyrrell, and we can never forget her alliance to the Bigges, of Bigelow Hall.'

Miss Matty cared much more for the little circumstance of her being a very good card-player.

'Mrs Fitz-Adam – I suppose –'

'No, madam. I must draw a line somewhere. Mrs Jamieson would not, I think, like to meet Mrs Fitz-Adam. I have the greatest respect for Mrs Fitz-Adam – but I cannot think her fit society for such ladies as Mrs Jamieson and Miss Matilda Jenkyns.'

Miss Betty Barker bowed low to Miss Matty, and pursed up her mouth. She looked at me with sidelong dignity, as much as to say, although a retired milliner, she was no democrat, and understood the difference of ranks.

'May I beg you to come as near half-past six, to my little dwelling, as possible, Miss Matilda? Mrs Jamieson dines at five, but has kindly promised not to delay her visit beyond that time –

half-past six.' And with a swimming curtsey Miss Betty Barker took her leave.

My prophetic soul foretold a visit that afternoon from Miss Pole, who usually came to call on Miss Matilda after any event – or indeed in sight of any event – to talk it over with her.

'Miss Betty told me it was to be a choice and select few,' said Miss Pole, as she and Miss Matty compared notes.

'Yes, so she said. Not even Mrs Fitz-Adam.'

Now Mrs Fitz-Adam was the widowed sister of the Cranford surgeon, whom I have named before. Their parents were respectable farmers, content with their station. The name of these good people was Hoggins. Mr Hoggins was the Cranford doctor now; we disliked the name, and considered it coarse; but, as Miss Jenkyns said, if he changed it to Piggins it would not be much better. We had hoped to discover a relationship between him and that Marchioness of Exeter whose name was Molly Hoggins;[6] but the man, careless of his own interests, utterly ignored and denied any such relationship; although, as dear Miss Jenkyns had said, he had a sister called Mary, and the same Christian names were very apt to run in families.

Soon after Miss Mary Hoggins married Mr Fitz-Adam, she disappeared from the neighbourhood for many years. She did not move in a sphere in Cranford society sufficiently high to make any of us care to know what Mr Fitz-Adam was. He died and was gathered to his fathers, without our ever having thought about him at all. And then Mrs Fitz-Adam reappeared in Cranford ('as bold as a lion,' Miss Pole said), a well-to-do widow, dressed in rustling black silk, so soon after her husband's death, that poor Miss Jenkyns was justified in the remark she made, that 'bombazine would have shown a deeper sense of her loss'.[7]

I remember the convocation of ladies, who assembled to decide whether or not Mrs Fitz-Adam should be called upon by the old blue-blooded inhabitants of Cranford. She had taken a large rambling house, which had been usually considered to confer a patent of gentility upon its tenant; because, once upon a time, seventy or eighty years before, the spinster daughter of an earl had resided in it. I am not sure if the inhabiting this house was not also believed to convey some unusual power of intellect; for the earl's daughter, Lady Jane, had a sister, Lady Anne, who had married a general officer, in the time of the American war; and this general officer had written one or two comedies, which were still acted on the London boards; and which, when we saw them advertised, made us all draw up, and feel that Drury Lane was paying a very pretty compliment to Cranford. Still, it was not at all a settled thing that Mrs Fitz-Adam was to be visited, when dear Miss Jenkyns died; and, with her, something of the clear knowledge of the strict code of gentility went out too. As Miss Pole observed, 'As most of the ladies of good family in Cranford were elderly spinsters, or widows without children, if we did not relax a little, and become less exclusive, by-and-by we should have no society at all.'

Mrs Forrester continued on the same side.

'She had always understood that Fitz meant something aristo-cratic;[8] there was Fitz-Roy – she thought that some of the King's children had been called Fitz-Roy; and there was Fitz-Clarence now – they were the children of dear good King William the Fourth. Fitz-Adam! – it was a pretty name; and she thought it very probably meant "Child of Adam." No one, who had not some good blood in their veins, would dare to be called Fitz; there was a deal in a name – she had had a cousin who spelt his name with two little ffs – ffoulkes, – and he always looked down upon capital letters, and said they belonged to lately-invented families. She had been afraid he would die a batchelor, he was so very choice. When he met with a Mrs ffarringdon, at a watering-place, he took to her immediately; and a very pretty genteel woman she was – a widow with a very good fortune; and "my cousin," Mr ffoulkes, married her; and it was all owing to her two little ffs.'

Mrs Fitz-Adam did not stand a chance of meeting with a Mr Fitz-anything in Cranford, so that could not have been her motive for settling there. Miss Matty thought it might have been the hope of being admitted in the society of the place, which would certainly be a very agreeable rise for ci-devant[9] Miss Hog-gins; and if this had been her hope, it would be cruel to dis-appoint her.

So everybody called upon Mrs Fitz-Adam – everybody but Mrs

Jamieson, who used to show how honourable she was by never
seeing Mrs Fitz-Adam, when they met at the Cranford parties.
There would be only eight or ten ladies in the room, and Mrs
Fitz-Adam was the largest of all, and she invariably used to stand
up when Mrs Jamieson came in, and curtsey very low to her
whenever she turned in her direction – so low, in fact, that I
think Mrs Jamieson must have looked at the wall above her, for
she never moved a muscle of her face, no more than if she had
not seen her. Still Mrs Fitz-Adam persevered.

The spring evenings were getting bright and long, when three
or four ladies in calashes met at Miss Barker's door. Do you know
what a calash is? It is a covering worn over caps, not unlike the
heads fastened on old-fashioned gigs; but sometimes it is not
quite so large. This kind of head-gear always made an awful impression on the children in Cranford; and now two or three left
off their play in the quiet sunny little street, and gathered, in
wondering silence, round Miss Pole, Miss Matty, and myself. We
were silent too, so that we could hear loud, suppressed whispers,
inside Miss Barker's house: 'Wait, Peggy! wait till I've run up-
stairs, and washed my hands. When I cough, open the door; I'll
not be a minute.'

And, true enough, it was not a minute before we heard a noise,
between a sneeze and a crow; on which the door flew open.
Behind it stood a round-eyed maiden, all aghast at the honourable
company of calashes, who marched in without a word. She recovered presence of mind enough to usher us into a small room,
which had been the shop, but was now converted into a tem-
porary dressing-room. There we unpinned and shook ourselves,
and arranged our features before the glass into a sweet and gracious company-face; and then, bowing backwards with 'After
you, ma'am,' we allowed Mrs Forrester to take precedence up the
narrow staircase that led to Miss Barker's drawing-room. There
she sat, as stately and composed as though we had never heard
that odd-sounding cough, from which her throat must have been
even then sore and rough. Kind, gentle, shabbily-dressed Mrs
Forrester was immediately conducted to the second place of honour – a seat arranged something like Prince Albert's near the
Queen's – good, but not so good. The place of pre-eminence was,

of course, reserved for the Honourable Mrs Jamieson, who presently came panting up the stairs – Carlo rushing round her on her progress, as if he meant to trip her up.

And now, Miss Betty Barker was a proud and happy woman! She stirred the fire, and shut the door, and sat as near to it as she could, quite on the edge of her chair. When Peggy came in, tottering under the weight of the tea-tray, I noticed that Miss Barker was sadly afraid lest Peggy should not keep her distance sufficiently. She and her mistress were on very familiar terms in their every-day intercourse, and Peggy wanted now to make several little confidences to her, which Miss Barker was on thorns to hear; but which she thought it her duty, as a lady, to repress. So she turned away from all Peggy's asides and signs; but she made one or two very mal-apropos answers to what was said; and at last, seized with a bright idea, she exclaimed, 'Poor sweet Carlo! I'm forgetting him. Come down stairs with me, poor little doggie, and it shall have its tea, it shall!'

In a few minutes she returned, bland and benignant as before; but I thought she had forgotten to give the 'poor little doggie' anything to eat; judging by the avidity with which he swallowed down chance pieces of cake. The tea-tray was abundantly loaded. I was pleased to see it, I was so hungry; but I was afraid the ladies present might think it vulgarly heaped up. I know they would have done at their own houses; but somehow the heaps disappeared here. I saw Mrs Jamieson eating seed-cake, slowly and considerately, as she did everything; and I was rather surprised, for I knew she had told us, on the occasion of her last party, that she never had it in her house, it reminded her so much of scented soap. She always gave us Savoy biscuits.[10] However, Mrs Jamieson was kindly indulgent to Miss Barker's want of knowledge of the customs of high life; and, to spare her feelings, ate three large pieces of seed-cake, with a placid, ruminating expression of countenance, not unlike a cow's.

After tea there was some little demur and difficulty. We were six in number; four could play at Preference, and for the other two there was Cribbage.[11] But all, except myself – (I was rather afraid of the Cranford ladies at cards, for it was the most earnest and serious business they ever engaged in) – were anxious to be

111

of the 'pool.' Even Miss Barker, while declaring she did not know Spadille from Manille,[12] was evidently hankering to take a hand. The dilemma was soon put an end to by a singular kind of noise. If a Baron's daughter-in-law could ever be supposed to snore, I should have said Mrs Jamieson did so then; for, overcome by the heat of the room, and inclined to doze by nature, the temptation of that very comfortable armchair had been too much for her, and Mrs Jamieson was nodding. Once or twice she opened her eyes with an effort, and calmly but unconsciously smiled upon us; but, by-and-by, even her benevolence was not equal to this exertion, and she was sound asleep.

'It is very gratifying to me,' whispered Miss Barker at the card-table to her three opponents, whom, notwithstanding her ignorance of the game, she was 'basting'[13] most unmercifully – 'very gratifying indeed, to see how completely Mrs Jamieson feels at home in my poor little dwelling; she could not have paid me a greater compliment.'

Miss Barker provided me with some literature in the shape of three or four handsomely-bound fashion-books ten or twelve years old, observing, as she put a little table and a candle for my especial benefit, that she knew young people liked to look at pictures. Carlo lay, and snorted, and started at his mistress's feet. He, too, was quite at home.

The card-table was an animated scene to watch; four ladies' heads, with niddle-noddling caps, all nearly meeting over the middle of the table, in their eagerness to whisper quick enough and loud enough: and every now and then came Miss Barker's 'Hush, ladies! if you please, hush! Mrs Jamieson is asleep.'

It was very difficult to steer clear between Mrs Forrester's deafness and Mrs Jamieson's sleepiness. But Miss Barker managed her arduous task well. She repeated the whisper to Mrs Forrester, distorting her face considerably, in order to show, by the motions of her lips, what was said; and then she smiled kindly all round at us, and murmured to herself, 'Very gratifying, indeed; I wish my poor sister had been alive to see this day.'

Presently the door was thrown wide open; Carlo started to his feet, with a loud snapping bark, and Mrs Jamieson awoke: or, perhaps, she had not been asleep – as she said almost directly, the room had been so light she had been glad to keep her eyes shut, but had been listening with great interest to all our amusing and agreeable conversation. Peggy came in once more, red with importance. Another tray! 'Oh, gentility!' thought I, 'can you endure this last shock?' For Miss Barker had ordered (nay, I doubt not, prepared, although she did say, 'Why! Peggy, what have you brought us?' and looked pleasantly surprised at the unexpected pleasure) all sorts of good things for supper – scalloped oysters, potted lobsters, jelly, a dish called 'little Cupids' (which was in great favour with the Cranford ladies, although too expensive to be given, except on solemn and state occasions – maccaroons sopped in brandy, I should have called it, if I had not known its more refined and classical name). In short, we were evidently to be feasted with all that was sweetest and best; and we thought it better to submit graciously, even at the cost of our gentility – which never ate suppers in general – but which, like most non-supper-eaters, was particularly hungry on all special occasions.

Miss Barker, in her former sphere, had, I dare say, been made acquainted with the beverage they call cherry-brandy. We none of us had ever seen such a thing, and rather shrank back when she proffered it us – 'just a little, leetle glass, ladies; after the oysters and lobsters, you know. Shell-fish are sometimes thought not very wholesome.' We all shook our heads like female mandarins![14] but, at last, Mrs Jamieson suffered herself to be persuaded, and we followed her lead. It was not exactly unpalatable, though so hot and so strong that we thought ourselves bound to give evidence that we were not accustomed to such things, by coughing terribly – almost as strangely as Miss Barker had done, before we were admitted by Peggy.

'It's very strong,' said Miss Pole, as she put down her empty glass; 'I do believe there's spirit in it.'

'Only a little drop – just necessary to make it keep,' said Miss Barker. 'You know we put brandy-paper over preserves to make them keep. I often feel tipsy myself from eating damson tart.'

I question whether damson tart would have opened Mrs

Jamieson's heart as the cherry-brandy did; but she told us of a coming event, respecting which she had been quite silent till that moment.

'My sister-in-law, Lady Glenmire, is coming to stay with me.'

There was a chorus of 'Indeed!' and then a pause. Each one rapidly reviewed her wardrobe, as to its fitness to appear in the presence of a Baron's widow; for, of course, a series of small festivals were always held in Cranford on the arrival of a visitor at any of our friends' houses. We felt very pleasantly excited on the present occasion.

Not long after this, the maids and the lanterns were announced. Mrs Jamieson had the sedan chair, which had squeezed itself into Miss Barker's narrow lobby with some difficulty, and most literally 'stopped the way.'[15] It required some skilful manoeuvring on the part of the old chairmen (shoemakers by day; but when summoned to carry the sedan, dressed up in a strange old livery – long great-coats, with small capes, coeval with the sedan, and similar to the dress of the class in Hogarth's pictures) to edge, and back, and try at it again, and finally to succeed in carrying their burden out of Miss Barker's front door. Then we heard their quick pit-a-pat along the quiet little street, as we put on our calashes, and pinned up our gowns; Miss Barker hovering about us with offers of help; which, if she had not remembered her former occupation, and wished us to forget it, would have been much more pressing.

CHAPTER VIII

Your Ladyship

EARLY the next morning – directly after twelve – Miss Pole made her appearance at Miss Matty's. Some very trifling piece of business was alleged as a reason for the call; but there was evidently something behind. At last out it came.

'By the way, you'll think I'm strangely ignorant; but, do you really know, I am puzzled how we ought to address Lady Glenmire. Do you say, "Your Ladyship," where you would say "you" to a common person? I have been puzzling all morning; and are we to say "My lady," instead of "Ma'am?" Now, you knew Lady Arley – will you kindly tell me the most correct way of speaking to the Peerage?'

Poor Miss Matty! she took off her spectacles and she put them on again – but how Lady Arley was addressed, she could not remember.

'It is so long ago,' she said. 'Dear! dear! how stupid I am! I don't think I ever saw her more than twice. I know we used to call Sir Peter, "Sir Peter," – but he came much oftener to see us than Lady Arley did. Deborah would have known in a minute. My lady – your ladyship. It sounds very strange, and as if it was not natural. I never thought of it before; but, now you have named it, I am all in a puzzle.'

It was very certain Miss Pole would obtain no wise decision from Miss Matty, who got more bewildered every moment, and more perplexed as to etiquettes of address.

'Well, I really think,' said Miss Pole, 'I had better just go and tell Mrs Forrester about our little difficulty. One sometimes grows nervous; and yet one would not have Lady Glenmire think we were quite ignorant of the etiquettes of high life in Cranford.'

'And will you just step in here, dear Miss Pole, as you come back, please; and tell me what you decide upon? Whatever you and Mrs Forrester fix upon, will be quite right, I'm sure. "Lady

Arley," "Sir Peter," ' said Miss Matty, to herself, trying to recall the old forms of words.

'Who is Lady Glenmire?' asked I.

'Oh! she's the widow of Mr Jamieson – that's Mrs Jamieson's late husband, you know – widow of his eldest brother. Mrs Jamieson was a Miss Walker, daughter of Governor Walker. Your ladyship. My dear, if they fix on that way of speaking, you must just let me practise a little on you first, for I shall feel so foolish and hot, saying it the first time to Lady Glenmire.'

It was really a relief to Miss Matty when Mrs Jamieson came on a very unpolite errand. I notice that apathetic people have more quiet impertinence than others; and Mrs Jamieson came now to insinuate pretty plainly that she did not particularly wish that the Cranford ladies should call upon her sister-in-law. I can hardly say how she made this clear; for I grew very indignant and warm, while with slow deliberation she was explaining her wishes to Miss Matty, who, a true lady herself, could hardly understand the feeling which made Mrs Jamieson wish to appear to her noble sister-in-law as if she only visited 'county' families. Miss Matty remained puzzled and perplexed long after I had found out the object of Mrs Jamieson's visit.

When she did understand the drift of the honourable lady's call, it was pretty to see with what quiet dignity she received the intimation thus uncourteously given. She was not in the least hurt – she was of too gentle a spirit for that; nor was she exactly conscious of disapproving of Mrs Jamieson's conduct; but there was something of this feeling in her mind, I am sure, which made her pass from the subject to others, in a less flurried and more composed manner than usual. Mrs Jamieson was, indeed, the more flurried of the two, and I could see she was glad to take her leave.

A little while afterwards, Miss Pole returned, red and indignant. 'Well! to be sure! You've had Mrs Jamieson here, I find from Martha; and we are not to call on Lady Glenmire. Yes! I met Mrs Jamieson, half-way between here and Mrs Forrester's, and she told me; she took me so by surprise, I had nothing to say. I wish I had thought of something very sharp and sarcastic; I dare say I shall to-night. And Lady Glenmire is but the widow of a

Scotch baron after all! I went on to look at Mrs Forrester's Peerage, to see who this lady was, that is to be kept under a glass case: widow of a Scotch peer – never sat in the House of Lords[1] – and as poor as Job, I dare say; and she – fifth daughter of some Mr Campbell or other. You are the daughter of a rector, at any rate, and related to the Arleys; and Sir Peter might have been Viscount Arley, every one says.'

Miss Matty tried to soothe Miss Pole, but in vain. That lady, usually so kind and good-humoured, was now in a full flow of anger.

'And I went and ordered a cap this morning, to be quite ready,' said she, at last, – letting out the secret which gave sting to Mrs Jamieson's intimation. 'Mrs Jamieson shall see if it is so easy to get me to make fourth at a pool, when she has none of her fine Scotch relations with her!'

In coming out of church, the first Sunday on which Lady Glenmire appeared in Cranford, we sedulously talked together, and turned our backs on Mrs Jamieson and her guest. If we might not call on her, we would not even look at her, though we were dying with curiosity to know what she was like. We had the comfort of questioning Martha in the afternoon. Martha did not belong to a sphere of society whose observation could be an implied compliment to Lady Glenmire, and Martha had made good use of her eyes.

'Well, ma'am! is it the little lady with Mrs Jamieson, you mean? I thought you would like more to know how young Mrs Smith was dressed, her being a bride.' (Mrs Smith was the butcher's wife.)

Miss Pole said, 'Good gracious me! as if we cared about a Mrs Smith;' but was silent, as Martha resumed her speech.

'The little lady in Mrs Jamieson's pew had on, ma'am, rather an old black silk, and a shepherd's plaid cloak, ma'am, and very bright black eyes she had, ma'am, and a pleasant, sharp face; not over young, ma'am, but yet, I should guess, younger than Mrs Jamieson herself. She looked up and down the church, like a bird, and nipped up her petticoats, when she came out, as quick and sharp as ever I see. I'll tell you what, ma'am, she's more like Mrs Deacon, at the "Coach and Horses," nor any one.'

'Hush, Martha!' said Miss Matty, 'that's not respectful.'

'Isn't it, ma'am? I beg pardon, I'm sure; but Jem Hearn said so as well. He said, she was just such a sharp, stirring sort of a body —'

'Lady,' said Miss Pole.

'Lady — as Mrs Deacon.'

Another Sunday passed away, and we still averted our eyes from Mrs Jamieson and her guest, and made remarks to ourselves that we thought were very severe — almost too much so. Miss Matty was evidently uneasy at our sarcastic manner of speaking.

Perhaps by this time Lady Glenmire had found out that Mrs Jamieson's was not the gayest, liveliest house in the world; perhaps Mrs Jamieson had found out that most of the county families were in London, and that those who remained in the country were not so alive as they might have been to the circumstance of Lady Glenmire being in their neighbourhood. Great events spring out of small causes; so I will not pretend to say what induced Mrs Jamieson to alter her determination of excluding the Cranford ladies, and send notes of invitation all round for a small party, on the following Tuesday. Mr Mulliner himself brought them round. He *would* always ignore the fact of there being a back-door to any house, and gave a louder rat-tat than his mistress, Mrs Jamieson. He had three little notes, which he carried in a large basket, in order to impress his mistress with an idea of their great weight, though they might easily have gone into his waistcoat pocket.

Miss Matty and I quietly decided we would have a previous engagement at home: — it was the evening on which Miss Matty usually made candle-lighters of all the notes and letters of the week; for on Mondays her accounts were always made straight — not a penny owing from the week before; so, by a natural arrangement, making candle-lighters fell upon a Tuesday evening and gave us a legitimate excuse for declining Mrs Jamieson's invitation. But before our answer was written, in came Miss Pole, with an open note in her hand.

'So!' she said. 'Ah! I see you have got your note, too. Better late than never. I could have told my Lady Glenmire she would be glad enough of our society before a fortnight was over.'

'Yes,' said Miss Matty, 'we're asked for Tuesday evening. And perhaps you would just kindly bring your work across and drink tea with us that night. It is my usual regular time for looking over the last week's bills, and notes, and letters, and making candle-lighters of them; but that does not seem quite reason enough for saying I have a previous engagement at home, though I meant to make it do. Now, if you would come, my conscience would be quite at ease, and luckily the note is not written yet.'

I saw Miss Pole's countenance change while Miss Matty was speaking.

'Don't you mean to go then?' asked she.

'Oh, no!' said Miss Matty, quietly. 'You don't either, I suppose?'

'I don't know,' replied Miss Pole. 'Yes, I think I do,' said she, rather briskly; and, on seeing Miss Matty looked surprised, she added, 'You see, one would not like Mrs Jamieson to think that anything she could do, or say, was of consequence enough to give offence; it would be a kind of letting down of ourselves, that I, for one, should not like. It would be too flattering to Mrs Jamieson, if we allowed her to suppose that what she had said affected us a week, nay ten days afterwards.'

'Well! I suppose it is wrong to be hurt and annoyed so long about anything; and, perhaps, after all, she did not mean to vex us. But I must say, I could not have brought myself to say the things Mrs Jamieson did about our not calling. I really don't think I shall go.'

'Oh, come! Miss Matty, you must go; you know our friend Mrs Jamieson is much more phlegmatic than most people, and does not enter into the little delicacies of feeling which you possess in so remarkable a degree.'

'I thought you possessed them too, that day Mrs Jamieson called to tell us not to go,' said Miss Matty, innocently.

But Miss Pole, in addition to her delicacies of feeling, possessed a very smart cap, which she was anxious to show to an admiring world; and so she seemed to forget all her angry words uttered not a fortnight before, and to be ready to act on what she called the great Christian principle of 'Forgive and forget;' and she lectured dear Miss Matty so long on this head, that she absolutely ended by assuring her it was her duty as a deceased rector's daughter, to buy a new cap, and go to the party at Mrs Jamieson's. So 'we were most happy to accept,' instead of 'regretting that we were obliged to decline.'

The expenditure on dress in Cranford was principally in that one article referred to. If the heads were buried in smart new caps, the ladies were like ostriches, and cared not what became of their bodies. Old gowns, white and venerable collars, any number of brooches, up and down and everywhere (some with dogs' eyes painted in them; some that were like small picture-frames with mausoleums and weeping-willows neatly executed in hair inside; some, again, with miniatures of ladies and gentlemen sweetly smiling out of a nest of stiff muslin) – old brooches for a permanent ornament, and new caps to suit the fashion of the day; the ladies of Cranford always dressed with chaste elegance and propriety, as Miss Barker once prettily expressed it.

And with three new caps, and a greater array of brooches than had ever been seen together at one time, since Cranford was a town, did Mrs Forrester, and Miss Matty, and Miss Pole appear on that memorable Tuesday evening. I counted seven brooches myself on Miss Pole's dress. Two were fixed negligently in her cap (one was a butterfly made of Scotch pebbles, which a vivid imagination might believe to be the real insect); one fastened her net neck-kerchief; one her collar; one ornamented the front of her gown, midway between her throat and waist; and another adorned the point of her stomacher.[2] Where the seventh was I have forgotten, but it was somewhere about her, I am sure.

But I am getting on too fast, in describing the dresses of the company. I should first relate the gathering, on the way to Mrs Jamieson's. That lady lived in a large house just outside the town. A road which had known what it was to be a street, ran right before the house, which opened out upon it, without any intervening garden or court. Whatever the sun was about, he never shone on the front of that house. To be sure, the living-rooms were at the back, looking on to a pleasant garden; the front windows only belonged to kitchens and house-keepers' rooms, and pantries; and in one of them Mr Mulliner was reported to sit. Indeed, looking askance, we often saw the back of a head covered with hair-powder, which also extended itself over his coat-collar down to his very waist; and this imposing back was always engaged in reading the *St James's Chronicle*, opened wide, which, in some degree, accounted for the length of time the said newspaper was in reaching us – equal subscribers with Mrs Jamieson, though, in right of her honourableness, she always had the reading of it first. This very Tuesday, the delay in forwarding the last number had been particularly aggravating; just when both Miss Pole and Miss Matty, the former more especially, had been wanting to see it, in order to coach up the court news, ready for the evening's interview with aristocracy. Miss Pole told us she had absolutely taken time by the forelock, and been dressed by five o'clock, in order to be ready, if the *St James's Chronicle* should come in at the last moment – the very *St James's Chronicle* which the powdered-head was tranquilly and composedly reading as we passed the accustomed window this evening.

'The impudence of the man!' said Miss Pole, in a low indignant whisper. 'I should like to ask him, whether his mistress pays her quarter-share for his exclusive use.'

We looked at her in admiration of the courage of her thought; for Mr Mulliner was an object of great awe to all of us. He seemed never to have forgotten his condescension in coming to live at Cranford. Miss Jenkyns, at times, had stood forth as the undaunted champion of her sex, and spoken to him on terms of equality; but even Miss Jenkyns could get no higher. In his pleasantest and most gracious moods he looked like a sulky cockatoo. He did not speak except in gruff monosyllables. He would wait in the hall when we begged him not to wait, and then looked deeply offended because we had kept him there, while, with trembling, hasty hands, we prepared ourselves for appearing in company.

Miss Pole ventured on a small joke as we went upstairs, intended, though addressed to us, to afford Mr Mulliner some slight amusement. We all smiled, in order to seem as if we felt at our ease, and timidly looked for Mr Mulliner's sympathy. Not a muscle of that wooden face had relaxed; and we were grave in an instant.

Mrs Jamieson's drawing-room was cheerful; the evening sun

came streaming into it, and the large square window was clustered round with flowers. The furniture was white and gold; not the later style, Louis Quatorze, I think they call it, all shells and twirls; no, Mrs Jamieson's chairs and tables had not a curve or bend about them.[3] The chair and table legs diminished as they neared the ground, and were straight and square in all their corners. The chairs were all a-row against the walls, with the exception of four or five which stood in a circle round the fire. They were railed with white bars across the back, and knobbed with gold; neither the railings nor the nobs invited to ease. There was a japanned table[4] devoted to literature on which lay a Bible, a Peerage, and a Prayer-Book. There was another square Pembroke table[5] dedicated to the Fine Arts, on which were a kaleidoscope,[6] conversation-cards, puzzle-cards[7] (tied together to an interminable length with faded pink satin ribbon), and a box painted in fond imitation of the drawings which decorate tea-chests.[8] Carlo lay on the worsted-worked rug, and ungraciously barked at us as we entered. Mrs Jamieson stood up, giving us each a torpid smile of welcome, and looking helplessly beyond us at Mr Mulliner, as if she hoped he would place us in chairs, for if he did not, she never could. I suppose he thought we could find our way to the circle round the fire, which reminded me of Stonehenge, I don't know why. Lady Glenmire came to the rescue of our hostess; and, somehow or other, we found ourselves for the first time placed agreeably, and not formally, in Mrs Jamieson's house. Lady Glenmire, now we had time to look at her, proved to be a bright little woman of middle age, who had been very pretty in the days of her youth, and who was even yet very pleasant-looking. I saw Miss Pole appraising her dress in the first five minutes; and I take her word, when she said the next day:

'My dear! ten pounds would have purchased every stitch she had on – lace and all.'

It was pleasant to suspect that a peeress could be poor, and partly reconciled us to the fact that her husband had never sat in the House of Lords; which, when we first heard of it, seemed a kind of swindling us out of our respect on false pretences; a sort of 'A Lord and No Lord' business.[9]

We were all very silent at first. We were thinking what we

could talk about, that should be high enough to interest My Lady. There had been a rise in the price of sugar, which, as preserving-time was near, was a piece of intelligence to all our housekeeping hearts, and would have been the natural topic if Lady Glenmire had not been by. But we were not sure if the Peerage ate preserves – much less knew how they were made. At last, Miss Pole, who had always a great deal of courage and *savoir faire*, spoke to Lady Glenmire, who on her part had seemed just as much puzzled to know how to break the silence as we were.

'Has your ladyship been to Court lately?' asked she; and then gave a little glance round at us, half timid and half triumphant, as much as to say, 'See how judiciously I have chosen a subject befitting the rank of the stranger!'

'I never was there in my life,' said Lady Glenmire, with a broad Scotch accent, but in a very sweet voice. And then, as if she had been too abrupt, she added, 'We very seldom went to London; only twice, in fact, during all my married life; and before I was married, my father had far too large a family' – (fifth daughter of Mr Campbell was in all our minds, I am sure) – 'to take us often from our home, even to Edinburgh. Ye'll have been in Edinburgh, maybe?' said she, suddenly brightening up with the hope of a common interest. We had none of us been there; but Miss Pole had an uncle who once had passed a night there, which was very pleasant.

Mrs Jamieson, meanwhile, was absorbed in wonder why Mr Mulliner did not bring the tea; and at length the wonder oozed out of her mouth.

'I had better wring the bell, my dear, had not I?' said Lady Glenmire, briskly.

'No – I think not – Mulliner does not like to be hurried.'

We should have liked our tea, for we dined at an earlier hour than Mrs Jamieson. I suspect Mr Mulliner had to finish the *St James's Chronicle* before he chose to trouble himself about tea. His mistress fidgeted and fidgeted, and kept saying, 'I can't think why Mulliner does not bring tea. I can't think what he can be about.' And Lady Glenmire at last grew quite impatient, but it was a pretty kind of impatience after all; and she rang the bell rather sharply, on receiving a half permission from her sister-in-law to do so. Mr Mulliner appeared in dignified surprise. 'Oh!' said Mrs Jamieson, 'Lady Glenmire rang the bell; I believe it was for tea.'

In a few minutes tea was brought. Very delicate was the china, very old the plate, very thin the bread and butter, and very small the lumps of sugar. Sugar was evidently Mrs Jamieson's favourite economy. I question if the little filigree sugar-tongs,[10] made something like scissors, could have opened themselves wide enough to take up an honest, vulgar, good-sized piece; and when I tried to seize two little minnikin pieces at once, so as not to be detected in too many returns to the sugar-basin, they absolutely dropped one, with a little sharp clatter, quite in a malicious and unnatural manner. But before this happened, we had a slight disappointment. In the little silver jug was cream, in the larger one was milk. As soon as Mr Mulliner came in, Carlo began to beg, which was a thing our manners forbade us to do, though I am sure we were just as hungry; and Mrs Jamieson said she was certain we would excuse her if she gave her poor dumb Carlo his tea first. She accordingly mixed a saucer-full for him, and put it down for him to lap; and then she told us how intelligent and sensible the dear little fellow was; he knew cream quite well, and constantly refused tea with only milk in it: so the milk was left for us; but we silently thought we were quite as intelligent and sensible as Carlo, and felt as if insult were added to injury, when we were called upon to admire the gratitude evinced by his wagging his tail for the cream, which should have been ours.

After tea we thawed down into common-life subjects. We were thankful to Lady Glenmire for having proposed some more bread and butter, and this mutual want made us better acquainted with her than we should ever have been with talking about the Court, though Miss Pole did say she had hoped to know how the dear Queen was from some one who had seen her.

The friendship, begun over bread and buter, extended on to cards. Lady Glenmire played Preference to admiration, and was a complete authority as to Ombre and Quadrille.[11] Even Miss Pole quite forgot to say 'my lady,' and 'your ladyship,' and said 'Basto! ma'am;'[12] 'you have Spadille, I believe,' just as quietly as

if we had never held the great Cranford parliament on the subject
of the proper mode of addressing a peeress.

As a proof of how thoroughly we had forgotten that we were in
the presence of one who might have sat down to tea with a coro-
net, instead of a cap, on her head, Mrs Forrester related a curious
little fact to Lady Glenmire – an anecdote known to the circle of
her intimate friends, but of which even Mrs Jamieson was not
aware. It related to some fine old lace, the sole relic of better days,
which Lady Glenmire was admiring on Mrs Forrester's collar.

'Yes,' said that lady, 'such lace cannot be got now for either
love or money; made by the nuns abroad, they tell me. They say
that they can't make it now, even there. But perhaps they can
now they've passed the Catholic Emancipation Bill.[13] I should not
wonder. But, in the mean time, I treasure up my lace very much.
I daren't even trust the washing of it to my maid' (the little
charity school-girl I have named before, but who sounded well as
'my maid'). 'I always wash it myself. And once it had a narrow
escape. Of course, your ladyship knows that such lace must never
be starched or ironed. Some people wash it in sugar and water;
and some in coffee, to make it the right yellow colour; but I myself have a very good receipt for washing it in milk, which stiffens
it enough, and gives it a very good creamy colour. Well, ma'am, I
had tacked it together (and the beauty of this fine lace is, that
when it is wet, it goes into a very little space), and put it to soak
in milk, when, unfortunately, I left the room; on my return, I
found pussy on the table, looking very like a thief, but gulping
very uncomfortably, as if she was half choked with something
she wanted to swallow, and could not. And would you believe it?
At first, I pitied her, and said, "Poor pussy! poor pussy!" till, all
at once, I looked and saw the cup of milk empty – cleaned out!
"You naughty cat!" said I; and I believe I was provoked enough
to give her a slap, which did no good, but only helped the lace
down – just as one slaps a choking child on the back. I could have
cried, I was so vexed; but I determined I would not give the lace
up without a struggle for it. I hoped the lace might disagree with
her, at any rate; but it would have been too much for Job, if he
had seen, as I did, that cat come in, quite placid and purring, not
a quarter of an hour after, and almost expecting to be stroked.

"No, pussy!" said I; "if you have any conscience, you ought not to expect that!" And then a thought struck me; and I rang the bell for my maid, and sent her to Mr Hoggins, with my compliments, and would he be kind enough to lend me one of his top-boots[14] for an hour? I did not think there was anything odd in the message; but Jenny said, the young men in the surgery laughed as if they would be ill, at my wanting a top-boot. When it came, Jenny and I put pussy in, with her fore-feet straight down, so that they were fastened, and could not scratch, and we gave her a teaspoonful of current-jelly, in which (your ladyship must excuse me) I had mixed some tartar emetic. I shall never forget how anxious I was for the next half-hour. I took pussy to my own room, and spread a clean towel on the floor. I could have kissed her when she returned the lace to sight, very much as it had gone down. Jenny had boiling water ready, and we soaked it and soaked it, and spread it on a lavender-bush in the sun, before I could touch it again, even to put it in milk. But now, your ladyship would never guess that it had been in pussy's inside.'

We found out, in the course of the evening, that Lady Glenmire was going to pay Mrs Jamieson a long visit, as she had given up her apartments in Edinburgh, and had no ties to take her back there in a hurry. On the whole, we were rather glad to hear this, for she had made a pleasant impression upon us; and it was also very comfortable to find, from things which dropped out in the course of conversation, that, in addition to many other genteel qualities, she was far removed from the 'vulgarity of wealth.'

'Don't you find it very unpleasant walking?' asked Mrs Jamieson, as our respective servants were announced. It was a pretty regular question from Mrs Jamieson, who had her own carriage in the coach-house, and always went out in a sedan-chair to the very shortest distances. The answers were nearly as much a matter of course.

'Oh dear, no! it is so pleasant and still at night!' 'Such a refreshment after the excitement of a party!' 'The stars are so beautiful!' This last from Miss Matty.

'Are you fond of astronomy?' Lady Glenmire asked.

'Not very,' replied Miss Matty, rather confused at the moment to remember which was astronomy and which was astrology –

but the answer was true under either circumstance, for she read, and was slightly alarmed at, Francis Moore's astrological predictions;[15] and, as to astronomy, in a private and confidential conversation, she had told me, she never could believe that the earth was moving constantly, and that she would not believe it if she could, it made her feel so tired and dizzy whenever she thought about it.

In our pattens, we picked our way home with extra care that night; so refined and delicate were our perceptions after drinking tea with 'my lady.'

CHAPTER IX

Signor Brunoni

SOON after the events of which I gave an account in my last paper, I was summoned home by my father's illness; and for a time I forgot, in anxiety about him, to wonder how my dear friends at Cranford were getting on, or how Lady Glenmire could reconcile herself to the dulness of the long visit which she was still paying to her sister-in-law, Mrs Jamieson. When my father grew a little stronger I accompanied him to the sea-side, so that altogether I seemed banished from Cranford, and was deprived of the opportunity of hearing any chance intelligence of the dear little town for the greater part of that year.

Late in November – when we had returned home again, and my father was once more in good health – I received a letter from Miss Matty; and a very mysterious letter it was. She began many sentences without ending them, running them one into another, in much the same confused sort of way in which written words run together on blotting-paper. All I could make out was, that if my father was better (which she hoped he was), and would take warning and wear a great-coat from Michaelmas to Lady-day,[1] if turbans were in fashion,[2] could I tell her? Such a piece of gaiety was going to happen as had not been seen or known of since Wombwell's lions came,[3] when one of them ate a little child's arm; and she was, perhaps, too old to care about dress, but a new cap she must have; and, having heard that turbans were worn, and some of the county families likely to come, she would like to look tidy, if I would bring her a cap from the milliner I employed; and oh, dear ! how careless of her to forget that she wrote to beg I would come and pay her a visit next Tuesday; when she hoped to have something to offer me in the way of amusement, which she would not now particularly describe, only sea-green was her favourite colour. So she ended her letter; but in a P.S. she added, she thought she might as well tell me what was the peculiar attraction to Cranford just now; Signor Brunoni was going to exhibit his wonderful magic in the Cranford Assembly Rooms, on Wednesday and Friday evening in the following week.

I was very glad to accept the invitation from my dear Miss Matty, independently of the conjuror, and most particularly anxious to prevent her from disfiguring her small gentle mousey face with a great Saracen's head turban; and accordingly, I bought her a pretty, neat, middle-aged cap, which, however, was rather a disappointment to her when, on my arrival, she followed me into my bedroom, ostensibly to poke the fire, but in reality, I do believe, to see if the sea-green turban was not inside the cap-box with which I had travelled. It was in vain that I twirled the cap round on my hand to exhibit back and side fronts: her heart had been set upon a turban, and all she could do was to say, with resignation in her look and voice:

'I am sure you did your best, my dear. It is just like the caps all the ladies in Cranford are wearing, and they have had theirs for a year, I dare say. I should have liked something newer, I confess – something more like the turbans Miss Betty Barker tells me Queen Adelaide wears; but it is very pretty, my dear. And I dare say lavender will wear better than sea-green. Well, after all, what is dress, that we should care about it! You'll tell me if you want anything, my dear. Here is the bell. I suppose turbans have not got down to Drumble yet?'

So saying, the dear old lady bemoaned herself out of the room, leaving me to dress for the evening, when, as she informed me, she expected Miss Pole and Mrs Forrester, and she hoped I should not feel myself too much tired to join the party. Of course I should not; and I made some haste to unpack and arrange my dress; but, with all my speed, I heard the arrivals and the buzz of conversation in the next room before I was ready. Just as I opened the door, I caught the words – 'I was foolish to expect anything very genteel out of the Drumble shops – poor girl! she did her best, I've no doubt.' But for all that, I had rather that she blamed Drumble and me than disfigured herself with a turban.

Miss Pole was always the person, in the trio of Cranford ladies now assembled, to have had adventures. She was in the habit of spending the morning in rambling from shop to shop; not to purchase anything (except an occasional reel of cotton, or a piece of tape), but to see the new articles and report upon them, and to collect all the stray pieces of intelligence in the town. She had a way, too, of demurely popping hither and thither into all sorts of places to gratify her curiosity on any point; a way which, if she had not looked so very genteel and prim, might have been considered impertinent. And now, by the expressive way in which she cleared her throat, and waited for all minor subjects (such as caps and turbans) to be cleared off the course, we knew she had something very particular to relate, when the due pause came – and I defy any people, possessed of common modesty, to keep up a conversation long, where one among them sits up aloft in silence, looking down upon all the things they chance to say as trivial and contemptible compared to what they could disclose, if properly entreated. Miss Pole began :

'As I was stepping out of Gordon's shop to-day, I chanced to go into the George (my Betty has a second-cousin who is chambermaid there, and I thought Betty would like to hear how she was), and, not seeing any one about, I strolled up the staircase, and found myself in the passage leading to the Assembly Room – (you and I remember the Assembly Room, I am sure, Miss Matty ! and the *menuets de la cour* !)[4] – so I went on, not thinking of what I was about, when, all at once, I perceived that I was in the middle of the preparations for to-morrow night – the room being divided with great clothes-maids,[5] over which Crosby's men were tacking red flannel; very dark and odd it seemed; it quite bewildered me, and I was going on behind the screens, in my absence of mind, when a gentleman (quite the gentleman, I can assure you) stepped forwards and asked if I had any business he could arrange for me. He spoke such pretty broken English, I could not help thinking of Thaddeus of Warsaw, and the Hungarian Brothers, and Santo Sebastiani;[6] and while I was busy picturing his past life to myself, he had bowed me out of the room. But wait a minute ! You have not heard half my story yet ! I was going downstairs, when who should I meet but Betty's second-cousin. So, of course, I stopped to speak to her for Betty's sake; and she told me that I had really seen the conjuror; the gentleman who spoke broken English was Signor Brunoni himself. Just at this moment he passed us on the stairs, making such a graceful bow! in reply to which I dropped a curtsey – all foreigners have such polite manners, one catches something of it. But when he had gone downstairs, I bethought me that I had dropped my glove in the Assembly Room (it was safe in my muff all the time, but I never found it till afterwards); so I went back, and, just as I was creeping up the passage left on one side of the great screen that goes nearly across the room, who should I see but the very same gentleman that had met me before, and passed me on the stairs, coming forwards from the inner part of the room, to which there is no entrance – you remember, Miss Matty: – and just repeating, in his pretty broken English, the inquiry if I had any business there – I don't mean that he put it quite so bluntly, but he seemed very determined that I should not pass the screen – so, of course, I explained about my glove, which, curiously enough, I found at that very moment.'

Miss Pole then had seen the conjuror – the real live conjuror! and numerous were the questions we all asked her. 'Had he a beard?' 'Was he young or old?' 'Fair or dark?' 'Did he look' – (unable to shape my question prudently, I put it in another form) – 'How did he look?' In short, Miss Pole was the heroine of the evening, owing to her morning's encounter. If she was not the rose (that is to say, the conjuror), she had been near it.[7]

Conjuration, sleight of hand, magic, witchcraft were the subjects of the evening. Miss Pole was slightly sceptical, and inclined to think there might be a scientific solution found for even the proceedings of the Witch of Endor.[8] Mrs Forrester believed everything, from ghosts to death-watches.[9] Miss Matty ranged between the two – always convinced by the last speaker. I think she was naturally more inclined to Mrs Forrester's side, but a desire of proving herself a worthy sister to Miss Jenkyns kept her equally balanced – Miss Jenkyns, who would never allow a servant to call the little rolls of tallow that formed themselves round candles 'winding-sheets,' but insisted on their being spoken of as 'roley-poleys!' A sister of hers to be superstitious! It would never do.

After tea, I was despatched downstairs into the dining-parlour for that volume of the old Encyclopaedia which contained the nouns beginning with C, in order that Miss Pole might prime herself with scientific explanation for the tricks of the following evening. It spoilt the pool at Preference which Miss Matty and Mrs Forrester had been looking forward to, for Miss Pole became so much absorbed in her subject, and the plates by which it was illustrated, that we felt it would be cruel to disturb her, otherwise than by one or two well-timed yawns, which I threw in now and then, for I was really touched by the meek way in which the two ladies were bearing their disappointment. But Miss Pole only read the more zealously, imparting to us no more interesting information than this:

'Ah! I see; I comprehend perfectly. A represents the ball. Put A between B and D – no! between C and F, and turn the second joint of the third finger of your left hand over the wrist of your right H. Very clear indeed! My dear Mrs Forrester, conjuring and witchcraft is a mere affair of the alphabet. Do let me read you this one passage?'

Mrs Forrester implored Miss Pole to spare her, saying, from a child upwards, she never could understand being read aloud to; and I dropped the pack of cards, which I had been shuffling very audibly; and by this discreet movement, I obliged Miss Pole to perceive that Preference was to have been the order of the evening, and to propose, rather unwillingly, that the pool should commence. The pleasant brightness that stole over the other two ladies' faces on this! Miss Matty had one or two twinges of self-reproach for having interrupted Miss Pole in her studies: and did not remember her cards well, or give her full attention to the game, until she had soothed her conscience by offering to lend the volume of the Encyclopaedia to Miss Pole, who accepted it thankfully, and said Betty should take it home when she came with the lantern.

The next evening we were all in a little gentle flutter at the idea of the gaiety before us. Miss Matty went up to dress betimes, and hurried me until I was ready, when we found we had an hour and a half to wait before the 'doors opened at seven precisely.' And we had only twenty yards to go! However, as Miss Matty said, it would not do to get too much absorbed in anything, and forget the time; so, she thought we had better sit quietly, without lighting the candles, till five minutes to seven. So Miss Matty dozed, and I knitted.

At length we set off; and at the door, under the carriage-way at the George, we met Mrs Forrester and Miss Pole: the latter was discussing the subject of the evening with more vehemence than ever, and throwing A's and B's at our heads like hail-stones. She had even copied one or two of the 'receipts' – as she called them – for the different tricks, on backs of letters, ready to explain and detect Signor Brunoni's arts.

We went into the cloak-room adjoining the Assembly Room; Miss Matty gave a sigh or two to her departed youth, and the remembrance of the last time she had been there, as she adjusted her pretty new cap before the strange, quaint old mirror in the cloak-room! The Assembly Room had been added to the inn about a hundred years before, by the different county families, who met together there once a month during the winter, to dance and play cards. Many a county beauty had first swam through the minuet, that she afterwards danced before Queen Charlotte,[10] in this very room. It was said that one of the Gunnings[11] had graced the apartment with her beauty; it was certain that a rich and beautiful widow, Lady Williams, had here been smitten with the noble figure of a young artist, who was staying with some family in the neighbourhood for professional purposes, and accompanied his patrons to the Cranford Assembly. And a pretty bargain poor Lady Williams had of her handsome husband, if all tales were true! Now, no beauty blushed and dimpled along the sides of the Cranford Assembly Room; no handsome artist won hearts by his bow, *chapeau bras*[12] in hand; the old room was dingy; the salmon-coloured paint had faded into a drab; great pieces of plaster had chipped off from the white wreaths and festoons on its walls; but still a mouldy odour of aristocracy lingered about the place, and a dusty recollection of the days that were gone made Miss Matty and Mrs Forrester bridle up as they entered, and walk mincingly up the room, as if there were a number of genteel observers, instead of two little boys, with a stick of toffy between them with which to beguile the time.

We stopped short at the second front row; I could hardly understand why, until I heard Miss Pole ask a stray waiter if any of the county families were expected; and when he shook his head, and believed not, Mrs Forrester and Miss Matty moved forwards, and our party represented a conversational square. The front row was soon augmented and enriched by Lady Glenmire and Mrs Jamieson. We six occupied the two front rows, and our aristocratic seclusion was respected by the groups of shopkeepers who strayed in from time to time, and huddled together on the back benches. At least I conjectured so, from the noise they made, and the sonorous bumps they gave in sitting down; but when, in weariness of the obstinate green curtain, that would not draw up, but would stare at me with two odd eyes, seen through holes, as in the old tapestry story, I would fain have looked round at the merry chattering people behind me, Miss Pole clutched my arm, and begged me not to turn, for 'it was not the thing.' What 'the thing' was, I never could find out, but it must have been something eminently dull and tiresome. However, we all sat eyes right, square front, gazing at the tantalizing curtain, and hardly speaking intelligibly, we were so afraid of being caught in the vulgarity of making any noise in a place of public amusement. Mrs Jamieson was the most fortunate, for she fell asleep.

At length the eyes disappeared – the curtain quivered – one side went up before the other, which stuck fast; it was dropped again, and, with a fresh effort, and a vigorous pull from some unseen hand, it flew up, revealing to our sight a magnificent gentleman in the Turkish costume, seated before a little table, gazing at us (I should have said with the same eyes that I had last seen through the hole in the curtain) with calm and condescending dignity, 'like a being of another sphere,' as I heard a sentimental voice ejaculate behind me.

'That's not Signor Brunoni!' said Miss Pole, decidedly, and so audibly that I am sure he heard, for he glanced down over his flowing beard at our party with an air of mute reproach. 'Signor Brunoni had no beard – but perhaps he'll come soon.' So she lulled herself into patience. Meanwhile, Miss Matty had reconnoitred through her eye-glass; wiped it, and looked again. Then she turned round, and said to me, in a kind, mild, sorrowful tone:

'You see, my dear, turbans *are* worn.'

But we had no time for more conversation. The Grand Turk, as Miss Pole chose to call him, arose and announced himself as Signor Brunoni.

'I don't believe him!' exclaimed Miss Pole, in a defiant manner. He looked at her again, with the same dignified upbraiding in his countenance. 'I don't!' she repeated, more positively than ever. 'Signor Brunoni had not got that muffy sort of thing about his chin, but looked like a close-shaved Christian gentleman.'

Miss Pole's energetic speeches had the good effect of wakening up Mrs Jamieson, who opened her eyes wide, in sign of the deepest attention – a proceeding which silenced Miss Pole, and encouraged the Grand Turk to proceed, which he did in very broken English – so broken that there was no cohesion between the parts of his sentences, a fact which he himself perceived at last, and so left off speaking and proceeded to action.

Now we were astonished. How he did his tricks I could not imagine; no, not even when Miss Pole pulled out her pieces of paper and began reading aloud – or at least in a very audible whisper – the separate 'receipts' for the most common of his tricks. If ever I saw a man frown, and look enraged, I saw the Grand Turk frown at Miss Pole; but, as she said, what could be expected but unchristian looks from a Mussulman? [13] If Miss Pole was sceptical, and more engrossed with her receipts and diagrams than with his tricks, Miss Matty and Mrs Forrester were mystified and perplexed to the highest degree. Mrs Jamieson kept taking her spectacles off and wiping them, as if she thought it was something defective in them which made the legerdemain; and Lady Glenmire, who had seen many curious sights in Edinburgh, was very much struck with the tricks, and would not at all agree with Miss Pole, who declared that anybody could do them with a little practice – and that she would, herself, undertake to do all he did, with two hours given to study the Encyclopaedia and make her third finger flexible.

At last, Miss Matty and Mrs Forrester became perfectly awestruck. They whispered together. I sat just behind them, so I could not help hearing what they were saying. Miss Matty asked Mrs Forrester 'if she thought it was quite right to have come to see such things? She could not help fearing they were lending

encouragement to something that was not quite –' a little shake
of the head filled up the blank. Mrs Forrester replied, that the
same thought had crossed her mind; she, too, was feeling very
uncomfortable; it was so very strange. She was quite certain that
it was her pocket-handkerchief which was in that loaf just now;
and it had been in her own hand not five minutes before. She
wondered who had furnished the bread? She was sure it could
not be Dakin, because he was the churchwarden. Suddenly, Miss
Matty half turned towards me:

'Will you look, my dear – you are a stranger in the town, and
it won't give rise to unpleasant reports – will you just look round
and see if the rector is here? If he is, I think we may conclude
that this wonderful man is sanctioned by the Church, and that
will be a great relief to my mind.'

I looked, and I saw the tall, thin, dry, dusty rector, sitting
surrounded by National School boys,[14] guarded by troops of his
own sex from any approach of the many Cranford spinsters.
His kind face was all agape with broad smiles, and the boys
around him were in chinks of laughing.[15] I told Miss Matty that
the Church was smiling approval, which set her mind at
ease.

I have never named Mr Hayter, the rector, because I, as a well-
to-do and happy young woman, never came in contact with him.
He was an old bachelor, but as afraid of matrimonial reports getting abroad about him as any girl of eighteen : and he would rush
into a shop, or dive down an entry, sooner than encounter any of
the Cranford ladies in the street; and, as for the Preference
parties, I did not wonder at his not accepting invitations to them.
To tell the truth, I always suspected Miss Pole of having given
very vigorous chase to Mr Hayter when he first came to Cranford; and not the less, because now she appeared to share so vividly
in his dread lest her name should ever be coupled with his. He
found all his interests among the poor and helpless; he had treated
the National School boys this very night to the performance; and
virtue was for once its own reward, for they guarded him right
and left, and clung round him as if he had been the queen-bee,
and they the swarm. He felt so safe in their environment, that he
could even afford to give our party a bow as we filed out. Miss

Pole ignored his presence, and pretended to be absorbed in convincing us that we had been cheated, and had not seen Signor Brunoni after all.

CHAPTER X

The Panic

I THINK a series of circumstances dated from Signor Brunoni's visit to Cranford, which seemed at the time connected in our minds with him, though I don't know that he had anything really to do with them. All at once all sorts of uncomfortable rumours got afloat in the town. There were one or two robberies – real *bonâ fide* robberies; men had up before the magistrates and committed for trial; and that seemed to make us all afraid of being robbed; and for a long time at Miss Matty's, I know, we used to make a regular expedition all round the kitchens and cellars every night, Miss Matty leading the way, armed with the poker, I following with the hearth-brush, and Martha carrying the shovel and fire-irons with which to sound the alarm: and by the accidental hitting together of them she often frightened us so much that we bolted ourselves up, all three together, in the back kitchen, or store-room, or wherever we happened to be, till, when our affright was over, we recollected ourselves, and set out afresh with double valiance. By day we heard strange stories from the shopkeepers and cottagers, of carts that went about in the dead of night, drawn by horses shod with felt, and guarded by men in dark clothes, going round the town, no doubt in search of some unwatched house or some unfastened door.[1]

Miss Pole, who affected great bravery herself, was the principal person to collect and arrange these reports, so as to make them assume their most fearful aspect. But we discovered that she had begged one of Mr Hoggins's worn-out hats to hang up in her lobby, and we (at least I) had my doubts as to whether she really would enjoy the little adventure of having her house broken into, as she protested she should. Miss Matty made no secret of being an arrant coward; but she went regularly through her housekeeper's duty of inspection – only the hour for this became earlier and earlier, till at last we went the rounds at half-past six, and

Miss Matty adjourned to bed soon after seven, 'in order to get the night over the sooner.'

Cranford had so long piqued itself on being an honest and moral town, that it had grown to fancy itself too genteel and well-bred to be otherwise, and felt the stain upon its character at this time doubly. But we comforted ourselves with the assurance which we gave to each other, that the robberies could never have been committed by any Cranford person; it must have been a stranger or strangers who brought this disgrace upon the town, and occasioned as many precautions as if we were living among the Red Indians or the French.[2]

This last comparison of our nightly state of defence and fortification was made by Mrs Forrester, whose father had served under General Burgoyne[3] in the American war, and whose husband had fought the French in Spain. She indeed inclined to the idea that, in some way, the French were connected with the small thefts, which were ascertained facts, and the burglaries and highway robberies, which were rumours. She had been deeply impressed with the idea of French spies, at some time in her life; and the notion could never be fairly eradicated, but sprang up again from time to time. And now her theory was this: the Cranford people respected themselves too much, and were too grateful to the aristocracy who were so kind as to live near the town, ever to disgrace their bringing up by being dishonest or immoral; therefore, we must believe that the robbers were strangers — if strangers, why not foreigners? — if foreigners, who so likely as the French? Signor Brunoni spoke broken English like a Frenchman, and, though he wore a turban like a Turk, Mrs Forrester had seen a print of Madame de Staël with a turban on,[4] and another of Mr Denon[5] in just such a dress as that in which the conjuror had made his appearance; showing clearly that the French, as well as the Turks, wore turbans: there could be no doubt Signor Brunoni was a Frenchman — a French spy, come to discover the weak and undefended places of England; and, doubtless, he had his accomplices: for her part, she, Mrs Forrester, had always had her own opinion of Miss Pole's adventure at the George Inn — seeing two men where only one was believed to be: French people had ways and means, which, she was thankful to say, the English knew nothing about; and she had never felt quite easy in her mind about going to see that conjuror; it was rather too much like a forbidden thing, though the rector was there. In short, Mrs Forrester grew more excited than we had ever known her before; and, being an officer's daughter and widow, we looked up to her opinion, of course.

Really I do not know how much was true or false in the reports which flew about like wildfire just at this time; but it seemed to me then that there was every reason to believe that at Mardon (a small town about eight miles from Cranford) houses and shops were entered by holes made in the walls, the bricks being silently carried away in the dead of the night, and all done so quietly that no sound was heard either in or out of the house. Miss Matty gave it up in despair when she heard of this. 'What was the use,' said she, 'of locks and bolts, and bells to the windows, and going round the house every night? That last trick was fit for a conjuror. Now she did believe that Signor Brunoni was at the bottom of it.'

One afternoon, about five o'clock, we were startled by a hasty knock at the door. Miss Matty bade me run and tell Martha on no account to open the door till she (Miss Matty) had reconnoitred through the window; and she armed herself with a footstool to drop down on the head of the visitor, in case he should show a face covered with black crape, as he looked up in answer to her inquiry of who was there. But it was nobody but Miss Pole and Betty. The former came up-stairs, carrying a little hand-basket, and she was evidently in a state of great agitation.

'Take care of that!' said she to me, as I offered to relieve her of her basket. 'It's my plate. I am sure there is a plan to rob my house to-night. I am come to throw myself on your hospitality, Miss Matty. Betty is going to sleep with her cousin at the George. I can sit up here all night, if you will allow me; but my house is so far from my neighbours; and I don't believe we could be heard if we screamed ever so!'

'But,' said Miss Matty, 'what has alarmed you so much? Have you seen any men lurking about the house?'

'Oh yes!' answered Miss Pole. 'Two very bad-looking men have gone three times past the house, very slowly; and an Irish beggarwoman came not half an hour ago,[6] and all but forced herself in past Betty, saying her children were starving, and she must speak to the mistress. You see, she said "mistress," though there was a hat hanging up in the hall, and it would have been more natural to have said "master." But Betty shut the door in her face, and came up to me, and we got the spoons together, and sat in the parlour-window watching, till we saw Thomas Jones going from his work, when we called to him and asked him to take care of us into the town.'

We might have triumphed over Miss Pole, who had professed such bravery until she was frightened; but we were too glad to perceive that she shared in the weaknesses of humanity to exult over her; and I gave up my room to her very willingly, and shared Miss Matty's bed for the night. But before we retired, the two ladies rummaged up, out of the recesses of their memory, such horrid stories of robbery and murder, that I quite quaked in my shoes. Miss Pole was evidently anxious to prove that such terrible events had occurred within her experience that she was justified in her sudden panic; and Miss Matty did not like to be outdone, and capped every story with one yet more horrible, till it reminded me, oddly enough, of an old story I had read somewhere, of a nightingale and a musician,[7] who strove one against the other which could produce the most admirable music, till poor Philomel dropped down dead.

One of the stories that haunted me for a long time afterwards, was of a girl, who was left in charge of a great house in Cumberland, on some particular fair-day, when the other servants all went off to the gaieties. The family were away in London, and a pedlar came by, and asked to leave his large and heavy pack in the kitchen, saying he would call for it again at night; and the girl (a gamekeeper's daughter), roaming about in search of amusement, chanced to hit upon a gun hanging up in the hall, and took it down to look at the chasing; and it went off through the open kitchen door, hit the pack, and a slow dark thread of blood came oozing out. (How Miss Pole enjoyed this part of the story, dwelling on each word as if she loved it!) She rather hurried over the further account of the girl's bravery, and I have but a confused idea that, somehow, she baffled the robbers with Italian irons,[8] heated red hot, and then restored to blackness by being dipped in grease.

We parted for the night with an awe-struck wonder as to what we should hear of in the morning – and on my part, with a vehement desire for the night to be over and gone: I was so afraid lest the robbers should have seen, from some dark lurking-place, that Miss Pole had carried off her plate, and thus have a double motive for attacking the house.

But, until Lady Glenmire came to call next day, we heard of nothing unusual. The kitchen fire-irons were in exactly the same position against the back door, as when Martha and I had skilfully piled them up like spillikins,[9] ready to fall with an awful clatter, if only a cat had touched the outside panels. I had wondered what we should do if thus awakened and alarmed, and had proposed to Miss Matty that we should cover up our faces under the bed-clothes, so that there should be no danger of the robbers thinking that we could identify them; but Miss Matty, who was trembling very much, scouted this idea, and said we owed it to society to apprehend them, and that she should certainly do her best to lay hold of them, and lock them up in the garret till morning.

When Lady Glenmire came, we almost felt jealous of her. Mrs Jamieson's house had really been attacked; at least there were men's footsteps to be seen on the flower-borders, underneath the kitchen windows, 'where nae men should be;'[10] and Carlo had barked all through the night as if strangers were abroad. Mrs Jamieson had been awakened by Lady Glenmire, and they had rung the bell which communicated with Mr Mulliner's room, in the third story, and when his nightcapped head had appeared over the bannisters, in answer to the summons, they had told him of their alarm, and the reasons for it; whereupon he retreated into his bedroom, and locked the door (for fear of draughts, as he informed them in the morning), and opened the window, and called out valiantly to say, if the supposed robbers would come to him he would fight them; but, as Lady Glenmire observed, that was but poor comfort, since they would have to pass by Mrs Jamieson's room and her own, before they could reach him, and must be of a very pugnacious disposition indeed, if they neglected the opportunities of robbery presented by the unguarded lower stories, to go up to a garret, and there force a door to get at the champion of the house. Lady Glenmire, after waiting and listening for some time in the drawing-room, had proposed to Mrs Jamieson that they should go to bed; but that lady said she should not feel comfortable unless she sat up and watched; and, accordingly, she packed herself warmly up on the sofa, where she was found by the housemaid, when she came into the room at six o'clock, fast asleep; but Lady Glenmire went to bed, and kept awake all night.

When Miss Pole heard of this, she nodded her head in great satisfaction. She had been sure we should hear of something happening in Cranford that night; and we had heard. It was clear enough they had first proposed to attack her house; but when they saw that she and Betty were on their guard, and had carried off the plate, they had changed their tactics and gone to Mrs Jamieson's, and no one knew what might have happened if Carlo had not barked, like a good dog as he was!

Poor Carlo! his barking days were nearly over. Whether the gang who infested the neighbourhood were afraid of him; or whether they were revengeful enough, for the way in which he had baffled them on the night in question, to poison him; or whether, as some among the more uneducated people thought, he died of apoplexy, brought on by too much feeding and too little exercise; at any rate, it is certain that, two days after this eventful night, Carlo was found dead, with his poor little legs stretched out stiff in the attitude of running, as if by such unusual exertion he could escape the sure pursuer, Death.

We were all sorry for Carlo, the old familiar friend who had snapped at us for so many years; and the mysterious mode of his death made us very uncomfortable. Could Signor Brunoni be at the bottom of this? He had apparently killed a canary with only a word of command; his will seemed of deadly force; who knew but what he might yet be lingering in the neighbourhood willing all sorts of awful things!

We whispered these fancies among ourselves in the evenings; but in the mornings our courage came back with the daylight, and in a week's time we had got over the shock of Carlo's death;

all but Mrs Jamieson. She, poor thing, felt it as she had felt no event since her husband's death; indeed, Miss Pole said, that as the Honourable Mr Jamieson drank a good deal, and occasioned her much uneasiness, it was possible that Carlo's death might be the greater affliction. But there was always a tinge of cynicism in Miss Pole's remarks. However, one thing was clear and certain; it was necessary for Mrs Jamieson to have some change of scene; and Mr Mulliner was very impressive on this point, shaking his head whenever we inquired after his mistress, and speaking of her loss of appetite and bad nights very ominously; and with justice too, for if she had two characteristics in her natural state of health, they were a facility for eating and sleeping. If she could neither eat nor sleep, she must be indeed out of spirits and out of health.

Lady Glenmire (who had evidently taken very kindly to Cranford) did not like the idea of Mrs Jamieson's going to Cheltenham, and more than once insinuated pretty plainly that it was Mr Mulliner's doing, who had been much alarmed on the occasion of the house being attacked, and since had said, more than once, that he felt it a very responsible charge to have to defend so many women. Be that as it might, Mrs Jamieson went to Cheltenham, escorted by Mr Mulliner; and Lady Glenmire remained in possession of the house, her ostensible office being to take care that the maid-servants did not pick up followers. She made a very pleasant-looking dragon: and, as soon as it was arranged for her stay in Cranford, she found out that Mrs Jamieson's visit to Cheltenham was just the best thing in the world. She had let her house in Edinburgh, and was for the time houseless, so the charge of her sister-in-law's comfortable abode was very convenient and acceptable.

Miss Pole was very much inclined to instal herself as a heroine, because of the decided steps she had taken in flying from the two men and one woman, whom she entitled 'that murderous gang.' She described their appearance in glowing colours, and I noticed that every time she went over the story some fresh trait of villany was added to their appearance. One was tall – he grew to be gigantic in height before we had done with him; he of course had black hair – and by-and-by, it hung in elf-locks[11] over his forehead and down his back. The other was short and broad – and a hump sprouted out on his shoulder before we heard the last of him; he had red hair – which deepened into carroty; and she was almost sure he had a cast in the eye – a decided squint. As for the woman, her eyes glared, and she was masculine-looking – a perfect virago; most probably a man dressed in woman's clothes: afterwards, we heard of a beard on her chin, and a manly voice and a stride.

If Miss Pole was delighted to recount the events of that afternoon to all inquirers, others were not so proud of their adventures in the robbery line. Mr Hoggins, the surgeon, had been attacked at his own door by two ruffians, who were concealed in the shadow of the porch, and so effectually silenced him, that he was robbed in the interval between ringing his bell and the servant's answering it. Miss Pole was sure it would turn out that this robbery had been committed by 'her men,' and went the very day she heard the report to have her teeth examined, and to question Mr Hoggins. She came to us afterwards; so we heard what she had heard, straight and direct from the source, while we were yet in the excitement and flutter of the agitation caused by the first intelligence; for the event had only occurred the night before.

'Well!' said Miss Pole, sitting down with the decision of a person who has made up her mind as to the nature of life and the world – (and such people never tread lightly, or seat themselves without a bump) – 'Well, Miss Matty! men will be men. Every mother's son of them wishes to be considered Samson and Solomon rolled into one – too strong ever to be beaten or discomfited – too wise ever to be outwitted. If you will notice, they have always foreseen events, though they never tell one for one's warning before the events happen; my father was a man, and I know the sex pretty well.'

She had talked herself out of breath, and we should have been very glad to fill up the necessary pause as chorus, but we did not exactly know what to say, or which man had suggested this diatribe against the sex; so we only joined in generally, with a grave shake of the head, and a soft murmur of 'They are very incomprehensible, certainly!'

'Now only think,' said she. 'There I have undergone the risk of having one of my remaining teeth drawn (for one is terribly at the mercy of any surgeon-dentist; and I, for one, always speak them fair till I have got my mouth out of their clutches), and after all, Mr Hoggins is too much of a man to own that he was robbed last night.'

'Not robbed!' exclaimed the chorus.

'Don't tell me!' Miss Pole exclaimed, angry that we could be for a moment imposed upon. 'I believe he was robbed, just as Betty told me, and he is ashamed to own it: and, to be sure, it was very silly of him to be robbed just at his own door; I dare say, he feels that such a thing won't raise him in the eyes of Cranford society, and is anxious to conceal it – but he need not have tried to impose upon me, by saying I must have heard an exaggerated account of some petty theft of a neck of mutton, which, it seems, was stolen out of the safe in his yard last week; he had the impertinence to add, he believed that that was taken by the cat. I have no doubt, if I could get to the bottom of it, it was that Irishman dressed up in women's clothes, who came spying about my house, with the story about the starving children.'

After we had duly condemned the want of candour which Mr Hoggins had evinced, and abused men in general, taking him for the representative and type, we got round to the subject about which we had been talking when Miss Pole came in – namely, how far, in the present disturbed state of the country, we could venture to accept an invitation which Miss Matty had just received from Mrs Forrester, to come as usual and keep the anniversary of her wedding-day, by drinking tea with her at five o'clock, and playing a quiet pool afterwards. Mrs Forrester had said, that she asked us with some diffidence, because the roads were, she feared, very unsafe. But she suggested that perhaps one of us would not object to take the sedan; and that the others, by walking briskly, might keep up with the long trot of the chairmen, and so we might all arrive safely at Over Place, a suburb of the town. (No. That is too large an expression: a small cluster of houses separated from Cranford by about two hundred yards of a dark and lonely lane.) There was no doubt but that a similar note was awaiting Miss Pole at home; so her call was a very fortunate affair, as it enabled us to consult together. We would all much rather have declined this invitation; but we felt that it would not be quite kind to Mrs Forrester, who would otherwise be left to a solitary retrospect of her not very happy or fortunate life. Miss Matty and Miss Pole had been visitors on this occasion for many years; and now they gallantly determined to nail their colours to the mast, and to go through Darkness-lane rather than fail in loyalty to their friend.

But when the evening came, Miss Matty (for it was she who was voted into the chair, as she had a cold), before being shut down in the sedan, like jack-in-the-box, implored the chairmen, whatever might befal, not to run away and leave her fastened up there, to be murdered; and even after they had promised, I saw her tighten her features into the stern determination of a martyr, and she gave me a melancholy and ominous shake of the head through the glass. However, we got there safely, only rather out of breath, for it was who could trot hardest through Darkness-lane, and I am afraid poor Miss Matty was sadly jolted.

Mrs Forrester had made extra preparations, in acknowledgment of our exertion in coming to see her through such dangers. The usual forms of genteel ignorance as to what her servants might send up were all gone through; and harmony and Preference seemed likely to be the order of the evening, but for an interesting conversation that began I don't know how, but which had relation, of course, to the robbers who infested the neighbourhood of Cranford.

Having braved the dangers of Darkness-lane, and thus having a little stock of reputation for courage to fall back upon; and also, I dare say, desirious of proving ourselves superior to men (*videlicet*[12] Mr Hoggins) in the article of candour, we began to relate our individual fears, and the private precautions we each of us took. I owned that my pet apprehension was eyes – eyes looking at me, and watching me, glittering out from some dull flat wooden surface; and that if I dared to go up to my looking-glass when I was panic-stricken, I should certainly turn it round, with its back towards me, for fear of seeing eyes behind me looking out of the darkness. I saw Miss Matty nerving herself up for a confession; and at last out it came. She owned that, ever since she had been a girl, she had dreaded being caught by her last leg, just as she was getting into bed, by some one concealed under it. She said, when she was younger and more active, she used to take a flying leap from a distance, and so bring both her legs up safely into bed at once; but that this always annoyed Deborah, who piqued herself upon getting into bed gracefully, and she had given it up in consequence. But now the old terror would often come over her, especially since Miss Pole's house had been attacked (we had got quite to believe in the fact of the attack having taken place), and yet it was very unpleasant to think of looking under a bed, and seeing a man concealed, with a great fierce face staring out at you; so she had bethought herself of something – perhaps I had noticed that she had told Martha to buy her a penny ball, such as children play with – and now she rolled this ball under the bed every night; if it came out on the other side, well and good; if not she always took care to have her hand on the bell-rope, and meant to call out John and Harry, just as if she expected men-servants to answer her ring.

We all applauded this ingenious contrivance, and Miss Matty sank back into satisfied silence, with a look at Mrs Forrester as if to ask for *her* private weakness.

Mrs Forrester looked askance at Miss Pole, and tried to change the subject a little, by telling us that she had borrowed a boy from one of the neighbouring cottages and promised his parents a hundredweight of coals at Christmas, and his supper every evening, for the loan of him at nights. She had instructed him in his possible duties when he first came; and, finding him sensible, she had given him the Major's sword (the Major was her late husband), and desired him to put it very carefully behind his pillow at night, turning the edge towards the head of the pillow. He was a sharp lad, she was sure; for, spying out the Major's cocked hat, he had said, if he might have that to wear he was sure he could frighten two Englishmen, or Four Frenchmen, any day. But she had impressed upon him anew that he was to lose no time in putting on hats or anything else; but, if he heard any noise, he was to run at it with his drawn sword. On my suggesting that some accident might occur from such slaughterous and indiscriminate directions, and that he might rush on Jenny getting up to wash, and have spitted her before he had discovered that she

was not a Frenchman, Mrs Forrester said she did not think that
that was likely, for he was a very sound sleeper, and generally
had to be well shaken, or cold-pigged[13] in a morning before they
could rouse him. She sometimes thought such dead sleep must be
owing to the hearty suppers the poor lad ate, for he was half-
starved at home, and she told Jenny to see that he got a good meal
at night.

Still this was no confession of Mrs Forrester's peculiar timidity,
and we urged her to tell us what she thought would frighten her
more than anything. She paused, and stirred the fire, and snuffed
the candles, and then she said, in a sounding whisper.

'Ghosts !'

She looked at Miss Pole, as much as to say she had declared
it, and would stand by it. Such a look was a challenge in itself.
Miss Pole came down upon her with indigestion, spectral illusions,
optical delusions, and a great deal out of Dr Ferrier and Dr Hibbert besides.[14] Miss Matty had rather a leaning to ghosts, as I have
mentioned before, and what little she did say, was well on Mrs
Forrester's side, who, emboldened by sympathy, protested that
ghosts were a part of her religion; that surely she, the widow of a
major in the army, knew what to be frightened at, and what not;
in short, I never saw Mrs Forrester so warm either before or since,
for she was a gentle, meek, enduring old lady in most things. Not
all the elder-wine that ever was mulled could this night wash out
the remembrance of this difference between Miss Pole and her
hostess. Indeed, when the elder-wine was brought in, it gave rise to
a new burst of discussion : for Jenny, the little maiden who
staggered under the tray, had to give evidence of having seen a
ghost with her own eyes, not so many nights ago, in Darkness-
lane – the very lane we were to go through on our way home.

In spite of the uncomfortable feeling which this last consideration gave me, I could not help being amused at Jenny's position,
which was exceedingly like that of a witness being examined and
cross-examined by two counsel who are not at all scrupulous
about asking leading questions. The conclusion I arrived at was,
that Jenny had certainly seen something beyond what a fit of
indigestion would have caused. A lady all in white, and without
her head, was what she deposed and adhered to, supported by a

consciousness of the secret sympathy of her mistress under the withering scorn with which Miss Pole regarded her. And not only she, but many others, had seen this headless lady, who sat by the roadside wringing her hands as in deep grief. Mrs Forrester looked at us from time to time, with an air of conscious triumph; but then she had not to pass through Darkness-lane before she could bury herself beneath her own familiar bed-clothes.

We preserved a discreet silence as to the headless lady while we were putting on our things to go home, for there was no knowing how near the ghostly head and ears might be, or what spiritual connexion they might be keeping up with the unhappy body in Darkness-lane; and therefore, even Miss Pole felt that it was as well not to speak lightly on such subjects, for fear of vexing or insulting that woe-begone trunk. At least, so I conjecture; for, instead of the busy clatter usual in the operation, we tied on our cloaks as sadly as mutes at a funeral.[15] Miss Matty drew the curtains round the windows of the chair to shut out disagreeable sights; and the men (either because they were in spirits that their labours were so nearly ended, or because they were going down hill) set off at such a round and merry pace, that it was all Miss Pole and I could do to keep up with them. She had breath for nothing but an imploring 'Don't leave me!' uttered as she clutched my arm so tightly that I could not have quitted her, ghost or no ghost. What a relief it was when the men, weary of their burden and their quick trot, stopped just where Headingley-causeway branches off from Darkness-lane! Miss Pole unloosed me and caught at one of the men.

'Could not you – could not you take Miss Matty round by Headingley-causeway? – the pavement in Darkness-lane jolts so, and she is not very strong.'

A smothered voice was heard from the inside of the chair:

'Oh! pray go on! What is the matter? What is the matter? I will give you sixpence more to go on very fast; pray don't stop here.'

'And I'll give you a shilling,' said Miss Pole, with tremulous dignity, 'if you'll go by Headingley-causeway.'

The two men grunted acquiescence and took up the chair and went along the causeway, which certainly answered Miss Pole's kind purpose of saving Miss Matty's bones; for it was covered with soft thick mud, and even a fall there would have been easy, till the getting up came, when there might have been some difficulty in extrication.

CHAPTER XI

Samuel Brown

THE next morning I met Lady Glenmire and Miss Pole, setting out on a long walk to find some old woman who was famous in the neighbourhood for her skill in knitting woollen stockings. Miss Pole said to me, with a smile half kindly and half contemptuous upon her countenance, 'I have been just telling Lady Glenmire of our poor friend Mrs Forrester, and her terror of ghosts. It comes from living so much alone, and listening to the bug-a-boo[1] stories of that Jenny of hers.' She was so calm and so much above superstitious fears herself, that I was almost ashamed to say how glad I had been of her Headingley-causeway proposition the night before, and turned off the conversation to something else.

In the afternoon Miss Pole called on Miss Matty to tell her of the adventure – the real adventure they had met with on their morning's walk. They had been perplexed about the exact path which they were to take across the fields, in order to find the knitting old woman, and had stopped to inquire at a little wayside public-house, standing on the high road to London, about three miles from Cranford. The good woman had asked them to sit down and rest themselves, while she fetched her husband, who could direct them better than she could; and, while they were sitting in the sanded parlour, a little girl came in. They thought that she belonged to the landlady, and began some trifling conversation with her; but, on Mrs Roberts's return, she told them that the little thing was the only child of a couple who were staying in the house. And then she began a long story, out of which Lady Glenmire and Miss Pole could only gather one or two decided facts; which were, that, about six weeks ago, a light spring-cart had broken down just before their door, in which there were two men, one woman, and this child. One of the men was seriously hurt – no bones broken, only 'shaken,' the landlady called it; but he had probably sustained some severe internal injury, for he had languished in their house ever since, attended by his wife, the mother of this little girl. Miss Pole had asked what he was, what he looked like. And Mrs Roberts had made answer that he was not like a gentleman, nor yet like a common person; if it had not been that he and his wife were such decent, quiet people, she could almost have thought he was a mountebank, or something of that kind, for they had a great box in the cart, full of she did not know what. She had helped to unpack it, and take out their linen and clothes, when the other man – his twin brother, she believed he was – had gone off with the horse and cart.

Miss Pole had begun to have her suspicions at this point, and expressed her idea that it was rather strange that the box and cart and horse and all should have disappeared; but good Mrs Roberts seemed to have become quite indignant at Miss Pole's implied suggestion; in fact, Miss Pole said, she was as angry as if Miss Pole had told her that she herself was a swindler. As the best way of convincing the ladies, she bethought her of begging them to see the wife; and, as Miss Pole said, there was no doubting the honest, worn, bronze face of the woman, who, at the first tender word from Lady Glenmire, burst into tears, which she was too weak to check, until some word from the landlady made her swallow down her sobs, in order that she might testify to the Christian kindness shown by Mr and Mrs Roberts. Miss Pole came round with a swing to as vehement a belief in the sorrowful tale as she had been sceptical before; and, as a proof of this, her energy in the poor sufferer's behalf was nothing daunted when she found out that he, and no other, was our Signor Brunoni, to whom all Cranford had been attributing all manner of evil this six weeks past! Yes! his wife said his proper name was Samuel Brown – 'Sam,' she called him – but to the last we preferred calling him 'the Signor;' it sounded so much better.

The end of their conversation with the Signora Brunoni was, that it was agreed that he should be placed under medical advice, and for any expense incurred in procuring this Lady Glenmire promised to hold herself responsible; and had accordingly gone to Mr Hoggins to beg him to ride over to the Rising Sun that very afternoon, and examine into the signor's real state; and as Miss Pole said, if it was desirable to remove him to Cranford to be

more immediately under Mr Hoggins's eye, she would undertake
to see for lodgings, and arrange about the rent. Mrs Roberts had
been as kind as could be all throughout; but it was evident that
their long residence there had been a slight inconvenience.

Before Miss Pole left us, Miss Matty and I were as full of the
morning's adventure as she was. We talked about it all the evening, turning it in every possible light, and we went to bed anxious
for the morning, when we should surely hear from some one what
Mr Hoggins thought and recommended. For, as Miss Matty
observed, though Mr Hoggins did say 'Jack's up,' 'a fig for his
heels,'[2] and called Preference 'Pref,' she believed he was a very
worthy man, and a very clever surgeon. Indeed, we were rather
proud of our doctor at Cranford, as a doctor. We often wished,
when we heard of Queen Adelaide or the Duke of Wellington
being ill, that they would send for Mr Hoggins; but, on consideration, we were rather glad they did not, for if we were ailing, what
should we do if Mr Hoggins had been appointed physician-in-
ordinary to the Royal Family? As a surgeon we were proud of
him; but as a man – or rather, I should say, as a gentleman – we
could only shake our heads over his name and himself, and wished
that he had read Lord Chesterfield's Letters[3] in the days when
his manners were susceptible of improvement. Nevertheless, we
all regarded his dictum in the signor's case as infallible; and
when he said that, with care and attention, he might rally, we
had no more fear for him.

But although we had no more fear, everybody did as much as
if there was great cause for anxiety – as indeed there was, until
Mr Hoggins took charge of him. Miss Pole looked out clean and
comfortable, if homely, lodging; Miss Matty sent the sedan-chair
for him; and Martha and I aired it well before it left Cranford, by
holding a warming-pan full of red-hot coals in it, and then
shutting it up close, smoke and all, until the time when he should
get into it at the Rising Sun. Lady Glenmire undertook the
medical department under Mr Hoggins's directions; and rummaged up all Mrs Jamieson's medicine glasses, and spoons, and
bed-tables, in a free and easy way, that made Miss Matty feel a
little anxious as to what that lady and Mr Mulliner might say,
if they knew. Mrs Forrester made some of the bread-jelly,[4] for

which she was so famous, to have ready as a refreshment in the lodgings when he should arrive. A present of this bread-jelly was the highest mark of favour dear Mrs Forrester could confer. Miss Pole had once asked her for the receipt, but she had met with a very decided rebuff; that lady told her that she could not part with it to any one during her life, and that after her death it was bequeathed, as her executors would find, to Miss Matty. What Miss Matty — or, as Mrs Forrester called her (remembering the clause in her will, and the dignity of the occasion), Miss Matilda Jenkyns — might choose to do with the receipt when it came into her possession — whether to make it public, or to hand it down as an heirloom — she did not know, nor would she dictate. And a mould of this admirable, digestible, unique bread-jelly was sent by Mrs Forrester to our poor sick conjuror. Who says that the aristocracy are proud? Here was a lady, by birth a Tyrrell,[5] and descended from the great Sir Walter that shot King Rufus, and in whose veins ran the blood of him who murdered the little princes in the Tower, going every day to see what dainty dishes she could prepare for Samuel Brown, a mountebank! But, indeed, it was wonderful to see what kind feelings were called out by this poor man's coming amongst us. And also wonderful to see how the great Cranford panic, which had been occasioned by his first coming in his Turkish dress, melted away into thin air on his second coming — pale and feeble, and with his heavy filmy eyes, that only brightened a very little when they fell upon the countenance of his faithful wife, or their pale and sorrowful little girl.

Somehow, we all forgot to be afraid. I dare say it was that finding out that he, who had first excited our love of the marvellous by his unprecedented arts, had not sufficient every-day gifts to manage a shying horse, made us feel as if we were ourselves again. Miss Pole came with her little basket at all hours of the evening, as if her lonely house, and the unfrequented road to it had never been infested by that 'murderous gang;' Mrs Forrester said, she thought that neither Jenny nor she need mind the headless lady who wept and wailed in Darkness-lane, for surely the power was never given to such beings to harm those who went about to try to do what little good was in their power; to which Jenny, trembling, assented; but the mistress's theory had little effect on

155

the maid's practice, until she had sewed two pieces of red flannel, in the shape of a cross, on her inner garment.[6]

I found Miss Matty covering her penny ball – the ball that she used to roll under her bed – with gay-coloured worsted in rainbow stripes.

'My dear,' said she, 'my heart is sad for that little careworn child. Although her father is a conjuror, she looks as if she had never had a good game of play in her life. I used to make very pretty balls in this way when I was a girl, and I thought I would try if I could not make this one smart and take it to Phœbe this afternoon. I think "the gang" must have left the neighbourhood, for one does not hear any more of their violence and robbery now.'

We were all of us far too full of the Signor's precarious state to talk about either robbers or ghosts. Indeed, Lady Glenmire said, she never had heard of any actual robberies, except that two little boys had stolen some apples from Farmer Benson's orchard, and that some eggs had been missed on market-day off Widow Hayward's stall. But that was expecting too much of us; we could not acknowledge that we had only had this small foundation for all our panic. Miss Pole drew herself up at this remark of Lady Glenmire's, and said 'that she wished she could agree with her as to the very small reason we had had for àlarm; but, with the recollection of a man disguised as a woman, who had endeavoured to force himself into her house, while his confederates waited outside; with the knowledge gained from Lady Glenmire herself, of the footprints seen on Mrs Jamieson's flower borders; with the fact before her of the audacious robbery committed on Mr Hoggins at his own door –' But here Lady Glenmire broke in with a very strong expression of doubt as to whether this last story was not an entire fabrication, founded upon the theft of a cat; she grew so red while she was saying all this, that I was not surprised at Miss Pole's manner of bridling up, and I am certain if Lady Glenmire had not been 'her Ladyship,' we should have had a more emphatic contradiction than the 'Well, to be sure!' and similar fragmentary ejaculations, which were all that she ventured upon in my lady's presence. But when she was gone, Miss Pole began a long congratulation to Miss Matty that so far they had escaped marriage, which she noticed always made people credulous to the last degree; indeed, she thought it argued great natural credulity in a woman if she could not keep herself from being married; and in what Lady Glenmire had said about Mr Hoggins's robbery, we had a specimen of what people came to, if they gave way to such a weakness; evidently, Lady Glenmire would swallow anything, if she could believe the poor vamped-up story about a neck of mutton and a pussy, with which he had tried to impose on Miss Pole, only she had always been on her guard against believing too much of what men said.

We were thankful, as Miss Pole desired us to be, that we had never been married; but I think, of the two, we were even more thankful that the robbers had left Cranford; at least I judge so from a speech of Miss Matty's that evening, as we sat over the fire, in which she evidently looked upon a husband as a great protector against thieves, burglars, and ghosts; and said, that she did not think that she should dare to be always warning young people against matrimony, as Miss Pole did continually; – to be sure, marriage was a risk, as she saw now she had had some experience; but she remembered the time when she had looked forward to being married as much as any one.

'Not to any particular person, my dear,' said she, hastily checking herself up as if she were afraid of having admitted too much; 'only the old story, you know, of ladies always saying, "When I marry," and gentlemen, "If I marry." ' It was a joke spoken in rather a sad tone, and I doubt if either of us smiled; but I could not see Miss Matty's face by the flickering fire-light. In a little while she continued :

'But after all I have not told you the truth. It is so long ago, and no one ever knew how much I thought of it at the time, unless, indeed, my dear mother guessed; but I may say that there was a time when I did not think I should have been only Miss Matty Jenkyns all my life; for even if I did meet with any one who wished to marry me now (and as Miss Pole says, one is never too safe), I could not take him – I hope he would not take it too much to heart, but I could *not* take him – or any one but the person I once thought I should be married to, and he is dead and gone, and he never knew how it all came about that I said "No," when I had thought many and many a time – Well, it's no matter what I thought. God ordains it all, and I am very happy, my dear. No one has such kind friends as I,' continued she, taking my hand and holding it in hers.

If I had never known of Mr. Holbrook, I could have said something in this pause, but as I had, I could not think of anything that would come in naturally, and so we both kept silence for a little time.

'My father once made us,' she began, 'keep a diary, in two columns; on one side we were to put down in the morning what we thought would be the course and events of the coming day, and at night we were to put down on the other side what really happened. It would be to some people rather a sad way of telling their lives' – (a tear dropped upon my hand at these words) – 'I don't mean that mine has been sad, only so very different to what I expected. I remember, one winter's evening, sitting over our bed-room fire with Deborah – I remember it as if it were yesterday – and we were planning our future lives – both of us were planning, though only she talked about it. She said she should like to marry an archdeacon, and write his charges;[7] and you know, my dear, she never was married, and, for aught I know, she never spoke to an unmarried archdeacon in her life. I never was ambitious, nor could I have written charges, but I thought I could manage a house (my mother used to call me her right hand), and I was always so fond of little children – the shyest babies would stretch out their little arms to come to me; when I was a girl, I was half my leisure time nursing in the neighbouring cottages – but I don't know how it was, when I grew sad and grave – which I did a year or two after this time – the little things drew back from me, and I am afraid I lost the knack, though I am just as fond of children as even and have a strange yearning at my heart whenever I see a mother with her baby in her arms. Nay, my dear' – (and by a sudden blaze which sprang up from a fall of the unstirred coals, I saw that her eyes were full of tears – gazing intently on some vision of what might have been) – 'do you know, I dream sometimes that I have a little child – always the same – a little girl of about two years old; she never grows older, though I have dreamt about her for many years. I don't think I ever dream of any words or sound she makes; she is very noiseless and still, but she comes to me when she is very sorry or very glad, and I have wakened with the clasp of her dear little arms round my neck. Only last night – perhaps because I had gone to sleep thinking of this ball for Phœbe – my little darling came in my dream, and put up her mouth to be kissed, just as I have seen real babies do to real mothers before going to bed. But all this is nonsense, dear! only don't be frightened by Miss Pole from being married. I can fancy it may be a very happy state, and a little credulity helps one on through life very smoothly, – better than always doubting and doubting, and seeing difficulties and disagreeables in everything.'

If I had been inclined to be daunted from matrimony, it would not have been Miss Pole to do it; it would have been the lot of poor Signor Brunoni and his wife. And yet again, it was an encouragement to see how, through all their cares and sorrows, they thought of each other and not of themselves; and how keen were their joys, if they only passed through each other, or through the little Phœbe.

The Signora told me, one day, a good deal about their lives up to this period. It began by my asking her whether Miss Pole's story of the twin brothers was true; it sounded so wonderful a likeness, that I should have had my doubts, if Miss Pole had not been unmarried. But the Signora, or (as we found out she preferred to be called) Mrs Brown, said it was quite true; that her brother-in-law was by many taken for her husband, which was of great assistance to them in their profession; 'though,' she continued, 'how people can mistake Thomas for the real Signor Brunoni, I can't conceive; but he says they do; so I suppose I must believe him. Not but what he is a very good man; I am sure I don't know how we should have paid our bill at the Rising Sun but for the money he sends; but people must know very little about art, if they can take him for my husband. Why, miss, in the ball trick, where my husband spreads his fingers, wide, and throws out his little finger with quite an air and a grace, Thomas just clumps up his hand like a fist, and might have ever so many balls hidden in it. Besides, he has never been in India, and knows nothing of the proper sit of a turban.'

'Have you been in India?' said I, rather astonished.

'Oh, yes! many a year, ma'am. Sam was a sergeant in the 31st; and when the regiment was ordered to India, I drew a lot to go, and I was more thankful than I can tell; for it seemed as if it would only be a slow death to me to part from my husband. But, indeed, ma'am, if I had known all, I don't know whether I would not rather have died there and then, than gone through what I have done since. To be sure, I've been able to comfort Sam, and to be with him; but, ma'am, I've lost six children,' said she, looking up at me with those strange eyes, that I've never noticed but in mothers of dead children – with a kind of wild look in them, as if seeking for what they never more might find. 'Yes! Six children died off, like little buds nipped untimely, in that cruel India. I thought as each died, I never could – I never would – love a child again; and when the next came, it had not only its own love, but the deeper love that came from the thoughts of its little dead brothers and sisters. And when Phœbe was coming, I said to my husband, "Sam, when the child is born, and I am strong, I shall leave you; it will cut my heart cruel; but if this baby dies too, I shall go mad; the madness is in me now; but if you let me go down to Calcutta, carrying my baby step by step, it will maybe work itself off; and I will save, and I will hoard, and I will beg, – and I will die, to get a passage home to England, where our baby may live!" God bless him! he said I might go; and he saved up his pay, and I saved every pice[8] I could get for washing or any way; and when Phœbe came, and I grew strong again, I set off. It was very lonely; through the thick forests, dark again with their heavy trees – along by the river's side – (but I had been brought up near the Avon in Warwickshire, so that flowing noise sounded like home) – from station to station,[9] from Indian village to village, I went along, carrying my child. I had seen one of the officers' ladies, with a little picture, ma'am – done by a Catholic foreigner, ma'am – of the Virgin and the little Saviour, ma'am.[10] She had him on her arm, and her form was softly curled round him, and their cheeks touched. Well, when I went to bid good-by to this lady, for whom I had washed, she cried sadly; for she, too, had lost her children, but she had not another to save, like me; and I was bold enough to ask her, would she give me that print? And she cried the more, and said *her* children were with that little blessed Jesus; and gave it me, and told me she had heard it had been painted on the bottom of a cask, which made it have that round shape. And when my body was very weary, and my heart was sick – (for there were times when I misdoubted if I could ever reach my home, and there were times when I thought of my husband; and one time when I thought my baby was dying) – I took out that picture and looked at it, till I could have thought the mother spoke to me, and comforted me. And the natives were very kind. We could not understand one another; but they saw my baby on my breast, and they came out to me, and brought me rice and milk, and sometimes flowers – I have got some of the flowers dried. Then, the next morning, I was so tired! and they wanted me to stay with them – I could tell that – and tried to frighten me from going into the deep woods, which, indeed, looked very strange and dark; but it seemed to me as if Death was following me to take my baby away from me; and as if I must go on, and on – and I thought how God had cared for mothers ever since the world was made, and would care for me; so I bade them good-by, and set off afresh. And once when my baby was ill, and both she and I needed rest, He led me to a place where I found a kind Englishman lived, right in the midst of the natives.'

'And you reached Calcutta safely at last?'

'Yes! safely. Oh! when I knew I had only two days' journey more before me, I could not help it, ma'am – it might be idolatry, I cannot tell – but I was near one of the native temples, and I went in it with my baby to thank God for his great mercy; for it seemed to me that where others had prayed before to their God, in their joy or in their agony, was of itself a sacred place. And I got as servant to an invalid lady, who grew quite fond of my baby aboard-ship; and, in two years' time, Sam earned his discharge, and came home to me, and to our child. Then he had to fix on a trade; but he knew of none; and, once, once upon a time, he had learnt some tricks from an Indian juggler; so he set up conjuring, and it answered so well that he took Thomas to help him – as his man, you know, not as another conjuror, though Thomas has set it up now on his own hook. But it has been a great help to us that likeness between the twins, and made a good many tricks go off well that they made up together. And Thomas is a good brother, only he has not the fine carriage of my husband, so that I can't think how he can be taken for Signor Brunoni himself, as he says he is.'

'Poor little Phœbe!' said I, my thoughts going back to the baby she carried all those hundred miles.

'Ah! you may say so! I never thought I should have reared her, though, when she fell ill at Chunderabaddad; but that good, kind Aga Jenkyns[11] took us in, which I believe was the very saving of her.'

'Jenkyns!' said I.

'Yes! Jenkyns. I shall think all people of that name are kind; for here is that nice old lady who comes every day to take Phœbe a walk!'

But an idea had flashed through my head: could the Aga Jenkyns be the lost Peter? True, he was reported by many to be dead. But, equally true, some had said that he had arrived at the dignity of Great Lama of Thibet. Miss Matty thought he was alive. I would make further inquiry.

CHAPTER XII

Engaged to be Married

WAS the 'poor Peter' of Cranford the Aga Jenkyns of Chunderabaddad, or was he not? As somebody says, that was the question.[1]

In my own home, whenever people had nothing else to do, they blamed me for want of discretion. Indiscretion was my bugbear fault. Everybody has a bugbear fault; a sort of standing characteristic – a *pièce de résistance*[2] for their friends to cut at; and in general they cut and come again. I was tired of being called indiscreet and incautious; and I determined for once to prove myself a model of prudence and wisdom. I would not even hint my suspicions respecting the Aga. I would collect evidence and carry it home to lay before my father, as the family friend of the two Miss Jenkynses.

In my search after facts, I was often reminded of a description my father had once given of a Ladies' Committee that he had had to preside over. He said he could not help thinking of a passage in Dickens,[3] which spoke of a chorus in which every man took the tune he knew best, and sang it to his own satisfaction. So, at this charitable committee, every lady took the subject uppermost in her mind, and talked about it to her own great contentment, but not much to the advancement of the subject they had met to discuss. But even that committee could have been nothing to the Cranford ladies when I attempted to gain some clear and definite information as to poor Peter's height, appearance, and when and where he was seen and heard of last. For instance, I remember asking Miss Pole – (and I thought the question was very opportune, for I put it when I met her at a call at Mrs Forrester's, and both the ladies had known Peter, and I imagined that they might refresh each other's memories) – I asked Miss Pole what was the very last thing they had ever heard about him; and then she named the absurd report to which I have alluded, about his having been elected Great Lama of Thibet; and this was a signal for each lady to go off on her separate idea. Mrs Forrester's start was made in the veiled prophet in Lalla Rookh[4] – whether I thought he was meant for the Great Lama, though Peter was not so ugly, indeed rather handsome if he had not been freckled. I was thankful to see her double upon Peter; but, in a moment, the delusive lady was off upon Rowlands' Kalydor,[5] and the merits of cosmetics and hair oils in general, and holding forth so fluently that I turned to listen to Miss Pole, who (through the llamas, the beasts of burden) had got to Peruvian bonds,[6] and the share market, and her poor opinion of joint-stock banks in general, and of that one in particular in which Miss Matty's money was invested. In vain I put in 'When was it – in what year was it that you heard that Mr Peter was the Great Lama?' They only joined issue to dispute whether llamas were carnivorous animals or not; in which dispute they were not quite on fair grounds, as Mrs Forrester (after they had grown warm and cool again) acknowledged that she always confused carnivorous and graminivorous together, just as she did horizontal and perpendicular; but then she apologized for it very prettily, by saying that in her day the only use people made of four-syllabled words was to teach how they should be spelt.

The only fact I gained from this conversation was that certainly Peter had last been heard of in India, 'or that neighbourhood;' and that this scanty intelligence of his whereabouts had reached Cranford in the year when Miss Pole had bought her Indian muslin gown, long since worn out (we washed it and mended it, and traced its decline and fall into a window-blind, before we could go on); – and in a year when Wombwell came to Cranford,[7] because Miss Matty had wanted to see an elephant in order that she might the better imagine Peter riding on one; and had seen a boa-constrictor too, which was more than she wished to imagine in her fancy-pictures of Peter's locality; – and in a year when Miss Jenkyns had learnt some piece of poetry off by heart, and used to say, at all the Cranford parties, how Peter was 'surveying mankind from China to Peru,'[8] which everybody had thought very grand, and rather appropriate, because India was between China and Peru, if you took care to turn the globe to the left instead of the right.

I suppose, all these inquiries of mine, and the consequent curi-

osity excited in the minds of my friends, made us blind and deaf
to what was going on around us. It seemed to me as if the sun
rose and shone, and as if the rain rained on Cranford, just as
usual, and I did not notice any sign of the times that could be
considered as a prognostic of any uncommon event; and, to the
best of my belief, not only Miss Matty and Mrs Forrester, but
even Miss Pole herself, whom we looked upon as a kind of
prophetess, from the knack she had of foreseeing things before
they came to pass – although she did not like to disturb her
friends by telling them her foreknowledge – even Miss Pole herself was breathless with astonishment when she came to tell us
of the astounding piece of news. But I must recover myself; the
contemplation of it, even at this distance of time, has taken away
my breath and my grammar, and unless I subdue my emotion,
my spelling will go too.

We were sitting – Miss Matty and I – much as usual; she in
the blue chintz[9] easy-chair, with her back to the light, and her
knitting in her hand – I reading aloud the *St James's Chronicle*. A
few minutes more, and we should have gone to make the little
alterations in dress usual before calling time (twelve o'clock) in
Cranford. I remember the scene and the date well. We had been
talking of the signor's rapid recovery since the warmer weather
had set in, and praising Mr Hoggin's' skill, and lamenting his
want of refinement and manner – (it seems a curious coincidence
that this should have been our subject, but so it was) – when a
knock was heard: a caller's knock – three distinct taps – and we
were flying (that is to say, Miss Matty could not walk very fast,
having had a touch of rheumatism) to our rooms, to change cap
and collars, when Miss Pole arrested us by calling out as she
came up the stairs, 'Don't go – I can't wait – it is not twelve, I
know – but never mind your dress – I must speak to you.' We
did our best to look as if it was not we who had made the hurried
movement, the sound of which she had heard; for, of course, we
did not like to have it supposed that we had any old clothes that
it was convenient to wear out in the 'sanctuary of home,' as Miss
Jenkyns once prettily called the back parlour, where she was tying up preserves. So we threw our gentility with double force
into our manners, and very genteel we were for two minutes

while Miss Pole recovered breath, and excited our curiosity strongly by lifting up her hands in amazement, and bringing them down in silence, as if what she had to say was too big for words, and could only be expressed by pantomime.

'What do you think, Miss Matty? What *do* you think? Lady Glenmire is to marry – is to be married, I mean – Lady Glenmire – Mr Hoggins – Mr Hoggins is going to marry Lady Glenmire!'

'Marry!' said we. 'Marry! Madness!'

'Marry!' said Miss Pole, with the decision that belonged to her character. 'I said marry! as you do; and I also said, "What a fool my lady is going to make of herself!" I could have said "Madness!" but I controlled myself, for it was in a public shop that I heard of it. Where feminine delicacy is gone to, I don't know! You and I, Miss Matty, would have been ashamed to have known that our marriage was spoken of in a grocer's shop, in the hearing of shopmen!'

'But,' said Miss Matty, sighing as one recovering from a blow, 'perhaps it is not true. Perhaps we are doing her injustice.'

'No,' said Miss Pole. 'I have taken care to ascertain that. I went straight to Mrs Fitz-Adam, to borrow a cookery book which I knew she had; and I introduced my congratulations *à propos* of the difficulty gentlemen must have in housekeeping; and Mrs Fitz-Adam bridled up, and said that she believed it was true, though how and where I could have heard it she did not know. She said her brother and Lady Glenmire had come to an understanding at last. "Understanding!" such a coarse word! But my lady will have to come down to many a want of refinement. I have reason to believe Mr Hoggins sups on bread-and-cheese and beer every night.'

'Marry!' said Miss Matty once again. 'Well! I never thought of it. Two people that we know going to be married. It's coming very near!'

'So near that my heart stopped beating, when I heard of it, while you might have counted twelve,' said Miss Pole.

'One does not know whose turn may come next. Here, in Cranford, poor Lady Glenmire might have thought herself safe,' said Miss Matty, with a gentle pity in her tones.

'Bah!' said Miss Pole, with a toss of her head. 'Don't you remember poor dear Captain Brown's song "Tibbie Fowler," and the line –

> Set her on the Tintock Tap,
> The wind will blaw a man till her.'[10]

'That was because "Tibbie Fowler" was rich I think.'

'Well! there is a kind of attraction about Lady Glenmire that I, for one, should be ashamed to have.'

I put in my wonder.[11] 'But how can she have fancied Mr Hoggins? I am not surprised that Mr Hoggins has liked her.'

'Oh! I don't know. Mr Hoggins is rich, and very pleasant-looking,' said Miss Matty, 'and very good-tempered and kind-hearted.'

'She has married for an establishment, that's it. I suppose she takes the surgery with it,' said Miss Pole, with a little dry laugh at her own joke. But, like many people who think they have made a severe and sarcastic speech, which yet is clever of its kind, she began to relax in her grimness from the moment when she made this allusion to the surgery; and we turned to speculate on the way in which Mrs Jamieson would receive the news. The person whom she had left in charge of her house to keep off followers from her maids, to set up a follower of her own! And that follower a man whom Mrs Jamieson had tabooed as vulgar, and inadmissible to Cranford society; not merely on account of his name, but because of his voice, his complexion, his boots, smelling of the stable, and himself, smelling of drugs. Had he ever been to see Lady Glenmire at Mrs Jamieson's? Chloride of lime would not purify the house in its owner's estimation if he had. Or had their interviews been confined to the occasional meetings in the chamber of the poor sick conjuror, to whom, with all our sense of the *mésalliance*,[12] we could not help allowing that they had both been exceedingly kind? And now it turned out that a servant of Mrs Jamieson's had been ill, and Mr Hoggins had been attending her for some weeks. So the wolf had got into the fold, and now he was carrying off the shepherdess. What would Mrs Jamieson say? We looked into the darkness of futurity as a child gazes after a rocket up in the cloudy sky, full of wondering expectation of the rattle, the discharge, and the brilliant shower of sparks and light.

Then we brought ourselves down to earth and the present time, by questioning each other (being all equally ignorant, and all equally without the slightest data to build any conclusions upon) as to when IT would take place? Where? How much a year Mr Hoggins had? Whether she would drop her title? And how Martha and the other correct servants in Cranford would ever be brought to announce a married couple as Lady Glenmire and Mr Hoggins? But would they be visited? Would Mrs Jamieson let us. Or must we choose between the Honourable Mrs Jamieson and the degraded Lady Glenmire? We all liked Lady Glenmire the best. She was bright, and kind, and sociable, and agreeable; and Mrs Jamieson was dull, and inert, and pompous, and tiresome. But we had acknowledged the sway of the latter so long, that it seemed like a kind of disloyalty now even to meditate disobedience to the prohibition we anticipated.

Mrs Forrester surprised us in our darned caps and patched collars; and we forgot all about them in our eagerness to see how she would bear the information, which we honourably left to Miss Pole to impart, although, if we had been inclined to take unfair advantage, we might have rushed in ourselves, for she had a most out-of-place fit of coughing for five minutes after Mrs Forrester entered the room. I shall never forget the imploring expression of her eyes, as she looked at us over her pocket-handkerchief. They said, as plain as words could speak, 'Don't let nature deprive me of the treasure which is mine, although for a time I can make no use of it.' And we did not.

Mrs Forrester's surprise was equal to ours; and her sense of injury rather greater, because she had to feel for her Order,[13] and saw more fully than we could do how such conduct brought stains on the aristocracy.

When she and Miss Pole left us we endeavoured to subside into calmness; but Miss Matty was really upset by the intelligence she had heard. She reckoned it up, and it was more than fifteen years since she had heard of any of her acquaintance going to be married, with the one exception of Miss Jessie Brown; and, as she said, it gave her quite a shock, and made her feel as if she could not think what would happen next.

I don't know whether it is a fancy of mine, or a real fact, but

I have noticed that, just after the announcement of an engagement in any set, the unmarried ladies in that set flutter out in an unusual gaiety and newness of dress, as much as to say, in a tacit and unconscious manner, 'We also are spinsters.' Miss Matty and Miss Pole talked and thought more about bonnets, gowns, caps, and shawls, during the fortnight that succeeded this call, than I had known them do for years before. But it might be the spring weather, for it was a warm and pleasant March; and merinoes and beavers,[14] and woollen materials of all sorts, were but ungracious receptacles of the bright sun's glancing rays. It had not been Lady Glenmire's dress that had won Mr Hoggins's heart, for she went about on her errands of kindness more shabby than ever. Although in the hurried glimpses I caught of her at church or elsewhere she appeared rather to shun meeting many of her friends, her face seemed to have almost something of the flush of youth in it; her lips looked redder and more trembling full than in their old compressed state, and her eyes dwelt on all things with a lingering light, as if she was learning to love Cranford and its belongings. Mr Hoggins looked broad and radiant, and creaked up the middle aisle at church in a bran-new pair of top boots – an audible, as well as visible, sign of his purposed change of state; for the tradition went, that the boots he had worn till now were the identical pair in which he first set out on his rounds in Cranford twenty-five years ago; only they had been new-pieced, high and low, top and bottom, heel and sole, black leather and brown leather, more times than any one could tell.

None of the ladies in Cranford chose to sanction the marriage by congratulating either of the parties. We wished to ignore the whole affair until our liege lady,[15] Mrs Jamieson, returned. Till she came back to give us our cue, we felt that it would be better to consider the engagement in the same light as the Queen of Spain's legs – facts which certainly existed, but the less said about the better.[16] This restraint upon our tongues – for you see if we did not speak about it to any of the parties concerned, how could we get answers to the questions that we longed to ask? – was beginning to be irksome, and our idea of the dignity of silence was paling before our curiosity, when another direction was given to our thoughts, by an announcement on the part of the principal shopkeeper of Cranford, who ranged the trades from grocer and cheesemonger to man-milliner, as occasion required, that the Spring Fashions were arrived, and would be exhibited on the following Tuesday, at his rooms in High-street. Now Miss Matty had been only waiting for this before buying herself a new silk gown. I had offered, it is true, to send to Drumble for patterns, but she had rejected my proposal, gently implying that she had not forgotten her disappointment about the sea-green turban. I was thankful that I was on the spot now, to counteract the dazzling fascination of any yellow or scarlet silk.

I must say a word or two here about myself. I have spoken of my father's old friendship for the Jenkyns family; indeed, I am not sure if there was not some distant relationship. He had willingly allowed me to remain all the winter at Cranford, in consideration of a letter which Miss Matty had written to him about the time of the panic, in which I suspect she had exaggerated my powers and my bravery as a defender of the house. But, now that the days were longer and more cheerful, he was beginning to urge the necessity of my return; and I only delayed in a sort of odd forlorn hope that if I could obtain any clear information, I might make the account given by the signora of the Aga Jenkyns tally with that of 'poor Peter,' his appearance and disappearance, which I had winnowed out of the conversation of Miss Pole and Mrs Forrester.

CHAPTER XIII

Stopped Payment

THE very Tuesday morning on which Mr Johnson was going to show the fashions, the post-woman brought two letters to the house. I say the post-woman, but I should say the postman's wife. He was a lame shoemaker, a very clean, honest man, much respected in the town; but he never brought the letters round except on unusual occasions, such as Christmas Day, or Good Friday; and on those days the letters, which should have been delivered at eight in the morning, did not make their appearance until two or three in the afternoon; for every one liked poor Thomas, and gave him a welcome on these festive occasions. He used to say, 'He was welly stawed[1] wi' eating, for there were three or four houses where nowt would serve 'em but he must share in their breakfast;' and by the time he had done his last breakfast, he came to some other friend who was beginning dinner; but come what might in the way of temptation, Tom was always sober, civil, and smiling; and, as Miss Jenkyns used to say, it was a lesson in patience, that she doubted not would call out that precious quality in some minds, where, but for Thomas, it might have lain dormant and undiscovered. Patience was certainly very dormant in Miss Jenkyns's mind, She was always expecting letters, and always drumming on the table till the post-woman had called or gone past. On Christmas Day and Good Friday she drummed from breakfast till church, from church-time till two o'clock – unless when the fire wanted stirring, when she invariably knocked down the fire-irons, and scolded Miss Matty for it. But equally certain was the hearty welcome and the good dinner for Thomas; Miss Jenkyns standing over him like a bold dragoon, questioning him as to his children – what they were doing – what school they went to; upbraiding him if another was likely to make its appearance, but sending even the little babies the shilling and the mince-pie which was her gift to all the children, with half-a-crown in addition for both father and mother. The post was not half of so much consequence to dear Miss Matty; but not for the world would she have diminished Thomas's welcome and his dole, though I could see that she felt rather shy over the ceremony, which had been regarded by Miss Jenkyns as a glorious opportunity for giving advice and benefiting her fellow-creatures. Miss Matty would steal the money all in a lump into his hand, as if she were ashamed of herself. Miss Jenkyns gave him each individual coin separate, with a 'There! that's for yourself; that's for Jenny,' &c. Miss Matty would even beckon Martha out of the kitchen while he ate his food: and once, to my knowledge, winked at its rapid disappearance into a blue cotton pocket-handkerchief. Miss Jenkyns almost scolded him if he did not leave a clean plate, however heaped it might have been, and give an injunction with every mouthful.

I have wandered a long way from the two letters that awaited us on the breakfast-table that Tuesday morning. Mine was from my father. Miss Matty's was printed. My father's was just a man's letter; I mean it was very dull, and gave no information beyond that he was well, that they had had a good deal of rain, that trade was very stagnant, and there were many disagreeable rumours afloat. He then asked me if I knew whether Miss Matty still retained her shares in the Town and County Bank, as there were very unpleasant reports about it; though nothing more than he had always foreseen, and had prophesied to Miss Jenkyns years ago, when she would invest their little property in it – the only unwise step that clever woman had ever taken, to his knowledge (the only time she ever acted against his advice, I knew). However, if anything had gone wrong, of course I was not to think of leaving Miss Matty while I could be of any use, &c.

'Who is your letter from, my dear? Mine is a very civil invitation, signed Edwin Wilson, asking me to attend an important meeting of the shareholders of the Town and County Bank, to be held in Drumble, on Thursday the twenty-first. I am sure, it is very attentive of them to remember me.'

I did not like to hear of this 'important meeting,' for, though I did not know much about business, I feared it confirmed what my father said: however, I thought, ill news always came fast enough, so I resolved to say nothing about my alarm, and merely told her that my father was well, and sent his kind regards to her. She kept turning over and admiring her letter. At last she spoke, –

'I remember their sending one to Deborah just like this; but that I did not wonder at, for everybody knew she was so clear-headed. I am afraid I could not help them much; indeed, if they came to accounts, I should be quite in the way, for I never could do sums in my head. Deborah, I know, rather wished to go, and went so far as to order a new bonnet for the occasion; but when the time came she had a bad cold; so they sent her a very polite account of what they had done. Chosen a director, I think it was. Do you think they want me to help them to choose a director? I am sure I should choose your father at once.'

'My father has no shares in the bank,' said I.

'Oh, no! I remember. He objected very much to Deborah's buying any, I believe. But she was quite the woman of business, and always judged for herself; and here, you see, they have paid eight per cent, all these years.'

It was a very uncomfortable subject to me, with my half-knowledge; so I thought I would change the conversation, and I asked at what time she thought we had better go and see the fashions. 'Well, my dear,' she said, 'the thing is this; it is not etiquette to go till after twelve, but then, you see, all Cranford will be there, and one does not like to be too curious about dress and trimmings and caps, with all the world looking on. It is never genteel to be over-curious on these occasions. Deborah had the knack of always looking as if the latest fashion was nothing new to her; a manner she had caught from Lady Arley, who did see all the new modes in London, you know. So I thought we would just slip down this morning, soon after breakfast; for I do want half a pound of tea; and then we could go up and examine the things at our leisure, and see exactly how my new silk gown must be made; and then, after twelve, we could go with our minds disengaged, and free from thoughts of dress.'

We began to talk of Miss Matty's new silk gown. I discovered that it would be really the first time in her life that she had to choose anything of consequence for herself: for Miss Jenkyns had always been the more decided character, whatever her taste might have been; and it is astonishing how such people carry the world before them by the mere force of will. Miss Matty anticipated the sight of the glossy folds with as much delight as if the five sovereigns, set apart for the purchase, could buy all the silks in the shop; and (remembering my own loss of two hours in a toy-shop before I could tell on what wonder to spend a silver threepence) I was very glad that we were going early, that dear Miss Matty might have leisure for the delights of perplexity.

If a happy sea-green could be met with, the gown was to be sea-green: if not, she inclined to maize, and I to silver grey; and we discussed the requisite number of breadths until we arrived at the shop-door. We were to buy the tea, select the silk, and then clamber up the iron corkscrew stairs that led into what was once a loft, though now a fashion show-room.

The young men at Mr Johnson's had on their best looks, and their best cravats, and pivoted themselves over the counter with surprising activity. They wanted to show us upstairs at once; but on the principle of business first and pleasure afterwards, we stayed to purchase the tea. Here Miss Matty's absence of mind betrayed itself. If she was made aware that she had been drinking green tea at any time,[2] she always thought it her duty to lie awake half through the night afterward – (I have known her to take it in ignorance many a time without such effects) – and consequently green tea was prohibited the house; yet to-day she herself asked for the obnoxious article, under the impression that she was talking about the silk. However, the mistake was soon rectified; and then the silks were unrolled in good truth. By this time the shop was pretty well filled, for it was Cranford market-day, and many of the farmers and country people from the neighbourhood round came in, sleeking down their hair, and glancing shyly about from under their eyelids, as anxious to take back some notion of the unusual gaiety to the mistress or the lasses at home, and yet feeling that they were out of place among the smart shopmen and gay shawls and summer prints. One honest-looking man, however, made his way up to the counter at which we stood, and boldly asked to look at a shawl or two. The other country folk confined themselves to the grocery side; but our neighbour was evidently too full of some kind intention towards mistress, wife, or daughter, to be shy; and it soon became a question with me, whether he or Miss Matty would keep their shopman the longest time. He thought each shawl more beautiful than the last; and, as for Miss Matty, she smiled and sighed over each fresh bale that was brought out; one colour set off another, and the heap together would, as she said, make even the rainbow look poor.

'I am afraid,' said she, hesitating, 'whichever I choose I shall wish I had taken another. Look at this lovely crimson! it would be so warm in winter. But spring is coming on, you know. I wish I could have a gown for every occasion,' said she, dropping her voice – as we all did in Cranford whenever we talked of anything we wished for but could not afford. 'However,' she continued, in a louder and more cheerful tone, 'it would give me a great deal of trouble to take care of them if I had them; so, I think I'll only take one. But which must it be, my dear?'

And now she hovered over a lilac with yellow spots, while I pulled out a quiet sage-green that had faded into insignificance under the more brilliant colours, but which was nevertheless a good silk in its humble way. Our attention was called off to our neighbour. He had chosen a shawl of about thirty shillings' value; and his face looked broadly happy, under the anticipation, no doubt, of the pleasant surprise he should give to some Molly or Jenny at home; he had tugged a leathern purse out of his breeches-pocket, and had offered a five-pound note in payment for the shawl, and for some parcels which had been brought round to him from the grocery counter; and it was just at this point that he attracted our notice. The shopman was examining the note with a puzzled, doubtful air:

'Town and County Bank! I am not sure, sir, but I believe we have received a warning against notes issued by this bank only this morning. I will just step and ask Mr Johnson, sir; but I'm afraid I must trouble you for payment in cash, or in a note of a different bank.'

I never saw a man's countenance fall so suddenly into dismay and bewilderment. It was almost piteous to see the rapid change.

'Dang it!' said he, striking his fist down on the table, as if to try which was the harder, 'the chap talks as if notes were to be had for the picking up.'

Miss Matty had forgotten her silk gown in her interest for the man. I don't think she had caught the name of the bank, and in my nervous cowardice I was anxious that she should not; and so I began admiring the yellow-spotted lilac gown that I had been utterly condemning only a minute before. But it was of no use.

'What bank was it? I mean, what bank did your note belong to?'

'Town and County Bank.'

'Let me see it,' said she quietly to the shopman, gently taking it out of his hand, as he brought it back to return it to the farmer.

Mr Johnson was very sorry, but, from information he had received, the notes issued by that bank were little better than waste paper.

'I don't understand it,' said Miss Matty to me in a low voice. 'That is our bank, is it not? – the Town and County Bank?'

'Yes,' said I. 'This lilac silk will just match the ribbons in your new cap, I believe,' I continued, holding up the folds so as to catch the light, and wishing that the man would make haste and be gone, and yet having a new wonder, that had only just sprung up, how far it was wise or right in me to allow Miss Matty to make this expensive purchase, if the affairs of the bank were really so bad as the refusal of the note implied.

But Miss Matty put on the soft dignified manner peculiar to her, rarely used, and yet which became her so well, and laying her hand gently on mine, she said, –

'Never mind the silks for a few minutes, dear. I don't understand you, sir,' turning now to the shopman, who had been attending to the farmer. 'Is this a forged note?'

'Oh, no, ma'am. It is a true note of its kind; but you see, ma'am, it is a joint-stock bank,[3] and there are reports out that it is likely to break. Mr Johnson is only doing his duty, ma'am, as I am sure Mr Dobson knows.'

But Mr Dobson could not respond to the appealing bow by any answering smile. He was turning the note absently over in his fingers, looking gloomily enough at the parcel containing the lately chosen shawl.

'It's hard upon a poor man,' said he, 'as earns every farthing with the sweat of his brow. However, there's no help for it. You must take back your shawl, my man; Lizzie must do on with her cloak for a while. And yon figs for the little ones – I promised them to 'em – I'll take them; but the 'bacco, and the other things –'

'I will give you five sovereigns for your note, my good man,' said Miss Matty. 'I think there is some great mistake about it, for I am one of the shareholders, and I'm sure they would have told me if things had not been going on right.'

The shopman whispered a word or two across the table to Miss Matty. She looked at him with a dubious air.

'Perhaps so,' said she. 'But I don't pretend to understand business; I only know that if it is going to fail, and if honest people are to lose their money because they have taken our notes – I can't explain myself,' said she, suddenly becoming aware that she had got into a long sentence with four people in audience – 'only I would rather exchange my gold for the note, if you please,' turning to the farmer, 'and then you can take your wife the shawl. It is only going without my gown a few days longer,' she continued, speaking to me. 'Then, I have no doubt, everything will be cleared up.'

'But if it is cleared up the wrong way?' said I.

'Why! then it will only have been common honesty in me, as a shareholder, to have given this good man the money. I am quite clear about it in my own mind; but, you know, I can never speak quite as comprehensibly as others can; – only you must give me your note, Mr Dobson, if you please, and go on with your purchases with these sovereigns.'

The man looked at her with silent gratitude – too awkward to put his thanks into words; but he hung back for a minute or two, fumbling with his note.

'I'm loth to make another one lose instead of me, if it is a loss; but, you see, five pounds is a deal of money to a man with a family; and, as you say, ten to one in a day or two the note will be as good as gold again.'

'No hope of that, my friend,' said the shopman.

'The more reason why I should take it,' said Miss Matty, quietly. She pushed her sovereigns towards the man, who slowly laid his note down in exchange. 'Thank you. I will wait a day or two before I purchase any of these silks; perhaps you will then have a greater choice. My dear, will you come up-stairs?'

We inspected the fashions with as minute and curious an interest as if the gown to be made after them had been bought. I could not see that the little event in the shop below had in the least damped Miss Matty's curiosity as to the make of sleeves, or the sit of skirts. She once or twice exchanged congratulations with me on our private and leisurely view of the bonnets and shawls; but I was, all the time, not so sure that our examination was so utterly private, for I caught glimpses of a figure dodging behind the cloaks and mantles; and, by a dexterous move, I came face to face with Miss Pole, also in morning costume (the principal feature of which was her being without teeth,[4] and wearing a veil to conceal the deficiency), come on the same errand as ourselves. But she quickly took her departure, because, as she said, she had a bad headache, and did not feel herself up to conversation.

As we came down through the shop, the civil Mr Johnson was awaiting us; he had been informed of the exchange of the note for gold, and with much good feeling and real kindness, but with a little want of tact, he wished to condole with Miss Matty, and impress upon her the true state of the case. I could only hope that he had heard an exaggerated rumour, for he said that her shares were worse than nothing, and that the bank could not pay a shilling in the pound. I was glad that Miss Matty seemed still a little incredulous; but I could not tell how much of this was real or assumed, with that self-control which seemed habitual to ladies of Miss Matty's standing in Cranford, who would have thought their dignity compromised by the slightest expression of surprise, dismay, or any similar feeling to an inferior in station, or in a public shop. However, we walked home very silently. I am ashamed to say, I believe I was rather vexed and annoyed at Miss Matty's conduct in taking the note to herself so decidedly. I had so set my heart upon her having a new silk gown, which she wanted sadly; in general she was so undecided anybody might turn her round; in this case I had felt that it was no use attempting it, but I was not the less put out at the result.

Somehow, after twelve o'clock, we both acknowledged to a

sated curiosity about the fashions, and to a certain fatigue of body (which was, in fact, depression of mind) that indisposed us to go out again. But still we never spoke of the note; till, all at once, something possessed me to ask Miss Matty if she would think it her duty to offer sovereigns for all the notes of the Town and County bank she met with? I could have bitten my tongue out the minute I had said it. She looked up rather sadly, and as if I had thrown a new perplexity into her already distressed mind; and for a minute or two she did not speak. Then she said – my own dear Miss Matty – without a shade of reproach in her voice :

'My dear! I never feel as if my mind was what people call very strong; and it's often hard enough work for me to settle what I ought to do with the case right before me. I was very thankful to – I was very thankful, that I saw my duty this morning, with the poor man standing by me; but it's rather a strain upon me to keep thinking and thinking what I should do if such and such a thing happened; and, I believe, I had rather wait and see what really does come; and I don't doubt I shall be helped then, if I don't fidget myself, and get too anxious beforehand. You know, love, I'm not like Deborah. If Deborah had lived, I've no doubt she would have seen after them, before they had got themselves into this state.'

We had neither of us much appetite for dinner, though we tried to talk cheerfully about different things. When we returned into the drawing-room, Miss Matty unlocked her desk and began to look over her account-books. I was so penitent for what I had said in the morning, that I did not choose to take upon myself the presumption to suppose that I could assist her; I rather left her alone, as, with puzzled brow, her eye followed her pen up and down the ruled page. By-and-by she shut the book, locked her desk, and came and drew a chair to mine, where I sat in moody sorrow over the fire. I stole my hand into hers; she clasped it, but did not speak a word. At last she said, with forced composure in her voice, 'If that bank goes wrong, I shall lose one hundred and forty-nine pounds thirteen shillings and fourpence a year; I shall only have thirteen pounds a year left.' I squeezed her hand hard and tight. I did not know what to say. Presently (it was too dark to see her face) I felt her fingers work convulsively in my grasp; and I knew she was going to speak again. I heard the sobs in her voice as she said, 'I hope it's not wrong – not wicked – but, oh! I am so glad poor Deborah is spared this. She could not have borne to come down in the world, – she had such a noble, lofty spirit.'

This was all she said about the sister who had insisted upon investing their little property in that unlucky bank. We were later in lighting the candle than usual that night, and until that light shamed us into speaking, we sat together very silently and sadly.

However, we took to our work after tea with a kind of forced cheerfulness (which soon became real as far as it went), talking of that never-ending wonder, Lady Glenmire's engagement. Miss Matty was almost coming round to think it a good fortune.

'I don't mean to deny that men are troublesome in a house. I don't judge from my own experience, for my father was neatness itself, and wiped his shoes on coming in as carefully as any woman; but still a man has a sort of knowledge of what should be done in difficulties, that it is very pleasant to have one at hand ready to lean upon. No, Lady Glenmire, instead of being tossed about, and wondering where she is to settle, will be certain of a home among pleasant and kind people, such as our good Miss Pole and Mrs Forrester. And Mr Hoggins is really a very personable man; and as for his manners – why, if they are not very polished, I have known people with very good hearts, and very clever minds too, who were not what some people reckoned refined, but who were both true and tender.'

She fell off into a soft reverie about Mr Holbrook, and I did not interrupt her, I was so busy maturing a plan I had had in my mind for some days, but which this threatened failure of the bank had brought to a crisis. That night, after Miss Matty went to bed, I treacherously lighted the candle again, and sat down in the drawing-room to compose a letter to the Aga Jenkyns – a letter which should affect him if he were Peter, and yet seem a mere statement of dry facts if he were a stranger. The church clock pealed out two before I had done.

The next morning news came, both official and otherwise, that the Town and County Bank had stopped payment. Miss Matty was ruined.

She tried to speak quietly to me; but when she came to the actual fact that she would have but about five shillings a week to live upon, she could not restrain a few tears.

'I am not crying for myself, dear,' said she, wiping them away; 'I believe I am crying for the very silly thought of how my mother would grieve if she could know – she always cared for us so much more than for herself. But many a poor person has less; and I am not very extravagant, and, thank God, when the neck of mutton, and Martha's wages, and the rent are paid, I have not a farthing owing. Poor Martha ! I think she'll be sorry to leave me.'

Miss Matty smiled at me through her tears, and she would fain have had me see only the smile, not the tears.

CHAPTER XIV

Friends in Need

IT was an example to me, and I fancy it might be to many others, to see how immediately Miss Matty set about the retrenchment – which she knew to be right under her altered circumstances. While she went down to speak to Martha, and break the intelligence to her, I stole out with my letter to the Aga Jenkyns, and went to the signor's lodgings to obtain the exact address. I bound the signora to secrecy; and, indeed, her military manners had a degree of shortness and reserve in them which made her always say as little as possible, except when under the pressure of strong excitement. Moreover – (which made my secret doubly sure) – the signor was now so far recovered as to be looking forward to travelling and conjuring again in the space of a few days, when he, his wife, and little Phœbe, would leave Cranford. Indeed, I found him looking over a great black and red placard, in which the Signor Brunoni's accomplishments were set forth, and to which only the name of the town where he would next display them was wanting. He and his wife were so much absorbed in deciding where the red letters would come in with most effect (it might have been the Rubric for that matter),[1] that it was some time before I could get my question asked privately, and not before I had given several decisions, the wisdom of which I questioned afterwards with equal sincerity as soon as the signor threw in his doubts and reasons on the important subject. At last I got the address, spelt by sound; and very queer it looked! I dropped it in the post on my way home; and then for a minute I stood looking at the wooden pane with the gaping slit which divided me from the letter, but a moment ago in my hand. It was gone from me like life – never to be recalled. It would get tossed about on the sea, and stained with sea-waves perhaps; and be carried among palm-trees, and scented with all tropical fragrance; – the little piece of paper, but an hour ago so familiar and commonplace, had set out on its race to the strange wild countries beyond the Ganges! But I could not afford to lose much time on this speculation. I hastened home, that Miss Matty might not miss me. Martha opened the door to me, her face swollen with crying. As soon as she saw me she burst out afresh, and taking hold of my arm she pulled me in, and banged the door to, in order to ask me if indeed it was all true that Miss Matty had been saying.

'I'll never leave her! No! I won't. I told her so, and said I could not think how she could find in her heart to give me warning. I could not have had the face to do it, if I'd been her. I might ha' been just as good-for-nothing as Mrs Fitz-Adam's Rosy, who struck for wages after living seven years and a half in one place. I said I was not one to go and serve Mammon[2] at that rate; that I knew when I'd got a good missus, if she didn't know when she'd got a good servant –'

'But Martha,' said I, cutting in while she wiped her eyes.

'Don't "but Martha" me,' she replied to my deprecatory tone. 'Listen to reason –'

'I'll not listen to reason,' she said, now in full possession of her voice, which had been rather choked with sobbing. 'Reason always means what some one else has got to say. Now I think what I've got to say is good enough reason. But, reason or not, I'll say it, and I'll stick to it. I've money in the Savings Bank,[3] and I've a good stock of clothes, and I'm not going to leave Miss Matty. No! not if she gives me warning every hour in the day!'

She put her arms akimbo, as much as to say she defied me; and, indeed, I could hardly tell how to begin to remonstrate with her, so much did I feel that Miss Matty, in her increasing infirmity, needed the attendance of this kind and faithful woman.

'Well!' said I at last –

'I'm thankful you begin with "well!" If you'd ha' begun with "but," as you did afore, I'd not ha' listened to you. Now you may go on.'

'I know you would be a great loss to Miss Matty, Martha –'

'I told her so. A loss she'd never cease to be sorry for,' broke in Martha, triumphantly.

'Still, she will have so little – so very little – to live upon, that I don't see just now how she could find you food – she will even be pressed for her own. I tell you this, Martha, because I feel you are like a friend to dear Miss Matty – but you know she might not like to have it spoken about.'

Apparently this was even a blacker view of the subject than Miss Matty had presented to her; for Martha just sat down on the first chair that came to hand, and cried out loud – (we had been standing in the kitchen).

At last she put her apron down, and looking me earnestly in the face, asked, 'Was that the reason Miss Matty wouldn't order a pudding today? She said she had no fancy for sweet things, and you and she would just have a mutton-chop. But I'll be up to her. Never you tell, but I'll make her a pudding, and a pudding she'll like, too, and I'll pay for it myself; so mind you see she eats it. Many a one has been comforted in their sorrow by seeing a good dish come upon the table.'

I was rather glad that Martha's energy had taken the immediate and practical direction of pudding-making, for it staved off the quarrelsome discussion as to whether she should or should not leave Miss Matty's service. She began to tie on a clean apron, and otherwise prepare herself for going to the shop for the butter, eggs, and what else she might require; she would not use a scrap of the articles already in the house for her cookery, but went to an old teapot in which her private store of money was deposited, and took out what she wanted.

I found Miss Matty very quiet, and not a little sad; but by-and-by she tried to smile for my sake. It was settled that I was to write to my father, and ask him to come over and hold a consultation; and as soon as this letter was despatched we began to talk over future plans. Miss Matty's idea was to take a single room, and retain as much of her furniture as would be necessary to fit up this, and sell the rest; and there to quietly exist upon what would remain after paying the rent. For my part, I was more ambitious and less contented. I thought of all the things by which a woman, past middle age, and with the education common to ladies fifty years ago, could earn or add to a living, without materially losing caste; but at length I put even this last chance on one side, and wondered what in the world Miss Matty could do.

Teaching was, of course, the first thing that suggested itself. If

Miss Matty could teach children anything, it would throw her among the little elves in whom her soul delighted. I ran over her accomplishments. Once upon a time I had heard her say she could play 'Ah! vous dirai-je, maman?'[4] on the piano; but that was long, long ago; that faint shadow of musical acquirement had died out years before. She had also once been able to trace out patterns very nicely for muslin embroidery, by dint of placing a piece of silver-paper over the design to be copied, and holding both again the window-pane, while she marked the scollop and eyelet-holes. But that was her nearest approach to the accomplishment of drawing, and I did not think it would go very far. Then again, as the branches of a solid English education – fancy-work and the use of the globes – such as the mistress of the Ladies' Seminary, to which all the tradespeople in Cranford sent their daughters, professed to teach; Miss Matty's eyes were failing her, and I doubted if she could discover the number of threads in a worsted-work pattern, or rightly appreciate the different shades required for Queen Adelaide's face, in the loyal wool-work now fashionable in Cranford.[5] As for the use of the globes. I had never been able to find it out myself, so perhaps I was not a good judge of Miss Matty's capability of instructing in this branch of education; but it struck me that equators and tropics, and such mystical circles, were very imaginary lines indeed to her, and that she looked upon the signs of the Zodiac as so many remnants of the Black Art.

What she piqued herself upon, as arts, in which she excelled, was making candle-lighters, or 'spills' (as she preferred calling them), of coloured paper, cut so as to resemble feathers, and knitting garters in a variety of dainty stitches. I had once said, on receiving a present of an elaborate pair, that I should feel quite tempted to drop one of them in the street, in order to have it admired; but I found this little joke (and it was a very little one) was such a distress to her sense of propriety, and was taken with such anxious, earnest alarm, lest the temptation might some day prove too strong for me, that I quite regretted having ventured upon it. A present of these delicately-wrought garters, a bunch of gay 'spills,' or a set of cards on which sewing-silk was wound in a mystical manner, were the well-known tokens of Miss Matty's favour. But would any one pay to have their children taught these arts; or, indeed, would Miss Matty sell, for filthy lucre,[6] the knack and the skill with which she made trifles of value to those who loved her?

I had to come down to reading, writing, and arithmetic; and, in reading the chapter every morning, she always coughed before coming to long words. I doubted her power of getting through a genealogical chapter, with any number of coughs. Writing she did well and delicately; but spelling! She seemed to think that the more out-of-the-way this was, and the more trouble it cost her, the greater the compliment she paid to her correspondent; and words that she would spell quite correctly in her letters to me, became perfect enigmas when she wrote to my father.

No! there was nothing she could teach to the rising generation of Cranford; unless they had been quick learners and ready imitators of her patience, her humility, her sweetness, her quiet contentment with all that she could not do. I pondered and pondered until dinner was announced by Martha, with a face all blubbered and swollen with crying.

Miss Matty had a few little peculiarities, which Martha was apt to regard as whims below her attention, and appeared to consider as childish fancies, of which an old lady of fifty-eight should try and cure herself. But today everything was attended to with the most careful regard. The bread was cut to the imaginery pattern of excellence that existed in Miss Matty's mind, as being the way which her mother had preferred; the curtain was drawn so as to exclude the dead-brick wall of a neighbour's stables, and yet left so as to show every tender leaf of the poplar which was bursting into spring beauty. Martha's tone to Miss Matty was just such as that good, rough-spoken servant usually kept sacred for little children, and which I had never heard her use to any grown-up person.

I had forgotten to tell Miss Matty about the pudding, and I was afraid she might not do justice to it, for she had evidently very little appetite this day; so I seized the opportunity of letting her into the secret while Martha took away the meat. Miss Matty's eyes filled with tears, and she could not speak, either to express surprise or delight, when Martha returned, bearing it aloft, made in the most wonderful representation of a lion *couchant*[7] that ever was moulded. Martha's face gleamed with triumph, as she set it down before Miss Matty with an exultant 'There!' Miss Matty wanted to speak her thanks, but could not; so she took Martha's hand and shook it warmly, which set Martha off crying, and I myself could hardly keep up the necessary composure. Martha burst out of the room; and Miss Matty had to clear her voice once or twice before she could speak. At last she said, 'I should like to keep this pudding under a glass shade, my dear!' and the notion of the lion *couchant*, with his currant eyes, being hoisted up to the place of honour on a mantelpiece, tickled my hysterical fancy, and I began to laugh, which rather surprised Miss Matty.

'I am sure, dear, I have seen uglier things under a glass shade before now,' said she.[8]

So had I, many a time and oft; and I accordingly composed my countenance (and now I could hardly keep from crying), and we both fell to upon the pudding, which was indeed excellent – only every morsel seemed to choke us, our hearts were so full.

We had too much to think about to talk much that afternoon. It passed over very tranquilly. But when the tea-urn was brought in, a new thought came into my head. Why should not Miss Matty sell tea – be an agent to the East India Tea Company[9] which then existed? I could see no objections to this plan, while the advantages were many – always supposing that Miss Matty could get over the degradation of condescending to anything like trade. Tea was neither greasy, nor sticky – grease and stickiness being two of the qualities which Miss Matty could not endure. No shop-window would be required. A small genteel notification of her being licensed to sell tea, would, it is true, be necessary; but I hoped that it could be placed where no one would see it. Neither was tea a heavy article, so as to tax Miss Matty's fragile strength. The only thing against my plan was the buying and selling involved.

While I was giving but absent answers to the questions Miss Matty was putting – almost as absently – we heard a clumping sound on the stairs, and a whispering outside the door: which indeed once opened and shut as if by some invisible agency. After a little while, Martha came in, dragging after her a great tall young man, all crimson with shyness, and finding his only relief in perpetually sleeking down his hair.

'Please, ma'am, he's only Jem Hearn,' said Martha, by way of introduction; and so out of breath was she, that I imagine she had had some bodily struggle before she could overcome his reluctance to be presented on the courtly scene of Miss Matilda Jenkyns's drawing-room.

'And please, ma'am, he wants to marry me off-hand. And please, ma'am, we want to take a lodger – just one quiet lodger, to make our two ends meet; and we'd take any house conformable; and, oh dear Miss Matty, if I may be so bold, would you have any objections to lodging with us? Jem wants it as much as I do.' [To Jem:] 'You great oaf! why can't you back me? – But he does want it, all the same, very bad – don't you, Jem? – only, you see, he's dazed at being called on to speak before quality.'[10]

'It's not that,' broke in Jem. 'It's that you've taken me all on a sudden, and I didn't think for to get married so soon – and such quick work does flabbergast a man. It's not that I'm against it, ma'am' (addressing Miss Matty), 'only Martha has such quick ways with her, when once she takes a thing into her head; and marriage, ma'am – marriage nails a man, as one may say. I daresay I shan't mind it after it's once over.'

'Please, ma'am,' said Martha – who had plucked at his sleeve, and nudged him with her elbow, and otherwise tried to interrupt him all the time he had been speaking – 'don't mind him, he'll come to; 'twas only last night he was an-axing me, and an-axing me, and all the more because I said I could not think of it for years to come, and now he's only taken aback with the suddenness of the joy; but you know, Jem, you are just as full as me about wanting a lodger.' (Another great nudge.)

'Ay! if Miss Matty would lodge with us – otherwise I've no mind to be cumbered with strange folk in the house,' said Jem, with a want of tact which I could see enraged Martha, who was trying to represent a lodger as the great object they wished to obtain, and that, in fact, Miss Matty would be smoothing their path, and conferring a favour, if she would only come and live with them.

Miss Matty herself was bewildered by the pair; their, or rather

Martha's sudden resolution in favour of matrimony staggered her, and stood between her and the contemplation of the plan which Martha had at heart. Miss Matty began:

'Marriage is a very solemn thing, Martha.'

'It is indeed, ma'am,' quoth Jem. 'Not that I've no objections to Martha.'

'You've never let me a-be for asking me for a fix when I would be married,' said Martha – her face all afire, and ready to cry with vexation – 'and now you're shaming me before my missus and all.'

'Nay, now! Martha, don't ee! don't ee! only a man likes to have breathing-time,' said Jem, trying to possess himself of her hand, but in vain. Then seeing that she was more seriously hurt than he had imagined, he seemed to try to rally his scattered faculties, and with more straightforward dignity than, ten minutes before, I should have thought it possible for him to assume, he turned to Miss Matty, and said, 'I hope, ma'am, you know that I am bound to respect every one who has been kind to Martha. I always looked on her as to be my wife – some time; and she has often and often spoke of you as the kindest lady that ever was; and though the plain truth is I would not like to be troubled with lodgers of the common run, yet if, ma'am, you'd honour us by living with us, I'm sure Martha would do her best to make you comfortable; and I'd keep out of your way as much as I could, which I reckon would be the best kindness such an awkward chap as me could do.'

Miss Matty had been very busy with taking off her spectacles, wiping them, and replacing them; but all she could say was, 'Don't let any thought of me hurry you into marriage: pray don't! Marriage is such a very solemn thing!'

'But Miss Matilda will think of your plan, Martha,' said I, struck with the advantages that it offered, and unwilling to lose the opportunity of considering about it. 'And I'm sure neither she nor I can ever forget your kindness; nor yours either, Jem.'

'Why, yes, ma'am! I'm sure I mean kindly, though I'm a bit fluttered by being pushed straight a-head into matrimony, as it were, and mayn't express myself conformable. But I'm sure I'm willing enough, and give me time to get accustomed; so, Martha, wench, what's the use of crying so, and slapping me if I come near?'

This last was *sotto voce*, and had the effect of making Martha bounce out of the room, to be followed and soothed by her lover. Whereupon Miss Matty sat down and cried very heartily, and accounted for it by saying that the thought of Martha being married so soon gave her quite a shock, and that she should never forgive herself if she thought she was hurrying the poor creature. I think my pity was more for Jem, of the two; but both Miss Matty and I appreciated to the full the kindness of the honest couple, although we said little about this, and a good deal about the chances and dangers of matrimony.

The next morning, very early, I received a note from Miss Pole, so mysteriously wrapped up, and with so many seals on it to secure secrecy, that I had to tear the paper before I could unfold it. And when I came to the writing I could hardly understand the meaning, it was so involved and oracular. I made out, however, that I was to go to Miss Pole's at eleven o'clock; the number *eleven* being written in full length as well as in numerals, and A.M. twice dashed under, as if I were very likely to come at eleven at night, when all Cranford was usually a-bed and asleep by ten. There was no signature except Miss Pole's initials, reversed, P. E.; but as Martha had given me the note, 'with Miss Pole's kind regards,' it needed no wizard to find out who sent it; and if the writers's name was to be kept secret, it was very well that I was alone when Martha delivered it.

I went, as requested, to Miss Pole's. The door was opened to me by her little maid Lizzy, in Sunday trim, as if some grand event was impending over this workday. And the drawing-room up-stairs was arranged in accordance with this idea. The table was set out, with the best green card-cloth, and writing materials upon it. On the little chiffonier[11] was a tray with a newly-decanted bottle of cowslip wine, and some ladies'-finger biscuits.[12] Miss Pole herself was in solemn array, as if to receive visitors, although it was only eleven o'clock. Mrs Forrester was there, crying quietly and sadly, and my arrival seemed only to call forth fresh tears. Before we had finished our greetings, performed with lugubrious mystery of demeanour, there was another rat-tat-tat, and

Mrs Fitz-Adam appeared, crimson with walking and excitement. It seemed as if this was all the company expected; for now Miss Pole made several demonstrations of being about to open the business of the meeting, by stirring the fire, opening and shutting the door, and coughing and blowing her nose. Then she arranged us all round the table, taking care to place me opposite to her; and last of all, she inquired of me if the sad report was true, as she feared it was, that Miss Matty had lost all her fortune?

Of course, I had but one answer to make; and I never saw more unaffected sorrow depicted on any countenance than I did there on the three before me.

'I wish Mrs Jamieson was here!' said Mrs Forrester at last; but to judge from Mrs Fitz-Adam's face, she could not second the wish.

'But without Mrs Jamieson,' said Miss Pole, with just a sound of offended merit in her voice, 'we, the ladies of Cranford, in my drawing-room assembled, can resolve upon something. I imagine we are none of us what may be called rich, though we all possess a genteel competency, sufficient for tastes that are elegant and refined, and would not, if they could, be vulgarly ostentatious.' (Here I observed Miss Pole refer to a small card concealed in her hand, on which I imagine she had put down a few notes.)

'Miss Smith,' she continued, addressing me (familiarly known as 'Mary' to all the company assembled, but this was a state occasion), 'I have conversed in private – I made it my business to do so yesterday afternoon – with these ladies on the misfortune which has happened to our friend, – and one and all of us have agreed that, while we have a superfluity, it is not only a duty but a pleasure, – a true pleasure, Mary!' – her voice was rather choked just here, and she had to wipe her spectacles before she could go on – 'to give what we can to assist her – Miss Matilda Jenkyns. Only, in consideration of the feelings of delicate independence existing in the mind of every refined female'– I was sure she had got back to the card now – 'we wish to contribute our mites in a secret and concealed manner, so as not to hurt the feelings I have referred to. And our object in requesting you to meet us this morning, is, that believing you are the daughter – that your father is, in fact, her confidential adviser in all pecuniary matters, we imagined that, by consulting with him, you might devise some mode in which our contribution could be made to appear the legal due which Miss Matilda Jenkyns ought to receive from –. Probably, your father, knowing her investments, can fill up the blank.'

Miss Pole concluded her address, and looked round for approval and agreement.

'I have expressed your meaning, ladies, have I not? And while Miss Smith considers what reply to make, allow me to offer you some little refreshment.'

I had no great reply to make; I had more thankfulness at my heart for their kind thoughts than I cared to put into words; and so I only mumbled out something to the effect 'that I would name what Miss Pole had said to my father, and that if anything could be arranged for dear Miss Matty,' – and here I broke down utterly, and had to be refreshed with a glass of cowslip wine before I could check the crying which had been repressed for the last two or three days. The worst was, all the ladies cried in concert. Even Miss Pole cried, who had said a hundred times that to betray emotion before any one was a sign of weakness and want of self-control. She recovered herself into a slight degree of impatient anger, directed against me, as having set them all off; and, moreover, I think she was vexed that I could not make a speech back in return for hers; and if I had known beforehand what was to be said, and had a card on which to express the probable feelings that would rise in my heart, I would have tried to gratify her. As it was, Mrs Forrester was the person to speak when we had recovered our composure.

'I don't mind, among friends, stating that I – no! I'm not poor exactly, but I don't think I'm what you may call rich; I wish I were, for dear Miss Matty's sake – but, if you please, I'll write down, in a sealed paper, what I can give. I only wish it was more: my dear Mary, I do indeed.'

Now I saw why paper, pens, and ink were provided. Every lady wrote down the sum she could give annually, signed the paper, and sealed it mysteriously. If their proposal was acceded to, my father was to be allowed to open the papers, under pledge of secrecy. If not, they were to be returned to their writers.

When this ceremony had been gone through, I rose to depart;
but each lady seemed to wish to have a private conference with
me. Miss Pole kept me in the drawing-room to explain why, in
Mrs Jamieson's absence, she had taken the lead in this 'movement,' as she was pleased to call it, and also to inform me that
she had heard from good sources that Mrs Jamieson was coming
home directly in a state of high displeasure against her sister-in-
law, who was forthwith to leave her house; and was, she believed, to return to Edinburgh that very afternoon. Of course
this piece of intelligence could not be communicated before Mrs
Fitz-Adam, more especially as Miss Pole was inclined to think
that Lady Glenmire's engagement to Mr Hoggins could not possibly hold against the blaze of Mrs Jamieson's displeasure. A few
hearty inquiries after Miss Matty's health concluded my interview with Miss Pole.

On coming downstairs I found Mrs Forrester waiting for me at
the entrance to the dining parlour; she drew me in, and when the
door was shut, she tried two or three times to begin on some subject, which was so unapproachable apparently, that I began to
despair of our ever getting to a clear understanding. At last out
it came; the poor old lady trembling all the time as if it were a
great crime which she was exposing to daylight, in telling me
how very, very little she had to live upon; a confession which
she was brought to make from a dread lest we should think that
the small contribution named in her paper bore any proportion
to her love and regard for Miss Matty. And yet that sum which
she so eagerly relinquished was, in truth, more than a twentieth
part of what she had to live upon, and keep house, and a little
serving-maid, all as became one born a Tyrrell. And when the
whole income does not nearly amount to a hundred pounds, to
give up a twentieth of it will necessitate many careful economies, and many pieces of self-denial – small and insignificant in
the world's account, but bearing a different value in another
acccount-book that I have heard of.[13] She did so wish she was rich,
she said; and this wish she kept repeating, with no thought of
herself in it, only with a longing, yearning desire to be able to
heap up Miss Matty's measure of comforts.

It was some time before I could console her enough to leave

her; and then, on quitting the house, I was waylaid by Mrs Fitz-Adam, who had also her confidence to make of pretty nearly the opposite description. She had not liked to put down all that she could afford, and was ready to give. She told me she thought she never could look Miss Matty in the face again if she presumed to be giving her so much as she should like to do. 'Miss Matty!' continued she, 'that I thought was such a fine young lady, when I was nothing but a country girl, coming to market with eggs and butter, and such like things. For my father, though well to do, would always make me go on as my mother had done before me; and I had to come into Cranford every Saturday, and see after sales and prices, and what not. And one day, I remember, I met Miss Matty in the lane that leads to Combehurst; she was walking on the footpath, which, you know, is raised a good way above the road, and a gentleman rode beside her, and was talking to her, and she was looking down at some primroses she had gathered, and pulling them all to pieces, and I do believe she was crying. But after she had passed, she turned round and ran after me to ask – oh, so kindly – about my poor mother, who lay on her deathbed; and when I cried she took hold of my hand to comfort me – and the gentleman waiting for her all the time – and her poor heart very full of something, I am sure; and I thought it such an honour to be spoken to in that pretty way by the rector's daughter, who visited at Arley Hall. I have loved her ever since, though perhaps I'd no right to do it; but if you can think of any way in which I might be allowed to give a little more without any one knowing it, I should be so much obliged to you, my dear. And my brother would be delighted to doctor her for nothing – medicines, leeches, and all. I know that he and her ladyship – (my dear, I little thought, in the days I was telling you of, that I should ever come to be sister-in-law to a ladyship!) – would do anything for her. We all would.'

I told her I was quite sure of it, and promised all sorts of things, in my anxiety to get home to Miss Matty, who might well be wondering what had become of me, – absent from her two hours without being able to account for it. She had taken very little note of time, however, as she had been occupied in numberless little arrangements preparatory to the great step of giving up her house. It was evidently a relief to her to be doing something in the way of retrenchment; for, as she said, whenever she paused to think, the recollection of the poor fellow with his bad five-pound note came over her, and she felt quite dishonest; only if it made her so uncomfortable, what must it not be doing to the directors of the bank, who must know so much more of the misery consequent upon this failure? She almost made me angry by dividing her sympathy between these directors (whom she imagined overwhelmed by self-reproach for the mismanagement of other people's affairs) and those who were suffering like her. Indeed, of the two, she seemed to think poverty a lighter burden than self-reproach; but I privately doubted if the directors would agree with her.

Old hoards were taken out and examined as to their money value, which luckily was small, or else I don't know how Miss Matty would have prevailed upon herself to part with such things as her mother's wedding-ring, the strange uncouth brooch with which her father had disfigured his shirt-frill, &c. However, we arranged things a little in order as to their pecuniary estimation, and were all ready for my father when he came the next morning.

I am not going to weary you with the details of all the business we went through; and one reason for not telling about them is, that I did not understand what we were doing at the time, and cannot recollect it now. Miss Matty and I sat assenting to accounts, and schemes, and reports, and documents, of which I do not believe we either of us understood a word; for my father was clear-headed and decisive, and a capital man of business, and if we made the slightest inquiry, or expressed the slightest want of comprehension, he had a sharp way of saying, 'Eh? eh? it's as clear as daylight. What's your objection?' And as we had not comprehended anything of what he had proposed, we found it rather difficult to shape our objections; in fact, we never were sure if we had any. So, presently Miss Matty got into a nervously acquiescent state, and said, 'Yes,' and 'Certainly,' at every pause, whether required or not: but when I once joined in as chorus to a 'Decidedly,' pronounced by Miss Matty in a tremblingly dubious tone, my father fired round at me and asked me 'What there was to decide?' And I am sure, to this day, I have never known. But, in justice to him, I must say, he had come over from Drumble to help Miss Matty when he could ill spare the time, and when his own affairs were in a very anxious state.

While Miss Matty was out of the room, giving orders for luncheon – and sadly perplexed between her desire of honouring my father by a delicate dainty meal, and her conviction that she had no right, now that all her money was gone, to indulge this desire, – I told him of the meeting of the Cranford ladies at Miss Pole's the day before. He kept brushing his hand before his eyes as I spoke; – and when I went back to Martha's offer the evening before, of receiving Miss Matty as a lodger, he fairly walked away from me to the window, and began drumming with his fingers upon it. Then he turned abruptly round, and said, 'See, Mary, how a good innocent life makes friends all round. Confound it! I could make a good lesson out of it if I were a parson; but as it is, I can't get a tail to my sentences – only I'm sure you feel what I want to say. You and I will have a walk after lunch, and talk a bit more about these plans.'

The lunch – a hot savoury mutton-chop, and a little of the cold lion [14] sliced and fried – was now brought in. Every morsel of this last dish was finished, to Martha's great gratification. Then my father bluntly told Miss Matty he wanted to talk to me alone, and that he would stroll out and see some of the old places, and then I could tell her what plan we thought desirable. Just before we went out, she called me back and said, 'Remember, dear, I'm the only one left – I mean, there's no one to be hurt by what I do. I'm willing to do anything that's right and honest; and I don't think, if Deborah knows where she is, she'll care so very much if I'm not genteel; because, you see, she'll know all, dear. Only let me see what I can do, and pay the poor people as far as I'm able.'

I gave her a hearty kiss, and ran after my father. The result of our conversation was this. If all parties were agreeable, Martha and Jem were to be married with as little delay as possible, and they were to live on in Miss Matty's present abode; the sum which the Cranford ladies had agreed to contribute annually being sufficient to meet the greater part of the rent, and leaving

Martha free to appropriate what Miss Matty should pay for her lodgings to any little extra comforts required. About the sale, my father was dubious at first. He said the old rectory furniture, however carefully used and reverently treated, would fetch very little; and that little would be but as a drop in the sea of the debts of the Town and County Bank. But when I represented how Miss Matty's tender conscience would be soothed by feeling that she had done what she could, he gave way; especially after I had told him the five-pound note adventure, and he had scolded me well for allowing it. I then alluded to my idea that she might add to her small income by selling tea; and, to my surprise (for I had nearly given up the plan), my father grasped at it with all the energy of a tradesman. I think he reckoned his chickens before they were hatched, for he immediately ran up the profits of the sales that she could effect in Cranford to more than twenty pounds a-year. The small dining-parlour was to be converted into a shop, without any of its degrading characteristics; a table was to be the counter; one window was to be retained unaltered, and the other changed into a glass door. I evidently rose in his estimation for having made this bright suggestion. I only hoped we should not both fall in Miss Matty's.

But she was patient and content with all our arrangements. She knew, she said, that we should do the best we could for her; and she only hoped, only stipulated, that she should pay every farthing that she could be said to owe, for her father's sake, who had been so respected in Cranford. My father and I had agreed to say as little as possible about the bank, indeed never to mention it again, if it could be helped. Some of the plans were evidently a little perplexing to her; but she had seen me sufficiently snubbed in the morning for want of comprehension to venture on too many inquiries now; and all passed over well, with a hope on her part that no one would be harried into marraige on her account. When we came to the proposal that she should sell tea, I could see it was rather a shock to her; not on account of any personal loss of gentility involved, but only because she distrusted her own powers of action in a new line of life, and would timidly have preferred a little more privation to any exertion for which she feared she was unfitted. However, when she saw my father was bent upon it, she sighed, and said she would try; and if she did not do well, of course she might give it up. One good thing about it was, she did not think men ever bought tea; and it was of men particularly she was afraid. They had such sharp loud ways with them; and did up accounts, and counted their change so quickly! Now if she might only sell comfits to children, she was sure she could please them!

CHAPTER XV

A Happy Return

BEFORE I left Miss Matty at Cranford everything had been comfortably arranged for her. Even Mrs Jamieson's approval of her selling tea had been gained. That oracle had taken a few days to consider whether by so doing Miss Matty would forfeit her right to the privileges of society in Cranford. I think she had some little idea of mortifying Lady Glenmire by the decision she gave at last; which was to this effect; that whereas a married woman takes her husband's rank by the strict laws of precedence, an unmarried woman retains the station her father occupied. So Cranford was allowed to visit Miss Matty; and, whether allowed or not, it intended to visit Lady Glenmire.

But what was our surprise – our dismay – when we learnt that Mr and Mrs *Hoggins* were returning on the following Tuesday. Mrs Hoggins ! Had she absolutely dropped her title, and so, in a spirit of bravado, cut the aristocracy to become a Hoggins ! She, who might have been called Lady Glenmire to her dying day ! Mrs Jamieson was pleased. She said it only convinced her of what she had known from the first, that the creature had a low taste. But 'the creature' looked very happy on Sunday at church; nor did we see it necessary to keep our veils down on that side of our bonnets on which Mr and Mrs Hoggins sat, as Mrs Jamieson did; thereby missing all the smiling glory of his face, and all the becoming blushes of hers. I am not sure if Martha and Jem looked more radiant in the afternoon, when they too made their first appearance. Mrs Jamieson soothed the turbulence of her soul by having the blinds of her windows drawn down, as if for a funeral, on the day when Mr and Mrs Hoggins received callers: and it was with some difficulty that she was prevailed upon to continue the *St James's Chronicle* – so indignant was she with its having inserted the announcement of the marriage.

Miss Matty's sale went off famously. She retained the furniture of her sitting-room and bed-room; the former of which she was to occupy till Martha could meet with a lodger who might wish to take it; and into this sitting-room and bed-room she had to cram all sorts of things, which were (the auctioneer assured her) bought in for her at the sale by an unknown friend. I always suspected Mrs Fitz-Adam of this; but she must have had an accessory, who knew what articles were particularly regarded by Miss Matty on account of their association with her early days. The rest of the house looked rather bare, to be sure; all except one tiny bed-room, of which my father allowed me to purchase the furniture for my occasional use in case of Miss Matty's illness.

I had expended my own small store in buying all manner of comfits and lozenges, in order to tempt the little people whom Matty loved so much, to come about her. Tea in bright green canisters – and comfits in tumblers – Miss Matty and I felt quite proud as we looked round us on the evening before the shop was to be opened. Martha had scoured the boarded floor to a white cleanness, and it was adorned with a brilliant piece of oil-cloth, on which customers were to stand before the table-counter. The wholesome smell of plaster and whitewash pervaded the apartment. A very small 'Matilda Jenkyns, licensed to sell tea,' was hidden under the lintel of the new door, and two boxes of tea with cabalistic inscriptions all over them[1] stood ready to disgorge their contents into the canisters.

Miss Matty, as I ought to have mentioned before, had had some scruples of conscience at selling tea when there was already Mr Johnson in the town, who included it among his numerous commodities; and, before she could quite reconcile herself to the adoption of her new business, she had trotted down to his shop, unknown to me, to tell him of the project that was entertained, and to inquire if it was likely to injure his business. My father called this idea of hers 'great nonsense,' and 'wondered how tradespeople were to get on if there was to be a continual consulting of each other's interests, which would put a stop to all competition directly.' And, perhaps, it would not have done in Drumble, but in Cranford it answered very well; for not only did Mr Johnson kindly put at rest all Miss Matty's scruples, and fear of injuring his business, but, I have reason to know, he repeatedly sent customers to her, saying that the teas he kept were of a common kind, but that Miss Jenkyns had all the choice sorts. And expensive tea is a very favourite luxury with well-to-do tradespeople and rich farmers' wives, who turn up their noses at the Congou and Souchong prevalent at many tables of gentility, and will have nothing else than Gunpowder and Pekoe for themselves.[2]

But to return to Miss Matty. It was really very pleasant to see how her unselfishness and simple sense of justice called out the same good qualities in others. She never seemed to think any one would impose upon her, because she would be so grieved to do it to them. I have heard her put a stop to the asseverations of the man who brought her coals, by quietly saying, 'I am sure you would be sorry to bring me wrong weight;' and if the coals were short measure that time, I don't believe they ever were again. People would have felt as much ashamed of presuming on her good faith as they would have done on that of a child. But my father says, 'such simplicity might be very well in Cranford, but would never do in the world.' And I fancy the world must be very bad, for with all my father's suspicion of every one with whom he has dealings, and in spite of all his many precautions, he lost upwards of a thousand pounds by roguery only last year.

I just stayed long enough to establish Miss Matty in her new mode of life, and to pack up the library, which the rector had purchased. He had written a very kind letter to Miss Matty, saying, 'how glad he should be to take a library so well selected as he knew that the late Mr Jenkyns's must have been, at any valuation put upon them.' And when she agreed to this, with a touch of sorrowful gladness that they would go back to the rectory, and be arranged on the accustomed walls once more, he sent word that he feared that he had not room for them all, and perhaps Miss Matty would kindly allow him to leave some volumes on her shelves. But Miss Matty said that she had her *Bible* and *Johnson's Dictionary*, and should not have much time for reading, she was afraid. Still I retained a few books out of consideration for the rector's kindness.

The money which he had paid, and that produced by the sale, was partly expended in the stock of tea, and part of it was invested against a rainy day; i.e. old age or illness. It was but a small sum, it is true; and it occasioned a few evasions of truth and white lies (all of which I think very wrong indeed – in theory – and would rather not put them in practice), for we knew Miss Matty would be perplexed as to her duty if she were aware of any little reserve-fund being made for her while the debts of the bank remained un-paid. Moreover, she had never been told of the way in which her friends were contributing to pay the rent. I should have liked to tell her this; but the mystery of the affair gave a piquancy to their deed of kindness which the ladies were unwilling to give up; and at first Martha had to shirk many a perplexed question as to her ways and means of living in such a house; but by-and-by Miss Matty's prudent uneasiness sank down into acquiescence with the existing arrangement.

I left Miss Matty with a good heart. Her sales of tea during the first two days had surpassed my most sanguine expectations. The whole country round seemed to be all out of tea at once. The only alteration I could have desired in Miss Matty's way of doing business was, that she should not have so plaintively entreated some of her customers not to buy green tea – running it down as slow poison, sure to destroy the nerves, and produce all manner of evil. Their pertinacity in taking it, in spite of all her warnings, distressed her so much that I really thought she would relinquish the sale of it, and so lose half her custom; and I was driven to my wits' end for instances of longevity entirely attributable to a persevering use of green tea. But the final argument, which settled the question, was a happy reference of mine to the train oil [3] and tallow candles which the Esquimaux not only enjoy but digest. After that she acknowledged that 'one man's meat might be another man's poison,' and contented herself thenceforward with an occasional remonstrance, when she thought the purchaser was too young and innocent to be acquainted with the evil effects green tea produced on some constitutions; and an habitual sigh when old people old enough to choose more wisely would prefer it.

I went over from Drumble once a quarter at least, to settle the accounts, and see after the necessary business letters, And, speak-ing of letters, I began to be very much ashamed of remembering my letter to the Aga Jenkyns, and very glad I had never named my writing to any one. I only hoped the letter was lost. No answer came. No sign was made.

About a year after Miss Matty set up shop, I received one of Martha's hieroglyphics, begging me to come to Cranford very soon. I was afraid that Miss Matty was ill, and went off that very afternoon, and took Martha by surprise when she saw me on opening the door. We went into the kitchen, as usual, to have our confidential conference; and then Martha told me she was expecting her confinement very soon – in a week or two; and she did not think Miss Matty was aware of it; and she wanted me to break the news to her, 'for indeed, miss!' continued Martha, crying hysterically, 'I'm afraid she won't approve of it; and I'm sure I don't know who is to take care of her as she should be taken care of, when I am laid up.'

I comforted Martha by telling her I would remain till she was about again; and only wished she had told me her reason for this sudden summons, as then I would have brought the requisite stock of clothes. But Martha was so tearful and tender-spirited, and unlike her usual self, that I said as little as possible about myself, and endeavoured rather to comfort Martha under all the probable and possible misfortunes that came crowding upon her imagination.

I then stole out of the house-door, and made my appearance, as if I were a customer, in the shop, just to take Miss Matty by surprise, and gain an idea of how she looked in her new situation. It was warm May weather, so only the little half-door was closed; and Miss Matty sat behind her counter, knitting an elaborate pair of garters : elaborate they seemed to me, but the difficult stitch was no weight upon her mind, for she was singing in a low voice to herself as her needles went rapidly in and out. I call it singing, but I daresay a musician would not use that word to the tuneless yet sweet humming of the low worn voice. I found out from the words, far more than from the attempt at the tune, that it was the Old Hundredth[4] she was crooning to herself : but the quiet continuous sound told of content, and gave me a pleasant feeling, as I stood in the street just outside the door, quite in harmony with that soft May morning. I went in. At first she did not catch who it was, and stood up as if to serve me; but in another minute watchful pussy had clutched her knitting, which was dropped in eager joy at seeing me. I found, after we had had a little conversation, that it was as Martha said, and that Miss Matty had no idea of the approaching household event. So I thought I would let things take their course, secure that when I went to her with the baby in my arms I should obtain that forgiveness for Martha which she was needlessly frightening herself into believing that Miss Matty would withhold, under some notion that the new claimant would require attentions from its mother that it would be faithless treason to Miss Matty to render.

But I was right. I think that must be an hereditary quality, for my father says he is scarcely ever wrong. One morning, within a week after I arrived, I went to call Miss Matty, with a little bundle of flannel in my arms. She was very much awe-struck when I showed her what it was, and asked for her spectacles off the dressing-table, and looked at it curiously, with a sort of tender wonder at its small perfection of parts. She could not banish the thought of the surprise all day, but went about on tiptoe, and was very silent. But she stole up to see Martha, and they both cried with joy; and she got into a complimentary speech to Jem, and did not know how to get out of it again, and was only extricated from her dilemma by the sound of the shop-bell, which was an equal relief to the shy, proud, honest Jem, who shook my hand so vigorously when I congratulated him that I think I feel the pain of it yet.

I had a busy life while Martha was laid up. I attended on Miss Matty, and prepared her meals; I cast up her accounts, and examined into the state of her canisters and tumblers. I helped her too, occasionally, in the shop; and it gave me no small amusement, and sometimes a little uneasiness, to watch her ways there. If a little child came in to ask for an ounce of almond-comfits (and four of the large kind which Miss Matty sold weighed that much), she always added one more by 'way of make-weight' as she called it, although the scale was handsomely turned before; and when I remonstrated against this, her reply was, 'The little things like it so much!' There was no use in telling her that the fifth comfit weighed a quarter of an ounce, and made every sale into a loss to her pocket. So I remembered the green tea, and winged my shaft with a feather out of her own plumage. I told her how unwholesome almond-comfits were; and how ill excess in them might make the little children. This argument produced some effect; for, henceforward, instead of the fifth comfit, she always told them to hold out their tiny palms, into which she shook either peppermint or ginger lozenges, as a preventive to the dangers that might arise from the previous sale. Altogether the lozenge trade, conducted on these principles, did not promise to be remunerative; but I was happy to find that she had made more than twenty pounds during the last year by her sales of tea; and, moreover, that now she was accustomed to it, she did not dislike the employment, which brought her into kindly intercourse with many of the people round about. If she gave them good weight, they, in their turn, brought many a little country present to the 'old rector's daughter;' – a cream cheese, a few new-laid eggs, a little fresh ripe fruit, a bunch of flowers. The counter was quite loaded with these offerings sometimes, as she told me.

As for Cranford in general, it was going on much as usual. The Jamieson and Hoggins feud still raged, if a feud it could be called, when only one side cared much about it. Mr and Mrs Hoggins were very happy together; and, like most very happy people, quite ready to be friendly: indeed, Mrs Hoggins was really desirous to be restored to Mrs Jamieson's good graces, because of the former intimacy. But Mrs Jamieson considered their very happiness an insult to the Glenmire family, to which she had still the honour to belong; and she doggedly refused and rejected every advance. Mr Mulliner, like a faithful clansman, espoused his mistress' side with ardour. If he saw either Mr or Mrs Hoggins, he would cross the street, and appear absorbed in the contemplation of life in general, and his own path in particular, until he had passed them by. Miss Pole used to amuse herself with wondering what in the world Mrs Jamieson would do, if either she or Mr Mulliner, or any other member of her household, was taken ill; she could hardly have the face to call in Mr Hoggins after the way she had behaved to them. Miss Pole grew quite impatient for some indisposition or accident to befall Mrs Jamieson or her dependants, in order that Cranford might see how she would act under the perplexing circumstances.

Martha was beginning to go about again, and I had already fixed a limit, not very far distant, to my visit, when one after- noon, as I was sitting in the shop-parlour with Miss Matty – I remember the weather was colder now than it had been in May, three weeks before, and we had a fire, and kept the door fully closed – we saw a gentleman go slowly past the window, and then stand opposite to the door, as if looking out for the name which we had so carefully hidden. He took out a double eye-glass and peered for some time before he could discover it. Then he came in. And, all of a sudden, it flashed across me that it was the Aga himself! For his clothes had an out-of-the-way foreign cut about them; and his face was deep brown, as if tanned and re- tanned by the sun. His complexion contrasted oddly with his plentiful snow-white hair; his eyes were dark and piercing, and he had an odd way of contracting them, and puckering up his cheeks into innumerable wrinkles when he looked earnestly at objects. He did so to Miss Matty when he first came in. His glance had first caught and lingered a little upon me; but then turned, with the peculiar searching look I have described, to Miss Matty. She was a little flustered and nervous, but no more so than she always was when any man came into her shop. She thought that he would probably have a note, or a sovereign at least, for which she would have to give change, which was an operation she very much disliked to perform. But the present cus- tomer stood opposite to her, without asking for anything, only looking fixedly at her as he drummed upon the table with his fingers, just for all the world as Miss Jenkyns used to do. Miss Matty was on the point of asking him what he wanted (as she told me afterwards), when he turned sharp to me: 'Is your name Mary Smith?'

'Yes!' said I.

All my doubts as to his identity were set at rest; and I only wondered what he would say or do next, and how Miss Matty would stand the joyful shock of what he had to reveal. Appar- ently he was at a loss how to announce himself; for he looked at last in search of something to buy, so as to gain time; and, as it happened, his eye caught on the almond-comfits, and he boldly asked for a pound of 'those things.' I doubt if Miss Matty had a whole pound in the shop; and besides the unusual magnitude of the order, she was disressed with the idea of the indigestion they would produce, taken in such unlimited quantities. She looked up to remonstrate. Something of tender relaxation in his face struck home to her heart. She said, 'It is – oh sir! can you be Peter?' and trembled from head to foot. In a moment he was round the table, and had her in his arms, sobbing the tearless cries of old age. I brought her a glass of wine; for indeed her colour had changed so as to alarm me, and Mr Peter, too. He kept saying, 'I have been too sudden for you, Matty, – I have, my little girl.'

I proposed that she should go at once up into the drawing-room, and lie down on the sofa there; she looked wistfully at her brother, whose hand she had held tight, even when nearly fainting; but on his assuring her that he would not leave her, she allowed him to carry her up-stairs.

I thought that the best I could do was to run and put the kettle on the fire for early tea, and then to attend to the shop, leaving the brother and sister to exchange some of the many thousand things they must have to say. I had also to break the news to Martha, who received it with a burst of tears, which nearly infected me. She kept recovering herself to ask if I was sure it was indeed Miss Matty's brother; for I had mentioned that he had grey hair, and she had always heard that he was a very handsome young man. Something of the same kind perplexed Miss Matty at tea-time, when she was installed in the great easy-chair opposite to Mr Jenkyns's, in order to gaze her fill. She could hardly drink for looking at him; and as for eating, that was out of the question.

'I suppose hot climates age people very quickly,' said she, almost to herself. 'When you left Cranford you had not a grey hair in your head.'

'But how many years ago is that?' said Mr Peter, smiling.

'Ah! true! yes! I suppose you and I are getting old. But still I did not think we were so very old! But white hair is very becoming to you, Peter,' she continued – a little afraid lest she had hurt him by revealing how his appearance had impressed her.

'I suppose I forgot dates too, Matty, for what do you think I have brought for you from India? I have an Indian muslin gown and a pearl necklace for you somewhere in my chest at Portsmouth.' He smiled as if amused at the idea of the incongruity of his presents with the appearance of his sister; but this did not strike her all at once, while the elegance of the articles did. I could see that for a moment her imagination dwelt complacently on the idea of herself thus attired; and instinctively she put her hand up to her throat – that little delicate throat which (Miss Pole had told me) had been one of her youthful charms; but the hand met the touch of folds of soft muslin, in which she was always swathed up to her chin; and the sensation recalled a sense of the unsuitableness of a pearl necklace to her age. She said, 'I'm afraid I'm too old; but it was very kind of you to think of it. They are just what I should have liked years ago – when I was young.'

'So I thought, my little Matty. I remembered your tastes; they were so like my dear mother's.' At the mention of that name, the brother and sister clasped each other's hands yet more fondly; and although they were perfectly silent, I fancied they might have something to say if they were unchecked by my presence, and I got up to arrange my room for Peter's occupation that night, intending myself to share Miss Matty's bed. But at my movement he started up. 'I must go and settle about a room at the George. My carpet-bag is there too.'

'No!' said Miss Matty, in great distress – 'you must not go; please, dear Peter – pray, Mary – oh! you must not go!'

She was so much agitated, that we both promised everything she wished. Peter sat down again, and gave her his hand, which, for better security, she held in both of hers, and I left the room to accomplish my arrangements.

Long, long into the night, far, far into the morning, did Miss Matty and I talk. She had much to tell me of her brother's life and adventures, which he had communicated to her, as they had sat alone. She said all was thoroughly clear to her; but I never quite understood the whole story; and when in after days I lost my awe of Mr Peter enough to question him myself, he laughed at my curiosity, and told me stories that sounded so very much like Baron Munchausen's,[5] that I was sure he was making fun of me. What I heard from Miss Matty was that he had been a volun-

teer at the siege of Rangoon;[6] had been taken prisoner by the
Burmese; had somehow obtained favour and eventual freedom
from knowing how to bleed the chief of the small tribe in some
case of dangerous illness; that on his release from years of cap-
tivity he had had his letters returned from England with the
ominous word 'Dead' marked upon them; and, believing himself
to be the last of his race, he had settled down as an indigo planter,
and had proposed to spend the remainder of his life in the country
to whose inhabitants and modes of life he had become habituated,
when my letter had reached him; and with the odd vehemence
which characterized him in age as it had done in youth, he had
sold his land and all his possessions to the first purchaser, and
come home to the poor old sister, who was more glad and rich
than any princess when she looked at him. She talked me to sleep
at last, and then I was awakened by a slight sound at the door,
for which she begged my pardon as she crept penitently into bed;
but it seems that when I could no longer confirm her belief that
the long-lost was really here – under the same roof – she had
begun to fear lest it was only a waking dream of hers; that there
never had been a Peter sitting by her all that blessed evening –
but that the real Peter lay dead far away beneath some wild sea-
wave, or under some strange eastern tree. And so strong had this
nervous feeling of hers become, that she was fain to get up and
go and convince herself that he was really there by listening
through the door to his even regular breathing – I don't like to
call it snoring, but I heard it myself through two closed doors –
and by-and-by it soothed Miss Matty to sleep.

I don't believe Mr Peter came home from India as rich as a
Nabob;[7] he even considered himself poor, but neither he nor Miss
Matty cared much about that. At any rate, he had enough to live
upon 'very genteelly' at Cranford; he and Miss Matty together.
And a day or two after his arrival, the shop was closed, while
troops of little urchins gleefully awaited the shower of comfits
and lozenges that came from time to time down upon their faces
as they stood-up-gazing at Miss Matty's drawing-room windows.
Occasionally Miss Matty would say to them (half hidden behind
the curtains), 'My dear children, don't make yourselves ill;' but a
strong arm pulled her back, and a more rattling shower than ever

succeeded. A part of the tea was sent in presents to the Cranford ladies; and some of it was distributed among the old people who remembered Mr Peter in the days of his frolicsome youth. The muslin gown was reserved for darling Flora Gordon (Miss Jessie Brown's daughter). The Gordons had been on the continent for the last few years, but were now expected to return very soon; and Miss Matty, in her sisterly pride, anticipated great delight in the joy of showing them Mr Peter. The pearl necklace disappeared; and about that time many handsome and useful presents made their appearance in the households of Miss Pole and Mrs Forrester; and some rare and delicate Indian ornaments graced the drawing-rooms of Mrs Jamieson and Mrs Fitz-Adam. I myself was not forgotten. Among other things, I had the handsomest bound and best edition of Dr Johnson's works that could be procured; and dear Miss Matty, with tears in her eyes, begged me to consider it as a present from her sister as well as herself. In short, no one was forgotten; and what was more, every one, however insignificant, who had shown kindness to Miss Matty at any time, was sure of Mr Peter's cordial regard.

CHAPTER XVI

Peace to Cranford

IT was not surprising that Mr Peter became such a favourite at Cranford. The ladies vied with each other who should admire him most; and no wonder; for their quiet lives were astonishingly stirred up by the arrival from India – especially as the person arrived told more wonderful stories than Sinbad the Sailor; and, as Miss Pole said, was quite as good as an Arabian Night any evening.[1] For my own part, I had vibrated all my life between Drumble and Cranford, and I thought it was quite possible that all Mr Peter's stories might be true although wonderful; but when I found, that if we swallowed an anecdote of tolerable magnitude one week, we had the dose considerably increased the next, I began to have my doubts; especially as I noticed that when his sister was present the accounts of Indian life were comparatively tame; not that she knew more than we did, perhaps less. I noticed also that when the rector came to call, Mr Peter talked in a different way about the countries he had been in. But I don't think the ladies in Cranford would have considered him such a wonderful traveller if they had only heard him talk in the quiet way he did to him. They liked him the better, indeed, for being what they called 'so very Oriental.'

One day, at a select party in his honour, which Miss Pole gave, and from which, as Mrs Jamieson honoured it with her presence, and had even offered to send Mr Mulliner to wait, Mr and Mrs Hoggins and Mrs Fitz-Adam were necessarily excluded — one day at Miss Pole's, Mr Peter said he was tired of sitting upright against the hard-backed uneasy chairs, and asked if he might not indulge himself in sitting cross-legged. Miss Pole's consent was eagerly given, and down he went with the utmost gravity. But when Miss Pole asked me, in an audible whisper, 'if he did not remind me of the Father of the Faithful?'[2] I could not help thinking of poor Simon Jones the lame tailor; and while Mrs Jamieson slowly commented on the elegance and convenience of the attitude, I remembered how we had all followed that lady's lead in condemning Mr Hoggins for vulgarity because he simply crossed his legs as he sat still on his chair. Many of Mr Peter's ways of eating were a little strange amongst such ladies as Miss Pole, and Miss Matty, and Mrs Jamieson, especially when I recollected the untasted green peas and two-pronged forks at poor Mr Holbrook's dinner.

The mention of that gentleman's name recals to my mind a conversation between Mr Peter and Miss Matty one evening in the summer after he returned to Cranford. The day had been very hot, and Miss Matty had been much oppressed by the weather; in the heat of which her brother revelled. I remember that she had been unable to nurse Martha's baby; which had become her favourite employment of late, and which was as much at home in her arms as in its mother's, as long as it remained a light weight – portable by one so fragile as Miss Matty. This day to which I refer, Miss Matty had seemed more than usually feeble and languid, and only revived when the sun went down, and her sofa was wheeled to the open window, through which, although it looked into the principal street of Cranford, the fragrant smell of the neighbouring hayfields came in every now and then, borne by the soft breezes that stirred the dull air of the summer twilight, and then died away. The silence of the sultry atmosphere was lost in the murmuring noises which came in from many an open window and door; even the children were abroad in the street, late as it was (between ten and eleven), enjoying the game of play for which they had not had spirits during the heat of the day. It was a source of satisfaction to Miss Matty to see how few candles were lighted even in the apartments of those houses from which issued the greatest signs of life. Mr Peter, Miss Matty and I, had all been quiet, each with a separate reverie, for some little time, when Mr Peter broke in:

'Do you know, little Matty, I could have sworn you were on the high road to matrimony when I left England that last time! If anybody had told me you would have lived and died an old maid then, I should have laughed in their faces.'

Miss Matty made no reply; and I tried in vain to think of some subject which should effectively turn the conversation; but I was very stupid; and before I spoke, he went on :

'It was Holbrook; that fine manly fellow who lived at Woodley, that I used to think would carry off my little Matty. You would not think it now, I daresay, Mary ! but this sister of mine was once a very pretty girl – at least I thought so; and so I've a notion did poor Holbrook. What business had he to die before I came home to thank him for all his kindness to a good-for-nothing cub as I was? It was that that made me first think he cared for you; for in all our fishing expeditions it was Matty, Matty, we talked about. Poor Deborah ! What a lecture she read me on having asked him home to lunch one day, when she had seen the Arley carriage in the town, and thought that my lady might call. Well, that's long years ago; more than half a life-time ! and yet it seems like yesterday ! I don't know a fellow I should have liked better as a brother-in-law. You must have played your cards badly, my little Matty, somehow or another – wanted your brother to be a good go-between, eh ! little one?' said he, putting out his hand to take hold of hers as she lay on the sofa – 'Why, what's this? you're shivering and shaking, Matty, with that confounded open window. Shut it, Mary, this minute !'

I did so, and then stooped down to kiss Miss Matty, and see if she really were chilled. She caught at my hand, and gave it a hard squeeze – but unconsciously I think – for in a minute or two she spoke to us quite in her usual voice, and smiled our uneasiness away; although she patiently submitted to the prescriptions we enforced of a warm bed, and a glass of weak negus.[3] I was to leave Cranford the next day, and before I went I saw that all the effects of the open window had quite vanished. I had superintended most of the alterations necessary in the house and household during the latter weeks of my stay. The shop was once more a parlour; the empty resounding rooms again furnished up to the very garrets.

There has been some talk of establishing Martha and Jem in another house; but Miss Matty would not hear of this. Indeed, I never saw her so much roused as when Miss Pole had assumed it to be the most desirable arrangement. As long as Martha would remain with Miss Matty, Miss Matty was only too thankful to have her about her; yes, and Jem too, who was a very pleasant man to have in the house, for she never saw him from week's end to week's end. And as for the probable children, if they would all turn out such little darlings as her god-daughter Matilda, she should not mind the number, if Martha didn't. Besides, the next was to be called Deborah; a point which Miss Matty had reluctantly yielded to Martha's stubborn determination that her firstborn was to be Matilda. So Miss Pole had to lower her colours, and even her voice, as she said to me that as Mr and Mrs Hearn were still to go on living in the same house with Miss Matty, we had certainly done a wise thing in hiring Martha's niece as an auxiliary.

I left Miss Matty and Mr Peter most comfortable and contented; the only subject for regret to the tender heart of the one and the social friendly nature of the other being the unfortunate quarrel between Mrs Jamieson and the plebeian Hogginses and their following. In joke I prophesied one day that this would only last until Mrs Jamieson or Mr Mulliner were ill, in which case they would only be too glad to be friends with Mr Hoggins; but Miss Matty did not like me looking forward to anything like illness in so light a manner; and, before the year was out, all had come round in a far more satisfactory way.

I received two Cranford letters on one auspicious October morning. Both Miss Pole and Miss Matty wrote to ask me to come over and meet the Gordons, whdo had returned to England alive and well, with their two children, now almost grown up. Dear Jessie Brown had kept her old kind nature, although she had changed her name and station; and she wrote to say that she and Major Gordon expected to be in Cranford on the fourteenth, and she hoped and begged to be remembered to Mrs Jamieson (named first, as became her honourable station), Miss Pole, and Miss Matty – could she ever forget their kindness to her poor father and sister? – Mrs Forrester, Mr Hoggins (and here again came in an allusion to kindness shown to the dead long ago), his new wife, who as such must allow Mrs Gordon to desire to make her acquaintance, and who was moreover an old Scotch friend of her husband's. In short, every one was named, from the rector – who had been appointed to Cranford in the interim between Captain Brown's death and Miss Jessie's marriage, and was now associated with the latter event – down to Miss Barker; all were asked to the luncheon; all except Mrs Fitz-Adam, who had come to live in Cranford since Miss Jessie Brown's days, and whom I found rather moping on account of the omission. People wondered at Miss Barker's being included in the honourable list; but then, as Miss Pole said, we must remember the disregard of the genteel properties of life in which the poor captain had educated his girls; and for his sake we swallowed our pride; indeed, Mrs Jamieson rather took it as a compliment, as putting Miss Betty (formerly *her* maid)[4] on a level with 'those Hogginses.'

But when I arrived in Cranford, nothing was as yet ascertained of Mrs Jamieson's own intentions; would the honourable lady go, or would she not? Mr Peter declared that she should and she would; Miss Pole shook her head and desponded. But Mr Peter was a man of resources. In the first place, he persuaded Miss Matty to write to Mrs Gordon, and to tell her of Mrs Fitz-Adam's existence, and to beg that one so kind, and cordial, and generous, might be included in the pleasant invitation. An answer came back by return of post, with a pretty little note for Mrs Fitz-Adam, and a request that Miss Matty would deliver it herself and explain the previous omission. Mrs Fitz-Adam was as pleased as could be, and thanked Miss Matty over and over again. Mr Peter had said 'Leave Mrs Jamieson to me;' so we did; especially as we knew nothing that we could do to alter her determination if once formed.

I did not know, nor did Miss Matty, how things were going on, until Miss Pole asked me, just the day before Mrs Gordon came, if I thought there was anything between Mr Peter and Mrs Jamieson in the matrimonial line, for that Mrs Jamieson was really going to the lunch at the George. She had sent Mr Mulliner down to desire that there might be a footstool put to the warmest seat in the room, as she meant to come, and knew that their chairs were very high. Miss Pole had picked this piece of news up, and from it she conjectured all sorts of things, and bemoaned yet more. 'If Peter should marry, what would become of poor dear Miss Matty? And Mrs Jamieson of all people!' Miss

Pole seemed to think there were other ladies in Cranford who would have done more credit to his choice, and I think she must have had some one who was unmarried in her head, for she kept saying, 'It was so wanting in delicacy in a widow to think of such a thing.'

When I got back to Miss Matty's I really did begin to think that Mr Peter might be thinking of Mrs Jamieson for a wife; and I was as unhappy as Miss Pole about it. He had the proof sheet of a great placard in his hand. 'Signor Brunoni, Magician to the King of Delhi, the Rajah of Oude, and the great Lama of Thibet,' &c. &c. was going to 'perform in Cranford for one night only,' – the very next night; and Miss Matty, exultant, showed me a letter from the Gordons, promising to remain over this gaiety, which Miss Matty said was entirely Peter's doing. He had written to ask the signor to come, and was to be at all the expenses of the affair. Tickets were to be sent gratis to as many as the room would hold. In short, Miss Matty was charmed with the plan, and said that to-morrow Cranford would remind her of the Preston Guild,[5] to which she had been in her youth – a luncheon at the George, with the dear Gordons, and the signor in the Assembly Room in the evening. But I – I looked only at the fatal words :

'*Under the Patronage of the* HONOURABLE
MRS JAMIESON.'

She, then, was chosen to preside over this entertainment of Mr Peter's; she was perhaps going to displace my dear Miss Matty in his heart, and make her life lonely once more ! I could not look forward to the morrow with any pleasure; and every innocent anticipation of Miss Matty's only served to add to my annoyance.

So, angry, and irritated, and exaggerating every little incident which could add to my irritation, I went on till we were all assembled in the great parlour at the George. Major and Mrs Gordon and pretty Flora and Mr Ludovic were all as bright and handsome and friendly as could be; but I could hardly attend to them for watching Mr Peter, and I saw that Miss Pole was equally busy. I had never seen Mrs Jamieson so roused and animated before; her face looked full of interest in what Mr Peter was saying.

I drew near to listen. My relief was great when I caught that his words were not words of love, but that, for all his grave face, he was at his old tricks. He was telling her of his travels in India, and describing the wonderful height of the Himalaya mountains: one touch after another added to their size; and each exceeded the former in absurdity; but Mrs Jamieson really enjoyed all in perfect good faith. I suppose she required strong stimulants to excite her to come out of her apathy. Mr Peter wound up his account by saying that, of course, at that altitude there were none of the animals to be found that existed in the lower regions; the game – everything was different. Firing one day at some flying creature, he was very much dismayed, when it fell, to find that he had shot a cherubim! Mr Peter caught my eye at this moment, and gave me such a funny twinkle, that I felt sure he had no thought of Mrs Jamieson as a wife, from that time. She looked uncomfortably amazed:

'But, Mr Peter – shooting a cherubim – don't you think – I am afraid that was sacrilege!'

Mr Peter composed his countenance in a moment, and appeared shocked at the idea! which, as he said truly enough, was now presented to him for the first time; but then Mrs Jamieson must remember that he had been living for a long time among savages – all of whom were heathens – some of them, he was afraid, were downright Dissenters.[6] Then, seeing Miss Matty draw near, he hastily changed the conversation, and after a little while, turning to me, he said, 'Don't be shocked, prim little Mary, at all my wonderful stories. I consider Mrs Jamieson fair game, and besides, I am bent on propitiating her, and the first step towards it is keeping her well awake. I bribed her here by asking her to let me have her name as patroness for my poor conjuror this evening; and I don't want to give her time enough to get up her rancour against the Hogginses, who are just coming in. I want everybody to be friends, for it harasses Matty so much to hear these quarrels. I shall go to it again by-and-by, so you need not look shocked. I intend to enter the Assembly Room to-night with Mrs Jamieson on one side, and my lady Mrs Hoggins on the other. You see if I don't.'

Somehow or another he did; and fairly got them into conversation together. Major and Mrs Gordon helped at the good work with their perfect ignorance of any existing coolness between any of the inhabitants of Cranford.

Ever since that day there has been the old friendly sociability in Cranford society; which I am thankful for, because of my dear Miss Matty's love of peace and kindliness. We all love Miss Matty, and I somehow think we are all of us better when she is near us.

THE END

COUSIN PHILLIS

Part I

IT is a great thing for a lad when he is first turned into the independence of lodgings. I do not think I ever was so satisfied and proud in my life as when, at seventeen, I sate down in a little three-cornered room above a pastry-cook's shop in the county town of Eltham. My father had left me that afternoon, after delivering himself of a few plain precepts, strongly expressed, for my guidance in the new course of life on which I was entering. I was to be a clerk under the engineer who had undertaken to make the little branch line from Eltham to Hornby.[1] My father had got me this situation, which was in a position rather above his own in life; or perhaps I should say, above the station in which he was born and bred; for he was raising himself every year in men's consideration and respect. He was a mechanic by trade, but he had some inventive genius, and a great deal of perseverance, and had devised several valuable improvements in railway machinery. He did not do this for profit, though, as was reasonable, what came in the natural course of things was acceptable; he worked out his ideas, because, as he said, 'until he could put them into shape, they plagued him by night and by day.' But this is enough about my dear father; it is a good thing for a country where there are many like him. He was a sturdy Independent by descent and conviction;[2] and this it was, I believe, which made him place me in the lodgings at the pastry-cook's. The shop was kept by the two sisters of our minister at home; and this was considered as a sort of safeguard to my morals, when I was turned loose upon the

219

temptations of the county town, with a salary of thirty pounds a year.

My father had given up two precious days, and put on his Sunday clothes, in order to bring me to Eltham, and accompany me first to the office, to introduce me to my new master (who was under some obligations to my father for a suggestion), and next to take me to call on the Independent minister of the little congregation at Eltham. And then he left me; and though sorry to part with him, I now began to taste with relish the pleasure of being my own master. I unpacked the hamper that my mother had provided me with, and smelt the pots of preserve with all the delight of a possessor who might break into their contents at any time he pleased. I handled and weighed in my fancy the home-cured ham, which seemed to promise me interminable feasts; and, above all, there was the fine savour of knowing that I might eat of these dainties when I liked, at my sole will, not dependent on the pleasure of any one else, however indulgent. I stowed my eatables away in the little corner cupboard – that room was all corners, and everything was placed in a corner, the fire-place, the window, the cupboard; I myself seemed to be the only thing in the middle, and there was hardly room for me. The table was made of a folding leaf under the window, and the window looked out upon the market-place; so the studies for the prosecution of which my father had brought himself to pay extra for a sitting-room for me, ran a considerable chance of being diverted from books to men and women. I was to have my meals with the two elderly Miss Browns in the little parlour behind the three-cornered shop downstairs; my breakfasts and dinners at least, for, as my hours in an evening were likely to be uncertain, my tea or supper was to be an independent meal.

Then, after this pride and satisfaction, came a sense of desolation. I had never been from home before, and I was an only child; and though my father's spoken maxim had been, 'Spare the rod and spoil the child,'[3] yet, unconsciously, his heart had yearned after me, and his ways towards me were more tender than he knew, or would have approved of in himself could he have known. My mother, who never professed sternness, was far more severe than my father: perhaps my boyish faults annoyed her more; for

I remember, now that I have written the above words, how she pleaded for me once in my riper years, when I had really offended against my father's sense of right.

But I have nothing to do with that now. It is about cousin Phillis that I am going to write, and as yet I am far enough from even saying who cousin Phillis was.

For some months after I was settled in Eltham, the new employment in which I was engaged – the new independence of my life – occupied all my thoughts. I was at my desk by eight o'clock, home to dinner at one, back at the office by two. The afternoon work was more uncertain than the mornings; it might be the same, or it might be that I had to accompany Mr Holdsworth, the managing engineer, to some point on the line between Eltham and Hornby. This I always enjoyed, because of the variety, and because of the country we traversed (which was very wild and pretty), and because I was thrown into companionship with Mr Holdsworth, who held the position of hero in my boyish mind. He was a young man of five-and-twenty or so, and was in a station above mine, both by birth and education; and he had travelled on the Continent, and wore mustachios and whiskers of a somewhat foreign fashion. I was proud of being seen with him. He was really a fine fellow in a good number of ways, and I might have fallen into much worse hands.

Every Saturday I wrote home, telling of my weekly doings – my father had insisted upon this; but there was so little variety in my life that I often found it hard work to fill a letter. On Sundays I went twice to chapel, up a dark narrow entry, to hear droning hymns, and long prayers, and a still longer sermon, preached to a small congregation, of which I was, by nearly a score of years, the youngest member. Occasionally, Mr Peters, the minister would ask me home to tea after the second service. I dreaded the honour, for I usually sate on the edge of my chair all the evening, and answered solemn questions, put in a deep bass voice, until household prayer-time came, at eight o'clock, when Mrs Peters came in, smoothing down her apron, and the maid-of-all-work followed, and first a sermon, and then a chapter was read, and a long impromptu prayer followed, till some instinct told Mr Peters that supper-time had come, and we rose from our knees with hunger

for our predominant feeling. Over supper the minister did un-
bend a little into one or two ponderous jokes, as if to show me
that ministers were men, after all. And then at ten o'clock I went
home, and enjoyed my long-repressed yawns in the three-cornered
room before going to bed.

Dinah and Hannah Dawson, so their names were put on the
board above the shop-door – I always called them Miss Dawson
and Miss Hannah – considered these visits of mine to Mr Peters
as the greatest honour a young man could have; and evidently
thought that if, after such privileges, I did not work out my sal-
vation, I was a sort of modern Judas Iscariot. On the contrary,
they shook their heads over my intercourse with Mr Holdsworth.
He had been so kind to me in many ways, that when I cut into
my ham, I hovered over the thought of asking him to tea in my
room, more especially as the annual fair was being held in Eltham
market-place, and the sight of the booths, the merry-go-rounds, the
wild-beast shows, and such country pomps, was (as I thought at
seventeen) very attractive. But when I ventured to allude my
wish in even distant terms, Miss Hannah caught me up, and
spoke of the sinfulness of such sights, and something about wallowing in the mire,[4] and then vaulted into France[5] and spoke evil
of the nation, and all who had ever set foot therein, till, seeing
that her anger was concentrating itself into a point, and that
that point was Mr Holdsworth, I thought it would be better to
finish my breakfast, and make what haste I could out of the sound
of her voice. I rather wondered afterwards to hear her and Miss
Dawson counting up their weekly profits with glee, and saying
that a pastry-cook's shop in the corner of the market-place, in
Eltham fair week, was no such bad thing. However, I never ventured to ask Mr Holdsworth to my lodgings.

There is not much to tell about this first year of mine at
Eltham. But when I was nearly nineteen, and beginning to think
of whiskers on my own account, I came to know cousin Phillis,
whose very existence had been unknown to me till then. Mr
Holdsworth and I had been out to Heathbridge for a day, working
hard. Heathbridge was near Hornby, for our line of railway was
above half finished. Of course, a day's outing was a great thing to
tell about in my weekly letters; and I fell to describing the coun-

try – a fault I was not often guilty of. I told my father of the
bogs, all over wild myrtle and soft moss, and shaking ground over
which we had to carry our line; and how Mr Holdsworth and I
had gone for our mid-day meals – for we had to stay here for two
days and a night – to a pretty village hard by, Heathbridge proper;
and how I hoped we should often have to go there, for the shaking, uncertain ground was puzzling our engineers – one end of
the line going up as soon as the other was weighted down. (I had
no thought for the shareholders' interests, as may be seen; we had
to make a new line on firmer ground before the junction railway
was completed.) I told all this at great length, thankful to fill up
my paper. By return letter, I heard that a second-cousin of my
mother's was married to the Independent minister of Hornby,
Ebenezer Holman by name, and lived at Heathbridge proper; the
very Heathbridge I had described, or so my mother believed, for
she had never seen her cousin Phillis Green, who was something
of an heiress (my father believed), being her father's only child,
and old Thomas Green had owned an estate of near upon fifty
acres, which must have come to his daughter. My mother's feeling of kinship seemed to have been strongly stirred by the mention of Heathbridge; for my father said she desired me, if ever I
went thither again, to make inquiry for the Reverend Ebenezer
Holman; and if indeed he lived there, I was further to ask if he
had not married one Phillis Green; and if both these questions
were answered in the affirmative, I was to go and introduce myself as the only child of Margaret Manning, born Moncypenny.
I was enraged at myself for having named Heathbridge at all,
when I found what it was drawing down upon me. One Independent minister, as I said to myself, was enough for any man; and
here I knew (that is to say, I had been catechized on Sabbath
mornings by) Mr Hunter, our minister at home; and I had had to
be civil to old Peters at Eltham, and behave myself for five hours
running whenever he asked me to tea at his house; and now, just
as I felt the free air blowing about me up at Heathbridge, I was
to ferret out another minister, and I should perhaps have to be
catechized by him, or else asked to tea at his house. Besides, I did
not like pushing myself upon strangers, who perhaps had never
heard of my mother's name, and such an odd name as it was –

Moneypenny; and if they had, had never cared more for her than she had for them, apparently, until this unlucky mention of Heathbridge.

Still, I would not disobey my parents in such a trifle, however irksome it might be. So the next time our business took me to Heathbridge, and we were dining in the little sanded inn-parlour, I took the opportunity of Mr Holdsworth's being out of the room, and asked the questions which I was bidden to ask of the rosy-cheeked maid. I was either unintelligible or she was stupid; for she said she did not know, but would ask master; and of course the landlord came in to understand what it was I wanted to know; and I had to bring out all my stammering inquiries before Mr Holdsworth, who would never have attended to them, I dare say, if I had not blushed, and blundered, and made such a fool of myself.

'Yes,' the landlord said, 'the Hope Farm was in Heathbridge proper, and the owner's name was Holman, and he was an Independent minister, and, as far as the landlord could tell, his wife's name was Phillis, anyhow her maiden name was Green.'

'Relations of yours?' asked Mr Holdsworth.

'No, sir – only my mother's second-cousins. Yes, I suppose they are relations. But I never saw them in my life.'

'The Hope Farm is not a stone's throw from here,' said the officious landlord, going to the window. 'If you carry your eye over yon bed of hollyhocks, over the damson-trees in the orchard yonder, you may see a stack of queer-like stone chimneys. Them is the Hope Farm chimneys; it's an old place, though Holman keeps it in good order.'

Mr Holdsworth had risen from the table with more promptitude than I had, and was standing by the window, looking. At the landlord's last words, he turned round, smiling, – 'It is not often that parsons know how to keep land in order, is it?'

'Beg pardon, sir, but I must speak as I find; and Minister Holman – we call the Church clergymen here "parson," sir;[6] he would be a bit jealous if he heard a Dissenter called parson – Minister Holman knows what he's about as well as e'er a farmer in the neighbourhood. He gives up five days a week to his own work, and two to the Lord's; and it is difficult to say which he works hardest at. He spends Saturday and Sunday a-writing sermons and a-visiting his flock at Hornby; and at five o'clock on Monday morning he'll be guiding his plough in the Hope Farm yonder just as well as if he could neither read nor write. But your dinner will be getting cold, gentlemen.'

So we went back to table. After a while, Mr Holdsworth broke the silence: – 'If I were you, Manning, I'd look up these relations of yours. You can go and see what they're like while we're waiting for Dobson's estimates, and I'll smoke a cigar in the garden meanwhile.'

'Thank you, sir. But I don't know them, and I don't think I want to know them.'

'What did you ask all those questions for, then?' said he, looking quickly up at me. He had no notion of doing or saying things without a purpose. I did not answer, so he continued, – 'Make up your mind, and go off and see what this farmer-minister is like, and come back and tell me – I should like to hear.'

I was so in the habit of yielding to his authority, or influence, that I never thought of resisting, but went on my errand, though I remember feeling as if I would rather have had my head cut off. The landlord, who had evidently taken an interest in the event of our discussion in a way that country landlords have, accompanied me to the house-door, and gave me repeated directions, as if I was likely to miss my way in two hundred yards. But I listened to him, for I was glad of the delay, to screw up my courage for the effort of facing unknown people and introducing myself. I went along the lane, I recollect, switching at all the taller roadside weeds, till, after a turn or two, I found myself close in front of the Hope Farm. There was a garden between the house and the shady, grassy lane; I afterwards found that this garden was called the court; perhaps because there was a low wall round it, with an iron railing on the top of the wall, and two great gates between pillars crowned with stone balls for a state entrance to the flagged path leading up to the front door. It was not the habit of the place to go in either by these great gates or by the front door; the gates, indeed, were locked, as I found, though the door stood wide open. I had to go round by a side-path lightly worn on a broad grassy way, which led past the court-wall, past a horse-mount, half covered with stone-crop and the little wild yellow fumitory,[7] to another door – 'the curate,' as I found it was termed by the master of the house, while the front door, 'handsome and all for show,' was termed the 'rector.'[8] I knocked with my hand upon the 'curate' door; a tall girl, about my own age, as I thought, came and opened it, and stood there silent, waiting to know my errand. I see her now – cousin Phillis. The westering sun shone full upon her, and made a slanting stream of light into the room within. She was dressed in dark blue cotton of some kind; up to her throat, down to her wrists, with a little frill of the same wherever it touched her white skin. And such a white skin as it was! I have never seen the like. She had light hair, nearer yellow than any other colour. She looked me steadily in the face with large, quiet eyes, wondering, but untroubled by the sight of a stranger. I thought it odd that so old, so full-grown as she was, she should wear a pinafore over her gown.

Before I had quite made up my mind what to say in reply to her mute inquiry of what I wanted there, a woman's voice called out, 'Who is it, Phillis? If it is any one for butter-milk send them round to the back-door.'

I thought I could rather speak to the owner of that voice than to the girl before me; so I passed her, and stood at the entrance of a room, hat in hand, for this side-door opened straight into the hall or house-place where the family sate when work was done. There was a brisk little woman of forty or so ironing some huge muslin cravats under the light of a long vine-shaded casement window. She looked at me distrustfully till I began to speak. 'My name is Paul Manning,' said I; but I saw she did not know the name. 'My mother's name was Moneypenny,' said I, – 'Margaret Moneypenny.'

'And she married one John Manning, of Birmingham,' said Mrs Holman, eagerly. 'And you'll be her son. Sit down! I am right glad to see you. To think of your being Margaret's son! Why, she was almost a child not so long ago. Well, to be sure, it is five-and-twenty years ago. And what brings you into these parts?'

She sate down herself, as if oppressed by her curiosity as to all the five-and-twenty years that had passed by since she had seen my mother. Her daughter Phillis took up her knitting – a long grey worsted man's stocking, I remember – and knitted away without looking at her work. I felt that the steady gaze of those deep grey eyes was upon me, though once, when I stealthily raised mine to hers, she was examining something on the wall above my head.

When I had answered all my cousin Holman's questions, she heaved a long breath, and said, 'To think of Margaret Moneypenny's boy being in our house! I wish the minister was here. Phillis, in what field is thy father to-day?'

'In the five-acre; they are beginning to cut the corn.'

'He'll not like being sent for, then, else I should have liked you to have seen the minister. But the five-acre is a good step off. You shall have a glass of wine and a bit of cake before you stir from this house, though. You're bound to go, you say, or else the minister comes in mostly when the men have their four o'clock.'

'I must go – I ought to have been off before now.'

'Here, then, Phillis, take the keys.' She gave her daughter some whispered directions, and Phillis left the room.

'She is my cousin, is she not?' I asked. I knew she was, but somehow I wanted to talk of her, and did not know how to begin.

'Yes – Phillis Holman. She is our only child – now.'

Either from that 'now,' or from a strange momentary wistfulness in her eyes, I knew that there had been more children, who were now dead.

'How old is cousin Phillis?' said I, scarcely venturing on the new name, it seemed too prettily familiar for me to call her by it; but cousin Holman took no notice of it, answering straight to the purpose.

'Seventeen last May-day; but the minister does not like to hear me calling it May-day,'[9] said she, checking herself with a little awe. 'Phillis was seventeen on the first day of May last,' she repeated in an amended edition.

'And I am nineteen in another month,' thought I, to myself; I don't know why.

Then Phillis came in, carrying a tray with wine and cake upon it.

'We keep a house-servant,' said cousin Holman, 'but it is churning day, and she is busy.' It was meant as a little proud apology for her daughter's being the handmaiden.[10]

'I like doing it, mother,' said Phillis, in her grave, full voice.

I felt as if I were somebody in the Old Testament – who, I could not recollect – being served and waited upon by the daughter of the host. Was I like Abraham's steward, when Rebekah gave him to drink at the well?[11] I thought Isaac had not gone the pleasantest way to work in winning him a wife. But Phillis never thought about such things. She was a stately, gracious young woman, in the dress and with the simplicity of a child.

As I had been taught, I drank to the health of my new-found cousin and her husband; and then I ventured to name my cousin Phillis with a little bow of my head towards her; but I was too awkward to look and see how she took my compliment. 'I must go now,' said I, rising.

Neither of the women had thought of sharing in the wine; cousin Holman had broken a bit of cake for form's sake.

'I wish the minister had been within,' said his wife, rising too. Secretly I was very glad he was not. I did not take kindly to ministers in those days, and I thought he must be a particular kind of man, by his objecting to the term May-day. But before I went, cousin Holman made me promise that I would come back on the Saturday following and spend Sunday with them; when I should see something of 'the minister.'

'Come on Friday, if you can,' were her last words as she stood at the curate-door, shading her eyes from the sinking sun with her hand.

Inside the house sate cousin Phillis, her golden hair, her dazzling complexion, lighting up the corner of the vine-shadowed room. She had not risen when I bade her good-by; she had looked at me straight as she said her tranquil words of farewell.

I found Mr Holdsworth down at the line, hard at work superintending. As soon as he had a pause, he said, 'Well, Manning, what are the new cousins like? How do preaching and farming seem to get on together? If the minister turns out to be practical as well as reverend, I shall begin to respect him.'

But he hardly attended to my answer, he was so much more

occupied with directing his work-people. Indeed, my answer did not come very readily; and the most distinct part of it was the mention of the invitation that had been given to me.

'Oh, of course you can go – and on Friday, too, if you like; there is no reason why not this week; and you've done a long spell of work this time, old fellow.'

I thought that I did not want to go on Friday; but when the day came, I found that I should prefer going to staying away, so I availed myself of Mr Holdsworth's permission, and went over to Hope Farm some time in the afternoon, a little later than my first visit. I found the 'curate' open to admit the soft September air, so tempered by the warmth of the sun, that it was warmer out of doors than in, although the wooden log lay smouldering in front of a heap of hot ashes on the hearth. The vine-leaves over the window had a tinge more yellow, their hedges were here and there scorched and browned; there was no ironing about, and cousin Holman sate just outside the house, mending a shirt. Phillis was at her knitting indoors: it seemed as if she had been at it all the week. The many-speckled fowls were pecking about in the farmyard beyond, and the milk-cans glittered with brightness, hung out to sweeten. The court was so full of flowers that they crept out upon the low-covered wall and horse-mount, and were even to be found self-sown upon the turf that bordered the path to the back of the house. I fancied that my Sunday coat was scented for days afterwards by the bushes of sweetbriar and the fraxinella[12] that perfumed the air. From time to time cousin Holman put her hand into a covered basket at her feet, and threw handsful of corn down for the pigeons that cooed and fluttered in the air around, in expectation of this treat.

I had a thorough welcome as soon as she saw me. 'Now this is kind – this is right down friendly,' shaking my hand warmly. 'Phillis, your cousin Manning is come!'

'Call me Paul, will you?' said I; 'they call me so at home, and Manning in the office.'

'Well, Paul, then. Your room is all ready for you, Paul, for, as I said to the minister, "I'll have it ready whether he comes o' Friday or not." And the minister said he must go up to the Ashfield whether you were to come or not; but he would come home betimes to see if you were here. I'll show you to your room, and you can wash the dust off a bit.'

After I came down, I think she did not quite know what to do with me; or she might think I was dull; or she might have work to do in which I hindered her; for she called Phillis, and bade her put on her bonnet, and go with me to the Ashfield, and find father. So we set off, I in a little flutter of a desire to make myself agreeable, but wishing that my companion were not quite so tall; for she was above me in height. While I was wondering how to begin our conversation, she took up the words.

'I suppose, cousin Paul, you have to be very busy at your work all day long in general.'

'Yes, we have to be in the office at half-past eight; and we have an hour for dinner, and then we go at it again till eight or nine.'

'Then you have not much time for reading.'

'No,' said I, with a sudden consciousness that I did not make the most of what leisure I had.

'No more have I. Father always gets an hour before going a-field in the mornings, but mother does not like me to get up so early.'

'My mother is always wanting me to get up earlier when I am at home.'

'What time do you get up?'

'Oh! – ah! – sometimes half-past six; not often though;' for I remembered only twice that I had done so during the past summer.

She turned her head and looked at me.

'Father is up at three; and so was mother till she was ill. I should like to be up at four.'

'Your father up at three! Why, what has he to do at that hour?'

'What has he not to do? He has his private exercise in his own room; he always rings the great bell which calls the men to milking; he rouses up Betty, our maid; as often as not he gives the horses their feed before the man is up – for Jem, who takes care of the horses, is an old man; and father is always loth to disturb him; he looks at the calves, and the shoulders, heels, traces,[13] chaff, and corn before the horses go a-field; he has often to whip-cord the plough-whips;[14] he sees the hogs fed; he looks into the

swill-tubs, and writes his orders for what is wanted for food for
man and beast; yes, and for fuel, too. And then, if he has a bit of
time to spare, he comes in and reads with me – but only English;
we keep Latin for the evenings, that we may have time to enjoy
it; and then he calls in the man to breakfast, and cuts the boys'
bread and cheese; and sees their wooden bottles filled, and sends
them off to their work; – and by this time it is half-past six, and
we have our breakfast. There is father,' she exclaimed, pointing
out to me a man in his shirt-sleeves, taller by the head than the
other two with whom he was working. We only saw him
through the leaves of the ash-trees growing in the hedge, and I
thought I must be confusing the figures, or mistaken : that man
still looked like a very powerful labourer, and had none of the
precise demureness of appearance which I had always imagined
was the characteristic of a minister. It was the Reverend Ebenezer
Holman, however. He gave us a nod as we entered the stubble-
field; and I think he would have come to meet us but that he was
in the middle of giving some directions to his men. I could see
that Phillis was built more after his type than her mother's. He,
like his daughter, was largely made, and of a fair, ruddy complexion, whereas hers was brilliant and delicate. His hair had been
yellow or sandy, but now was grizzled. Yet his grey hairs be-
tokened no failure in strength. I never saw a more powerful man
– deep chest, lean flanks, well-planted head. By this time we were
nearly up to him; and he interrupted himself and stepped forwards; holding out his hand to me, but addressing Phillis.

'Well, my lass, this is cousin Manning, I suppose. Wait a
minute, young man, and I'll put on my coat, and give you a
decorous and formal welcome. But – Ned Hall, there ought to be
a water-furrow across this land : it's a nasty, stiff, clayey,
dauby[15] bit of ground, and thou and I must fall to, come next
Monday – I beg your pardon, cousin Manning – and there's old
Jem's cottage wants a bit of thatch; you can do that job to-
morrow while I am busy.' Then, suddenly changing the tone of
his deep bass voice to an odd suggestion of chapels and preachers,
he added, 'Now, I will give out the psalm, "Come all harmonious
tongues," to be sung to "Mount Ephraim" tune.'[16]

He lifted his spade in his hand, and began to beat time with it;

the two labourers seemed to know both words and music, though I did not; and so did Phillis : her rich voice followed her father's as he set the tune; and the men came in with more uncertainty, but still harmoniously. Phillis looked at me once or twice with a little surprise at my silence; but I did not know the words. There we five stood, bareheaded, excepting Phillis, in the tawny stubble-field, from which all the shocks of corn had not yet been carried – a dark wood on one side, where the woodpigeons were cooing; blue distance seen through the ash-trees on the other. Somehow, I think that if I had known the words, and could have sung, my throat would have been choked up by the feeling of the un-accustomed scene.

The hymn was ended, and the men had drawn off before I could stir. I saw the minister beginning to put on his coat, and looking at me with friendly inspection in his gaze, before I could rouse myself.

'I dare say you railway gentlemen don't wind up the day with singing a psalm together,' said he; 'but it is not a bad practice – not a bad practice. We have had it a bit earlier to-day for hos-pitality's sake – that's all.'

I had nothing particular to say to this, though I was thinking a great deal. From time to time I stole a look at my companion. His coat was black, and so was his waistcoat; neckcloth he had none, his strong full throat being bare above the snow-white shirt. He wore drab-coloured knee-breeches, grey worsted stockings (I thought I knew the maker), and strong-nailed shoes. He carried his hat in his hand, as if he liked to feel the coming breeze lifting his hair. After a while, I saw that the father took hold of the daughter's hand, and so, they holding each other, went along to-wards home. We had to cross a lane. In it were two little children, one lying prone on the grass in a passion of crying, the other standing stock still, with its finger in its mouth, the large tears slowly rolling down its cheeks for sympathy. The cause of their distress was evident; there was a broken brown pitcher, and a little pool of spilt milk on the road.

'Hollo ! Hollo ! What's all this?' said the minister. 'Why, what have you been about, Tommy,' lifting the little petticoated lad,[17] who was lying sobbing, with one vigorous arm. Tommy looked at him with surprise in his round eyes, but no affright – they were evidently old acquaintances.

'Mammy's jug!' said he, at last, beginning to cry afresh.

'Well! and will crying piece mammy's jug, or pick up spilt milk? How did you manage it, Tommy?'

'He' (jerking his head at the other) 'and me was running races.'

'Tommy said he could beat me,' put in the other.

'Now, I wonder what will make you two silly lads mind, and not run races again with a pitcher of milk between you,' said the minister, as if musing. 'I might flog you, and so save mammy the trouble; for I dare say she'll do it if I don't.' The fresh burst of whimpering from both showed the probability of this. 'Or I might take you to the Hope Farm and give you some more milk; but then you'd be running races again, and my milk would follow that to the ground, and make another white pool. I think the flogging would be best – don't you?'

'We would never run races no more,' said the elder of the two.

'Then you'd not be boys; you'd be angels.'

'No, we shouldn't.'

'Why not?'

They looked into each other's eyes for an answer to this puzzling question. At length, one said, 'Angels is dead folk.'

'Come; we'll not get too deep into theology. What do you think of my lending you a tin can with a lid to carry the milk in? That would not break, at any rate; though I would not answer for the milk not spilling if you ran races. That's it!'

He had dropped his daughter's hand, and now held out each of his to the little fellows. Phillis and I followed, and listened to the prattle which the minister's companions now poured out to him, and which he was evidently enjoying. At a certain point, there was a sudden burst of the tawny, ruddy-evenings landscape. The minister turned round and quoted a line or two of Latin.[18]

'It's wonderful,' said he, 'how exactly Virgil has hit the enduring epithets, nearly two thousand years ago, and in Italy; and yet how it describes to a T what is now lying before us in the parish of Heathbridge, county –, England.'

'I dare say it does,' said I, all aglow with shame, for I had forgotten the little Latin I ever knew.

The minister shifted his eyes to Phillis's face; it mutely gave him back the sympathetic appreciation that I, in my ignorance, could not bestow.

'Oh! this is worse than the catechism,'[19] thought I; 'that was only remembering words.'

'Phillis, lass, thou must go home with these lads, and tell their mother all about the race and the milk. Mammy must always know the truth,' now speaking to the children. 'And tell her, too, from me that I have got the best birch rod in the parish; and that if she ever thinks her children want a flogging she must bring them to me, and, if I think they deserve it, I'll give it them better than she can.' So Phillis led the children towards the dairy, somewhere in the back yard, and I followed the minister in through the 'curate' into the house-place.

'Their mother,' said he, 'is a bit of a vixen, and apt to punish her children without rhyme or reason. I try to keep the parish rod as well as the parish bull.'[20]

He sate down in the three-cornered chair by the fireside, and looked around the empty room.

'Where's the missus?' said he to himself. But she was there in a minute; it was her regular plan to give him his welcome home – by a look, by a touch, nothing more – as soon as she could after his return, and he had missed her now. Regardless of my presence, he went over the day's doings to her; and then, getting up, he said he must go and make himself 'reverend', and that then we would have a cup of tea in the parlour. The parlour was a large room with two casemented windows on the other side of the broad flagged passage leading from the rector-door to the wide staircase, with its shallow, polished oaken steps, on which no carpet was ever laid. The parlour-floor was covered in the middle by a home-made carpeting of needlework and list. One or two quaint family pictures of the Holman family hung round the walls; the fire-grate and irons were much ornamented with brass; and on a table against the wall between the windows, a great beau-pot[21] of flowers was placed upon the folio volumes of Matthew Henry's Bible.[22] It was a compliment to me to use this room, and I tried to be grateful for it; but we never had our meals there after that first day, and I was glad of it; for the large house-place, living-

room, dining-room, whichever you might like to call it, was twice
as comfortable and cheerful. There was a rug in front of the great
large fire-place, and an oven by the grate, and a crook, with the
kettle hanging from it, over the bright wood-fire; everything that
ought to be black and polished in that room was black and polished; and the flags, and window-curtains, and such things as
were to be white and clean, were just spotless in their purity. Opposite to the fire-place, extending the whole length of the room,
was an oaken shovel-board,[23] with the right incline for a skilful
player to send the weights into the prescribed space. There were
baskets of white work about, and a small shelf of books hung
against the wall, books used for reading, and not for propping up a
beau-pot of flowers. I took down one or two of those books once
when I was left alone in the house-place on the first evening – Virgil, Cæsar, a Greek grammar – oh, dear! ah, me! and Phillis Holman's name in each of them! I shut them up, and put them back in
their places, and walked as far away from the bookshelf as I
could. Yes, and I gave my cousin Phillis a wide berth, although
she was sitting at her work quietly enough, and her hair was
looking more golden, her dark eyelashes longer, her round pillar
of a throat whiter than ever. We had done tea, and we had returned into the house-place that the minister might smoke his
pipe without fear of contaminating the drab damask window-
curtains of the parlour. He had made himself 'reverend' by putting on one of the voluminous white muslin neckcloths that I had
seen cousin Holman ironing that first visit I had paid to the Hope
Farm, and by making one or two other unimportant changes in his
dress. He sate looking steadily at me, but whether he saw me or
not I cannot tell. At the time I fancied that he did, and was gauging me in some unknown fashion in his secret mind. Every now
and then he took his pipe out of his mouth, knocked out the ashes,
and asked me some fresh question. As long as these related to my
acquirements or my reading, I shuffled uneasily and did not know
what to answer. By-and-by he got round to the more practical
subject of railroads, and on this I was more at home. I really had
taken an interest in my work; nor would Mr Holdsworth, indeed,
have kept me in his employment if I had not given my mind as
well as my time to it; and I was, besides, full of the difficulties

which beset us just then, owing to our not being able to find a steady bottom on the Heathbridge moss, over which we wished to carry our line. In the midst of all my eagerness in speaking about this, I could not help being struck with the extreme pertinence of his questions. I do not mean that he did not show ignorance of many of the details of engineering : that was to have been expected; but on the premises he had got hold of, he thought clearly and reasoned logically. Phillis – so like him as she was both in body and mind – kept stopping her work and looking at me, trying to fully understand all that I said. I felt she did; and perhaps it made me take more pains in using clear expressions, and arranging my words, than I otherwise should.

'She shall see I know something worth knowing, though it mayn't be her dead-and-gone languages,' thought I.

'I see,' said the minister, at length. 'I understand it all. You've a clear, good head of your own, my lad, – choose how you came by it.'

'From my father,' said I, proudly. 'Have you not heard of his discovery of a new method of shunting?[24] It was in the *Gazette*. It was patented. I thought every one had heard of Manning's patent winch.'

'We don't know who invented the alphabet,' said he, half smiling, and taking up his pipe.

'No, I dare say not, sir,' replied I, half offended; 'that's so long ago.'

Puff – puff – puff.

'But your father must be a notable man. I heard of him once before; and it is not many a one fifty miles away whose fame reaches Heathbridge.'

'My father is a notable man, sir. It is not me that says so; it is Mr Holdsworth, and – and everybody.'

'He is right to stand up for his father,' said cousin Holman, as if she were pleading for me.

I chafed inwardly, thinking that my father needed no one to stand up for him. He was man sufficient for himself.

'Yes – he is right,' said the minister, placidly. 'Right, because it comes from his heart – right, too, as I believe, in point of fact. Else there is many a young cockerel that will stand upon a dunghill and crow about his father, by way of making his own plumage to shine. I should like to know thy father,' he went on, turning straight to me, with a kindly, frank look in his eyes.

But I was vexed, and would take no notice. Presently, having finished his pipe, he got up and left the room. Phillis put her work hastily down, and went after him. In a minute or two she returned, and sate down again. Not long after, and before I had quite recovered my good temper, he opened the door out of which he had passed, and called to me to come to him. I want across a narrow stone passage into a strange, many-cornered room, not ten feet in area, part study, part counting-house, looking into the farm-yard; with a desk to sit at, a desk to stand at, a spittoon, a set of shelves with old divinity books upon them; another, smaller, filled with books on farriery,[25] farming, manures, and such subjects, with pieces of paper containing memoranda stuck against the whitewashed walls with wafers, nails, pins, anything that came readiest to hand; a box of carpenter's tools on the floor, and some manuscripts in short-hand on the desk.

He turned round half laughing. 'That foolish girl of mine thinks I have vexed you' – putting his large, powerful hand on my shoulder. ' "Nay," says I; "kindly meant is kindly taken" – is it not so?'

'It was not quite, sir,' replied I, vanquished by his manner; 'but it shall be in future.'

'Come, that's right. You and I shall be friends. Indeed, it's not many a one I would bring in here. But I was reading a book this morning, and I could not make it out; it is a book that was left here by mistake one day; I had subscribed to Brother Robinson's sermons; and I was glad to see this instead of them, for sermons though they be, they're . . . well, never mind! I took 'em both, and made my old coat do a bit longer; but all's fish that comes to my net.[26] I have fewer books than leisure to read them, and I have a prodigious appetite. Here it is.'

It was a volume of stiff mechanics, involving many technical terms, and some rather deep mathematics. These last, which would have puzzled me, seemed easy enough to him; all that he wanted was the explanations of the technical words, which I could easily give.

While he was looking through the book to find the places where he had been puzzled, my wandering eye caught on some of the papers on the wall, and I could not help reading one, which has stuck by me ever since. At first, it seemed a kind of weekly diary; but then I saw that the seven days were portioned out for special prayers and intercessions: Monday for his family, Tuesday for enemies, Wednesday for the Independent churches, Thursday for all other churches, Friday for persons afflicted, Saturday for his own soul, Sunday for all wanderers and sinners, that they might be brought home to the fold.

We were called back into the house-place to have supper. A door opening into the kitchen was opened; and all stood up in both rooms, while the minister, tall, large, one hand resting on the spread table, the other lifted up, said, in a deep voice that would have been loud had it not been so full and rich, but with the peculiar accent or twang that I believed is considered devout by some people, 'Whether we eat or drink, or whatsoever we do, let us do all to the glory of God.'[27]

The supper was an immense meat-pie. We of the house-place were helped first; then the minister hit the handle of his buck-horn carving-knife on the table once, and said, –

'Now or never,' which meant, did any of us want any more; and when we had all declined, either by silence or by words, he knocked twice with his knife on the table, and Betty came in through the open door, and carried off the great dish to the kitchen, where an old man and a young one, and a help-girl, were awaiting their meal.

'Shut the door, if you will,' said the minister to Betty.

'That's in honour of you,' said cousin Holman, in a tone of satisfaction, as the door was shut. 'When we've no stranger with us, the minister is so fond of keeping the door open, and talking to the men and maids, just as much as to Phillis and me.'

'It brings us all together like a household just before we meet as a household in prayer,' said he, in explanation. 'But to go back to what we were talking about – can you tell me of any simple book on dynamics that I could put in my pocket, and study a little at leisure times in the day?'

'Leisure times, father?' said Phillis, with a nearer approach to a smile than I had yet seen on her face.

'Yes; leisure times, daughter. There is many an odd minute lost in waiting for other folk; and now that railroads are coming so near us, it behoves us to know something about them.'

I thought of his own description of his 'prodigious big appetite' for learning. And he had a good appetite of his own for the more material victual before him. But I saw, or fancied I saw, that he had some rule for himself in the matter both of food and drink.

As soon as supper was done the household assembled for prayer. It was a long impromptu evening prayer; and it would have seemed desultory enough had I not had a glimpse of the kind of day that preceded it, and so been able to find a clue to the thoughts that preceded the disjointed utterances; for he kept there kneeling down in the centre of a circle, his eyes shut, his outstretched hands pressed palm to palm – sometimes with a long pause of silence, as if waiting to see if there was anything else he wished to 'lay before the Lord' (to use his own expression) – before he concluded with the blessing. He prayed for the cattle and live creatures, rather to my surprise; for my attention had begun to wander, till it was recalled by the familiar words.

And here I must not forget to name an odd incident at the con-clusion of the prayer, and before we had risen from our knees (indeed before Betty was well awake, for she made a nightly prac-tice of having a sound nap, her weary head lying on her stalwart arms); the minister, still kneeling in our midst, but with his eyes wide open, and his arms dropped by his side, spoke to the elder man, who turned round on his knees to attend. 'John, didst see that Daisy had her warm mash to-night; for we must not neglect the means, John – two quarts of gruel, a spoonful of ginger, and a gill of beer – the poor beast needs it, and I fear it slipped out of my mind to tell thee; and here was I asking a blessing and neglect-ing the means, which is a mockery,' said he, dropping his voice.

Before we went to bed he told me he should see little or noth-ing more of me during my visit, which was to end on Sunday evening, as he always gave up both Saturday and Sabbath to his work in the ministry. I remembered that the landlord at the inn had told me this on the day when I first inquired about these new relations of mine; and I did not dislike the opportunity which I saw would be afforded me of becoming more acquainted with cousin Holman and Phillis, though I earnestly hoped that the latter would not attack me on the subject of the dead languages.

I went to bed, and dreamed that I was as tall as cousin Phillis, and had a sudden and miraculous growth of whisker, and a still more miraculous acquaintance with Latin and Greek. Alas! I wakened up still a short, beardless lad, with *'tempus fugit'*[28] for my sole remembrance of the little Latin I had once learnt. While I was dressing, a bright thought came over me: I could question cousin Phillis, instead of her questioning me, and so manage to keep the choice of subjects of conversation in my own power.

Early as it was, every one had breakfasted, and my basin of bread and milk was put on the oven-top to await my coming down. Every one was gone about their work. The first to come into the house-place was Phillis with a basket of eggs. Faithful to my resolution, I asked –

'What are those?'

She looked at me for a moment, and then said gravely – 'Potatoes!'

'No! they are not,' said I. 'They are eggs. What do you mean by saying they are potatoes?'

'What do you mean by asking me what they were, when they were plain to be seen?' retorted she.

We were both getting a little angry with each other.

'I don't know. I wanted to begin to talk to you; and I was afraid you would talk to me about books as you did yesterday. I have not read much; and you and the minster have read so much.'

'I have not,' said she. 'But you are our guest; and mother says I must make it pleasant to you. We won't talk of books. What must we talk about?'

'I don't know. How old are you?'

'Seventeen last May. How old are you?'

'I am nineteen. Older than you by nearly two years,' said I, drawing myself up to my full height.

'I should not have thought you were above sixteen,' she replied, as quietly as if she were not saying the most provoking thing she possibly could. Then came a pause.

'What are you going to do now?' asked I.

'I should be dusting the bed-chambers; but mother said I had better stay and make it pleasant to you,' said she, a little plaintively, as if dusting rooms was far the easiest task.

'Will you take me to see the live-stock? I like animals, though I don't know much about them.'

'Oh, do you? I am so glad! I was afraid you would not like animals, as you did not like books.'

I wondered why she said this. I think it was because she had begun to fancy all our tastes must be dissimilar. We went together all through the farm-yard; we fed the poultry, she kneeling down with her pinafore full of corn and meal, and tempting the little timid downy chickens upon it, much to the anxiety of the fussy ruffled hen, their mother. She called to the pigeons, who fluttered down at the sound of her voice. She and I examined the great sleek cart-horses; sympathized in our dislike of pigs; fed the calves; coaxed the sick cow, Daisy; and admired the others out at pasture; and came back tired and hungry and dirty at dinner-time, having quite forgotten that there were such things as dead languages, and consequently capital friends.

Part II

COUSIN HOLMAN gave me the weekly county newspaper to read aloud to her, while she mended stockings out of a high piled-up basket, Phillis helping her mother. I read and read, unregardful of the words I was uttering, thinking of all manner of other things; of the bright colour of Phillis's hair, as the afternoon sun fell on her bending head; of the silence of the house, which enabled me to hear the double tick of the old clock which stood half-way up the stairs; of the variety of inarticulate noises which cousin Holman made while I read, to show her sympathy, wonder, or horror at the newspaper intelligence. The tranquil monotony of that hour made me feel as if I had lived for ever, and should live for ever droning out paragraphs in that warm sunny room, with my two quiet hearers, and the curled-up pussy cat sleeping on the hearth-rug, and the clock on the house-stairs perpetually clicking out the passage of the moments. By-and-by Betty the servant came to the door into the kitchen, and made a sign to Phillis, who put her half-mended stocking down, and went away to the kitchen without a word. Looking at cousin Holman a minute or two afterwards, I saw that she had dropped her chin upon her breast, and had fallen fast asleep. I put the newspaper down, and was nearly following her example, when a waft of air from some unseen source, slightly opened the door of communication with the kitchen, that Phillis must have left unfastened; and I saw part of her figure as she sate by the dresser, peeling apples with quick dexterity of finger, but with repeated turnings of her head towards some book lying on the dresser by her. I softly rose, and as softly went into the kitchen, and looked over her shoulder; before she was aware of my neighbourhood. I had seen that the book was in a language unknown to me, and the running title was *L'Inferno.* Just as I was making out the relationship of this word to 'infernal,' she started and turned round, and, as if continuing her thought as she spoke, she sighed out, –

242

'Oh! it is so difficult! Can you help me?' putting her finger below a line.

'Me! I! Not I! I don't even know what language it is in!'

'Don't you see it is Dante?' she replied, almost petulantly; she did so want help.

'Italian, then?' said I, dubiously; for I was not quite sure.

'Yes. And I do so want to make it out. Father can help me a little, for he knows Latin; but then he has so little time.'

'You have not much, I should think, if you have often to try and do two things at once, as you are doing now.'

'Oh! that's nothing! Father bought a heap of old books cheap. And I knew something about Dante before; and I have always liked Virgil so much. Paring apples is nothing, if I could only make out this old Italian. I wish you knew it.'

'I wish I did,' said I, moved by her impetuosity of tone. 'If, now, only Mr Holdsworth were here; he can speak Italian like anything, I believe.'

'Who is Mr Holdsworth?' said Phillis, looking up.

'Oh, he's our head engineer. He's a regular first-rate fellow! He can do anything;' my hero-worship and my pride in my chief all coming into play. Besides, if I was not clever and book-learned myself, it was something to belong to some one who was.

'How is it that he speaks Italian?' asked Phillis.

'He had to make a railway through Piedmont, which is in Italy, I believe; and he had to talk to all the workmen in Italian; and I have heard him say that for nearly two years he had only Italian books to read in the queer outlandish places he was in.'

'Oh, dear!' said Phillis; 'I wish –' and then she stopped. I was not quite sure whether to say the next thing that came into my mind; but I said it.

'Could I ask him anything about your book, or your difficulties?'

She was silent for a minute or so, and then she made reply –

'No! I think not. Thank you very much, though. I can generally puzzle a thing out in time. And then, perhaps, I remember it

better than if some one had helped me. I'll put it away now, and
you must move off, for I've got to make the paste for the pigs; we
always have a cold dinner on Sabbaths.'

'But I may stay and help you, mayn't I?'

'Oh, yes; not that you can help at all, but I like to have you
with me.'

I was both flattered and annoyed at this straightforward avowal.
I was pleased that she liked me; but I was young coxcomb enough
to have wished to play the lover, and I was quite wise enough to
perceive that if she had any idea of the kind in her head she would
never have spoken out so frankly. I comforted myself immediately,
however, by finding out that the grapes were sour. A great tall
girl in a pinafore, half a head taller than I was, reading books
that I had never heard of, and talking about them too, as of far
more interest than any mere personal subjects; that was the last
day on which I ever thought of my dear cousin Phillis as the possible mistress of my heart and life. But we were all the greater
friends for this idea being utterly put away and buried out of
sight.

Late in the evening the minister came home from Hornby. He
had been calling on the different members of his flock; and unsatisfactory work it had proved to him, it seemed from the fragments that dropped out of his thoughts into his talk.

'I don't see the men; they are all at their business, their shops,
or their warehouses; they ought to be there. I have no fault to find
with them; only if a pastor's teaching or words of admonition are
good for anything, they are needed by the men as much as by the
women.'

'Cannot you go and see them in their places of business, and
remind them of their Christian privileges and duties, minister?'
asked cousin Holman, who evidently thought that her husband's
words could never be out of place.

'No!' said he, shaking his head. 'I judge them by myself. If
there are clouds in the sky, and I am getting in the hay just
ready for loading, and rain sure to come in the night, I should look
ill upon brother Robinson if he came into the field to speak about
serious things.'

'But, at any rate, father, you do good to the women, and perhaps they repeat what you have said to them to their husbands and children?'

'It is to be hoped they do, for I cannot reach the men directly; but the women are apt to tarry before coming to me, to put on ribbons and gauds;[1] as if they could hear the message I bear to them best in their smart clothes. Mrs Dobson to-day – Phillis, I am thankful thou dost not care for the vanities of dress!'

Phillis reddened a little as she said, in a low humble voice –

'But I do, father, I'm afraid. I often wish I could wear pretty-coloured ribbons round my throat like the squire's daughters.'

'It's but natural, minister!' said his wife; 'I'm not above liking a silk gown better than a cotton one myself!'

'The love of dress is a temptation and a snare,' said he, gravely. 'The true adornment is a meek and quiet spirit. And, wife,' said he, as a sudden thought crossed his mind, 'in that matter I, too, have sinned. I wanted to ask you, could we not sleep in the grey room, instead of our own?'

'Sleep in the grey room? – change our room at this time o' day?' cousin Holman asked, in dismay.

'Yes,' said he. 'It would save me from a daily temptation to anger. Look at my chin!' he continued; 'I cut it this morning – I cut it on Wednesday when I was shaving; I do not know how many times I have cut it of late, and all from impatience at seeing Timothy Cooper at his work in the yard.'

'He's a downright lazy tyke!' said cousin Holman. 'He's not worth his wage. There's but little he can do, and what he can do, he does badly.'

'True,' said the minister. 'But he is but, so to speak, a half-wit; and yet he has got a wife and children.'

'More shame for him!'

'But that is past change. And if I turn him off, no one else will take him on. Yet I cannot help watching him of a morning as he goes sauntering about his work in the yard; and I watch, and I watch, till the old Adam[2] rises strong within me at his lazy ways, and some day, I am afraid, I shall go down and send him about his business – let alone the way in which he makes me cut myself while I am shaving – and then his wife and children will starve. I wish we could move to the grey room.'

I do not remember much more of my first visit to the Hope Farm. We went to chapel in Heathbridge, slowly and decorously walking along the lanes, ruddy and tawny with the colouring of the coming autumn. The minister walked a little before us, his hands behind his back, his head bent down, thinking about the discourse to be delivered to his people, cousin Holman said; and we spoke low and quietly, in order not to interrupt his thoughts. But I could not help noticing the respectful greetings which he received from both rich and poor as we went along; greetings which he acknowledged with a kindly wave of his hand, but with no words of reply. As we drew near the town, I could see some of the young fellows we met cast admiring looks on Phillis; and that made me look too. She had on a white gown, and a short black silk cloak, according to the fashion of the day. A straw bonnet with brown ribbon strings; that was all. But what her dress wanted in colour, her sweet bonny face had. The walk made her cheeks bloom like the rose; the very whites of her eyes had a blue tinge in them, and her dark eyelashes brought out the depth of the blue eyes themselves. Her yellow hair was put away as straight as its natural curliness would allow. If she did not perceive the admiration she excited, I am sure cousin Holman did; for she looked as fierce and as proud as ever her quiet face could look, guarding her treasure, and yet glad to perceive that others could see that it was a treasure. That afternoon I had to return to Eltham to be ready for the next day's work I found out afterwards that the minister and his family were all 'exercised in spirit,' as to whether they did well in asking me to repeat my visits at the Hope Farm, seeing that of necessity I must return to Eltham on the Sabbath-day. However, they did go on asking me, and I went on visiting them, whenever my other engagements permitted me, Mr Holdsworth being in this case, as in all, a kind and indulgent friend. Nor did my new acquaintances oust him from my strong regard and admiration. I had room in my heart for all, I am happy to say, and as far as I can remember, I kept praising each to the other in a manner which, if I had been an older man, living more amongst people of the world, I should have thought unwise, as well as a little ridiculous. It was unwise, certainly, as it was almost sure to cause disappointment if ever they did become acquainted; and perhaps it was ridiculous, though I do not think we any of us thought it so at the time. The minister used to listen to my accounts of Mr Holdsworth's many accomplishments and various adventures in travel with the truest interest, and most kindly good faith; and Mr Holdsworth in return liked to hear about my visits to the farm, and description of my cousin's life there – liked it, I mean, as much as he liked anything that was merely narrative, without leading to action.

So I went to the farm certainly, on an average, once a month during that autumn; the course of life there was so peaceful and quiet, that I can only remember one small event, and that was one that I think I took more notice of than any one else: Phillis left off wearing the pinafores that had always been so obnoxious to me; I do not know why they were banished, but on one of my visits I found them replaced by pretty linen aprons in the morning, and a black silk one in the afternoon. And the blue cotton gown became a brown stuff one as winter drew on; this sounds like some book I once read, in which a migration from the blue bed to the brown was spoken of as a great family event.[3]

Towards Christmas my dear father came to see me, and to consult Mr Holdsworth about the improvement which has since been known as 'Manning's driving wheel.' Mr Holdsworth, as I think I have before said, had a very great regard for my father, who had been employed in the same great machine-shop in which Mr Holdsworth had served his apprenticeship; and he and my father had many mutual jokes about one of these gentlemen-apprentices who used to set about his smith's work in white wash-leather gloves, for fear of spoiling his hands. Mr Holdsworth often spoke to me about my father as having the same kind of genius for mechanical invention as that of George Stephenson,[4] and my father had come over now to consult him about several improvements, as well as an offer of partnership. It was a great pleasure to me to see the mutual regard of these two men. Mr Holdsworth, young, handsome, keen, well-dressed, an object of admiration to all the youth of Eltham; my father, in his decent but unfashionable Sunday clothes, his plain, sensible face full of hard lines, the marks of toil and thought, – his hands, blackened beyond the power of soap and water by years of labour in the foundry; speaking a strong Northern dialect, while Mr Holdsworth had a long soft drawl in his voice, as many of the Southerners have, and was reckoned in Eltham to give himself airs.

Although most of my father's leisure time was occupied with conversations about the business I have mentioned, he felt that he ought not to leave Eltham without going to pay his respects to the relations who had been so kind to his son. So he and I ran up on an engine along the incomplete line as far as Heathbridge, and went, by invitation, to spend a day at the farm.

It was odd and yet pleasant to me to perceive how these two men, each having led up to this point such totally dissimilar lives, seemed to come together by instinct, after one quiet straight look into each other's faces. My father was a thin, wiry man of five foot seven; the minister was a broad-shouldered, fresh-coloured man of six foot one; they were neither of them great talkers in general – perhaps the minister the most so – but they spoke much to each other. My father went into the fields with the minister; I think I see him now, with his hands behind his back, listening intently to all explanations of tillage,[5] and the different processes of farming; occasionally taking up an implement, as if unconsciously, and examining it with a critical eye, and now and then asking a question, which I could see was considered as pertinent by his companion. Then we returned to look at the cattle, housed and bedded in expectation of the snow-storm hanging black on the western horizon, and my father learned the points of a cow with as much attention as if he meant to turn farmer. He had his little book that he used for mechanical memoranda and measurements in his pocket, and he took it out to write down 'straight back,' 'small muzzle,' 'deep barrel,'[6] and I know not what else, under the head 'cow.' He was very critical on a turnip-cutting machine, the clumsiness of which first incited him to talk; and when we went into the house he sat thinking and quiet for a bit, while Phillis and her mother made the last preparations for tea, with a little unheeded apology from cousin Holman, because we were not sitting in the best parlour, which

she thought might be chilly on so cold a night. I wanted nothing
better than the blazing, crackling fire that sent a glow over all
the house-place, and warmed the snowy flags under our feet till
they seemed to have more heat than the crimson rug right in
front of the fire. After tea, as Phillis and I were talking together
very happily, I heard an irrepressible exclamation from cousin
Holman, –

'Whatever is the man about!'

And on looking round, I saw my father taking a straight
burning stick out of the fire, and, after waiting for a minute, and
examining the charred end to see if it was fitted for his purpose,
he went to the hard-wood dresser, scoured to the last pitch of
whiteness and cleanliness, and began drawing with the stick; the
best substitute for chalk or charcoal within his reach, for his
pocket-book pencil was not strong or bold enough for his purpose. When he had done, he began to explain his new model of a
turnip-cutting machine to the minister, who had been watching
him in silence all the time. Cousin Holman had, in the mean-
time, taken a duster out of a drawer, and, under pretence of
being as much interested as her husband in the drawing, was
secretly trying on an outside mark how easily it would come
off, and whether it would leave her dresser as white as before.
Then Phillis was sent for the book on dynamics, about which I
had been consulted during my first visit, and my father had to
explain many difficulties, which he did in language as clear as
his mind, making drawings with his stick wherever they were
needed as illustrations, the minister sitting with his massive head
restings on his hands, his elbows on the table, almost unconscious
of Phillis, leaning over and listening greedily, with her hand on
his shoulder, sucking in information like her father's own
daughter. I was rather sorry for cousin Holman; I had been so
once or twice before; for do what she would, she was completely
unable even to understand the pleasure her husband and
daughter took in intellectual pursuits, much less to care in the
least herself for the pursuits themselves, and was thus unavoid-
ably thrown out of some of their interests. I had once or twice
thought she was a little jealous of her own child, as a fitter companion for her husband than she was herself; and I fancied the

minister himself was aware of this feeling, for I had noticed an occasional sudden change of subject, and a tenderness of appeal in his voice as he spoke to her, which always made her look contented and peaceful again. I do not think that Phillis ever perceived these little shadows; in the first place, she had such complete reverence for her parents that she listened to them both as if they had been St Peter and St Paul,[7] and besides, she was always to much engrossed with any matter in hand to think about other people's manner and looks.

This night I could see, though she did not, how much she was winning on my father. She asked a few questions which showed that she had followed his explanations up to that point; possibly, too, her unusual beauty might have something to do with his favourable impression of her; but he made no scruple of expressing his admiration of her to her father and mother in her absence from the room; and from that evening I date a project of his which came out to me a day or two afterwards, as we sate in my little three-cornered room in Eltham.

'Paul,' he began, 'I never thought to be a rich man; but I think it's coming upon me. Some folk are making a deal of my new machine (calling it by its technical name), and Ellison, of the Borough Green Works, has gone so far as to ask me to be his partner.'

'Mr Ellison the Justice! – who lives in King Street? why, he drives his carriage!'[8] said I, doubting, yet exultant.

Ay, lad, John Ellison. But that's no sign that I shall drive my carriage. Though I should like to save thy mother walking, for she's not so young as she was. But that's a long way off, anyhow. I reckon I should start with a third profit. It might be seven hundred, or it might be more. I should like to have the power to work out some fancies o' mine. I care for that much more than for th' brass. And Ellison has no lads; and by nature the business would come to thee in course o' time. Ellison's lasses are but bits o' things, and are not like to come by husbands just yet; and when they do, maybe they'll not be in the mechanical line. It will be an opening for thee, lad, if thou art steady. Thou'rt not great shakes, I know, in th' inventing line; but many a one gets on better without having fancies for something he does not see and never has seen. I'm right down glad to see that mother's cousins are such uncommon folk for sense and goodness. I have taken the minister to my heart like a brother; and she is a womanly quiet sort of a body. And I'll tell you frank, Paul, it will be a happy day for me if ever you can come and tell me that Phillis Holman is like to be my daughter. I think if that lass had not a penny, she would be the making of a man; and she'll have yon house and lands, and you may be her match yet in fortune if all goes well.'

I was growing as red as fire; I did not know what to say, and yet I wanted to say something; but the idea of having a wife of my own at some future day, though it had often floated about in my own head, sounded so strange when it was thus first spoken about by my father. He saw my confusion, and half smiling said, –

'Well, lad, what dost say to the old father's plans? Thou art but young, to be sure; but when I was thy age, I would ha' given my right hand if I might ha' thought of the chance of wedding the lass I cared for –'

'My mother?' asked I, a little struck by the change of his tone of voice.

'No! not thy mother. Thy mother is a very good woman – none better. No! the lass I cared for at nineteen ne'er knew how I loved her, and a year or two after and she was dead, and ne'er knew. I think she would ha' been glad to ha' known it, poor Molly; but I had to leave the place where we lived for to try to earn my bread – and I meant to come back – but before ever I did, she was dead and gone: I ha' never gone there since. But if you fancy Phillis Holman, and can get her to fancy you, my lad, it shall go different with you, Paul, to what it did with your father.'

I took counsel with myself very rapidly, and I came to a clear conclusion.

'Father,' said I, 'if I fancied Phillis ever so much, she would never fancy me. I like her as much as I could like a sister; and she likes me as if I were her brother – her younger brother.'

I could see my father's countenance fall a little.

'You see she's so clever – she's more like a man than a woman – she knows Latin and Greek.'

'She'd forget 'em, if she'd a houseful of children,' was my father's comment on this.

'But she knows many a thing besides, and is wise as well as learned; she has been so much with her father. She would never think much of me, and I should like my wife to think a deal of her husband.'

'It is not just book-learning or the want of it as makes a wife think much or little of her husband,' replied my father, evidently unwilling to give up a project which had taken deep root in his mind. 'It's a something – I don't rightly know how to call it – if he's manly, and sensible, and straightforward; and I reckon you're that, my boy.'

'I don't think I should like to have a wife taller than I am, father,' said I, smiling; he smiled too, but not heartily.

'Well,' said he, after a pause. 'It's but a few days I've been thinking of it, but I'd got as fond of my notion as if it had been a new engine as I'd been planning out. Here's our Paul, thinks I to myself, a good sensible breed o' lad, as has never vexed or troubled his mother or me; with a good business opening out before him, age nineteen, not so bad-looking, though perhaps not to call handsome, and here's his cousin, not too near a cousin, but just nice, as one may say; aged seventeen, good and true, and well brought up to work with her hands as well as her head; a scholar – but that can't be helped, and is more her misfortune than her fault, seeing she is the only child of a scholar – and as I said afore, once she's a wife and a mother she'll forget it all, I'll be bound – with a good fortune in land and house when it shall please the Lord to take her parents to himself; with eyes like poor Molly's for beauty, a colour that comes and goes on a milk-white skin, and as pretty a mouth –'

'Why, Mr Manning, what fair lady are you describing?' asked Mr Holdsworth, who had come quickly and suddenly upon our *tête-à-tête*, and had caught my father's last words as he entered the room.

Both my father and I felt rather abashed; it was such an odd subject for us to be talking about; but my father, like a straight-forward simple man as he was, spoke out the truth.

'I've been telling Paul of Ellison's offer, and saying how good an opening it made for him –'

'I wish I'd as good,' said Mr Holdsworth. 'But has the business a "pretty mouth?" '

'You're always so full of your joking, Mr Holdsworth,' said my father. 'I was going to say that if he and cousin Phillis Holman liked to make it up between them, I would put no spoke in the wheel.'

'Phillis Holman!' said Mr Holdsworth. 'Is she the daughter of the minister-farmer out at Heathbridge? Have I been helping on the course of true love by letting you go there so often? I knew nothing of it.'

'There is nothing to know,' said I, more annoyed than I chose to show. 'There is no more true love in the case than may be between the first brother and sister you may choose to meet. I have been telling father she would never think of me; she's a great deal taller and cleverer; and I'd rather be taller and more learned than my wife when I have one.'

'And it is she, then, that has the pretty mouth your father spoke about? I should think that would be an antidote to the cleverness and learning. But I ought to apologize for breaking in upon your last night; I came upon business to your father.'

And then he and my father began to talk about many things that had no interest for me just then, and I began to go over again my conversation with my father. The more I thought about it, the more I felt that I had spoken truly about my feelings towards Phillis Holman. I loved her dearly as a sister, but I could never fancy her as my wife. Still less could I think of her ever – yes, *condescending*, that is the word – condescending to marry me. I was roused from a reverie on what I should like my possible wife to be, by hearing my father's warm praise of the minister, as a most unusual character; how they had got back from the diameter of driving-wheels to the subject of the Holmans I could never tell; but I saw that my father's weighty praises were exciting some curiosity in Mr Holdsworth's mind; indeed, he said, almost in a voice of reproach, –

'Why, Paul, you never told me what kind of a fellow this minister-cousin of yours was!'

'I don't know that I found out, sir,' said I. 'But if I had, I don't think you'd have listened to me, as you have done to my father.'

'No! most likely not, old fellow,' replied Mr Holdsworth, laughing. And again and afresh I saw what a handsome pleasant clear face his was; and though this evening I had been a bit put out with him – through his sudden coming, and his having heard my father's open-hearted confidence – my hero resumed all his empire over me by his bright merry laugh.

And if he had not resumed his old place that night, he would have done so the next day, when, after my father's departure, Mr Holdsworth spoke about him with such just respect for his character, such ungrudging admiration of his great mechanical genius, that I was compelled to say, almost unawares, –

'Thank you, sir. I am very much obliged to you.'

'Oh, you're not at all. I am only speaking the truth. Here's a Birmingham workman, self-educated, one may say – having never associated with stimulating minds, or had what advantages travel and contact with the world may be supposed to afford – working out his own thoughts into steel and iron, making a scientific name for himself – a fortune, if it pleases him to work for money – and keeping his singleness of heart, his perfect simplicity of manner; it puts me out of patience to think of my expensive schooling, my travels hither and thither, my heaps of scientific books, and I have done nothing to speak of. But it's evidently good blood; there's that Mr Holman, that cousin of yours, made of the same stuff.'

'But he's only cousin because he married my mother's second cousin,' said I.

'That knocks a pretty theory on the head, and twice over, too. I should like to make Holman's acquaintance.'

'I am sure they would be glad to see you at Hope Farm,' said I, eagerly. 'In fact, they've asked me to bring you several times: only I thought you would find it dull.'

'Not at all. I can't go yet though, even if you do get me an invitation; for the —— —— Company want me to go to the —— Valley, and look over the ground a bit for them, to see if it would do for a branch line; it's a job which may take me away for some time; but I shall be backwards and forwards, and you're quite up to doing what is needed in my absence; the only work that may be beyond you is keeping old Jevons from drinking.'

He went on giving me directions about the management of the men employed on the line, and no more was said then, or for several months, about his going to Hope Farm. He went off into ——Valley, a dark overshadowed dale, where the sun seemed to set behind the hills before four o'clock on midsummer afternoon.

Perhaps it was this that brought on the attack of low fever which he had soon after the beginning of the new year; he was very ill for many weeks, almost many months; a married sister – his only relation, I think – came down from London to nurse him, and I went over to him when I could, to see him, and give him 'masculine news,' as he called it; reports of the progress of the line, which, I am glad to say, I was able to carry on in his absence, in the slow gradual way which suited the company best, while trade was in a languid state, and money dear in the market. Of course, with this occupation for my scanty leisure, I did not often go over to Hope Farm. Whenever I did go, I met with a thorough welcome; and many inquiries were made as to Holdsworth's illness, and the progress of his recovery.

At length, in June I think it was, he was sufficiently recovered to come back to his lodgings at Eltham, and resume part at least of his work. His sister, Mrs Robinson, had been obliged to leave him some weeks before, owing to some epidemic amongst her own children. As long as I had seen Mr Holdsworth in the rooms at the little inn at Hensleydale, where I had been accustomed to look upon him as an invalid, I had not been aware of the visible shake his fever had given to his health. But, once back in the old lodgings, where I had always seen him so buoyant, eloquent, decided, and vigorous in former days, my spirits sank at the change in one whom I had always regarded with a strong feeling of admiring affection. He sank into silence and despondency after the least exertion; he seemed as if he could not make up his mind to any action, or else that, when it was made up, he lacked strength to carry out his purpose. Of course, it was but the natural state of slow convalescence, after so sharp an illness; but, at the time, I did not know this, and perhaps I represented his state as more serious than it was to my kind relations at Hope Farm; who, in their grave, simple, eager way, immediately thought of the only help they could give.

'Bring him out here,' said the minister. 'Our air here is good to a proverb; the June days are fine; he may loiter away his time in the hay-field, and the sweet smells will be a balm in themselves – better than physic.'

'And,' said cousin Holman, scarcely waiting for her husband to finish his sentence, 'tell him there is new milk and fresh eggs to be had for the asking; it's luck Daisy has just calved, for her milk is always as good as other cow's cream; and there is the plaid room with the morning sun all streaming in.'

Phillis said nothing, but looked as much interested in the project as any one. I took it upon myself. I wanted them to see him; him to know them. I proposed it to him when I got home. He was too languid after the day's fatigue, to be willing to make the little exertion of going amongst strangers; and disappointed me by almost declining to accept the invitation I brought. The next morning it was different; he apologized for his ungraciousness of the night before; and told me that he would get all things in train, so as to be ready to go out with me to Hope Farm on the following Saturday.

'For you must go with me, Manning,' said he; 'I used to be as impudent a fellow as need be, and rather liked going amongst strangers, and making my way; but since my illness I am almost like a girl, and turn hot and cold with shyness, as they do, I fancy.'

So it was fixed. We were to go out to Hope Farm on Saturday afternoon; and it was also understood that if the air and the life suited Mr Holdsworth, he was to remain there for a week or ten days, doing what work he could at that end of the line, while I took his place at Eltham to the best of my ability. I grew a little nervous, as the time drew near, and wondered how the brilliant Holdsworth would agree with the quiet quaint family of the minister; how they would like him, and many of his half-foreign ways. I tried to prepare him, by telling him from time to time little things about the goings-on at Hope Farm.

'Manning,' said he, 'I see you don't think I am half good enough for your friends. Out with it, man.'

'No,' I replied, boldly. 'I think you are good; but I don't know if you are quite of their kind of goodness.'

'And you've found out already that there is greater chance of disagreement between two "kinds of goodness," each having its own idea of right, than between a given goodness and a moderate degree of naughtiness – which last often arises from an indifference to right?'

'I don't know. I think you're talking metaphysics, and I am sure that is bad for you.'

' " When a man talks to you in a way that you don't understand about a thing which he does not understand, them's metaphysics." You remember the clown's definition, don't you, Manning?'[9]

'No, I don't,' said I. 'But what I do understand is, that you must go to bed; and tell me at what time we must start to-morrow, that I may go to Hepworth, and get those letters written we were talking about this morning.'

'Wait till to-morrow, and let us see what the day is like,' he answered, with such languid indecision as showed me he was over-fatigued. So I went my way.

The morrow was blue and sunny, and beautiful; the very perfection of an early summer's day. Mr Holdsworth was all impatience to be off into the country; morning had brought back his freshness and strength, and consequent eagerness to be doing. I was afraid we were going to my cousin's farm rather too early, before they would expect us; but what could I do with such a restless vehement man as Holdsworth was that morning? We came down upon the Hope Farm before the dew was off the grass on the shady side of the lane; the great house-dog was loose, basking in the sun, near the closed side door. I was surprised at the door being shut, for all summer long it was open from morning to night; but it was only on latch. I opened it, Rover watching me with half-suspicious, half-trustful eyes. The room was empty.

'I don't know where they can be,' said I. 'But come in and sit down while I go and look for them. You must be tired.'

'Not I. This sweet balmy air is like a thousand tonics. Besides, this room is hot, and smells of those pungent wood-ashes. What are we to do?'

'Go round to the kitchen. Betty will tell us where they are.'

So we went round into the farmyard, Rover accompanying us out of a grave sense of duty. Betty was washing out her milk-pans in the cold bubbling spring-water that constantly trickled in and out of a stone trough. In such weather as this most of her kitchen-work was done out of doors.

'Eh, dear!' said she, 'the minister and missus is away at Hornby! They ne'er thought of your coming so betimes!' The missus had some errands to do, and she thought as she'd walk with the minister and be back by dinner-time.'

'Did not they expect us to dinner?' said I.

'Well, they did, and they did not, as I may say. Missus said to me the cold lamb would do well enough if you did not come; and if you did I was to put on a chicken and some bacon to boil; and I'll go do it now, for it is hard to boil bacon enough.'

'And is Phillis gone, too?' Mr Holdsworth was making friends with Rover.

'No! She's just somewhere about. I reckon you'll find her in the kitchen-garden, getting peas.'

'Let us go there,' said Holdsworth, suddenly leaving off his play with the dog.

So I led the way to the kitchen-garden. It was in the first promise of a summer profuse in vegetables and fruits. Perhaps it was not so much cared for as other parts of the property; but it was more attended to than most kitchen-gardens belonging to farm-houses. There were borders of flowers along each side of the gravel walks; and there was an old sheltering wall on the north side covered with tolerably choice fruit-trees; there was a slope down to the fish-pond at the end, where there were great strawberry-beds; and raspberry bushes and rose-bushes grew wherever there was a space; it seemed a chance which had been planted. Long rows of peas stretched at right angles from the main walk, and I saw Phillis stooping down among them, before she saw us. As soon as she heard our cranching[10] steps on the gravel, she stood up, and shading her eyes from the sun, recognized us. She was quite still for a moment, and then came slowly towards us, blushing a little from evident shyness. I had never seen Phillis shy before.

'This is Mr Holdsworth, Phillis,' said I, as soon as I had shaken hands with her. She glanced up at him, and then looked down, more flushed than ever at his grand formality of taking his hat off and bowing; such manners had never been seen at Hope Farm before.

'Father and mother are out. They will be so sorry; you did not write, Paul, as you said you would.'

'It was my fault,' said Holdsworth, understanding what she meant as well as if she had put it more fully into words. 'I have not yet given up all the privileges of an invalid; one of which is indecision. Last night, when your cousin asked me at what time we were to start, I really could not make up my mind.'

Phillis seemed as if she could not make up her mind as to what to do with us. I tried to help her –

'Have you finished getting peas?' taking hold of the half-filled basket she was unconsciously holding in her hand; 'or may we stay and help you?'

'If you would. But perhaps it will tire you, sir?' added she, speaking now to Holdsworth.

'Not a bit,' said he. 'It will carry me back twenty years of my life, when I used to gather peas in my grandfather's garden. I suppose I may eat a few as I go along?'

'Certainly, sir. But if you went to the strawberry-beds you would find some strawberries ripe, and Paul can show you where they are.'

'I am afraid you distrust me. I can assure you I know the exact fulness at which peas should be gathered. I take great care not to pluck them when they are unripe. I will not be turned off, as unfit for my work.'

This was a style of half-joking talk that Phillis was not accustomed to. She looked for a moment as if she would have liked to defend herself from the playful charge of distrust made against her, but she ended by not saying a word. We all plucked our peas in busy silence for the next five minutes. Then Holdsworth lifted himself up from between rows, and said, a little wearily, –

'I am afraid I must strike work. I am not as strong as I fancied myself.'

Phillis was full of penitence immediately. He did, indeed, look pale; and she blamed herself for having allowed him to help her. 'It was very thoughtless of me. I did not know – I thought, perhaps, you really liked it. I ought to have offered you something to eat, sir. Oh, Paul, we have gathered quite enough; how stupid I was to forget that Mr Holdsworth had been ill!' And in a blushing hurry she led the way towards the house. We went in, and she moved a heavy cushioned chair forwards, into which Mr Holdsworth was only too glad to sink. Then with deft and quiet speed she brought in a little tray, wine, water, cake, home-made bread, and newly-churned butter. She stood by in some anxiety till, after bite and sup, the colour returned to Mr Holdsworth's face, and he would fain have made us some laughing apologies for the fright he had given us But then Phillis drew back from her innocent show of care and interest, and relapsed into the cold shyness habitual to her when she was first thrown into the company of strangers She brought out the last week's county paper (which Mr Holdsworth had read five days ago), and then quietly withdrew; and then he subsided into languor, leaning back and shutting his eyes as if he would go to sleep. I stole into the kitchen after Phillis: but she had made the round of the corner of the house outside, and I found her sitting on the horse-mount, with her basket of peas, and a basin into which she was shelling them. Rover lay at her feet, snapping now and then at the flies. I went to her, and tried to help her, but somehow the sweet crisp young peas found their way more frequently into my mouth than into the basket, while we talked together in a low tone, fearful of being overheard through the open casements of the house-place in which Holdsworth was resting

'Don't you think him handsome?' asked I

'Perhaps – yes – I have hardly looked at him,' she replied 'But is not he very like a foreigner?'

'Yes, he cuts his hair foreign fashion,' said I.

'I like an Englishman to look like an Englishman.'

'I don't think he thinks about it. He says he began that way when he was in Italy, because everybody wore it so, and it is natural to keep it on in England.'

'Not if he began it in Italy because everybody there wore it so. Everybody here wears it differently.'

I was a little offended with Phillis's logical fault-finding with my friend; and I determined to change the subject.

'When is your mother coming home?'

'I should think she might come any time now; but she had to go and see Mrs Morton, who was ill, and she might be kept, and not be home till dinner. Don't you think you ought to go and see how Mr Holdsworth is going on, Paul? He may be faint again.'

I went at her bidding; but there was no need for it. Mr Holdsworth was up, standing by the window, his hands in his pockets; he had evidently been watching us. He turned away as I entered.

'So that is the girl I found your good father planning for your wife, Paul, that evening when I interrupted you! Are you of the same coy mind still? It did not look like it a minute ago.'

'Phillis and I understand each other,' I replied, sturdily. 'We are like brother and sister. She would not have me as a husband if there was not another man in the world; and it would take a deal to make me think of her – as my father wishes' (somehow I did not like to say 'as a wife'), 'but we love each other dearly.'

'Well, I am rather surprised at it – not at your loving each other in a brother-and-sister kind of way – but at finding it so impossible to fall in love with such a beautiful woman.'

Woman! beautiful woman! I had thought of Phillis as a comely but awkward girl; and I could not banish the pinafore from my mind's eye when I tried to picture her to myself. Now I turned, as Mr Holdsworth had done, to look at her again out of the window: she had just finished her task, and was standing up, her back to us, holding the basket, and the basin in it, high in the air, out of Rover's reach, who was giving vent to his delight at the probability of a change of place by glad leaps and barks, and snatches at what he imagined to be a withheld prize. At length she grew tired of their mutual play, and with a feint of striking him, and a 'Down, Rover! do hush!' she looked towards the window where we were standing, as if to reassure herself that no one had been disturbed by the noise, and seeing us, she coloured all over, and hurried away, with Rover still curving in sinuous lines about her as she walked.

'I should have liked to have sketched her,' said Mr Holdsworth, as he turned away. He went back to his chair, and rested in silence for a minute or two. Then he was up again.

'I would give a good deal for a book,' he said. 'It would keep me quiet.' He began to look round; there were a few volumes at one end of the shovel-board.

'Fifth volume of Matthew Henry's *Commentary*.' said he, reading their titles aloud. '*Housewife's complete Manual; Berridge on Prayer; L'Inferno* – Dante!' in great surprise. 'Why, who reads this?'

'I told you Phillis reads it. Don't you remember? She knows Latin and Greek, too.'

'To be sure! I remember! But somehow I never put two and two together. That quiet girl, full of household work, is the wonderful scholar, then, that put you to rout with her questions when you first began to come here. To be sure, "Cousin Phillis!" What's here: a paper with the hard, obsolete words written out. I wonder what sort of a dictionary she has got. Baretti[11] won't tell her all these words. Stay! I have got a pencil here. I'll write down the most accepted meanings, and save her a little trouble.'

So he took her book and the paper back to the little round table, and employed himself in writing explanations and definitions of the words which had troubled her. I was not sure if he was not taking a liberty: it did not quite please me, and yet I did not know why. He had only just done, and replaced the paper in the book, and put the latter back in its place, when I heard the sound of wheels stopping in the lane, and looking out, I saw cousin Holman getting out of a neighbour's gig, making her little curtsey of acknowledgment, and then coming towards the house. I went to meet her.

'Oh, Paul!' said she, 'I am so sorry I was kept; and then Thomas Dobson said if I would wait a quarter of an hour he would – But where's your friend Mr Holdsworth? I hope he is come?'

Just then he came out, and with his pleasant cordial manner

took her hand, and thanked her for asking him to come out here to get strong.

'I'm sure I am very glad to see you, sir. It was the minister's thought. I took it into my head you would be dull in our quiet house, for Paul says you've been such a great traveller; but the ministers said that dullness would perhaps suit you while you were but ailing, and that I was to ask Paul to be here as much as he could. I hope you'll find yourself happy with us, I'm sure, sir. Has Phillis given you something to eat and drink, I wonder? there's a deal in eating a little often, if one has to get strong after an illness.' And then she began to question him as to the details of his indisposition in her simple motherly way. He seemed at once to understand her, and to enter into friendly relations with her. It was not quite the same in the evening when the minister came home. Men have always a little natural antipathy to get over when they first meet as strangers. But in this case each was disposed to make an effort to like the other; only each was to each a specimen of an unknown class. I had to leave the Hope Farm on Sunday afternoon, as I had Mr Holdsworth's work as well as my own to look to in Eltham; and I was not at all sure how things would go on during the week that Holdsworth was to remain on his visit; I had been once or twice in hot water already at the near clash of opinions between the minister and my much-vaunted friend. On the Wednesday I received a short note from Holdsworth; he was going to stay on, and return with me on the following Sunday, and he wanted me to send him a certain list of books, his theodolite,[12] and other surveying instruments, all of which could easily be conveyed down the line to Heathbridge. I went to his lodgings and picked out the books. Italian, Latin, trigonometry; a pretty considerable parcel they made, besides the implements. I began to be curious as to the general progress of affairs at Hope Farm, but I could not go over till the Saturday. At Heathbridge I found Holdsworth, come to meet me. He was looking quite a different man to what I had left him; embrowned, sparkles in his eyes, so languid before. I told him how much stronger he looked.

'Yes!' said he. 'I am fidging fain to be at work again.[13] Last week I dreaded the thoughts of my employment; now I am full of desire to begin. This week in the country has done wonders for me.'

'You have enjoyed yourself, then?'

'Oh! it has been perfect in its way. Such a thorough country life! and yet removed from the dulness which I always used to fancy accompanied country life, by the extraordinary intelligence of the minister. I have fallen into calling him "the minister," like every one else.'

'You get on with him, then?' said I. 'I was a little afraid.'

'I was on the verge of displeasing him once or twice, I fear, with random assertions and exaggerated expressions, such as one always uses with other people, and thinks nothing of; but I tried to check myself when I saw how it shocked the good man; and really it is very wholesome exercise, this trying to make one's words represent one's thoughts, instead of merely looking to their effect on others.'

'Then you are quite friends now?' I asked.

'Yes, thoroughly; at any rate as far as I go. I never met with a man with such a desire for knowledge. In information, as far as it can be gained from books, he far exceeds me on most subjects; but then I have travelled and seen – Were not you surprised at the list of things I sent for?'

'Yes; I thought it did not promise much rest.'

'Oh! some of the books were for the minister, and some for his daughter. (I call her Phillis to myself, but I use euphemisms in speaking about her to others. I don't like to seem familiar, and yet Miss Holman is a term I have never heard used.)'

'I thought the Italian books were for her.'

'Yes! Fancy her trying at Dante for her first book in Italian! I had a capital novel by Manzoni, *I Promessi Sposi*,[14] just the thing for a beginner; and if she must still puzzle out Dante, my dictionary is far better than hers.'

'Then she found out you had written those definitions on her list of words?'

'Oh! yes' – with a smile of amusement and pleasure. He was going to tell me what had taken place, but checked himself.

'But I don't think the minister will like your having given her a novel to read?'[15]

'Pooh! What can be more harmless? Why make a bugbear of a word?[16] It is as pretty and innocent a tale as can be met with. You don't suppose they take *Virgil* for gospel?'

By this time we were at the farm. I think Phillis gave me a warmer welcome than usual, and cousin Holman was kindness itself. Yet somehow I felt as if I had lost my place, and that Holdsworth had taken it. He knew all the ways of the house; he was full of little filial attentions to cousin Holman; he treated Phillis with the affectionate condescension of an elder brother; not a bit more; not in any way different. He questioned me about the progress of affairs in Eltham with eager interest.

'Ah!' said cousin Holman, 'you'll be spending a different kind of time next week to what you have done this! I can see how busy you'll make yourself! But if you don't take care you'll be ill again, and have to come back to our quiet ways of going on.'

'Do you suppose I shall need to be ill to wish to come back here?' he answered warmly. 'I am only afraid you have treated me so kindly that I shall always be turning up on your hands.'

'That's right,' she replied. 'Only don't go and make yourself ill by over-work. I hope you'll go on with a cup of new milk every morning, for I am sure that is the best medicine; and put a teaspoonful of rum in it, if you like; many a one speaks highly of that, only we had no rum in the house.'

I brought with me an atmosphere of active life which I think he had begun to miss; and it was natural that he should seek my company, after his week of retirement. Once I saw Phillis looking at us as we talked together with a kind of wistful curiosity; but as soon as she caught my eye, she turned away, blushing deeply.

That evening I had a little talk with the minister. I strolled along the Hornby road to meet him; for Holdsworth was giving Phillis an Italian lesson, and cousin Holman had fallen asleep over her work.

Somehow, and not unwillingly on my part, our talk fell on the friend whom I had introduced to the Hope Farm.

'Yes! I like him!' said the minister, weighing his words a little as he spoke. 'I like him. I hope I am justified in doing it, but he takes hold of me, as it were; and I have almost been afraid lest he carries me away, in spite of my judgment.'

'He is a good fellow; indeed he is,' said I. 'My father thinks well of him; and I have seen a deal of him. I would not have had him come here if I did not know that you would approve of him.'

'Yes,' (once more hesitating,) 'I like him, and I think he is an upright man; there is a want of seriousness in his talk at times, but, at the same time, it is wonderful to listen to him! He makes Horace and Virgil living, instead of dead, by the stories he tells me of his sojourn in the very countries where they lived, and where to this day, he says – But it is like dram-drinking.[17] I listen to him till I forget my duties, and am carried off my feet. Last Sabbath evening he led us away into talk on profane subjects ill befitting the day.'

By this time we were at the house, and our conversation stopped. But before the day was out, I saw the unconscious hold that my friend had got over all the family. And no wonder: he had seen so much and done so much as compared to them, and he told about it all so easily and naturally, and yet as I never heard any one else do; and his ready pencil was out in an instant to draw on scraps of paper all sorts of illustrations – modes of drawing up water in Northern Italy, wine-carts, buffaloes, stone-pines,[18] I know not what. After we had all looked at these drawings, Phillis gathered them together, and took them.

It is many years since I have seen thee, Edward Holdsworth, but thou wast a delightful fellow! Ay, and a good one too; though much sorrow was caused by thee!

Part III

JUST after this I went home for a week's holiday. Everything was prospering there; my father's new partnership gave evident satisfaction to both parties. There was no display of increased wealth in our modest household; but my mother had a few extra comforts provided for her by her husband. I made acquaintance with Mr and Mrs Ellison, and first saw pretty Margaret Ellison, who is now my wife. When I returned to Eltham, I found that a step was decided upon, which had been in contemplation for some time; that Holdsworth and I should remove our quarters to Hornby; our daily presence, and as much of our time as possible, being required for the completion of the line at that end.

Of course this led to greater facility of intercourse with the Hope Farm people. We could easily walk out there after our day's work was done, and spend a balmy evening hour or two, and yet return before the summer's twilight had quite faded away. Many a time, indeed, we would fain have stayed longer – the open air, the fresh and pleasant country, made so agreeable a contrast to the close town lodgings which I shared with Mr Holdsworth; but early hours, both at eve and morn, were an imperative necessity with the minister, and he made no scruple at turning either or both of us out of the house directly after evening prayer, or 'exercise,' as he called it. The remembrance of many a happy day, and of several little scenes, comes back upon me as I think of that summer. They rise like pictures to my memory, and in this way I can date their succession; for I know that corn harvest must have come after hay-making, apple-gathering after corn-harvest.

The removal to Hornby took up some time, during which we had neither of us any leisure to go out to the Hope Farm. Mr Holdsworth had been out there once during my absence at home. One sultry evening, when work was done, he proposed our walking out and paying the Holmans a visit. It so happened that I had omitted to write my usual weekly letter home in our press of business, and I wished to finish that before going out. Then he said that he would go, and that I could follow him if I liked. This I did in about an hour; the weather was so oppressive, I remember, that I took off my coat as I walked, and hung it over my arm. All the doors and windows at the farm were open when I arrived there, and every tiny leaf on the trees was still. The silence of the place was profound; at first I thought that it was entirely deserted; but just as I drew near the door I heard a weak sweet voice begin to sing; it was cousin Holman, all by herself in the house-place, piping up a hymn, as she knitted away in the clouded light. She gave me a kindly welcome, and poured out all the small domestic news of the fortnight past upon me, and, in return, I told her about my own people and my visit at home.

'Where were the rest?' at length I asked.

Betty and the men were in the field helping with the last load of hay, for the minister said there would be rain before the morning. Yes, and the minister himself, and Phillis, and Mr Holdsworth, were all there helping. She thought that she herself could have done something; but perhaps she was the least fit for hay-making of any one; and somebody must stay at home and take care of the house, there were so many tramps about; if I had not had something to do with the railroad she would have called them navvies.[1] I asked her if she minded being left alone, as I should like to go and help; and having her full and glad permission to leave her alone, I went off, following her directions: through the farmyard, past the cattle-pond, into the ash-field, beyond into the higher field with two holly-bushes in the middle. I arrived there: there was Betty with all the farming men, and a cleared field, and a heavily laden cart; one man at the top of the great pile ready to catch the fragrant hay which the others threw up to him with their pitchforks; a little heap of cast-off clothes in a corner of the field (for the heat, even at seven o'clock, was insufferable), a few cans and baskets, and Rover lying by them panting, and keeping watch. Plenty of loud, hearty, cheerful talking; but no minister, no Phillis, no Mr Holdsworth. Betty saw me first, and understanding who it was that I was in search of, she came towards me.

'They're out yonder – agait[2] wi' them things o' Measter Holdsworth's.'

So 'out yonder' I went; out on to a broad upland common, full of red sand-banks, and sweeps and hollows; bordered by dark firs, purple in the coming shadows, but near at hand all ablaze with flowering gorse, or, as we call it in the south, furze-bushes, which, seen against the belt of distant trees, appeared brilliantly golden. On this heath, a little way from the field-gate, I saw the three. I counted their heads, joined together in an eager group over Holdsworth's theodolite. He was teaching the minister the practical art of surveying and taking a level. I was wanted to assist, and was quickly set to work to hold the chain. Phillis was as intent as her father; she had hardly time to greet me, so desirous was she to hear some answer to her father's question.

So we went on, the dark clouds still gathering, for perhaps five minutes after my arrival. Then came the blinding lightning and the rumble and quick-following peal of thunder right over our heads. It came sooner than I expected, sooner than they had looked for: the rain delayed not; it came pouring down; and what were we to do for shelter? Phillis had nothing on but her indoor things – no bonnet, no shawl. Quick as the darting lightning around us, Holdsworth took off his coat and wrapped it round her neck and shoulders, and almost without a word, hurried us all into such poor shelter as one of the overhanging sand-banks could give. There we were, cowered down, close together, Phillis innermost, almost too tightly packed to free her arms enough to divest herself of the coat, which she, in her turn, tried to put lightly over Holdsworth's shoulders. In doing so she touched his shirt.

'Oh, how wet you are!' she cried, in pitying dismay; 'and you've hardly got over your fever! Oh, Mr Holdsworth, I am so sorry!' He turned his head a little, smiling at her.

'If I do catch cold, it is all my fault for having deluded you into staying out here!' but she only murmured again, 'I am so sorry.'

The minister spoke now. 'It is a regular downpour. Please God that the hay is saved! But there is no likelihood of its ceasing, and I had better go home at once, and send you all some wraps; umbrellas will not be safe with yonder thunder and lightning.'

Both Holdsworth and I offered to go instead of him; but he was resolved, although perhaps it would have been wiser if Holdsworth, wet as he already was, had kept himself in exercise. As he moved off, Phillis crept out, and could see on to the storm-swept heath. Part of Holdsworth's apparatus still remained exposed to all the rain. Before we could have any warning, she had rushed out of the shelter and collected the various things, and brought them back in triumph to where we crouched. Holdsworth had stood up, uncertain whether to go to her assistance or not. She came running back, her long lovely hair floating and dripping, her eyes glad and bright, and her colour freshened to a glow of health by the exercise and the rain.

'Now, Miss Holman, that's what I call wilful,' said Holdsworth, as she gave them to him. 'No, I won't thank you' (his looks were thanking her all the time). 'My little bit of dampness annoyed you, because you thought I had got wet in your service; so you were determined to make me as uncomfortable as you were yourself. It was an unchristian piece of revenge!'

His tone of badinage (as the French call it) would have been palpable enough to any one accustomed to the world; but Phillis was not, and it distressed or rather bewildered her. 'Unchristian' had to her a very serious meaning; it was not a word to be used lightly; and though she did not exactly understand what wrong it was that she was accused of doing, she was evidently desirous to throw off the imputation. At first her earnestness to disclaim unkind motives amused Holdsworth; while his light continuance of the joke perplexed her still more; but at last he said something gravely, and in too low a tone for me to hear, which made her all at once become silent, and called out her blushes. After a while, the minister came back, a moving mass of shawls, cloaks, and umbrellas. Phillis kept very close to her father's side on our return to the farm. She appeared to me to be shrinking away from Holdsworth, while he had not the slightest variation in his manner from what it usually was in his graver moods; kind, protecting, and thoughtful towards her. Of course, there was a great commotion about our wet clothes; but I name the little events of that evening now because I wondered at the time what he had said in that low voice to silence Phillis so effectually, and because, in thinking of their intercourse by the light of future events, that evening stands out with some prominence.

I have said that after our removal to Hornby our communications with the farm became almost of daily occurrence. Cousin Holman and I were the two who had least to do with this intimacy. After Mr Holdsworth regained his health, he too often talked above her head in intellectual matters, and too often in his light bantering tone for her to feel quite at her ease with him. I really believe that he adopted this latter tone in speaking to her because he did not know what to talk about to a purely motherly woman, whose intellect had never been cultivated, and whose loving heart was entirely occupied with her husband, her child, her household affairs, and, perhaps, a little with the concerns of the members of her husband's congregation, because they, in a way, belonged to her husband. I had noticed before that she had fleeting shadows of jealousy even of Phillis, when her daughter and her husband appeared to have strong interests and sympathies in things which were quite beyond her comprehension. I had noticed it in my first acquaintance with them, I say, and had admired the delicate tact which made the minister, on such occasions, bring the conversation back to such subjects as those on which his wife, with her practical experience of every-day life, was an authority; while Phillis, devoted to her father, unconsciously followed his lead, totally unaware, in her filial reverence, of his motive for doing so.

To return to Holdsworth. The minister had at more than one time spoken of him to me with slight distrust, principally occasioned by the suspicion that his careless words were not always those of soberness and truth. But it was more as a protest against the fascination which the younger man evidently exercised over the elder one – more as it were to strengthen himself against yielding to this fascination – that the minister spoke out to me about this failing of Holdsworth's, as it appeared to him. In return Holdsworth was subdued by the minister's uprightness and goodness, and delighted with his clear intellect – his strong healthy craving after further knowledge. I never met two men who took more thorough pleasure and relish in each other's society. To Phillis his relation continued that of an elder brother: he directed her studies into new paths, he patiently drew out the expression of many of her thoughts, and perplexities, and unformed theories

– scarcely even now falling into the vein of banter which she was slow to understand.

One day – harvest-time – he had been drawing on a loose piece of paper – sketching ears of corn, sketching carts drawn by bullocks and laden with grapes – all the time talking with Phillis and me, cousin Holman putting in her not pertinent remarks, when suddenly he said to Phillis, –

'Keep your head still; I see a sketch! I have often tried to draw your head from memory, and failed; but I think I can do it now. If I succeed I will give it to your mother. You would like a portrait of your daughter as Ceres,[3] would you not, ma'am?'

'I should like a picture of her; yes, very much, thank you, Mr Holdsworth, but if you put that straw in her hair,' (he was holding some wheat ears above her passive head, looking at the effect with an artistic eye,) 'you'll ruffle her hair. Phillis, my dear, if you're to have your picture taken, go upstairs, and brush your hair smooth.'

'Not on any account. I beg your pardon, but I want hair loosely flowing.'

He began to draw, looking intently at Phillis; I could see this stare of his discomposed her – her colour came and went, her breath quickened with the consciousness of his regard; at last, when he said, 'Please look at me for a minute or two, I want to get in the eyes,' she looked up at him, quivered, and suddenly got up and left the room. He did not say a word, but went on with some other part of the drawing; his silence was unnatural, and his dark cheek blanched a little. Cousin Holman looked up from her work, and put her spectacles down.

'What's the matter? Where is she gone?'

Holdsworth never uttered a word, but went on drawing. I felt obliged to say something; it was stupid enough, but stupidity was better than silence just then.

'I'll go and call her,' said I. So I went into the hall, and to the bottom of the stairs; but just as I was going to call Phillis, she came down swiftly with her bonnet on, and saying, 'I'm going to father in the five-acre,' passed out by the open 'rector,' right in front of the house-place windows, and out at the little white side-gate. She had been seen by her mother and Holdsworth, as she passed; so there was no need for explanation, only cousin Holman and I had a long discussion as to whether she could have found the room too hot, or what had occasioned her sudden departure. Holdsworth was very quiet during all the rest of that day; nor did he resume the portrait-taking by his own desire, only at my cousin Holman's request the next time that he came; and then he said he should not require any more formal sittings for only such a slight sketch as he felt himself capable of making. Phillis was just the same as ever the next time I saw her after her abrupt passing me in the hall. She never gave any explanation of her rush out of the room.

So all things went on, at least as far as my observation reached at the time, or memory can recall now, till the great apple-gathering of the year. The nights were frosty, the mornings and evenings were misty, but at mid-day all was sunny and bright, and it was one mid-day that both of us being on the line near Heathbridge, and knowing that they were gathering apples at the farm, we resolved to spend the men's dinner-hour in going over there. We found the great clothes-baskets full of apples, scenting the house, and stopping up the way; and an universal air of merry contentment with this the final produce of the year. The yellow leaves hung on the trees ready to flutter down at the slightest puff of air; the great bushes of Michaelmas daisies in the kitchen-garden were making their last show of flowers. We must needs taste the fruit off the different trees, and pass our judgment as to their flavour; and we went away with our pockets stuffed with those that we liked best. As we had passed to the orchard, Holdsworth had admired and spoken about some flower which he saw; it so happened he had never seen this old-fashioned kind since the days of his boyhood. I do not know whether he had thought anything more about this chance speech of his, but I know I had not – when Phillis, who had been missing just at the last moment of our hurried visit, re-appeared with a little nosegay of this same flower, which she was tying up with a blade of grass. She offered it to Holdsworth as he stood with her father on the point of departure. I saw their faces. I saw for the first time an unmistakable look of love in his black eyes; it was more than gratitude for the little attention; it was tender and beseeching – passionate. She shrank from it in confusion, her glance fell on me; and, partly to hide her emotion, partly out of real kindness at what might appear ungracious neglect of an older friend, she flew off to gather me a few late-blooming China roses. But it was the first time she had ever done anything of the kind for me.

We had to walk fast to be back on the line before the men's return, so we spoke but little to each other, and of course the afternoon was too much occupied for us to have any talk. In the evening we went back to our joint lodgings in Hornby. There, on the table, lay a letter for Holdsworth, which had been forwarded to him from Eltham. As our tea was ready, and I had had nothing to eat since morning, I fell to directly without paying much attention to my companion as he opened and read his letter. He was very silent for a few minutes; at length he said, –

'Old fellow! I'm going to leave you!'

'Leave me!' said I. 'How? When?'

'This letter ought to have come to hand sooner. It is from Greathed the engineer' (Greathed was well known in those days; he is dead now, and his name half-forgotten); 'he wants to see me about some business; in fact, I may as well tell you, Paul, this letter contains a very advantageous proposal for me to go out to Canada, and superintend the making of a line there.'

I was in utter dismay.

'But what will our company say to that?'

'Oh, Greathed has the superintendence of this line, you know; and he is going to be engineer in chief to this Canadian line; many of the shareholders in this company are going in for the other, so I fancy they will make no difficulty in following Greathed's lead. He says he has a young man ready to put in my place.'

'I hate him,' said I.

'Thank you,' said Holdsworth, laughing.

'But you must not,' he resumed; 'for this is a very good thing for me, and, of course, if no one can be found to take my inferior work, I can't be spared to take the superior. I only wish I had received this letter a day sooner. Every hour is of consequence, for Greathed says they are threatening a rival line. Do you know, Paul, I almost fancy I must go up to-night? I can take an engine

274

back to Eltham, and catch the night train. I should not like Greathed to think me lukewarm.'

'But you'll come back?' I asked, distressed at the thought of
this sudden parting.

'Oh, yes! At least I hope so. They may want me to go out by
the next steamer, that will be on Saturday.' He began to eat and
drink standing, but I think he was quite unconscious of the
nature of either his food or his drink.

'I will go to-night. Activity and readiness go a long way in our
profession. Remember that, my boy! I hope I shall come back,
but if I don't, be sure and recollect all the words of wisdom that
have fallen from my lips. Now where's the portmanteau? If I can
gain half an hour for a gathering up of my things in Eltham, so
much the better. I'm clear of debt anyhow; and what I owe for
my lodgings you can pay for me out of my quarter's salary, due
November 4th.'

'Then you don't think you will come back?' I said, despond-
ingly.

'I will come back some time, never fear,' said he, kindly. 'I may
be back in a couple of days, having been found incompetent for
the Canadian work; or I may not be wanted to go out so soon as
I now anticipate. Anyhow you don't suppose I am going to forget
you, Paul – this work out there ought not to take me above two
years, and, perhaps, after that, we may be employed together
again.'

Perhaps! I had very little hope. The same kind of happy days
never returns. However, I did all I could in helping him : clothes,
papers, books, instruments; how we pushed and struggled – how I
stuffed. All was done in a much shorter time than we had calculated upon, when I had run down to the sheds to order the
engine. I was going to drive him to Eltham. We sat ready for a
summons. Holdsworth took up the little nosegay that he had
brought away from the Hope Farm, and had laid on the mantelpiece on first coming into the room. He smelt at it, and caressed it
with his lips.

'What grieves me is that I did not know – that I have not said
good-by to – to them.'

He spoke in a grave tone, the shadow of the coming separation falling upon him at last.

'I will tell them,' said I. 'I am sure they will be very sorry.' Then we were silent.

'I never liked any family so much.'

'I knew you would like them.'

'How one's thoughts change, – this morning I was full of a hope, Paul.' He paused, and then he said, –

'You put that sketch in carefully?'

'That outline of a head?' asked I. But I knew he meant an abortive sketch of Phillis, which had not been successful enough for him to complete it with shading or colouring.

'Yes. What a sweet innocent face it is! and yet so – Oh, dear!'

He sighed and got up, his hands in his pockets, to walk up and down the room in evident disturbance of mind. He suddenly stopped opposite to me.

'You'll tell them how it all was. Be sure and tell the good minister that I was so sorry not to wish him good-by, and to thank him and his wife for all their kindness. As for Phillis, – please God in two years I'll be back and tell her myself all in my heart.'

'You love Phillis, then?' said I.

'Love her! – Yes, that I do. Who could help it, seeing her as I have done? Her character as unusual and rare as her beauty! God bless her! God keep her in her high tranquillity, her pure innocence. – Two years! It is a long time. – But she lives in such seclusion, almost like the sleeping beauty,[4] Paul,' – (he was smiling now, though a minute before I had thought him on the verge of tears,) – 'but I shall come back like a prince from Canada, and waken her to my love. I can't help hoping that it won't be difficult, eh, Paul?'

This touch of coxcombry displeased me a little, and I made no answer. He went on, half apologetically, –

'You see, the salary they offer me is large; and beside that, this experience will give me a name which will entitle me to expect a still larger in any future undertaking.'

'That won't influence Phillis.'

'No! but it will make me more eligible in the eyes of her father and mother.'

I made no answer.

'You give me your best wishes, Paul,' said he, almost pleading. 'You would like me for a cousin?'

I heard the scream and whistle of the engine ready down at the sheds.

'Ay, that I should,' I replied, suddenly softened towards my friend now that he was going away. 'I wish you were to be married to-morrow, and I were to be best man.'

'Thank you, lad. Now for this cursed portmanteau (how the minister would be shocked); but it is heavy!' and off we sped into the darkness.

He only just caught the night train at Eltham, and I slept, desolately enough, at my old lodgings at Miss Dawson's, for that night. Of course the next few days I was busier than ever, doing both his work and my own. Then came a letter from him, very short and affectionate. He was going out in the Saturday steamer, as he had more than half expected; and by the following Monday the man who was to succeed him would be down at Eltham. There was a P.S., with only these words: —

'My nosegay goes with me to Canada; but I do not need it to remind me of Hope Farm.'

Saturday came; but it was very late before I could go out to the farm. It was a frosty night, the stars shone clear above me, and the road was crisping beneath my feet. They must have heard my footsteps before I got up to the house. They were sitting at their usual employments in the house-place when I went in. Phillis's eyes went beyond me in their look of welcome, and then fell in quiet disappointment on her work.

'And where's Mr Holdsworth?' asked cousin Holman, in a minute or two. 'I hope his cold is not worse, — I did not like his short cough.'

I laughed awkwardly; for I felt that I was the bearer of unpleasant news.

'His cold had need be better — for he's gone — gone away to Canada!'

I purposely looked away from Phillis, as I thus abruptly told my news.

'To Canada!' said the minister.

'Gone away!' said his wife.

But no word from Phillis.

'Yes!' said I. 'He found a letter at Hornby when we got home the other night – when we got home from here; he ought to have got it sooner; he was ordered to go up to London directly, and to see some people about a new line in Canada, and he's gone to lay it down; he has sailed to-day. He was sadly grieved not to have time to come out and wish you all good-by; but he started for London within two hours after he got that letter. He bade me thank you most gratefully for all your kindnesses; he was very sorry not to come here once again.'

Phillis got up and left the room with noiseless steps.

'I am very sorry,' said the minister.

'I am sure so am I!' said cousin Holman. 'I was real fond of that lad ever since I nursed him last June after that bad fever.'

The minister went on asking me questions respecting Holdsworth's future plans; and brought out a large old-fashioned atlas, that he might find out the exact places between which the new railroad was to run. Then supper was ready; it was always on the table as soon as the clock on the stairs struck eight, and down came Phillis – her face white and set, her dry eyes looking defiance to me, for I am afraid I hurt her maidenly pride by my glance of sympathetic interest as she entered the room. Never a word did she say – never a question did she ask about the absent friend, yet she forced herself to talk.

And so it was all the next day. She was as pale as could be, like one who has received some shock; but she would not let me talk to her, and she tried hard to behave as usual. Two or three times I repeated, in public, the various affectionate messages to the family with which I was charged by Holdsworth; but she took no more notice of them than if my words had been empty air. And in this mood I left her on the Sabbath evening.

My new master was not half so indulgent as my old one. He kept up strict discipline as to hours, so that it was some time before I could again go out, even to pay a call at the Hope Farm.

It was a cold misty evening in November. The air even indoors, seemed full of haze; yet there was a great log burning on the hearth, which ought to have made the room cheerful. Cousin Holman and Phillis were sitting at the little round table before the fire, working away in silence. The minister had his books out on the dresser, seemingly deep in study, by the light of his solitary candle; perhaps the fear of disturbing him made the unusual stillness of the room. But a welcome was ready for me from all; not noisy, not demonstrative – that it never was; my damp wrappers were taken off, the next meal was hastened, and a chair placed for me on one side of the fire, so that I pretty much commanded a view of the room. My eye caught on Phillis, looking so pale and weary, and with a sort of aching tone (if I may call it so) in her voice. She was doing all the accustomed things – fulfilling small household duties, but somehow differently – I can't tell you how, for she was just as deft and quick in her movements, only the light spring was gone out of them. Cousin Holman began to question me; even the minister put aside his books, and came and stood on the opposite side of the fire-place, to hear what waft of intelligence I brought. I had first to tell them why I had not been to see them for so long – more than five weeks. The answer was simple enough; business and the necessity of attending strictly to the orders of a new superintendent, who had not yet learned trust, much less indulgence. The minister nodded his approval of my conduct, and said, –

'Right, Paul ! "Servants, obey in all things your master according to the flesh."[5] I have had my fears lest you had too much licence under Edward Holdsworth.'

'Ah,' said cousin Holman, 'poor Mr Holdsworth, he'll be on the salt seas by this time !'

'No, indeed,' said I, 'he's landed. I have had a letter from him from Halifax.'

Immediately a shower of questions fell thick upon me. When? How? What was he doing? How did he like it? What sort of a voyage? &c.

'Many is the time we have thought of him when the wind was blowing so hard; the old quince-tree is blown down, Paul, that on the right-hand of the great pear-tree; it was blown down last Monday week, and it was that night that I asked the minister to pray in an especial manner for all them that went down in ships upon the great deep,[6] and he said then, that Mr Holdsworth might be already landed; but I said, even if the prayer did not fit him, it was sure to be fitting somebody out at sea, who would need the Lord's care. Both Phillis and I thought he would be a month on the seas.'

Phillis began to speak, but her voice did not come rightly at first. It was a little higher pitched than usual, when she said, –

'We thought he would be a month if he went in a sailing-vessel, or perhaps longer. I suppose he went in a steamer?'[7]

'Old Obadiah Grimshaw was more than six weeks in getting to America,' observed cousin Holman.

'I presume he cannot as yet tell how he likes his new work?' asked the minister.

'No! he is but just landed; it is but one page long. I'll read it to you, shall I? –

DEAR PAUL, –

'WE are safe on shore, after a rough passage, Thought you would like to hear this, but homeward-bound steamer is making signals for letters. Will write again soon. It seems a year since I left Hornby. Longer since I was at the farm. I have got my nosegay safe. Remember me to the Holmans.

'Yours,   'E. H.'

'That's not much, certainly,' said the minister. 'But it's a comfort to know he's on land these blowy nights.'

Phillis said nothing. She kept her head bent down over her work; but I don't think she put a stitch in, while I was reading the letter. I wondered if she understood what nosegay was meant; but I could not tell. When next she lifted up her face, there were two spots of brilliant colour on the cheeks that had been so pale before. After I had spent an hour or two there, I was bound to return back to Hornby. I told them I did not know when I could come again, as we – by which I mean the company – had undertaken the Hensleydale line; that branch for which poor Holdsworth was surveying when he caught his fever.

'But you'll have a holiday at Christmas,' said my cousin. 'Surely they'll not be such heathens as to work you then?'

'Perhaps the lad will be going home,' said the minister, as if to mitigate his wife's urgency; but for all that, I believe he wanted me to come. Phillis fixed her eyes on me with a wistful expression, hard to resist. But, in deed, I had no thought of resisting. Under my new master I had no hope of a holiday long enough to enable me to go to Birmingham and see my parents with any comfort; and nothing could be pleasanter to me than to find myself at home at my cousin's for a day or two, then. So it was fixed that we were to meet in Hornby Chapel on Christmas Day, and that I was to accompany them home after service, and if possible to stay over the next day.

I was not able to get to chapel till late on the appointed day, and so I took a seat near the door in considerable shame, although it really was not my fault. When the service was ended, I went and stood in the porch to await the coming out of my cousins. Some worthy people belonging to the congregation clustered into a group just where I stood, and exchanged the good wishes of the season. It had just begun to snow, and this occasioned a little delay, and they fell into further conversation. I was not attending to what was not meant for me to hear, till I caught the name of Phillis Holman. And then I listened; where was the harm?

'I never saw any one so changed!'

'I asked Mrs Holman,' quoth another, ' "Is Phillis well?" and she just said she had been having a cold which had pulled her down; she did not seem to think anything of it.'

'They had best take care of her,' said one of the oldest of the good ladies; 'Phillis comes of a family as is not long-lived. Her mother's sister, Lydia Green, her own aunt as was, died of a decline just when she was about this lass's age.'

This ill-omened talk was broken in upon by the coming out of the minister, his wife and daughter, and the consequent interchange of Christmas compliments. I had had a shock, and felt heavy-hearted and anxious, and hardly up to making the appropriate replies to the kind greetings of my relations. I looked askance at Phillis. She had certainly grown taller and slighter, and was thinner; but there was a flush of colour on her face which deceived me for a time, and made me think she was looking as well as ever. I only saw her paleness after we had returned to the farm, and she had subsided into silence and quiet. Her grey eyes looked hollow and sad; her complexion was of a dead white. But she went about just as usual; at least, just as she had done the last time I was there, and seemed to have no ailment; and I was inclined to think that my cousin was right when she had answered the inquiries of the good-natured gossips, and told them that Phillis was suffering from the consequences of a bad cold, nothing more.

I have said that I was to stay over the next day; a great deal of snow had come down, but not all, they said, though the ground was covered deep with the white fall. The minister was anxiously housing his cattle, and preparing all things for a long continuance of the same kind of weather. The men were chopping wood, sending wheat to the mill to be ground before the road should become impassable for a cart and horse. My cousin and Phillis had gone upstairs to the apple-room to cover up the fruit from the frost. I had been out the greater part of the morning, and came in about an hour before dinner. To my surprise, knowing how she had planned to be engaged, I found Phillis sitting at the dresser, resting her head on her two hands and reading, or seeming to read. She did not look up when I came in, but murmured something about her mother having sent her down out of the cold. It flashed across me that she was crying, but I put it down to some little spirit of temper; I might have known better than to suspect the gentle, serene Phillis of crossness, poor girl; I stooped down, and began to stir and build up the fire, which appeared to have been neglected. While my head was down I heard a noise which made me pause and listen – a sob, an unmistakable, irrepressible sob. I started up.

'Phillis!' I cried, going towards her, with my hand out, to take hers for sympathy and her sorrow, whatever it was. But she was too quick for me, she held her hand out of my grasp, for fear of my detaining her; as she quickly passed out of the house, she said, –

'Don't, Paul! I cannot bear it!' and passed me, still sobbing, and went out into the keen, open air.

I stood still and wondered. What could have come to Phillis?

The most perfect harmony prevailed in the family, and Phillis especially, good and gentle as she was, was so beloved that if they had found out that her finger ached, it would have cast a shadow over their hearts. Had I done anything to vex her? No: she was crying before I came in. I went to look at her book – one of those unintelligible Italian books. I could make neither head nor tail of it. I saw some pencil-notes on the margin, in Holdsworth's handwriting.

Could that be it? Could that be the cause of her white looks, her weary eyes, her wasted figure, her struggling sobs? This idea came upon me like a flash of lightning on a dark night, making all things so clear we cannot forget them afterwards when the gloomy obscurity returns. I was still standing with the book in my hand when I heard cousin Holman's footsteps on the stairs, and as I did not wish to speak to her just then, I followed Phillis's example, and rushed out of the house. The snow was lying on the ground; I could track her feet by the marks they had made; I could see where Rover had joined her. I followed on till I came to a great stack of wood in the orchard – it was built up against the back wall of the outbuildings, – and I recollected then how Phillis had told me, that first day when we strolled together, that underneath this stack had been her hermitage, her sanctuary, when she was a child; how she used to bring her book to study there, or her work, when she was not wanted in the house; and she had now evidently gone back to this quiet retreat of her childhood, forgetful of the clue given me by her footmarks on the new-fallen snow. The stack was built up very high; but through the interstices of the sticks I could see her figure, although I did not all at once perceive how I could get to her. She was sitting on a log of wood, Rover by her. She had laid her cheek on Rover's head, and had her arm round his neck, partly for a pillow, partly from an instinctive craving for warmth on that bitter cold day. She was making a low moan, like an animal in pain, or perhaps more like the sobbing of the wind. Rover, highly flattered by her caress, and also, perhaps, touched by sympathy, was flapping his heavy tail against the ground, but not otherwise moving a hair, until he heard my approach with his quick erected ears. Then, with a short, abrupt bark of distrust, he sprang up as if to leave his mistress. Both he and I were immovably still for a moment. I was not sure if what I longed to do was wise: and yet I could not bear to see the sweet serenity of my dear cousin's life so disturbed by a suffering which I thought I could assuage. But Rover's ears were sharper than my breathing was noiseless: he heard me, and sprang out from under Phillis's restraining hand.

'Oh, Rover, don't you leave me, too,' she plained out.

'Phillis!' said I, seeing by Rover's exit that the entrance to where she sat was to be found on the other side of the stack. 'Phillis, come out! You have got a cold already; and it is not fit for you to sit there on such a day as this. You know how displeased and anxious it would make them all.'

She sighed, but obeyed; stooping a little, she came out, and stood upright, opposite to me in the lonely, leafless orchard. Her face looked so meek and so sad that I felt as if I ought to beg her pardon for my necessarily authoritative words.

'Sometimes I feel the house so close,' she said; 'and I used to sit under the wood-stack when I was a child. It was very kind of you, but there was no need to come after me. I don't catch cold easily.'

'Come with me into this cow-house, Phillis. I have got something to say to you; and I can't stand this cold, if you can.'

I think she would have fain run away again; but her fit of energy was all spent. She followed me unwillingly enough – that I could see. The place to which I took her was full of the fragrant breath of the cows, and was a little warmer than the outer air. I put her inside, and stood myself in the doorway, thinking how I could best begin. At last I plunged into it.

'I must see that you don't get cold for more reasons than one; if you are ill, Holdsworth will be so anxious and miserable out there' (by which I meant Canada) –

She shot one penetrating look at me, and then turned her face away with a slightly impatient movement. If she could have run away then she would, but I held the means of exit in my own power. 'In for a penny in for a pound,' I thought, and I went on rapidly, anyhow.

'He talked so much about you, just before he left – that night after he had been here, you know – and you had given him those flowers.' She put her hands up to hide her face, but she was listening now – listening with all her ears.

'He had never spoken much about you before, but the sudden going away unlocked his heart, and he told me how he loved you, and how he hoped on his return that you might be his wife.'

'Don't,' said she, almost gasping out the word, which she had tried once or twice before to speak; but her voice had been choked. Now she put her hand backwards; she had quite turned away from me, and felt for mine. She gave it a soft lingering pressure; and then she put her arms down on the wooden division, and laid her head on it, and cried quiet tears. I did not understand her at once, and feared lest I had mistaken the whole case, and only annoyed her. I went up to her. 'Oh, Phillis! I am so sorry – I thought you would, perhaps, have cared to hear it; he did talk so feelingly, as if he did love you so much, and somehow I thought it would give you pleasure.'

She lifted up her head and looked at me. Such a look! Her eyes, glittering with tears as they were, expressed an almost heavenly happiness; her tender mouth was curved with rapture – her colour vivid and blushing; but as if she was afraid her face expressed too much, more than the thankfulness to me she was essaying to speak, she hid it again almost immediately. So it was all right then, and my conjecture was well-founded! I tried to remember something more to tell her of what he had said, but again she stopped me.

'Don't,' she said. She still kept her face covered and hidden. In half a minute she added, in a very low voice, 'Please, Paul, I think I would rather not hear any more – I don't mean but what I have – but what I am very much obliged – Only – only, I think I would rather hear the rest from himself when he comes back.'

And then she cried a little more, in quite a different way. I did not say any more, I waited for her. By-and-by she turned towards me – not meeting my eyes, however; and putting her hand in mine just as if we were two children, she said, –

'We had best go back now – I don't look as if I had been crying, do I?'

'You look as if you had a bad cold,' was all the answer I made.

'Oh! but I am – I am quite well, only cold; and a good run will warm me. Come along, Paul.'

So we ran, hand in hand, till, just as we were on the threshold of the house, she stopped –

'Paul, please, we won't speak about *that* again.'

Part IV

WHEN I went over on Easter Day I heard the chapel-gossips complimenting cousin Holman on her daughter's blooming looks, quite forgetful of their sinister prophecies three months before. And I looked at Phillis, and did not wonder at their words. I had not seen her since the day after Christmas Day. I had left the Hope Farm only a few hours after I had told her the news which had quickened her heart into renewed life and vigour. The remembrance of our conversation in the cow-house was vividly in my mind as I looked at her when her bright healthy appearance was remarked upon. As her eyes met mine our mutual recollections flashed intelligence from one to the other. She turned away, her colour heightening as she did so. She seemed to be shy of me for the first few hours after our meeting, and I felt rather vexed with her for her conscious avoidance of me after my long absence. I had stepped a little out of my usual line in telling her what I did; not that I had received any charge of secrecy, or given even the slightest promise to Holdsworth that I would not repeat his words. But I had an uneasy feeling sometimes when I thought of what I had done in the excitement of seeing Phillis so ill and in so much trouble. I meant to have told Holdsworth when I wrote next to him; but when I had my half-finished letter before me I sate with my pen in my hand hesitating. I had more scruple in revealing what I had found out or guessed at of Phillis's secret than in repeating to her his spoken words. I did not think I had any right to say out to him what I believed – namely, that she loved him dearly, and had felt his absence even to the injury of her health. Yet to explain what I had done in telling her how he had spoken about her that last night, it would be necessary to give my reasons, so I had settled within myself to leave it alone. As she had told me she should like to hear all the details and fuller particulars and more explicit declarations first from him, so he should have the pleasure of extracting the delicious tender

287

secret from her maidenly lips. I would not betray my guesses, my
surmises, my all but certain knowledge of the state of her heart.
I had received two letters from him after he had settled to his
business; they were full of life and energy; but in each there had
been a message to the family at the Hope Farm of more than
common regard; and a slight but distinct mention of Phillis herself, showing that she stood single and alone in his memory.
These letters I had sent on to the minister, for he was sure to care
for them, even supposing he had been unacquainted with their
writer, because they were so clever and so picturesquely worded
that they brought, as it were, a whiff of foreign atmosphere into
his circumscribed life. I used to wonder what was the trade or
business in which the minister would not have thriven, mentally
I mean, if it had so happened that he had been called into that
state. He would have made a capital engineer, that I know; and
he had a fancy for the sea, like many other land-locked men to
whom the great deep is a mystery and a fascination. He read law-
books with relish; and, once happening to borrow *De Lolme on
the British Constitution* (or some such title),[1] he talked about
jurisprudence till he was far beyond my depth. But to return to
Holdsworth's letters. When the minister sent them back he also
wrote out a list of questions suggested by their perusal, which I
was to pass on in my answers to Holdsworth, until I thought of
suggesting direct correspondence between the two. That was the
state of things as regarded the absent one when I went to the
farm for my Easter visit, and when I found Phillis in that state
of shy reserve towards me which I have named before. I thought
she was ungrateful; for I was not quite sure if I had done wisely
in having told her what I did. I had committed a fault, or a folly,
perhaps, and all for her sake; and here was she, less friends with
me than she had even been before. This little estrangement only
lasted a few hours. I think that as soon as she felt pretty sure of
there being no recurrence, either by word, look, or allusion, to the
one subject that was predominant in her mind, she came back to
her old sisterly ways with me. She had much to tell me of her
own familiar interests; how Rover had been ill, and how anxious
they had all of them been, and how, after some little discussion
between her father and her, both equally grieved by the sufferings

of the old dog, he had been 'remembered in the household prayers,' and how he had begun to get better only the very next day, and then she would have led me into a conversation on the right ends of prayer, and on special providences, and I know not what; only I 'jibbed' like their old cart-horse, and refused to stir a step in that direction. Then we talked about the different broods of chickens, and she showed me the hens that were good mothers, and told me the characters of all the poultry with the utmost good faith; and in all good faith I listened, for I believe there was a good deal of truth in all she said. And then we strolled on into the wood beyond the ash-meadow, and both of us sought for early primroses, and the fresh green crinkled leaves. She was not afraid of being alone with me after the first day. I never saw her so lovely, or so happy. I think she hardly knew why she was so happy all the time. I can see her now, standing under the budding branches of the gray trees, over which a tinge of green seemed to be deepening day after day, her sun-bonnet fallen back on her neck, her hands full of delicate wood-flowers, quite unconscious of my gaze, but intent on sweet mockery of some bird in neighbouring bush or tree. She had the art of warbling, and replying to the notes of different birds, and knew their song, their habits and ways, more accurately than any one else I ever knew. She had often done it at my request the spring before; but this year she really gurgled, and whistled, and warbled just as they did, out of the very fulness and joy of her heart. She was more than ever the very apple of her father's eye; her mother gave her both her own share of love, and that of the dead child who had died in infancy. I have heard cousin Holman murmur, after a long dreamy look at Phillis, and tell herself how like she was growing to Johnnie, and soothe herself with plaintive inarticulate sounds, and many gentle shakes of the head, for the aching sense of loss she would never get over in this world. The old servants about the place had the dumb loyal attachment to the child of the land, common to most agricultural labourers; not often stirred into activity or expression. My cousin Phillis was like a rose that had come to full bloom on the sunny side of a lonely house, sheltered from storms. I have read in some book of poetry –

> A maid whom there were none to praise,
> And very few to love.[2]

And somehow those lines always reminded me of Phillis; yet they were not true of her either. I never heard her praised; and out of her own household there were very few to love her; but though no one spoke out their approbation, she always did right in her parents' eyes, out of her natural simple goodness and wisdom. Holdsworth's name was never mentioned between us when we were alone; but I had sent on his letters to the minister, as I have said; and more than once he began to talk about our absent friend, when he was smoking his pipe after the day's work was done. Then Phillis hung her head a little over her work, and listened in silence.

'I miss him more than I thought for; no offence to you, Paul. I said once his company was like dram-drinking; that was before I knew him; and perhaps I spoke in a spirit of judgment. To some men's minds everything presents itself strongly, and they speak accordingly; and so did he. And I thought in my vanity of censorship that his were not true and sober words; they would not have been if I had used them, but they were so to a man of his class of perceptions. I thought of the measure with which I had been meting to him when Brother Robinson was here last Thursday, and told me that a poor little quotation I was making from the *Georgics*[3] savoured of vain babbling and profane heathenism He went so far as to say that by learning other languages than our own, we were flying in the face of the Lord's purpose when He had said, at the building of the Tower of Babel,[4] that he would confound their languages so that they should not understand each other's speech. As Brother Robinson was to me, so was I to the quick wits, bright senses, and ready words of Holdsworth.'

The first little cloud upon my peace came in the shape of a letter from Canada, in which there were two or three sentences that troubled me more than they ought to have done, to judge merely from the words employed. It was this: – 'I should feel dreary enough in this out-of-the-way place if it were not for a friendship I have formed with a French Canadian of the name of Ventadour. He and his family are a great resource to me in the long evenings. I never heard such delicious vocal music as the voices of these Ventadour boys and girls in their part songs; and the foreign element retained in their characteristics and manner of living reminds me of some of the happiest days of my life. Lucille, the second daughter, is curiously like Phillis Holman.' In vain I said to myself that it was probably this likeness that made him take pleasure in the society of the Ventadour family. In vain I told my anxious fancy that nothing could be more natural than this intimacy, and that there was no sign of its leading to any consequence that ought to disturb me. I had a presentiment, and I was disturbed; and I could not reason it away. I dare say my presentiment was rendered more persistent and keen by the doubts which would force themselves into my mind, as to whether I had done well in repeating Holdsworth's words to Phillis. Her state of vivid happiness this summer was markedly different to the peaceful serenity of former days. If in my thoughtfulness at noticing this I caught her eye, she blushed and sparkled all over, guessing that I was remembering our joint secret. Her eyes fell before mine, as if she could hardly bear me to see the revelation of their bright glances. And yet I considered again, and comforted myself by the reflection that, if this change had been anything more than my silly fancy, her father or her mother would have perceived it. But they went on in tranquil unconsciousness and undisturbed peace.

A change in my own life was quickly approaching. In the July of this year my occupation on the — railway and its branches came to an end. The lines were completed, and I was to leave —shire, to return to Birmingham, where there was a niche already provided for me in my father's prosperous business. But before I left the north it was an understood thing amongst us all that I was to go and pay a visit of some weeks at the Hope Farm. My father was as much pleased at this plan as I was; and the dear family of cousins often spoke of things to be done, and sights to be shown me, during this visit. My want of wisdom in having told 'that thing' (under such ambiguous words I concealed the injudicious confidence I had made to Phillis) was the only drawback to my anticipations of pleasure.

The ways of life were too simple at the Hope Farm for my coming to them to make the slightest disturbance. I knew my room,

like a son of the house. I knew the regular course of their days,
and that I was expected to fall into it, like one of the family.
Deep summer peace brooded over the place; the warm golden air
was filled with the murmur of insects near at hand, the more
distant sound of voices out in the fields, the clear far-away rumble
of carts over the stone-paved lanes miles away. The heat was too
great for the birds to be singing; only now and then one might
hear the wood-pigeons in the trees beyond the ash-field. The cattle
stood knee-deep in the pond, flicking their tails about to keep off
the flies. The minister stood in the hay-field, without hat or
cravat, coat or waistcoat, panting and smiling. Phillis had been
leading the row of farm-servants, turning the swathes of fragrant
hay with measured movement. She went to the end – to the
hedge, and then, throwing down her rake, she came to me with her
free sisterly welcome. 'Go, Paul!' said the minister. 'We need all
hands to make use of the sunshine to-day. "Whatsoever thine
hand findeth to do, do it with all thy might."[5] It will be a healthy
change of work for thee, lad; and I find my best rest in change of
work.' So off I went, a willing labourer, following Phillis's lead;
it was the primitive distinction of rank; the boy who frightened
the sparrows off the fruit was the last in our rear. We did not
leave off till the red sun was gone down behind the fir-trees bor-
dering the common. Then we went home to supper – prayers – to
bed; some bird singing far into the night, as I heard it through
my open window, and the poultry beginning their clatter and
cackle in the earliest morning. I had carried what luggage I immediately needed with me from my lodgings, and the rest was to
be sent by the carrier. He brought it to the farm betimes that
morning, and along with it he brought a letter or two that had
arrived since I had left. I was talking to cousin Holman – about
my mother's ways of making bread, I remember; cousin Holman
was questioning me, and had got me far beyond my depth – in
the house-place, when the letters were brought in by one of the
men, and I had to pay the carrier for his trouble before I could
look at them. A bill – a Canadian letter! What instinct made me
so thankful that I was alone with my dear unobservant cousin?
What made me hurry them away into my coat-pocket? I do not
know. I felt strange and sick, and made irrelevant answers, I am

afraid. Then I went to my room, ostensibly to carry up my boxes. I sate on the side of my bed and opened my letter from Holdsworth. It seemed to me as if I had read its contents before, and knew exactly what he had got to say. I knew he was going to be married to Lucille Ventadour; nay, that he *was* married; for this was the 5th of July, and he wrote word that his marriage was fixed to take place on the 29th of June. I knew all the reasons he gave, all the raptures he went into. I held the letter loosely in my hands, and looked into vacancy, yet I saw a chaffinch's nest on the lichen-covered trunk of an old apple-tree opposite my window, and saw the mother-bird come fluttering in to feed her brood, – and yet I did not see it, although it seemed to me afterwards as if I could have drawn every fibre, every feather. I was stirred up to action by the merry sound of voices and the clamp of rustic feet coming home for the mid-day meal. I knew I must go down to dinner; I knew, too, I must tell Phillis; for in his happy egotism, his new-fangled foppery, Holdsworth had put in a P.S., saying that he should send wedding-cards to me and some other Hornby and Eltham acquaintances, and 'to his kind friends at Hope Farm.' Phillis had faded away to one among several 'kind friends.' I don't know how I got through dinner that day. I remember forcing myself to eat, and talking hard; but I also recollect the wondering look in the minister's eyes. He was not one to think evil without cause; but many a one would have taken me for drunk. As soon as I decently could I left the table, saying I would go out for a walk. At first I must have tried to stun reflection by rapid walking, for I had lost myself on the high moorlands far beyond the familiar gorse-covered common, before I was obliged for very weariness to slacken my pace. I kept wishing – oh ! how fervently wishing I had never committed that blunder; that the one little half-hour's indiscretion could be blotted out. Alternating with this was anger against Holdsworth; unjust enough, I dare say. I suppose I stayed in that solitary place for a good hour or more, and then I turned homewards, resolving to get over the telling Phillis at the first opportunity, but shrinking from the fulfilment of my resolution so much that when I came into the house and saw Phillis (doors and windows open wide in the sultry weather) alone in the kitchen, I became quite sick with apprehension. She was standing by the dresser, cutting up a great household loaf into hunches of bread for the hungry labourers who might come in any minute, for the heavy thunder-clouds were overspreading the sky. She looked round as she heard my step.

'You should have been in the field, helping with the hay,' said she, in her calm, pleasant voice. I had heard her as I came near the house softly chanting some hymn-tune, and the peacefulness of that seemed to be brooding over her now.

'Perhaps I should. It looks as if it was going to rain.'

'Yes; there is thunder about. Mother has had to go to bed with one of her bad headaches. Now you are come in –'

'Phillis,' said I, rushing at my subject and interrupting her, 'I went a long walk to think over a letter I had this morning – a letter from Canada. You don't know how it has grieved me.' I held it out to her as I spoke. Her colour changed a little, but it was more the reflection of my face, I think, than because she formed any definite idea from my words. Still she did not take the letter. I had to bid her to read it, before she quite understood what I wished. She sate down rather suddenly as she received it into her hands; and, spreading it on the dresser before her, she rested her forehead on the palms of her hands, her arms supported on the table, her figure a little averted, and her countenance thus shaded. I looked out of the open window; my heart was very heavy. How peaceful it all seemed in the farmyard! Peace and plenty. How still and deep was the silence of the house! Tick-tick went the unseen clock on the wide staircase. I had heard the rustle once, when she turned over the page of thin paper. She must have read to the end. Yet she did not move, or say a word, or even sigh. I kept on looking out of the window, my hands in my pockets. I wonder how long that time really was? It seemed to me interminable – unbearable. At length I looked round at her. She must have felt my look, for she changed her attitude with a quick sharp movement, and caught my eyes.

'Don't look so sorry, Paul,' she said. 'Don't, please. I can't bear it. There is nothing to be sorry for. I think not, at least. You have not done wrong, at any rate.' I felt that I groaned, but I don't think she heard me. 'And he, – there's no wrong in his marrying, is there? I'm sure I hope he'll be happy. Oh! how I hope it!'

These last words were like a wail; but I believe she was afraid of breaking down, for she changed the key in which she spoke, and hurried on. 'Lucille – that's our English Lucy, I suppose?[6] Lucille Holdsworth! It's a pretty name; and I hope – I forget what I was going to say. Oh! it was this. Paul, I think we need never speak about this again; only remember you are not to be sorry. You have not done wrong; you have been very, *very* kind; and if I see you looking grieved I don't know what I might do; – I might break down, you know.'

I think she was on the point of doing so then, but the dark storm came dashing down, and the thunder-cloud broke right above the house, as it seemed. Her mother, roused from sleep, called out for Phillis; the men and women from the hayfield came running into shelter, drenched through. The minister followed, smiling, and not unpleasantly excited by the war of elements; for, by dint of hard work through the long summer's day, the greater part of the hay was safely housed in the barn in the field. Once or twice in the succeeding bustle I came across Phillis, always busy, and, as it seemed to me, always doing the right thing. When I was alone in my own room at night I allowed myself to feel relieved; and to believe that the worst was over, and was not so very bad after all. But the succeeding days were very miserable. Sometimes I thought it must be my fancy that falsely represented Phillis to me as strangely changed, for surely, if this idea of mine was well-founded, her parents – her father and mother – her own flesh and blood – would have been the first to perceive it. Yet they went on in their household peace and content; if anything, a little more cheerfully than usual, for the 'harvest of the first-fruits,'[7] the the minister called it, had been more bounteous than usual, and there was plenty all around in which the humblest labourer was made to share. After the one thunderstorm, came one or two lovely serene days, during which the hay was all carried; and then succeeded long soft rains filling the ears of corn, and causing the mown grass to spring afresh. The minister allowed himself a few more hours of relaxation and home enjoyment than usual during this wet spell: hard earth-bound frost was his winter holiday; these wet days, after the hay harvest, his summer holiday. We sate with open windows, the fragrance and the freshness called out by the soft-falling rain filling the house-place; while the quiet ceaseless patter among the leaves outside ought to have had the same lulling effect as all other gentle perpetual sounds, such as mill-wheels and bubbling springs, have on the nerves of happy people. But two of us were not happy. I was sure of myself for one. I was worse than sure, – I was wretchedly anxious about Phillis. Ever since that day of the thunderstorm there had been a new, sharp, discordant sound to me in her voice, a sort of jangle in her tone; and her restless eyes had no quietness in them; and her colour came and went without a cause that I could find out. The minister, happy in ignorance of what most concerned him, brought out his books; his learned volumes and classics. Whether he read and talked to Phillis, or to me, I do not know; but feeling by instinct that she was not, could not be, attending to the peaceful details, so strange and foreign to the turmoil in her heart, I forced myself to listen, and if possible to understand.

'Look here!' said the minister, tapping the old vellum-bound book he held; 'in the first *Georgic* he speaks of rolling and irrigation:[8] a little further on he insists on choice of the best seed, and advises us to keep the drains clear. Again, no Scotch farmer could give shrewder advice than to cut light meadows while the dew is on, even though it involve night-work. It is all living truth in these days.' He began beating time with a ruler upon his knee, to some Latin lines he read aloud just then. I suppose the monotonous chant irritated Phillis to some irregular energy, for I remember the quick knotting and breaking of the thread with which she was sewing. I never heard that snap repeated now, without suspecting some sting or stab troubling the heart of the worker. Cousin Holman, at her peaceful knitting, noticed the reason why Phillis had so constantly to interrupt the progress of her seam.

'It is bad thread, I'm afraid,' she said, in a gentle sympathetic voice. But it was too much for Phillis.

'The thread is bad – everything is bad – I am so tired of it all!' And she put down her work, and hastily left the room. I do not suppose that in all her life Phillis had ever shown so much temper before. In many a family the tone, the manner, would not have been noticed; but here it fell with a sharp surprise upon the sweet, calm atmosphere of home. The minister put down ruler and book, and pushed his spectacles up to his forehead. The mother looked distressed for a moment, and then smoothed her features and said in an explanatory tone, – 'It's the weather, I think. Some people feel it different to others. It always brings on a headache with me.' She got up to follow her daughter, but half-way to the door she thought better of it, and came back to her seat. Good mother! she hoped the better to conceal the unusual spirit of temper, by pretending not to take much notice of it. 'Go on, minister,' she said; 'it is very interesting what you are reading about, and when I don't quite understand it, I like the sound of your voice.' So he went on, but languidly and irregularly, and beat no more time with his ruler to any Latin lines. When the dusk came on, early that July night because of the cloudy sky, Phillis came softly back, making as though nothing had happened. She took up her work, but it was too dark to do many stitches; and she dropped it soon. Then I saw how her hand stole into her mother's, and how this latter fondled it with quiet caresses, while the minister, as fully aware as I was of this tender pantomime, went on talking in a happier tone of voice about things as uninteresting to him, at the time, I verily believe, as they were to me; and that is saying a good deal, and shows how much more real what was passing before him was, even to a farmer, than the agricultural customs of the ancients.

I remember one thing more, – an attack which Betty the servant made upon me one day as I came in through the kitchen where she was churning, and stopped to ask her for a drink of buttermilk.

'I say, cousin Paul,' (she had adopted the family habit of addressing me generally as cousin Paul, and always speaking to me in that form,) 'something's amiss with our Phillis, and I reckon you've a good guess what it is. She's not one to take up wi' such as you,' (not complimentary, but that Betty never was, even to those for whom she felt the highest respect,) 'but I'd as lief yon Holdsworth had never come near us. So there you've a bit o' my mind.'

And a very unsatisfactory bit it was. I did not know what to answer to the glimpse at the real state of the case implied in the

shrewd woman's speech; so I tried to put her off by assuming surprise at her first assertion.

'Amiss with Phillis! I should like to know why you think
anything is wrong with her. She looks as blooming as any one
can do.'

'Poor lad! you're but a big child after all; and you've likely
never heard of a fever-flush. But you know better nor that, my
fine fellow! so don't think for to put me off wi' blooms and blos-
soms and such-like talk. What makes her walk about for hours
and hours o' nights when she used to be abed and asleep? I sleep
next room to her, and hear her plain as can be. What makes her
come in panting and ready to drop into that chair,' – nodding to
one close to the door, – 'and it's "Oh! Betty, some water, please?"
That's the way she comes in now, when she used to come back as
fresh and bright as she went out. If yon friend o' yours has played
her false, he's a deal for t' answer for; she's a lass who's as sweet
and as sound as a nut, and the very apple of her father's eye, and
of her mother's too, only wi' her she ranks second to th' minister.
You'll have to look after yon chap, for I, for one, will stand no
wrong to our Phillis.'

What was I to do or to say? I wanted to justify Holdsworth, to
keep Phillis's secret, and to pacify the woman all in the same
breath. I did not take the best course, I'm afraid.

'I don't believe Holdsworth ever spoke a word of – of love to
her in all his life. I'm sure he didn't.'

'Ay, ay! but there's eyes, and there's hands, as well as tongues;
and a man has two o' th' one and but one o' t'other.'

'And she's so young; do you suppose her parents would not
have seen it?'

'Well! if you axe me that, I'll say out boldly, "No." They've
called her "the child" so long – "the child" is always their name
for her when they talk on her between themselves, as if never
anybody else had a ewe-lamb before them – that she's grown up
to be a woman under their very eyes, and they look on her still
as if she were in her long clothes. And you ne'er heard on a man
falling in love wi' a babby in long clothes!'

'No!' said I, half laughing. But she went on as grave as a judge.

'Ay! you see you'll laugh at the bare thought on it – and I'll be bound th' minister, though he's not a laughing man, would ha' sniggled⁹ at th' notion of falling in love wi' the child. Where's Holdsworth off to?'

'Canada,' said I, shortly.

'Canada here, Canada there,' she replied testily. 'Tell me how far he's off, instead of giving me your gibberish. Is he a two days' journey away? or a three? or a week?'

'He's ever so far off – three weeks at the least,' cried I in despair. 'And he's either married, or just going to be. So there!' I expected a fresh burst of anger. But no; the matter was too serious. Betty sate down, and kept silence for a minute or two. She looked so miserable and downcast, that I could not help going on, and taking her a little into my confidence.

'It is quite true what I said. I know he never spoke a word to her. I think he liked her, but it's all over now. The best thing we can do – the best and kindest for her – and I know you love her, Betty –'

'I nursed her in my arms; I gave her little brother his last taste o' earthly food,' said Betty, putting her apron up to her eyes.

'Well! don't let us show her we guess that she is grieving; she'll get over it the sooner. Her father and mother don't even guess at it, and we must make as if we didn't. It's too late now to do anything else.'

'I'll never let on; I know nought. I've known true love mysel', in my day. But I wish he'd been farred¹⁰ before he ever came near this house, with his "Please Betty" this, and "Please Betty" that, and drinking up our new milk as if he'd been a cat. I hate such beguiling ways.'

I thought it was as well to let her exhaust herself in abusing the absent Holdsworth; if it was shabby and treacherous in me, I came in for my punishment directly.

'It's a caution to a man how he goes about beguiling. Some men do it as easy and innocent as cooing doves. Don't you be none of 'em, my lad. Not that you've got the gifts to do it, either; you're no great shakes to look at, neither for figure, nor yet for face, and it would need be a deaf adder to be taken in wi' your words,¹¹ though there may be no great harm in 'em.' A lad of nineteen or twenty is not flattered by such an out-spoken opinion even from the oldest and ugliest of her sex; and I was only too glad to change the subject by my repeated injunctions to keep Phillis's secret. The end of our conversation was this speech of hers : –

'You great gaupus,[12] for all you're called cousin o' th' minister – many a one is cursed wi' fools for cousins – d'ye think I can't see sense except through your spectacles? I give you leave to cut out my tongue, and nail it up on th' barn-door for a caution to magpies,[13] if I let out on that poor wench, either to herself, or any one that is hers, as the Bible says. Now you've heard me speak Scripture language, perhaps you'll be content, and leave me my kitchen to myself.'

During all these days, from the 5th of July to the 17th, I must have forgotten what Holdsworth had said about sending cards. And yet I think I could not have quite forgotten; but, once having told Phillis about his marriage, I must have looked upon the after consequence of cards as of no importance. At any rate they came upon me as a surprise at last. The penny-post reform, as people call it, had come into operation a short time before;[14] but the never-ending stream of notes and letters which seem now to flow in upon most households had not yet begun its course; at least in those remote parts. There was a post-office at Hornby; and an old fellow, who stowed away the few letters in any or all his pockets, as it best suited him, was the letter-carrier to Heathbridge and the neighbourhood. I have often met him in the lanes thereabouts, and asked him for letters. Sometimes I have come upon him, sitting on the hedge-bank resting; and he has begged me to read him an address, too illegible for his spectacled eyes to decipher. When I used to inquire if he had anything for me, or for Holdsworth (he was not particular to whom he gave up the letters, so that he got rid of them somehow, and could set off homewards), he would say he thought that he had, for such was his invariable safe form of answer; and would fumble in breast-pockets, waistcoat-pockets, breeches-pockets, and, as a last resource, in coat-tail pockets; and at length try to comfort me, if I looked disappointed, by telling me, 'Hoo had missed this toime, but was sure to write to-morrow;' 'Hoo'[15] representing an imaginery sweetheart.

Sometimes I had seen the minister bring home a letter which he had found lying for him at the little shop that was the post-office at Heathbridge, or from the grander establishment at Hornby. Once or twice Josiah, the carter, remembered that the old letter-carrier had trusted him with an epistle to 'Measter,'[16] as they had met in the lanes. I think it must have been about ten days after my arrival at the farm, and my talk to Phillis cutting bread-and-butter at the kitchen dresser, before the day on which the minister suddenly spoke at the dinner-table, and said –

'By-the-by, I've got a letter in my pocket. Reach me my coat here, Phillis.' The weather was still sultry, and for coolness and ease the minister was sitting in his shirt-sleevees. 'I went to Heathbridge about the paper they had sent me, which spoils all the pens – and I called at the post-office, and found a letter for me, unpaid, – and they did not like to trust it to old Zekiel. Ay! here it is! Now we shall hear news of Holdsworth, – I thought I'd keep it till we were all together.' My heart seemed to stop beating, and I hung my head over my plate, not daring to look up. What would come of it now? What was Phillis doing? How was she looking? A moment of suspense, – and then he spoke again. 'Why! what's this? Here are two visiting tickets with his name on, no writing at all. No! it's not his name on both. Mrs Holdsworth! The young man has gone and got married.' I lifted my head at these words; I could not help looking just for one instant at Phillis. It seemed to me as if she had been keeping watch over my face and ways. Her face was brilliantly flushed; her eyes were dry and glittering; but she did not speak; her lips were set together almost as if she was pinching them tight to prevent words or sounds coming out. Cousin Holman's face expressed surprise and interest.

'Well!' she said, 'who'd ha' thought it! He's made quick work of his wooing and wedding. I'm sure I wish him happy. Let me see' – counting on her fingers, – 'October, November, December, January, February, March, April, May, June, July, – at least we're at the 28th, – it is nearly ten months after all, and reckon a month each way off –'

'Did you know of this news before?' said the minister, turning sharp round on me, surprised, I suppose, at my silence, – hardly suspicious, as yet.

'I knew – I had heard – something. It is to a French Canadian young lady,' I went on, forcing myself to talk. 'Her name is Ventadour.'

'Lucille Ventadour!' said Phillis, in a sharp voice, out of tune.

'Then you knew too!' exclaimed the minister.

We both spoke at once. I said, 'I heard of the probability of –, and told Phillis.' She said, 'He is married to Lucille Ventadour, of French descent; one of a large family near St Meurice; am not I right?' I nodded. 'Paul told me, – that is all we know, is not it? Did you see the Howsons, father, in Heathbridge?' and she forced herself to talk more than she had done for several days, asking many questions, trying, as I could see, to keep the conversation off the one raw surface, on which to touch was agony. I had less self-command; but I followed her lead. I was not so much absorbed in the conversation but what I could see that the minister was puzzled and uneasy; though he seconded Phillis's efforts to prevent her mother from recurring to the great piece of news, and uttering continual exclamations of wonder and surprise. But with that one exception we were all disturbed out of our natural equanimity, more or less. Every day, every hour, I was reproaching myself more and more for my blundering officiousness. If only I had held my foolish tongue for that one half-hour; if only I had not been in such impatient haste to do something to relieve pain! I could have knocked my stupid head against the wall in my remorse. Yet all I could do now was to second the brave girl in her efforts to conceal her disappointment and keep her maidenly secret. But I thought that dinner would never, never come to an end. I suffered for her, even more than for myself. Until now everything which I had heard spoken in that happy household were simple words of true meaning. If we had aught to say, we said it; and if any one preferred silence, nay if all did so, there would have been no spasmodic, forced efforts to talk for the sake of talking, or to keep off intrusive thoughts or suspicions.

At length we got up from our places, and prepared to disperse; but two or three of us had lost our zest and interest in the daily labour. The minister stood looking out of the window in silence, and when he roused himself to go out to the fields where his labourers were working, it was with a sigh; and he tried to avert his troubled face as he passed us on his way to the door. When he had left us, I caught sight of Phillis's face, as, thinking herself unobserved, her countenance relaxed for a moment or two into sad, woful weariness. She started into briskness again when her mother spoke, and hurried away to do some little errand at her bidding. When we two were alone, cousin Holman recurred to Holdsworth's marriage. She was one of those people who like to view an event from every side of probability, or even possibility; and she had been cut short from indulging herself in this way during dinner.

'To think of Mr Holdsworth's being married! I can't get over it, Paul. Not but what he was a very nice young man! I don't like her name, though; it sounds foreign. Say it again, my dear. I hope she'll know how to take care of him, English fashion. He is not strong, and if she does not see that his things are well aired, I should be afraid of the old cough.'

'He always said he was stronger than he had ever been before, after that fever.'

'He might think so, but I have my doubts. He was a very pleasant young man, but he did not stand nursing very well. He got tired of being coddled, as he called it. I hope they'll soon come back to England, and then he'll have a chance for his health. I wonder now, if she speaks English; but, to be sure, he can speak foreign tongues like anything, as I've heard the minister say.'

And so we went on for some time, till she became drowsy over her knitting, on the sultry summer afternoon; and I stole away for a walk, for I wanted some solitude in which to think over things, and, alas! to blame myself with poignant stabs of remorse.

I lounged lazily as soon as I got to the wood. Here and there the bubbling, brawling brook circled round a great stone, or a root of an old tree, and made a pool; otherwise it coursed brightly over the gravel and stones. I stood by one of these for more than half an hour, or, indeed, longer, throwing bits of wood or pebbles into the water, and wondering what I could do to remedy the present state of things. Of course all my meditation was of no use; and at length the distant sound of the horn employed to tell the men far afield to leave off work, warned me that it was six o'clock, and time for me to go home. Then I caught wafts of the loud-voiced singing of the evening psalm. As I was crossing the ash-field, I saw the minister at some distance talking to a man. I could not hear what they were saying, but I saw an impatient or dissentient (I could not tell which) gesture on the part of the former, who walked quickly away, and was apparently absorbed in his thoughts, for though he passed within twenty yards of me, as both our paths converged towards home, he took no notice of me. He passed the evening in a way which was even worse than dinner-time. The minister was silent, depressed, even irritable. Poor cousin Holman was utterly perplexed by this unusual frame of mind and temper in her husband; she was not well herself, and was suffering from the extreme and sultry heat, which made her less talkative than usual. Phillis, usually so reverently tender to her parents, so soft, so gentle, seemed now to take no notice of the unusual state of things, but talked to me – to any one, on indifferent subjects, regardless of her father's gravity, of her mother's piteous looks of bewilderment. But once my eyes fell upon her hands, concealed under the table, and I could see the passionate, convulsive manner in which she laced and interlaced her fingers perpetually, wringing them together from time to time, wringing till the compressed flesh became perfectly white. What could I do? I talked with her, as I saw she wished; her grey eyes had dark circles round them, and a strange kind of dark light in them; her cheeks were flushed, but her lips were white and wan. I wondered that others did not read these signs as clearly as I did. But perhaps they did; I think, from what came afterwards, the minister did.

Poor cousin Holman! she worshipped her husband; and the outward signs of his uneasiness were more patent to her simple heart than were her daughter's. After a while she could bear it no longer. She got up, and, softly laying her hand on his broad stooping shoulder, she said, –

'What is the matter, minister? Has anything gone wrong?'

He started as if from a dream. Phillis hung her head, and caught her breath in terror at the answer she feared. But he, looking round with a sweeping glance, turned his broad, wise face up to his anxious wife, and forced a smile, and took her hand in a re-assuring manner.

'I am blaming myself, dear. I have been overcome with anger this afternoon. I scarcely knew what I was doing, but I turned away Timothy Cooper. He has killed the Ribstone pippin at the corner of the orchard; gone and piled the quicklime for the mortar for the new stable wall against the trunk of the tree – stupid fellow ! killed the tree outright – and it loaded with apples !'

'And Ribstone pippins are so scarce,' said sympathetic cousin Holman.

'Ay ! But Timothy is but a half-wit; and he has a wife and children. He had often put me to it sore, with his slothful ways, but I had laid it before the Lord, and striven to bear with him. But I will not stand it any longer, it's past my patience. And he has notice to find another place. Wife, we won't talk more about it.' He took her hand gently off his shoulder, touched it with his lips; but relapsed into a silence as profound, if not quite so morose in appearance, as before. I could not tell why, but this bit of talk between her father and mother seemed to take all the factitious spirits out of Phillis. She did not speak now, but looked out of the open casement at the calm large moon, slowly moving through the twilight sky. Once I thought her eyes were filling with tears; but, if so, she shook them off, and arose with alacrity when her mother, tired and dispirited, proposed to go to bed immediately after prayers. We all said good-night in our separate ways to the minister, who still sat at the table with the great Bible open before him, not much looking up at any of our salutations, but returning them kindly. But when I, last of all, was on the point of leaving the room, he said, still scarcely looking up –

'Paul, you will oblige me by staying here a few minutes. I would fain have some talk with you.'

I knew what was coming, all in a moment. I carefully shut-to the door, put out my candle, and sat down to my fate. He seemed to find some difficulty in beginning, for, if I had not heard that he wanted to speak to me, I should never have guessed it, he seemed so much absorbed in reading a chapter to the end. Suddenly he lifted his head up and said, –

'It is about that friend of yours, Holdsworth! Paul, have you any reason for thinking he has played tricks upon Phillis?'

I saw that his eyes were blazing with such a fire of anger at the bare idea, that I lost all my presence of mind, and only repeated, –

'Played tricks on Phillis!'

'Ay! you know what I mean: made love to her, courted her, made her think that he loved her, and then gone away and left her. Put it as you will, only give me an answer of some kind or another – a true answer, I mean – and don't repeat my words, Paul.'

He was shaking all over as he said this. I did not delay a moment in answering him, –

'I do not believe that Edward Holdsworth ever played tricks on Phillis, ever made love to her; he never, to my knowledge, made her believe that he loved her.'

I stopped; I wanted to nerve up my courage for a confession, yet I wished to save the secret of Phillis's love for Holdsworth as much as I could; that secret which she had so striven to keep sacred and safe; and I had need of some reflection before I went on with what I had to say.

He began again before I had quite arranged my manner of speech. It was almost as if to himself, – 'She is my only child; my little daughter! She is hardly out of childhood; I have thought to gather her under my wings for years to come; her mother and I would lay down our lives to keep her from harm and grief.' Then, raising his voice, and looking at me, he said, 'Something has gone wrong with the child; and it seemed to me to date from the time she heard of that marriage. It is hard to think that you may know more of her secret cares and sorrows than I do, – but perhaps you do, Paul, perhaps you do, – only, if it be not a sin, tell me what I can do to make her happy again; tell me.'

'It will not do much good, I am afraid,' said I, 'but I will own how wrong I did; I don't mean wrong in the way of sin, but in the way of judgment. Holdsworth told me just before he went that he loved Phillis, and hoped to make her his wife, and I told her.'

There! it was out; all my part in it, at least; and I set my lips together, and waited for the words to come. I did not see his face; I looked straight at the wall opposite; but I heard him once begin to speak, and then turn over the leaves in the book before him. How awfully still that room was! The air outside, how still it was! The open windows let in no rustle of leaves, no twitter or movement of birds – no sound whatever. The clock on the stairs – the minister's hard breathing – was it to go on for ever? Impatient beyond bearing at the deep quiet, I spoke again, –

'I did it for the best, as I thought.'

The minister shut the book to hastily, and stood up. Then I saw how angry he was.

'For the best, do you say? It was best, was it, to go and tell a young girl what you never told a word of to her parents, who trusted you like a son of their own?'

He began walking about, up and down the room close under the open windows, churning up his bitter thoughts of me.

'To put such thoughts into the child's head,' continued he; 'to spoil her peaceful maidenhood with talk about another man's love; and such love, too,' he spoke scornfully now – 'a love that is ready for any young woman. Oh, the misery in my poor little daughter's face to-day at dinner – the misery, Paul! I thought you were one to be trusted – your father's son too, to go and put such thoughts into the child's mind; you two talking together about that man wishing to marry her.'

I could not help remembering the pinafore, the childish garment which Phillis wore so long, as if her parents were unaware of her progress towards womanhood. Just in the same way the minister spoke and thought of her now, as a child, whose innocent peace I had spoiled by vain and foolish talk. I knew that the truth was different, though I could hardly have told it now; but, indeed, I never thought of trying to tell; it was far from my mind to add one iota to the sorrow which I had caused. The minister went on walking, occasionally stopping to move things on the table, or articles of furniture, in a sharp, impatient, meaningless way, then he began again, –

'So young, so pure from the world! how could you go and talk to such a child, raising hopes, exciting feelings – all to end thus; and best so, even though I saw her poor piteous face look as it did. I can't forgive you, Paul; it was more than wrong – it was wicked – to go and repeat that man's words.'

His back was now to the door, and, in listening to his low angry tones, he did not hear it slowly open, nor did he see Phillis, standing just within the room, until he turned round; then he stood still. She must have been half undressed; but she had covered herself with a dark winter cloak, which fell in long folds to her white, naked, noiseless feet. Her face was strangely pale: her eyes heavy in the black circles round them. She came up to the table very slowly, and leant her hand upon it, saying mournfully, –

'Father, you must not blame Paul. I could not help hearing a great deal of what you were saying. He did tell me, and perhaps it would have been wiser not, dear Paul! But – oh, dear! oh, dear! I am so sick with shame! He told me out of his kind heart, because he saw – that I was so very unhappy at *his* going away.'

She hung her head, and leant more heavily than before on her supporting hand.

'I don't understand,' said her father; but he was beginning to understand. Phillis did not answer till he asked her again. I could have struck him now for his cruelty; but then I knew all.

'I loved him, father!' she said at length, raising her eyes to the minister's face.

'Had he ever spoken of love to you? Paul says not!'

'Never.' She let fall her eyes, and drooped more than ever. I almost thought she would fall.

'I could not have believed it,' said he, in a hard voice, yet sighing the moment he had spoken. A dead silence for a moment. 'Paul! I was unjust to you. You deserved blame, but not all that I said.' Then again a silence. I thought I saw Phillis's white lips moving, but it might be the flickering of the candlelight – a moth had flown in through the open casement, and was fluttering round the flame; I might have saved it, but I did not care to do so, my heart was too full of other things. At any rate, no sound was heard for long endless minutes. Then he said, – 'Phillis! did we not make you happy here? Have we not loved you enough?'

She did not seem to understand the drift of this question; she looked up as if bewildered, and her beautiful eyes dilated with a painful, tortured expression. He went on, without noticing the look on her face; he did not see it, I am sure.

'And yet you would have left us, left your home, left your father and your mother, and gone away with this stranger, wandering over the world.'

He suffered, too; there were tones of pain in the voice in which he uttered this reproach. Probably the father and daughter were never so far apart in their lives, so unsympathetic. Yet some new terror came over her, and it was to him she turned for help. A shadow came over her face, and she tottered towards her father; falling down, her arms across his knees, and moaning out, –

'Father, my head! my head!' and then she slipped through his quick-enfolding arms, and lay on the ground at his feet.

I shall never forget his sudden look of agony while I live; never! We raised her up; her colour had strangely darkened; she was insensible. I ran through the back-kitchen to the yard pump, and brought back water. The minister had her on his knees, her head against his breast, almost as though she were a sleeping child. He was trying to rise up with his poor precious burden, but the momentary terror had robbed the strong man of his strength, and he sank back in his chair with sobbing breath.

'She is not dead, Paul! is she?' he whispered, hoarse, as I came near him.

I, too, could not speak, but I pointed to the quivering of the muscles round her mouth. Just then cousin Holman, attracted by some unwonted sound, came down. I remember I was surprised at the time at her presence of mind, she seemed to know so much better what to do than the minister, in the midst of the sick affright which blanched her countenance, and made her tremble all over. I think now that it was the recollection of what had gone before; the miserable thought that possibly his words had brought on this attack, whatever it might be, that so unmanned the minister. We carried her up-stairs, and while the women were putting her to bed, still unconscious, still slightly convulsed, I slipped out, and saddled one of the horses, and rode as fast as the heavy-trotting beast could go, to Hornby, to find the doctor there, and bring him back. He was out, might be detained the whole night. I remember saying, 'God help us all!' as I sate on my horse, under the window, through which the apprentice's head had appeared to answer my furious tugs at the night-bell. He was a good-natured fellow. He said, –

'He may be home in half an hour, there's no knowing; but I daresay he will. I'll send him out to the Hope Farm directly he comes in. It's that good-looking young woman, Holman's daughter, that's ill, isn't it?'

'Yes.'

'It would be a pity if she was to go. She's an only child, isn't she? I'll get up, and smoke a pipe in the surgery, ready for the governor's coming home. I might go to sleep if I went to bed again.'

'Thank you, you're a good fellow!' and I rode back almost as quickly as I came.

It was a brain fever. The doctor said so, when he came in the early summer morning. I believe we had come to know the nature of the illness in the night-watches that had gone before. As to hope of ultimate recovery, or even evil prophecy of the probable end, the cautious doctor would be entrapped into neither. He gave his directions, and promised to come again; so soon, that this one thing showed his opinion of the gravity of the case.

By God's mercy she recovered, but it was a long, weary time first. According to previously made plans, I was to have gone home at the beginning of August. But all such ideas were put aside now, without a word being spoken. I really think that I was necessary in the house, and especially to the minister at this time; my father was the last man in the world under such circumstances, to expect me home.

I say, I think I was necessary in the house. Every person (I had almost said every creature, for all the dumb beasts seemed to know and love Phillis) about the place went grieving and sad, as though a cloud was over the sun. They did their work, each striving to steer clear of the temptation to eye-service, in fulfilment of the trust reposed in them by the minister. For the day after Phillis had been taken ill, he had called the men employed on the farm into the empty barn; and there he had entreated their prayers for

his only child; and then and there he had told them of his present incapacity for thought about any other thing in this world
but his little daughter, lying nigh unto death, and he had asked
them to go on with their daily labours as best they could, without
his direction. So, as I say, these honest men did their work to the
best of their ability, but they slouched along with sad and careful
faces, coming one by one in the dim mornings to ask news of the
sorrow that overshadowed the house; and receiving Betty's intelligence, always darkened by passing through her mind, with slow
shakes of the head, and a dull wistfulness of sympathy. But, poor
fellows, they were hardly fit to be trusted with hasty messages,
and here my poor services came in. One time I was to ride hard
to Sir William Bentinck's, and petition for ice out of his ice-house,
to put on Phillis's head. Another it was to Eltham I must go, by
train, horse, anyhow, and bid the doctor there come for a consultation, for fresh symptoms appeared, which Mr Brown, of Hornby, considered unfavourable. Many an hour have I sate on the
window-seat, half-way up the stairs, close by the old clock, listening in the hot stillness of the house for the sounds in the sick-
room. The minister and I met often, but spoke together seldom.
He looked so old – so old! He shared the nursing with his wife;
the strength that was needed seemed to be given to them both in
that day. They required no one else about their child. Every office
about her was sacred to them; even Betty only went into the
room for the most necessary purposes. Once I saw Phillis through
the open door; her pretty golden hair had been cut off long
before; her head was covered with wet cloths, and she was moving
it backwards and forwards on the pillow, with weary, never-
ending motion, her poor eyes shut, trying in the old accustomed
way to croon out a hymn tune, but perpetually breaking it up
into moans of pain. Her mother sate by her, tearless, changing
the cloths upon her head with patient solicitude. I did not see the
minister at first, but there he was in a dark corner, down upon
his knees, his hands clasped together in passionate prayer. Then
the door shut, and I saw no more.

One day he was wanted; and I had to summon him. Brother
Robinson and another minister, hearing of his 'trial,' had come to

see him. I told him this upon the stair-landing in a whisper. He was strangely troubled.

'They will want me to lay bare my heart. I cannot do it. Paul, stay with me. They mean well; but as for spiritual help at such a time – it is God only, God only, who can give it.'

So I went in with him. They were two ministers from the neighbourhood; both older than Ebenezer Holman; but evidently inferior to him in education and worldly position. I thought they looked at me as if I were an intruder, but remembering the minister's words I held my ground, and took up one of poor Phillis's books (of which I could not read a word) to have an ostensible occupation. Presently I was asked to 'engage in prayer,' and we all knelt down; Brother Robinson 'leading,' and quoting largely as I remember from the Book of Job. He seemed to take for his text, if texts are ever taken for prayers, 'Behold thou hast instructed many; but now it is come upon thee, and thou faintest, it toucheth thee and thou art troubled.'[17] When we others rose up, the minister continued for some minutes on his knees. Then he too got up, and stood facing us, for a moment, before we all sate down in conclave. After a pause Robinson began –

'We grieve for you, Brother Holman, for your trouble is great. But we would fain have you remember you are as a light set on a hill;[18] and the congregations are looking at you with watchful eyes. We have been talking as we came along on the two duties required of you in this strait; Brother Hodgson and me. And we have resolved to exhort you on these two points. First, God has given you the opportunity of showing forth an example of resignation.' Poor Mr Holman visibly winced at this word. I could fancy how he had tossed aside such brotherly preachings in his happier moments; but now his whole system was unstrung, and 'resignation' seemed a term which presupposed that the dreaded misery of losing Phillis was inevitable. But good stupid Mr Robinson went on. 'We hear on all sides that there are scarce any hopes of your child's recovery; and it may be well to bring you to mind of Abraham; and how he was willing to kill his only child when the Lord commanded. Take example by him, Brother Holman. Let us hear you say, "The Lord giveth and the Lord taketh away. Blessed be the name of the Lord!"'[19]

There was a pause of expectancy. I verily believe the minister tried to feel it; but he could not. Heart of flesh was too strong. Heart of stone he had not.

'I will say it to my God, when He gives me strength, – when the day comes,' he spoke at last.

The other two looked at each other, and shook their heads. I think the reluctance to answer as they wished was not quite unexpected. The minister went on: 'There are hopes yet,' he said, as if to himself. 'God has given me a great heart for hoping, and I will not look forward beyond the hour.' Then turning more to them, and speaking louder, he added: 'Brethren, God will strengthen me when the times comes, when such resignation as you speak of is needed. Till then I cannot feel it; and what I do not feel I will not express; using words as if they were a charm.' He was getting chafed, I could see.

He had rather put them out by these speeches of his; but after a short time and some more shakes of the head, Robinson began again, –

'Secondly, we would have you listen to the voice of the rod, and ask yourself for what sins this trial has been laid upon you; whether you may not have been too much given up to your farm and your cattle; whether this world's learning has not puffed you up to vain conceit and neglect of the things of God; whether you have not made an idol of your daughter?'

'I cannot answer – I will not answer!' exclaimed the minister. 'My sins I confess to God.[20] But if they were scarlet (and they are so in His sight,' he added, humbly), 'I hold with Christ that afflictions are not sent by God in wrath as penalties for sin.'

'Is that orthodox, Brother Robinson?' asked the third minister, in a deferential tone of inquiry.

Despite the minister's injunction not to leave him, I thought matters were getting so serious that a little homely interruption would be more to the purpose than my continued presence, and I went round to the kitchen to ask for Betty's help.

"Od rot 'em!' said she; 'they're always a-coming at illconvenient times; and they have such hearty appetites, they'll make nothing of what would have served master and you since our poor lass has been ill. I've but a bit of cold beef in th' house; but

I'll do some ham and eggs, and that'll rout 'em from worrying the minister. They're a deal quieter after they've had their victual. Last time as old Robinson came, he was very reprehensible upon master's learning, which he couldn't compass to save his life, so he needn't have been afeard of that temptation, and used words long enough to have knocked a body down; but after me and missus had given him his fill of victual, and he'd had some good ale and a pipe, he spoke just like any other man, and could crack a joke with me.'

Their visit was the only break in the long weary days and nights. I do not mean that no other inquiries were made. I believe that all the neighbours hung about the place daily till they could learn from some out-comer how Phillis Holman was. But they knew better than to come up to the house, for the August weather was so hot that every door and window was kept constantly open, and the least sound outside penetrated all through. I am sure the cocks and hens had a sad time of it; for Betty drove them all into an empty barn, and kept them fastened up in the dark for several days, with very little effect as regarded their crowing and clacking. At length came a sleep which was the crisis, and from which she wakened up with a new faint life. Her slumber had lasted many, many hours. We scarcely dared to breathe or move during the time; we had striven to hope so long, that we were sick at heart, and durst not trust in the favourable signs : the even breathing, the moistened skin, the slight return of delicate colour into the pale, wan lips. I recollect stealing out that evening in the dusk, and wandering down the grassy lane, under the shadow of the over-arching elms to the little bridge at the foot of the hill, where the lane to the Hope Farm joined another road to Hornby. On the low parapet of that bridge I found Timothy Cooper, the stupid, half-witted labourer, sitting, idly throwing bits of mortar into the brook below. He just looked up at me as I came near, but gave me no greeting, either by word or gesture. He had generally made some sign of recognition to me, but this time I thought he was sullen at being dismissed. Nevertheless I felt as if it would be a relief to talk a little to some one, and I sate down by him. While I was thinking how to begin, he yawned weariedly.

'You are tired, Tim?' said I.

'Ay,' said he. 'But I reckon I may go home now.'

'Have you been sitting here long?'

'Welly all day long.[21] Leastways sin' seven i' th' morning.'

'Why what in the world have you been doing?'

'Nought.'

'Why have you been sitting here, then?'

'T' keep carts off.' He was up now, stretching himself, and shaking his lubberly limbs.

'Carts! what carts?'

'Carts as might ha' wakened yon wench! It's Hornby market-day. I reckon yo're no better nor a half-wit yoursel'.' He cocked his eye at me as if he were gauging my intellect.

'And have you been sitting here all day to keep the lane quiet?'

'Aye. I've nought else to do. Th' minister has turned me adrift. Have yo' heard how th' lass is faring to-night?'

'They hope she'll waken better for this long sleep. Good-night to you, and God bless you, Timothy,' said I.

He scarcely took any notice of my words, as he lumbered across a stile that led to his cottage. Presently I went home to the farm. Phillis had stirred, had spoken two or three faint words. Her mother was with her, dropping nourishment into her scarce conscious mouth. The rest of the household were summoned to evening prayer for the first time for many days. It was a return to the daily habits of happiness and health. But in these silent days our very lives had been an unspoken prayer. Now we met in the house-place, and looked at each other with strange recognition of the thankfulness on all our faces. We knelt down; we waited for the minister's voice. He did not begin as usual. He could not; he was choking. Presently we heard the strong man's sob. Then old John turned round on his knees, and said –

'Minister, I reckon we have blessed the Lord wi' all our souls, though we've ne'er talked about it; and maybe He'll not need spoken words this night. God bless us all, and keep our Phillis safe from harm! Amen.'

Old John's impromptu prayer was all we had that night.

'Our Phillis,' as he called her, grew better day by day from that time. Not quickly; I sometimes grew desponding, and feared that she would never be what she had been before; no more she has, in some ways.

I seized an early opportunity to tell the minister about Timothy Cooper's unsolicited watch on the bridge during the long summer's day.

'God forgive me!' said the minister. 'I have been too proud in my own conceit. The first steps I take out of this house shall be to Cooper's cottage.'

I need hardly say Timothy was reinstated in his place on the farm; and I have often since admired the patience with which his master tried to teach him how to do the easy work which was henceforward carefully adjusted to his capacity.

Phillis was carried downstairs, and lay for hour after hour quite silent on the great sofa, drawn up under the windows of the house-place. She seemed always the same, gentle, quiet, and sad. Her energy did not return with her bodily strength. It was sometimes pitiful to see her parents' vain endeavours to rouse her to interest. One day the minister brought her a set of blue ribbons, reminding her with a tender smile of a former conversation in which she had owned to a love of such feminine vanities. She spoke gratefully to him, but when he was gone she laid them on one side, and languidly shut her eyes. Another time I saw her mother bring her the Latin and Italian books that she had been so fond of before her illness – or, rather, before Holdsworth had gone away. That was worst of all. She turned her face to the wall, and cried as soon as her mother's back was turned. Betty was laying the cloth for the early dinner. Her sharp eyes saw the state of the case.

'Now, Phillis!' said she, coming up to the sofa; 'we ha' done a' we can for you, and th' doctors has done a' they can for you, and I think the Lord has done a' He can for you, and more than you deserve, too, if you don't do something for yourself. If I were you, I'd rise up and snuff the moon, sooner than break your father's and your mother's hearts wi' watching and waiting till it pleases you to fight your own way back to cheerfulness. There, I never favoured long preachings, and I've said my say.'

A day or two after Phillis asked me, when we were alone, if I thought my father and mother would allow her to go and stay with them for a couple of months. She blushed a little as she faltered out her wish for change of thought and scene.

'Only for a short time, Paul. Then – we will go back to the peace of the old days. I know we shall; I can, and I will!'

APPENDIX A

The Last Generation in England

I HAVE just taken up by chance an old number of the Edinburgh Review (April 1848), in which it is said that Southey had proposed to himself to write a 'history of English domestic life.'[1] I will not enlarge upon the infinite loss we have had in the non-fulfilment of this plan; every one must in some degree feel its extent who has read those charming glimpses of home scenes contained in the early volumes of the 'Doctor, &c.'[2] This quarter of an hour's chance reading has created a wish in me to put upon record some of the details of country town life, either observed by myself, or handed down to me by older relations; for even in small towns, scarcely removed from villages, the phases of society are rapidly changing; and much will appear strange, which yet occurred only in the generation immediately preceding ours. I must however say before going on, that although I choose to disguise my own identity, and to conceal the name of the town to which I refer, every circumstance and occurrence which I shall relate is strictly and truthfully told without exaggeration. As for classing the details with which I am acquainted under any heads, that will be impossible from their heterogeneous nature; I must write them down as they arise in my memory.

The town in which I once resided is situated in a district inhabited by large landed proprietors of very old family. The daughters of these families, if unmarried, retired to live in — on their annuities, and gave the ton[3] to the society there, stately ladies they were, remembering etiquette and precedence in every occurrence of life, and having their genealogy at their tongue's end. Then there were the widows of the cadets[4] of these same families; also poor, and also proud, but I think more genial and less given to recounting their pedigrees than the former. Then came the professional men and their wives; who were more wealthy than the ladies I have named, but who always treated them with deference and respect, sometimes even amounting to obsequiousness; for was there not 'my brother, Sir John —,' and 'my uncle, Mr —, of —,' to give employment and patronage to the doctor or the attorney? A grade lower came a class of single or widow ladies; and again it was possible, not to say probable, that their pecuniary circumstances were in better condition than those of the aristocratic dames, who nevertheless refused to meet in general society the *ci-devant*[5] housekeepers, or widows of stewards, who had been employed by their fathers and brothers, they would occasionally condescend to ask 'Mason,' or 'that good Bentley,' to a private tea-drinking, at which I doubt not much gossip relating to former days at the hall would pass; but that was patronage; to associate with them at another person's house, would have been an acknowledgment of equality.

Below again came the shopkeepers, who dared to be original; who gave comfortable suppers after the very early dinners of that day, not checked by the honourable Mr D—'s precedent of a seven o'clock tea on the most elegant and economical principles, and a supperless turn-out at nine. There were the usual respectable and disrespectable poor; and hanging on the outskirts of society were a set of young men, ready for mischief and brutality, and every now and then dropping off the pit's brink into crime. The habits of this class (about forty years ago) were much such as those of the Mohawks a century before.[6] They would stop ladies returning from the card-parties, which were the staple gaiety of the place, and who were only attended by a maidservant bearing a lantern, and whip them; literally whip them as you whip a little child; until administering such chastisement to a good, precise old lady of high family, 'my brother, the magistrate,' came forward and put down such proceedings with a high hand.

Certainly there was more individuality of character in those days than now; no one even in a little town of two thousand inhabitants would now be found to drive out with a carriage full of dogs; each dressed in the male or female fashion of the day, as the case might be; each dog provided with a pair of house-shoes, for which his carriage boots were changed on his return. No old lady would be so oblivious of 'Mrs Grundy's' existence now as to dare to invest her favourite cow, after its unlucky fall into a lime-pit, in flannel waistcoat and drawers, in which the said cow paraded the streets of — to the day of its death.

There were many regulations which were strictly attended to in the society of —, and which probably checked more manifestations of eccentricity. Before a certain hour in the morning calls were never paid, nor yet after a certain hour in the afternoon; the consequence was that everybody was out, calling on everybody at the same time, for it was *de rigueur* that morning calls should be returned within three days; and accordingly, making due allowance for our proportion of rain in England, every fine morning was given up to this employment. A quarter of an hour was the limit of a morning call.

Before the appointed hour of reception, I fancy the employment of many of the ladies was fitting up their laces and muslins (which, for the information of all those whom it may concern, were never ironed, but carefully stretched, and pinned, thread by thread, with most Lilliputian pieces, on a board covered with flannel). Most of these scions of quality had many pounds' worth of valuable laces descended to them from mothers and grand-mothers, which must be 'got up' by no hands, as you may guess, but those of Fairly Fair. Indeed when muslin and net were a guinea a yard, this was not to be wondered at. The lace was washed in buttermilk, which gave rise to an odd little circumstance. One lady left her lace, basted up,[7] in some not very sour buttermilk; and unluckily the cat lapped it up, lace and all (one would have thought the lace would have choked her, but so it was); the lace was too valuable to be lost, so a small dose of tartar emetic was administered to the poor cat; the lace returned to view was carefully darned, and decked the good lady's best cap for many a year after; and many a time did she tell the story, gracefully bridling up in a prim sort of way, and giving a little cough, as if preliminary to a rather improper story. The first sentence of it was always, I remember, 'I do not think you can guess where the lace on my cap has been;' dropping her voice, 'in pussy's inside, my dear!'

The dinner hour was three o'clock in all houses of any pretensions to gentility; and a very late hour it was considered to be.

Soon after four one or two inveterate card-players might be seen in calash and pattens,[8] picking their way along the streets to the house where the party of the evening was to be held. As soon as they arrived and had unpacked themselves, an operation of a good half-hour's duration in the dining-parlour, they were ushered into the drawing-room, where, unless in the very height of summer, it was considered a delicate attention to have the shutters closed, the curtains drawn, and the candles lighted. The card-tables were set out, each with two new packs of cards, for which it was customary to pay each person placing a shilling under one of the candlesticks.

The ladies settled down to Preference, and allowed of no interruption; even the tea-trays were placed on the middle of the card-tables, and tea hastily gulped down with a few remarks on the good or ill fortune of the evening. New arrivals were greeted with nods in the intervals of the game; and as people entered the room, they were pounced upon by the lady of the house to form another table. Cards were a business in those days, not a recreation. Their very names were to be treated with reverence. Some one came to — from a place where flippancy was in fashion; he called the knave 'Jack,' and everybody looked grave, and voted him vulgar; but when he was overheard calling Preference – the decorous, highly-respectable game of Preference, – Pref.,[9] why, what course remained for us but to cut him, and cut him we did.

About half-past eight, notices of servants having arrived for their respective mistresses were given : the games were concluded, accounts settled, a few parting squibs and crackers[10] let off at careless or unlucky partners, and the party separated. By ten o'clock all – was in bed and asleep. I have made no mention of gentlemen at these parties, because if ever there was an Amazonian town in England it was —. Eleven widows of respectability at one time kept house there; besides spinsters innumerable. The doctor preferred his arm-chair and slippers to the forms of society, such as I have described, and so did the attorney, who was besides not insensible to the charms of a hot supper. Indeed, I suppose it was because of the small incomes of the more aristocratic portion of our little society not sufficing both for style and luxury, but it was a fact, that as gentility decreased good living increased in proportion. We had the honour and glory of looking at old plate and delicate china at the *comme il faut*[11] tea-parties, but the slices of bread and butter were like wafers, and the sugar for coffee was rather of the brownest, still there was much gracious kindness among our *haute volée*.[12] In those times, good Mr Rigmarole, carriages were carriages, and there were not the infinite variety of broughams, droskys,[13] &c., &c., down to a wheelbarrow, which now make locomotion easy; nor yet were there cars and cabs and flys ready for hire in our little town. A post-chaise was the only conveyance besides *the* sedan-chair, of which more anon. So the widow of an earl's son, who possessed a proper old-fashioned coach and pair, would, on rainy nights, send her carriage, the only private carriage of —, round the town, picking up all the dowagers and invalids, and conveying them dry and safe to and from their evening engagement. The various other ladies who, in virtue of their relations holding manors and maintaining game-keepers, had frequent presents, during the season, of partridges, pheasants, &c., &c., would daintily carve off the tid-bits, and putting them carefully into a hot basin, bid Betty or Molly cover it up quickly, and carry it to Mrs or Miss So-and-so, whose appetite was but weakly and who required dainties to tempt it which she could not afford to purchase.

These poorer ladies had also their parties in turn; they were too proud to accept invitations if they might not return them, although various and amusing were their innocent make-shifts and imitations. To give you only one instance, I remember a card-party at one of these good ladies' lodgings; where, when tea-time arrived, the ladies sitting on the sofa had to be displaced for a minute, in order that the tea-trays, (plates of cake, bread and butter, and all,) might be extricated from their concealment under the valances of the couch.

You may imagine the subjects of the conversation amongst these ladies; cards, servants, relations, pedigrees, and last and best, much mutual interest about the poor of the town, to whom they were one and all kind and indefatigable benefactresses; cooking, sewing for, advising, doctoring, doing everything but educating them. One or two old ladies dwelt on the glories of former days; when — boasted of two earl's daughters as residents. Though it must be sixty years since they died, there are traces of their characters yet lingering about the place. Proud, precise, and generous; bitter tories they were. Their sister had married a General, more distinguished for a successful comedy, than for his mode of conducting the war in America; and, consequently, his sisters-in-law held the name of Washington in deep abhorrence. I can fancy the way in which they must have spoken of him, from the shudder of abomination with which their devoted admirers spoke years afterwards of 'that man Washington.' Lady Jane was moreover a benefactress to —. Before her day, the pavement of the footpath was composed of loose round stones, placed so far apart that a delicate ankle might receive a severe wrench from slipping between; but she left a sum of money in her will to make and keep in repair a flag pavement, on condition that it should only be broad enough for one to walk abreast, in order 'to put a stop to the indecent custom coming into vogue of ladies linking with gentlemen;' linking being the old-fashioned word for walking arm-in-arm. Lady Jane also left her sedan and money to pay the bearers for the use of the ladies of —, who were frequently like Adam and Eve in the weather-glass [14] in consequence, the first arrival at a party having to commence the order of returning when the last lady was only just entering upon the gaieties of the evening.

The old ladies were living hoards of family tradition and old custom. One of them, a Shropshire woman, had been to school in London about the middle of the last century. The journey from Shropshire took her a week. At the school to which she was sent, besides fine work of innumerable descriptions, pastry, and the art of confectionary were taught to those whose parents desired it. The dancing-master gave his pupils instructions in the art of using a fan properly. Although an only child, she had never sat down in her parents' presence without leave until she was married; and spoke with infinite disgust of the modern familiarity with which children treated their parents. 'In my days,' said she, 'when we wrote to our fathers and mothers, we began "Honoured Sir," or "Honoured Madam," none of your "Dear Mamas," or "Dear Papas" would have been permitted; and we ruled off our margin before beginning our letters, instead of cramming writing into every corner of the paper; and when we ended our letters we asked our parents' blessing if we were writing to them; and if we wrote to a friend we were content to "remain your affectionate friend," instead of hunting up some new-fangled expression, such as "your attached, your loving," &c. Fanny, my dear! I got a letter to-day signed "Yours cordially," like a dram-shop![15] what will this world come to?' Then she would tell how a gentleman having asked her to dance in her youth, never thought of such familiarity as offering her his arm to conduct her to her place, but taking up the flap of his silk-lined coat, he placed it over his open palm, and on it the lady daintily rested the tips of her fingers. To be sure, my dear old lady once confessed to a story neither so pretty nor so proper, namely, that one of the amusements of her youth was 'measuring noses' with some gentlemen, – not an uncommon thing in those days; and, as lips lie below noses, such measurements frequently ended in kisses. At her house there was a little silver basket-strainer, and once remarking on this, she showed me a silver saucer pierced through with holes, and told me it was a relic of the times when tea was first introduced into England; after it had been infused and the beverage drank, the leaves were taken out of the teapot and placed on this strainer, and then eaten by those who liked with sugar and butter, 'and very good they were,' she added. Another relic which she possessed was an old receipt-book, dating back to the middle of the sixteenth century. Our grandmothers must have been strong-headed women, for there were numerous receipts for 'ladies' beverages,' &c., generally beginning with 'Take a gallon of brandy, or any other spirit.' The puddings, too, were no light matters: one receipt, which I copied for the curiosity of the thing, begins with 'Take thirty eggs, two quarts of cream,' &c. These brobdignagian[16] puddings she explained by saying that the afternoon meal, before the introduction of tea, generally consisted of cakes and cold puddings, together with a glass of what we should now call liqueur, but which was then denominated bitters.

The same old lady advocated strongly the manner in which marriages were formerly often brought about. A young man went up to London to study for the bar, to become a merchant, or what not, and arrived at middle age without having thought about matrimony; when, finding himself rich and desirous of being married, he would frequently write to some college friend, or to the clergyman of his native place, asking him to recommend a wife; whereupon the friend would send a list of suitable ladies; the bachelor would make his selection, and empower his friend to wait upon the parents of the chosen one, who accepted or refused without much consultation of their daughter's wishes; often the first intelligence she had of the affair was by being told by her mother to adorn herself in her best, as the gentleman her parents proposed for her husband was expected by the night-coach to supper.

'And very happy marriages they turned out, my dear – very,' my venerable informant would add, sighing. I always suspected that her own had been of this description.

APPENDIX B

The Cage at Cranford

HAVE I told you anything about my friends at Cranford since the year 1856?[1] I think not.

You remember the Gordons, don't you? She that was Jessie Brown, who married her old love, Major Gordon: and from being poor became quite a rich lady: but for all that never forgot any of her old friends in Cranford.

Well! the Gordons were travelling abroad, for they were very fond of travelling; people who have had to spend part of their lives in a regiment always are, I think. They were now in Paris, in May, 1856, and were going to stop there, and in the neighbourhood all summer, but Mr Ludovic was coming to England soon; so Mrs Gordon wrote me word. I was glad she told me, for just then I was waiting to make a little present to Miss Pole, with whom I was staying; so I wrote to Mrs Gordon, and asked her to choose me out something pretty and new and fashionable, that would be acceptable to Miss Pole. Miss Pole had just been talking a great deal about Mrs Fitz-Adam's caps being so unfashionable, which I suppose made me put in that word fashionable; but afterwards I wished I had sent to say my present was not to be too fashionable; for there is such a thing, I can assure you! The price of my present was not to be more than twenty shillings, but that is a very handsome sum if you put it in that way, though it may not sound so much if you only call it a sovereign.

Mrs Gordon wrote back to me, pleased, as she always was, with doing anything for her old friends. She told me she had been out for a day's shopping before going into the country, and had got a cage for herself of the newest and most elegant description, and had thought that she could not do better than get another like it as my present for Miss Pole, as cages were so much better made in Paris than anywhere else. I was rather dismayed when I read this letter, for, however pretty a cage might be, it was something for Miss Pole's own self, and not for her parrot, that I had intended to get. Here had I been finding ever so many reasons against her buying a new cap at Johnsons' fashion-show, because I thought that the present which Mrs Gordon was to choose for me in Paris might turn out to be an elegant and fashionable head-dress; a kind of cross between a turban and a cap,[2] as I see those from Paris mostly are; and now I had to veer round, and advise her to go as fast as she could, and secure Mr Johnson's cap before any other purchaser snatched it up. But Miss Pole was too sharp for me.

'Why, Mary,' said she, 'it was only yesterday you were running down that cap like anything. You said, you know, that lilac was too old a colour for me; and green too young; and that the mixture was very unbecoming.'

'Yes, I know,' said I; 'but I have thought better of it. I thought about it a great deal last night, and I think – I thought – they would neutralise each other; and the shadows of any colour are, you know – something I know – complementary colours.' I was not sure of my own meaning, but I had an idea in my head, though I could not express it. She took me up shortly.

'Child, you don't know what you are saying. And besides, I don't want compliments at my time of life. I lay awake, too, thinking of the cap. I only buy one ready-made once a year, and of course it's a matter for consideration; and I came to the conclusion that you were quite right.'

'Oh! dear Miss Pole! I was quite wrong; if you only knew – I did think it a very pretty cap – only –'

'Well! do just finish what you've got to say. You're almost as bad as Miss Matty in your way of talking, without being half as good as she is in other ways; though I'm very fond of you, Mary, I don't mean I am not; but you must see you're very off and on, and very muddle-headed. It's the truth, so you will not mind my saying so.'

It was just because it did seem like the truth at that time that I did mind her saying so; and, in despair, I thought I would tell her all.

'I did not mean what I said; I don't think lilac too old or green too young; and I think the mixture very becoming to you; and I think you will never get such a pretty cap again, at least in Cranford.' It was fully out, so far, at least.

'Then, Mary Smith, will you tell me what you did mean, by speaking as you did, and convincing me against my will, and giving me a bad night?'

'I meant – oh, Miss Pole, I meant to surprise you with a present from Paris; and I thought it would be a cap. Mrs Gordon was to choose it, and Mr Ludovic to bring it. I dare say it is in England now; only it's not a cap. And I did not want you to buy Johnson's cap, when I thought I was getting another for you.'

Miss Pole found this speech 'muddle-headed,' I have no doubt, though she did not say so, only making an odd noise of perplexity. I went on: 'I wrote to Mrs Gordon, and asked her to get you a present – something new and pretty. I meant it to be a dress, but I suppose I did not say so; I thought it would be a cap, for Paris is so famous for caps, and it is –'

'You're a good girl, Mary' (I was past thirty, but did not object to being called a girl; and, indeed, I generally felt like a girl at Cranford, where everybody was so much older than I was), 'but when you want a thing, say what you want; it is the best way in general. And now I suppose Mrs Gordon has bought something quite different? – a pair of shoes, I dare say, for people talk a deal of Paris shoes. Anyhow, I'm just as much obliged to you, Mary, my dear. Only you should not go and spend your money on me.'

'It was not much money; and it was not a pair of shoes. You'll let me go and get the cap, won't you? It was so pretty – somebody will be sure to snatch it up.'

'I don't like getting a cap that's sure to be unbecoming.'

'But it is not; it was not. I never saw you look so well in anything,' said I.

'Mary, Mary, remember who is the father of lies!'

'But he's not my father,' exclaimed I, in a hurry, for I saw Mrs Fitz-Adam go down the street in the direction of Johnson's shop. 'I'll eat my words; they were all false: only just let me run down and buy you that cap – that pretty cap.'

'Well! run off, child. I liked it myself till you put me out of taste with it.'

I brought it back in triumph from under Mrs Fitz-Adam's very nose, as she was hanging in meditation over it; and the more we saw if it, the more we felt pleased with our purchase. We turned it on this side, and we turned it on that; and though we hurried it away into Miss Pole's bedroom at the sound of a double knock at the door, when we found it was only Miss Matty and Mr Peter, Miss Pole could not resist the opportunity of displaying it, and said in a solemn way to Miss Matty:

'Can I speak to you for a few minutes in private?' And I knew feminine delicacy too well to explain what this grave prelude was to lead to; aware how immediately Miss Matty's anxious tremor would be allayed by the sight of the cap. I had to go on talking to Mr Peter, however, when I would far rather have been in the bed-room, and heard the observations and comments.

We talked of the new cap all day; what gowns it would suit; whether a certain bow was not rather too coquettish for a woman of Miss Pole's age. 'No longer young,' as she called herself, after a little struggle with the words, though at sixty-five she need not have blushed as if she were telling a falsehood. But at last the cap was put away, and with a wrench we turned our thoughts from the subject. We had been silent for a little while, each at our work with a candle between us, when Miss Pole began:

'It was very kind of you, Mary, to think of giving me a present from Paris.'

'Oh, I was only too glad to be able to get you something! I hope you will like it, though it is not what I expected.'

'I am sure I shall like it. And a surprise is always so pleasant.'

'Yes; but I think Mrs Gordon has made a very odd choice.'

'I wonder what it is. I don't like to ask, but there's a great deal in anticipation; I remember hearing dear Miss Jenkyns say that "anticipation was the soul of enjoyment," or something like that. Now there is no anticipation in a surprise; that's the worst of it.'

'Shall I tell you what it is?'

'Just as you like, my dear. If it is any pleasure to you, I am quite willing to hear.'

'Perhaps I had better not. It is something quite different to what I expected, and meant to have got; and I'm not sure if I like it as well.'

'Relieve your mind, if you like, Mary. In all disappointments sympathy is a great balm.'

'Well, then, it's something not for you; it's for Polly. It's a cage. Mrs Gordon says they make such pretty ones in Paris.'

I could see that Miss Pole's first emotion was disappointment. But she was very fond of her cockatoo, and the thought of his smartness in his new habitation made her be reconciled in a moment; besides that she was really grateful to me for having planned a present for her.

'Polly! Well, yes; his old cage is very shabby; he is so continually pecking at it with his sharp bill. I dare say Mrs Gordon noticed it when she called here last October. I shall always think of you, Mary, when I see him in it. Now we can have him in the drawing-room, for I dare say a French cage will be quite an ornament to the room.'

And so she talked on, till we worked ourselves up into high delight at the idea of Polly in his new abode, presentable in it even to the Honourable Mrs Jamieson. The next morning Miss Pole said she had been dreaming of Polly with her new cap on his head, while she herself sat on a perch in the new cage and admired him. Then, as if ashamed of having revealed the fact of imagining 'such arrant nonsense' in her sleep, she passed on rapidly to the philosophy of dreams, quoting some book she had lately been reading, which was either too deep in itself, or too confused in her repetition for me to understand it. After breakfast, we had the cap out again; and that in its different aspects occupied us for an hour or so; and then, as it was a fine day, we turned into the garden, where Polly was hung on a nail outside the kitchen window. He clamoured and screamed at the sight of his mistress, who went to look for an almond for him. I examined his cage meanwhile, old discoloured wicker-work, clumsily made by a Cranford basket-maker. I took out Mrs Gordon's letter; it was dated the fifteenth, and this was the twentieth, for I had kept it secret for two days in my pocket. Mr Ludovic was on the point of setting out for England when she wrote.

'Poor Polly!' said I, as Miss Pole, returning, fed him with the almond.

'Ah! Polly does not know what a pretty cage he is going to

have,' said she, talking to him as she would have done to a child; and then turning to me, she asked when I thought it would come? We reckoned up dates, and made out that it might arrive that very day. So she called to her little stupid servant-maiden Fanny,[3] and bade her go out and buy a great brass-headed nail, very strong, strong enough to bear Polly and the new cage, and we all three weighed the cage in our hands, and on her return she was to come up into the drawing-room with the nail and a hammer.

Fanny was a long time, as she always was, over her errands; but as soon as she came back, we knocked the nail, with solemn earnestness, into the house-wall, just outside the drawing-room window; for, as Miss Pole observed, when I was not there she had no one to talk to, and as in summer-time she generally sat with the window open, she could combine two purposes, the giving air and sun to Polly-Cockatoo, and the having his agreeable companionship in her solitary hours.

'When it rains, my dear, or even in a very hot sun, I shall take the cage in. I would not have your pretty present spoilt for the world. It was very kind of you to think of it; I am quite come round to liking it better than any present of mere dress; and dear Mrs Gordon has shown all her usual pretty observation in remembering my Polly-Cockatoo.'

'Polly-Cockatoo' was his grand name; I had only once or twice heard him spoken of by Miss Pole in this formal manner, except when she was speaking to the servants; then she always gave him his full designation, just as most people call their daughters Miss, in speaking of them to strangers or servants. But since Polly was to have a new cage, and all the way from Paris too, Miss Pole evidently thought it necessary to treat him with unusual respect.

We were obliged to go out to pay some calls; but we left strict orders with Fanny what to do if the cage arrived in our absence, as (we had calculated) it might. Miss Pole stood ready bonneted and shawled at the kitchen door, I behind her, and cook behind Fanny, each of us listening to the conversation of the other two.

'And Fanny, mind if it comes you coax Polly-Cockatoo nicely into it. He is very particular, and may be attached to his old cage, though it is so shabby. Remember, birds have their feelings as much as we have! Don't hurry him in making up his mind.'

'Please, ma'am, I think an almond would help him to get over his feelings,' said Fanny, dropping a curtsey at every speech, as she had been taught to do at her charity school.

'A very good idea, very. If I have my keys in my pocket I will give you an almond for him. I think he is sure to like the view up the street from the window; he likes seeing people, I think.'

'It's but a dull look-out into the garden; nowt but dumb flowers,' said cook, touched by this allusion to the cheerfulness of the street, as contrasted with the view from her own kitchen window.

'It's a very good look-out for busy people,' said Miss Pole, severely. And then, feeling she was likely to get the worst of it in an encounter with her old servant, she withdrew with meek dignity, being deaf to some sharp reply; and of course I, being bound to keep order, was deaf too. If the truth must be told, we rather hastened our steps, until we had banged the street-door behind us.

We called on Miss Matty, of course; and then on Mrs Hoggins. It seemed as if ill-luck would have it that we went to the only two households of Cranford where there was the encumbrance of a man, and in both places the man was where he ought not to have been – namely, in his own house, and in the way. Miss Pole – out of civility to me, and because she really was full of the new cage for Polly, and because we all in Cranford relied on the sympathy of our neighbours in the veriest trifle that interested us – told Miss Matty, and Mr Peter, and Mr and Mrs Hoggins; he was standing in the drawing-room, booted and spurred, and eating his hunk of bread-and-cheese in the very presence of his aristocratic wife, my lady that was. As Miss Pole said afterwards, if refinement was not to be found in Cranford, blessed as it was with so many scions of county families, she did not know where to meet with it. Bread-and-cheese in a drawing-room! Onions next.

But for all Mr Hoggins's vulgarity, Miss Pole told him of the present she was about to receive.

'Only think! a new cage for Polly – Polly – Polly-Cockatoo,

you know, Mr Hoggins. You remember him, and the bite he gave me once because he wanted to be put back in his cage, pretty bird?'

'I only hope the new cage will be strong as well as pretty, for I must say a –' He caught a look from his wife, I think, for he stopped short. 'Well, we're old friends, Polly and I, and he put some practice in my way once. I shall be up the street this afternoon, and perhaps I shall step in and see this smart Parisian cage.'

'Do!' said Miss Pole, eagerly. 'Or, if you are in a hurry, look up at my drawing-room window; if the cage is come, it will be hanging out there, and Polly in it.'

We had passed the omnibus that met the train from London some time ago, so we were not surprised as we returned home to see Fanny half out of the window, and cook evidently either helping or hindering her. Then they both took their heads in; but there was no cage hanging up. We hastened up the steps.

Both Fanny and the cook met us in the passage.

'Please, ma'am,' said Fanny, 'there's no bottom to the cage, and Polly would fly away.'

'And there's no top,' exclaimed cook. 'He might get out at the top quite easy.'

'Let me see,' said Miss Pole, brushing past, thinking no doubt that her superior intelligence was all that was needed to set things to rights. On the ground lay a bundle, or a circle of hoops, neatly covered over with calico,[4] no more like a cage for Polly-Cockatoo than I am like a cage. Cook took something up between her finger and thumb, and lifted the unsightly present from Paris. How I wish it had stayed there! – but foolish ambition has brought people to ruin before now; and my twenty shillings are gone, sure enough, and there must be some use or some ornament intended by the maker of the thing before us.

'Don't you think it's a mousetrap, ma'am?' asked Fanny, dropping her little curtsey.

For reply, the cook lifted up the machine, and showed how easily mice might run out; and Fanny shrank back abashed. Cook was evidently set against the new invention, and muttered about its being all of a piece with French things[5] French cooks, French plums (nasty dried-up things), French rolls (as had no substance in 'em).

Miss Pole's good manners, and desire of making the best of things in my presence, induced her to try and drown cook's mutterings.

'Indeed, I think it will make a very nice cage for Polly-Cockatoo. How pleased he will be to go from one hoop to another, just like a ladder, and with a board or two at the bottom, and nicely tied up at the top –'

Fanny was struck with a new idea.

'Please, ma'am, my sister-in-law has got an aunt as lives lady's-maid with Sir John's daughter – Miss Arley. And they did say as she wore iron petticoats all made of hoops –'

'Nonsense, Fanny!' we all cried; for such a thing had not been heard of in all Drumble, let alone Cranford, and I was rather looked upon in the light of a fast young woman by all the laundresses of Cranford, because I had two corded petticoats.

'Go mind thy business, wench,' said cook, with the utmost contempt. 'I'll warrant we'll manage th' cage without thy help.'

'It is near dinner-time, Fanny, and the cloth not laid,' said Miss Pole, hoping the remark might cut two ways; but cook had no notion of going. She stood on the bottom step of the stairs, holding the Paris perplexity aloft in the air.

'It might do for a meat-safe,' said she. 'Cover it o'er wi' canvas, to keep th' flies out. It is a good framework, I reckon, anyhow!' She held her head on one side, like a connoisseur in meat-safes, as she was.

Miss Pole said, 'Are you sure Mrs Gordon called it a cage, Mary? Because she is a woman of her word, and would not have called it so if it was not.'

'Look here; I have the letter in my pocket.'

' "I have wondered how I could best fulfil your commission for me to purchase something to the value of" – um, um, never mind – "fashionable and pretty for dear Miss Pole, and at length I have decided upon one of the new kind of 'cages' " (look here, Miss Pole; here is the word, C.A.G.E.), "which are made so much lighter and more elegant in Paris than in England. Indeed, I am not sure if they have ever reached you, for it is not a month since I saw the first of the kind in Paris." '

'Does she say anything about Polly-Cockatoo?' asked Miss Pole. 'That would settle the matter at once, as showing that she had him in her mind.'

'No – nothing.'

Just then Fanny came along the passage with the tray full of dinner-things in her hands. When she had put them down, she stood at the door of the dining-room taking a distant view of the article. 'Please, ma'am, it looks like a petticoat without any stuff in it; indeed it does, if I'm to be whipped for saying it.'

But she only drew down upon herself a fresh objurgation from the cook; and sorry and annoyed, I seized the opportunity of taking the thing out of cook's hand, and carrying it upstairs, for it was full time to get ready for dinner. But we had very little appetite for our meal, and kept constantly making suggestions, one to the other, as to the nature and purpose of this Paris 'cage,' but as constantly snubbing poor little Fanny's reiteration of 'Please, ma'am, I do believe it's a kind of petticoat – indeed I do.' At length Miss Pole turned upon her with almost as much vehemence as cook had done, only in choicer language.

'Don't be so silly, Fanny. Do you think ladies are like children, and must be put in go-carts;[6] or need wire guards like fires to surround them; or can get warmth out of bits of whalebone and steel; a likely thing indeed! Don't keep talking about what you don't understand.'

So our maiden was mute for the rest of the meal. After dinner we had Polly brought upstairs in her old cage, and I held out the new one, and we turned it about in every way. At length Miss Pole said:

'Put Polly-Cockatoo back, and shut him up in his cage. You hold this French thing up' (alas! that my present should be called a 'thing'), 'and I'll sew a bottom on to it. I'll lay a good deal, they've forgotten to sew in the bottom before sending it off.' So I held and she sewed; and then she held and I sewed, till it was all done. Just as we had put Polly-Cockatoo in, and were closing up the top with a pretty piece of old yellow ribbon – and, indeed, it was not a bad-looking cage after all our trouble – Mr Hoggins came up-stairs, having been seen by Fanny before he had time to knock at the door.

'Hallo!' said he, almost tumbling over us, as we were sitting on the floor at our work. 'What's this?'

'It's this pretty present for Polly-Cockatoo,' said Miss Pole, raising herself up with as much dignity as she could, 'that Mary has had sent from Paris for me.' Miss Pole was in great spirits now we had got Polly in; I can't say that I was.

Mr Hoggins began to laugh in his boisterous vulgar way.

'For Polly – ha! ha! It's meant for you, Miss Pole – ha! ha! It's a new invention to hold your gowns out – ha! ha!'

'Mr Hoggins! you may be a surgeon, and a very clever one, but nothing – not even your profession – gives you a right to be indecent.'

Miss Pole was thoroughly roused, and I trembled in my shoes. But Mr Hoggins only laughed the more. Polly screamed in concert, but Miss Pole stood in stiff rigid propriety, very red in the face.

'I beg your pardon, Miss Pole, I am sure. But I am pretty certain I am right. It's no indecency that I can see; my wife and Mrs Fitz-Adam take in a Paris fashion-book between 'em, and I can't help seeing the plates of fashions sometimes – ha! ha! ha! Look, Polly has got out of his queer prison – ha! ha! ha!'

Just then Mr Peter came in; Miss Matty was so curious to know if the expected present had arrived. Mr Hoggins took them by the arm, and pointed to the poor thing lying on the ground, but could not explain for laughing. Miss Pole said:

'Although I am not accustomed to give an explanation of my conduct to gentlemen, yet, being insulted in my own house by – by Mr Hoggins, I must appeal to the brother of my old friend – my very oldest friend. Is this article a lady's petticoat, or a bird's cage?'

She held it up as she made this solemn inquiry. Mr Hoggins seized the moment to leave the room, in shame, as I supposed, but, in reality, to fetch his wife's fashion-book; and, before I had completed the narration of the story of my unlucky commission, he returned, and, holding the fashion-plate open by the side of the extended article, demonstrated the identity of the two.

But Mr Peter had always a smooth way of turning off anger, by either his fun or a compliment. 'It is a cage,' said he, bowing to Miss Pole; 'but it is a cage for an angel, instead of a bird! Come along, Hoggins, I want to speak to you!'

And, with an apology, he took the offending and victorious surgeon out of Miss Pole's presence. For a good while we said nothing; and we were now rather shy of little Fanny's superior wisdom when she brought up tea. But towards night our spirits revived, and we were quite ourselves again, when Miss Pole proposed that we should cut up the pieces of steel or whalebone – which, to do them justice, were very elastic – and make ourselves two very comfortable English calashes out of them with the aid of a piece of dyed silk which Miss Pole had by her.

NOTES

Cranford

CHAPTER I

1. *Amazons*: according to Greek legend, the members of an exclusively female state who were famous for their skill as warriors. The name means 'no breast' and describes the Amazons' supposed practice of removing the right breast in order to draw a bow more easily. The qualifying description of the Amazons as being 'holders of houses above a certain rent' may be a reference to the 1832 Reform Bill which gave the vote to £10 householders. It is certainly Mrs Gaskell's intention to make her Amazons solidly middle-class: as we see later (p. 64) Cranford is not short of working-class men. An identical situation is described in 'Mr Harrison's Confessions': 'You will find it a curious statistical fact, but five-sixths of our householders of a certain rank in Duncombe are women. We have widows and old maids in rich abundance. In fact, my dear sir, I believe that you and I are almost the only gentlemen in the place – Mr Bullock, of course, excepted. By gentlemen, I mean professional men.'

2. *Drumble*: Manchester, which, like Knutsford, appears in Mrs Gaskell's work under a variety of names. It is fifteen miles from Knutsford.

3. *Miss Tyler, of cleanly memory*: the aunt of Robert Southey (1774–1843) who looked after him as a child and had a passion for cleanliness. Southey was Poet Laureate in the period of time covered by *Cranford*.

4. *the last gigot, the last tight and scanty petticoat*: the gigot was a 'leg o'mutton' sleeve, wide at the shoulder, narrow at the wrist. These, together with straight skirts, were popular early in the nineteenth century. Speaking of the mid 1830s the young Mary Smith would have been attracted more to the fashionable hooped skirts, hence the joke in the next paragraph about an umbrella being like 'a stick in petticoats.' Fashions in umbrellas were also changing at this time, with silk being largely replaced by cotton.

5. *Manx laws . . . Tinwald Mount*: it was the custom in the Isle of

Man for all laws passed during the year to be read annually to the assembled population at Tynwald Hill in the centre of the island. There is a sonnet by Wordsworth called 'Tynwald Hill' on this aspect of the Isle of Man.

6. *one little charity-school maiden*: the number of domestic servants in a Victorian household was a reliable indication of a family's status and was rigidly codified by writers on social etiquette. One general and inexperienced maidservant from a charity-school (one of the purposes of which was to train children of the poor for precisely this work) would place Mrs Forrester low on the social scale. See Miss Matty's comments on the decline in her standard of living after her father's death (p. 103).

7. *tea-bread*: sweetened bread-rolls shaped into scrolls and whorls. E. P. Watson points out that these are a Cheshire speciality.

8. *pattens*: over-shoes, consisting of a wooden platform secured by straps: worn to protect the wearer's normal shoes from mud.

9. *half-pay captain*: an army officer retired from active service who remained on the reserve at half his normal pay.

10. *a neighbouring railroad*: at this time the railway system was still in its infancy, though Mrs Gaskell was writing *Cranford* during the boom years. Knutsford itself did not have a railway until 1862, but they were familiar in that area of the north west much earlier: the Liverpool and Manchester Railway, opened in 1830, was the first to rely completely on steam and set a model for future developments.

11. *sedan-chairs*: clearly unusual at this time but not quite anachronistic. This is also one of the many details Mrs Gaskell draws from life in Knutsford: 'Knutsford still keeps its sedan chair as a memento of bygone days, and it is used once a year at the May-Day celebrations.' Mrs Ellis H. Chadwick, *Mrs Gaskell: Haunts, Homes, and Stories*, 1910, p. 43.

12. *Miss Betty Barker*: the 1864 edition of *Cranford* gives Betsy instead of Betty here, though not subsequently, and, following E. P. Watson's example, I have altered this.

13. *louder than the clerk*: it was one of the jobs of the parish clerk to lead the responses in church services.

14. *'Preference'*: a version of whist played with thirty-two cards. Four players are involved initially but only three actually play, the dealer sitting out. Hence the narrator's remark about being the 'unlucky fourth'.

15. *'Jock of Hazeldean'*: a ballad by Sir Walter Scott (1816).

16. *numbers of 'The Pickwick Papers'*: *Pickwick Papers* was pub-

lished originally in twenty monthly parts, April 1836 to November 1837, the 'editor' being given as Boz, Dickens's pseudonym. Dickens was advised by his friend not to publish his book in this form as it was considered 'low' or 'vulgar', which is exactly Miss Jenkyns's response. When *Cranford* was serialized in *Household Words*, Dickens deleted references to himself and to *Pickwick* and substituted similar references to Thomas Hood and *Hood's Own*. The substitution was understandable (Dickens being editor of *Household Words*) and sensible (Hood being a well-known comic writer and editor), but the original references were important to Mrs Gaskell's purpose and were replaced in the first book edition of 1853.

17. *the 'swarry' which Sam Weller gave at Bath*: *Pickwick Papers*, chapter XXXVII, describes a 'soirée' given by the footmen of Bath to which Sam Weller is invited, and is chosen by Mrs Gaskell with characteristic thematic care. The footmen are pompous and overbearing: Sam mocks them, though they are too foolish to understand this, and morally his victory is one of common sense over misplaced pride. There are obvious parallels to be drawn with the present clash between Captain Brown and Miss Jenkyns.

18. *Rasselas*: published in 1759. It is hardly a work of 'light and agreeable fiction' as Miss Jenkyns later describes it (p. 50), but a series of dialogues on moral themes between Rasselas, the Prince of Abyssinia, and his teacher, Imlac, one of which Miss Jenkyns reads. The stately, slow-moving prose of *Rasselas* is totally unlike the verve and humour of *Pickwick*.

19. *The Rambler*: a periodical written mainly by Dr Johnson, published twice weekly for two years from March 1750. Captain Brown's point is that however much the styles of Boz and Johnson differ, the two authors shared a journalistic ability to write at speed for the general public.

20. *sotto voce*: in a low voice.

CHAPTER II

1. *bakehouse*: communal bakehouses were common throughout the period. They were used mainly, though not entirely, by the poor to cook any special meal (Sunday dinner in this instance) for which something more than an open fire was needed.

2. *Brutus wig*: a closely cropped or curly hair-style which was popular during the period of the French revolution.

3. *'But don't you forget the white worsted at Flint's'*: Flint's was a

London haberdasher's near the monument and sufficiently renowned throughout England to provide this refrain from a popular song, 'Country Commissions to my Cousin in Town'.

4. *Deborah*: Judges iv, 4.

5. *cravat . . . jockey-cap*: both unfashionable for women at this time, but used by Mrs Gaskell here to indicate Miss Jenkyns's masculine nature. At Captain Brown's funeral the jockey-cap becomes a 'helmet' (p. 57).

6. *'plumed wars'*: a strange reference, but, as Miss Jenkyns's letter is full of literary allusions, possibly to *Othello*, III, iii, 350–51: 'Farewell the plumed troop and the big wars / That make ambition virtue !'

7. *Brunonian*: an inflated version of Brown of the kind popularly, though often unfairly, associated with the Johnsonian style. Whether intentional or not, it is noticeable that in the next sentence the butcher's wife is called Mrs Johnson.

8. *'the feast of reason and the flow of soul'*: Pope, *Imitations of Horace*, Satire 1, Book II, 128.

9. *'the pure wells of English undefiled'*: the reference is to Chaucer, by Spenser, *Faerie Queene*, IV, ii, 32.

10. *pot-pourri*: a mixture of flower petals and perfume used to give pleasant scent and normally kept in a small jar. The more natural methods employed by the ladies of Cranford are totally unpretentious forms of elegant economy.

11. *many a rolling, three-piled sentence*: another ironic reference to Johnsonian style.

12. *where the weary are at rest*: Job iii, 17.

13. *'Though He slay me, yet will I trust in Him'*: Job xiii, 15. 'Though he slay me, yet will I wait for him.'

14. *arrowroot*: a starch taken from the tuberous roots of West Indian and South American plants. Widely used in Victorian cooking to thicken sauces, or as here, as a kind of gruel for invalids.

15. *Galignani*: *Galignani's Messenger*, an English newspaper published in Paris from 1814, and widely read by British tourists.

16. *'Old Poz'*: a play for children by Maria Edgeworth in *The Parent's Assistant* (1795). 'That's poz!' (i.e. positive or certain) is a catch phrase used by one of the characters in the play, and the angelic young heroine is called Lucy.

17. *Christmas Carol*: first published 1843. Dickens substituted the title of a comic poem by Hood, 'Miss Kilmansegg and her Golden Leg' when this episode appeared in *Household Words*.

CHAPTER III

1. *'Hortus Siccus'*: Latin: a dry garden, i.e. a collection of dried plants arranged in a book.

2. *forbidden, by the articles of her engagement, to have 'followers'*: the courting habits of servants seem to have obsessed Victorian employers. This was partly through fears of burglary, but even more from the thought of any sexual activity on the part of servants taking place in the house, and as in Cranford, employers would sometimes insist that servants should have no 'followers' without asking permission of the mistress of the house. Mary Smith's comments on the ridiculous nature of this is a neat illustration of how she represents a younger and less conventional generation than the ladies of Cranford.

3. *till Missus rings the bell for prayers at ten*: servants would commonly be expected to join in evening prayers with the family. See also *Cousin Phillis*, p. 239.

4. *I held up a screen*: a hand-screen normally used to shield the face from the heat of a fire, but serving here, as in 'Mr Harrison's Confessions', to avoid any potentially embarrassing situation.

5. *Blue Beard*: the folk-villain – best known from the story by Charles Perrault, first published in 1697 – who systematically murdered his wives and kept their bodies locked in his castle.

6. *the Scandinavian prophetess*: a reference to Thomas Gray's 'The Descent of Odin'. The prophetess is visited by Odin in the underworld where she tells him of the fate of his son Balder. The refrain 'Leave me, leave me to repose' expresses her unwillingness to answer Odin's questions.

7. *the 'pride which apes humility'*: from 'The Devil's Thoughts' by Coleridge and Southey, first published in the *Morning Post*, 6 September 1799.

8. *Esq . . . Mr . . . Yeoman*: the original title of Esquire (or Squire) was given to someone, usually high born, who attended a Knight, and was ranked next to him in the social scale. Mr Holbrook deplores the pretentious habit of using 'Esq' instead of 'Mr' and insists he is a yeoman, i.e. a small independent farmer who owns his own land.

9. *mousseline-de-laine*: literally 'muslin of wool': a fine woven material originally of wool, but later of mixed wool and cotton.

10. *sarsenet*: a fine silk material used mainly for linings.

CHAPTER IV

1. *fly*: a small fast-moving carriage.

2. *gilly-flowers*: wallflowers.

3. *As Goethe says*: source unknown and possibly not intended to be specific.

4. '*No broth, no ball; no ball, no beef*': ball is a dialect word for dumpling, and the practice of eating a suet or Yorkshire pudding before the main meat course is still followed in parts of the North of England. Mr Holbrook's adherence to his father's maxim in this respect, his scorn of the fashionable habit of eating sweet puddings before the main course, his old-fashioned eating utensils, and his rough table manners, are not merely employed to make him eccentric. They show in what ways the Jenkyns family thought that he was not 'enough of a gentleman' for Miss Matty, while his goodness of heart and greater awareness of more important aspects of modern life provide one of the strongest condemnations of the weak and snobbish sides of Cranford gentility.

5. *Aminé . . . Ghoul*: a gruesome story in the *Arabian Nights*. Aminé astonishes her husband, Sidi Nouman, by eating for dinner only a few grains of rice which she picks up one by one with a pin. He later learns that she is an enchantress who at night joins a female Ghoul in eating the flesh of corpses which they dig from their graves.

6. *calashes*: Mary Smith gives her own ironic definition of these later in the book, p. 110.

7. '*The cedar spreads his dark-green layers of shade*': Tennyson, 'The Gardener's Daughter', 1.115.

8. *the review of his poems in Blackwood*: 'The Gardener's Daughter' was first published in Tennyson's *Poems 1842*. They were reviewed enthusiastically by many periodicals, but not in *Blackwood's* until April 1849, and then with some reservations. It is possible that Mrs Gaskell has made a mistake over the title of the periodical, but more likely that she has in mind the praise given by Christopher North to Tennyson's earlier volumes of poetry (1830 and 1833) in *Blackwood's*.

9. *Black as ashbuds in March*: 'The Gardener's Daughter,' 1.28: 'More black than ashbuds in the front of March'.

10. *Locksley Hall*: also first published in *Poems 1842*, it tells of a broken love-affair, the woman being forced by family snobbery to

abandon the man she loves, and has therefore a certain thematic
relevance in this context.

11. *he should call on the ladies soon, and inquire how they got
home*: a common act of courtesy in the eighteenth and early nineteenth centuries, but also more than this. In a formal society it provided a means of courtship for young people, which is why Miss
Matty is 'pleased and fluttered'. See Jane Austen, *Pride and Prejudice*, chapter 15: 'Bingley was the principal spokesman, and Miss
Bennet the principal object. He was then, he said, on his way to
Longbourn on purpose to inquire after her.'

12. *Paris*: for many Victorians Paris was regarded with abhorrence as a city of sexual immorality and social revolutions, and Mrs
Gaskell frequently makes gentle fun of this attitude. See p. 139 where
the French are ironically equated with the Red Indians. Miss Matty
also associates the French with her fear in childhood that they were
about to invade England (p. 90).

13. *capable*: roomy.

14. *widows' caps*: in the 1830s these were usually made of plain
white stiffened muslin, and often worn with turned-down white
muslin collar and cuffs.

CHAPTER V

1. *the failure of a Joint-Stock Bank*: provincial joint stock banks
were allowed by an Act of Parliament in 1826, the first being opened
the following year. They were notoriously unstable, and the
references to them here and elsewhere in *Cranford* indicate the
financial uncertainty and dissatisfaction with the Bank of England
which existed prior to Peel's Bank Charter Act of 1844.

2. *envelopes . . . when they first came in*: gummed envelopes were
introduced as part of the Penny Post Reforms. See *Cousin Phillis*,
Part IV, note 14.

3. *to 'keep blind man's holiday'*: to sit in the dark, i.e. to make no
change in one's normal condition.

4. *Tonquin beans*: usually called Tonka beans. They come from
South America and were used for their pleasant scent.

5. *a huge full-bottomed wig*: fashionable in the mid eighteenth
century.

6. *'Paduasoy'*: a strong rich silk.

7. *parshality . . . bewty*: no special point is intended by Mrs

Jenkyns's poor spelling. This kind of spelling according to the sounds of words is often found in eighteenth-century letters.

8. *J. and J. Rivingtons*: an established London publishers, associated mainly with theological works.

9. *dum memor ipse mei, dum spiritus [hos] regit artus*: Virgil, *Aeneid*, IV, 336: 'While memory lasts, while the spirit still animates my frame.'

10. *carmen*: a song or poem.

11. *Gentleman's Magazine*: another link with Dr Johnson who worked for the *Gentleman's Magazine* during his early days in London.

12. *M. T. Ciceronis Epistolæ*: the letters of Marcus Tullius Cicero (106–43 B.C.), Roman orator and statesman.

13. *a rod in pickle*: a threat of a future scolding, just as a rod is laid in pickle to keep it ready for use.

14. *Mrs Chapone*: Hester Chapone (1727–1801), well-known 'Blue-stocking', friend of Dr Johnson and Richardson, a contributor to the *Rambler* and the *Gentleman's Magazine*, author of *Letters on the Improvement of the Mind* (1774).

15. *Mrs Carter*: Elizabeth Carter (1717–1806), like Mrs Chapone a member of the Blue-stocking circle and admired by Dr Johnson. Her translation of Epictetus was published in 1758.

16. *fashed*: vexed or bothered.

17. *the old original post*: letter paper. The 'stamp' described is a watermark.

18. *banished wafers from polite society*: a wafer was a small disc of red paper used to seal a letter. The reference here is to Maria Edgworth's *Patronage* (1813), Chapter VIII, in which the Duke of Greenwich is disgusted to receive a letter sealed with a wafer. Giving it to his secretary he says. 'Open that, if you please, sir – *I wonder how any man can have the impertinence to send me his spittle.*'

19. *franks . . . members of parliament*: members of Parliament were allowed the privilege of franking letters (i.e. sending them free of charge) a practice open to the kind of abuse described here.

20. *sesquipedalian*: measuring a foot and a half, containing many syllables.

21. *Herod*: Matthew xiv, 1. Herod was the Tetrarch (i.e. a Roman ruler of the fourth part of a kingdom) of Judea.

22. *the fable of the Boy and the Wolf*: false warning, after the story in Aesop's *Fables*: the French did not after all invade England, although they were widely expected to do so.

23. *David and Goliath*: I Samuel xvii.

24. *Apollyon and Abaddon*: the Greek and Hebrew names for the Angel of the Bottomless Pit (Revelation ix), frequently invoked during the period of the Napoleonic Wars.

25. '*Bonus Bernardus non videt omnia*': 'the good Bernard does not see everything'. The proverb refers to St Bernard of Clairvaux (1091–1153), a man famed for his knowledge and 'clear vision'.

CHAPTER VI

1. *St James's Chronicle*: a paper founded in 1760 which represented the views of the church and court. It was published originally three times a week, but later only once weekly.

2. *shovel-hat*: a broad-brimmed hat turned up at the sides, worn by the clergy.

3. *a new rhododendron*: E. P. Watson points out that this would have been quite unusual at the time, as they did not become popular until Sir Joseph Hooker's discovery of many new species, described in *Rhododendrons of the Sikkim Himalaya* (1849–51).

4. *Queen Esther and King Ahasuerus*: Esther 1–2.

5. *Dor*: editions of *Cranford* prior to that in the Oxford English Novels series have 'Don' here. E. P. Watson is surely right that the correct reading should be 'Dor' (a diminutive of Deborah) as given in *Household Words*.

6. *post-horses . . . gig*: post-horses were for hire at local inns, and offered a fast means of transport: a gig was a light, two-wheeled carriage drawn by one horse and much slower over a long distance.

7. *no overland route then*: a safe overland route to India, via the Red Sea, was established in the late 1830s, improving postal communication considerably. Until the Suez Canal was opened in 1869, the usual route was via the Cape of Good Hope.

8. *some great war in India*: Peter's own later description, p. 209, makes it clear that this was the first Burmese War, 1824–6. Rangoon was captured by British forces in 1824.

CHAPTER VII

1. *too patriotic and John Bullish to wear what the Mounseers wore*: John Bull, the symbol of strong and stolid Britain: Mounseers, an anglicized term of contempt for the French (i.e. monsieurs).

2. *Queen Adelaide*: the consort of William IV who was king 1830–37.

3. *delicate mess*: a prepared meal.

4. *passée*: old-fashioned.

5. *pool*: the stakes played for in a game, though here more the number of people required to make up a game. For Preference see Chapter I, note 14.

6. *Molly Higgins*: not Molly but Sarah, the daughter of a Shropshire labourer who became the second wife of Henry Cecil in 1791. He succeeded to the peerage two years later on the death of his uncle. Tennyson's poem 'The Lord of Burleigh' published in *Poems 1842* is based on this story.

7. *bombazine*: a dress material of mixed silk and wool used especially for mourning garments.

8. *she had always understood that Fitz meant something aristocratic*: it does, but not quite what Mrs Forrester has in mind. It means 'son of' and is often applied to the illegitimate children of royalty. Fitz-Clarence was the name given to the children born to Mrs Jordan, King William's mistress before his accession.

9. *ci-devant*: formerly.

10. *Savoy biscuits*: long thin biscuits of crisp sponge, sometimes joined together in pairs as 'ladies' fingers', often served with sweet wine.

11. *Cribbage*: a card game in which points scored are marked on a board with pegs.

12. *did not know Spadille from Manille*: Spadille is the ace of spades and Manille the second highest card in Ombre.

13. *basting*: beating or winning: 'Bastro' is the ace of clubs.

14. *female mandarins*: an allusion to china figures of mandarins with heads balanced so as to nod.

15. *'stopped the way'*: at the end of parties footmen would call out that a certain guest's carriage 'stopped the way' which indicated that it was time to go, and also that others were being hindered from leaving.

CHAPTER VIII

1. *Scotch peer – never sat in the House of Lords*: on the dissolution of the Scottish Parliament by the Act of Union 1707, the number of Scottish peers allowed to sit in the House of Lords was reduced to sixteen.

2. *stomacher*: an ornamental front to the bodice descending to a point at the waist.

3. *the furniture was white and gold ... not a curve or bend about them*: Mrs Jamieson's furniture seems to be in the neo-classical Louis Seize or Directoire style of the later eighteenth century, which became popular in England. The more ornate Louis Quatorze enjoyed a revival in the years after Waterloo.

4. *a japanned table*: a table with a top of lacquered black varnish, popular in England in the eighteenth century.

5. *Pembroke table*: a table with two folding leaves.

6. *kaleidoscope*: invented by Sir David Brewster, 1817.

7. *conversation-cards, puzzle-cards*: Mrs Gaskell describes these in 'Mr Harrison's Confessions', Chapter VIII: 'sheaves of slips of cardboard, with intellectual or sentimental questions on one set, and equally intellectual and sentimental answers on the other; and as the answers were fit to any and all the questions, you may think they were a characterless ... set of things'.

8. *the drawings which decorate tea-chests*: Chinese writing on the wooden chests of imported tea.

9. *a sort of 'A Lord and No Lord' business*: an obscure allusion, but probably referring back to Tennyson's poem 'The Lord of Burleigh' (see Chapter VII, note 6) in which a painter courts and marries a village girl before revealing to her that he is 'Lord of Burleigh': 'Not a Lord in all the county/is so great a Lord as he', lines 59–60. There is also an anonymous ballad, 'A Lord and no Lord' of c. 1726.

10. *filigree sugar-tongs*: made of an ornamental lace-like tracery of gold or silver.

11. *Ombre and Quadrille*: card games especially popular in the eighteenth century played with a pack of 40 cards.

12. *Basto*: the ace of clubs. See Chapter VII, note 13.

13. *the Catholic Emancipation Bill*: passed in 1829, it repealed earlier legislation imposing civil and public restrictions on Catholics. Mrs Forrester's interpretation of the possible effects of the Act is characteristically confused.

14. *top-boots*: boots reaching to just below the knee with turnover tops.

15. *Francis Moore's astrological predictions*: Francis Moore (1657–1715) was an astrologer and physician who published an almanac prophesying the weather, 1699, to advertise his pills. The following year he published the Vox *Stellarum*, later, and still, known as 'Old Moore's Almanac'.

CHAPTER IX

1. *from Michaelmas to Lady-day*: from 29 September to 25 March.

2. *if turbans were in fashion*: fashionable at various times from the late eighteenth century, but in England especially during the Napoleonic Wars, influenced by the Egyptian campaigns.

3. *Wombwell's Lions*: George Wombwell (1778–1850) owner of a famous travelling menagerie.

4. *menuets de la cour*: court minuets.

5. *clothes-maids*: now usually called clothes-horses; wooden frames on which clothes are hung to dry.

6. *Thaddeus of Warsaw, and the Hungarian Brothers, and Santo Sebastiana*: heroes of popular romances. *Thaddeus of Warsaw* (1803) by Jane Porter, and *The Hungarian Brothers* (1807) and *Don Sebastian* (1809) by her sister Anna Maria Porter.

7. *If she was not the rose . . . she had been near it*: an allusion to *Gulistan* by the Persian poet Sa'di (1215–1292) translated into English by Francis Gladwin, 1806; 'a worthless piece of clay, but having for a season associated with the rose, the virtue of my companion was communicated to me'.

8. *the Witch of Endor*: who was asked by Saul to call up the spirit of Samuel; I Samuel xxviii.

9. *death-watches*: the sound of the death-watch beetle is popularly supposed to foretell death.

10. *Queen Charlotte*: consort of King George III (1760–1830), died 1818.

11. *one of the Gunnings*: Maria Gunning (1733–60) and her sister Elizabeth (1734–90) were famous 'beauties' – they were actually nicknamed 'The Beauties' – of the mid eighteenth century, both of whom married into the aristocracy.

12. *chapeau bras*: a three-cornered silk hat which could be folded and carried under the arm: fashionable in the late eighteenth century.

13. *Mussulman*: Muslim, usually a Turk or Persian.

14. *National School boys*: who would have attended day school provided by the National Society for the Education of the Poor in the Principles of the Established Church which was founded in 1811.

15. *in chinks of laughing*: convulsive fits.

CHAPTER X

1. *in search of some unwatched house or some unfastened door*: the kind of fear described by Mrs Gaskell although in this instance misguided was real enough for many small country towns. Miss Mitford describes a similar situation: 'During many weeks, the neighbourhood had been infested by a gang of bold, sturdy pilferers, roving vagabonds, begging by day, stealing and poaching by night – who had committed such extensive devastations amongst the poultry and linen of the village, as well as game in the preserves, that the whole population was on the alert.' 'Jesse Cliffe', *Country Stories* (1837). See also 'The Last Generation', p. 320.

2. *Red Indians or the French*: see Chapter IV, note 12.

3. *General Burgoyne*: (1722–92) he was commander of the British troops at the surrender of Saratoga, 1777, in the American War of Independence.

4. *Madame de Staël*: French writer (1766–1817) and critic of Napoleon during the years following the French Revolution. For the popularity of turbans, see Chapter IX, note 1. The portrait referred to here was probably by François Gerard.

5. *Mr Denon*: Baron Dominique-Vivant Denon (1747–1825), French archaeologist and writer, who accompanied Napoleon on his Egyptian campaign.

6. *Irish beggar-woman*: Irish beggars were a common sight in early Victorian England, driven to leave Ireland by the dreadful series of famines. There is a possible connection here with the railway as many Irishmen worked as navvies. See *Cousin Phillis*, Part III, note 1.

7. *an old story . . . of a nightingale and a musician*: this story is told in John Ford's play *The Lover's Melancholy* (1629), and the relevant passage quoted in full in Miss Mitford's *Our Village* (1824), pp. 141–3, a book which is often claimed as an influence on Cranford.

8. *Italian irons*: used for ironing frills and goffering.

9. *spillikins*: splinters of wood, bone, or ivory, used in a children's game of the same name.

10. *'where nae men should be'*: from an old Scottish ballad 'Our Goodman Came Home at E'en'.

11. *elf-locks*: tangled hair supposed to have been made by Queen Mab. It was considered unlucky to disentangle them.

12. *videlicet*: Latin, usually written viz., namely, or such as.

13. *cold-pigged*: doused with water; pig is a dialect word for pitcher.

14. *Dr Ferrier and Dr Hibbert*: John Ferrier (1761–1815) and Samuel Hibbert (1782–1848) were both authorities on apparitions.

15. *mutes at a funeral*: professional attendants, dressed in deep mourning cloths, hired to give the sense of solemnity and grandeur which was characteristic of Victorian funerals.

CHAPTER XI

1. *bug-a-boo*: goblin.

2. *'Jack's up,' 'a fig for his heels'*: expressions from cribbage. When the 'Jack' or 'knave' is turned up an extra point is awarded. Mrs Gaskell had used this same anecdote in 'The Last Generation', see p. 322.

3. *Lord Chesterfield's Letters*: Chesterfield's letters to his son were first published in 1774. They are famous for their advice on behaviour and manners.

4. *bread-jelly*: a mixture of bread crumbs, gelantine, and cinnamon or lemon rind, set in a mould. It was sometimes reheated and served as a drink.

5. *by birth a Tyrrell*: Walter Tyrrell was reputed to have shot the arrow that killed William Rufus, King of England (1087–1100); and Sir James Tyrrell was beheaded in 1502 for treason after confessing to the murder of the princes in the Tower of London.

6. *two pieces of red flannel, in the shape of a cross, on her inner garment*: a more extreme form of superstition than those usually recorded by Mrs Gaskell in *Cranford*. Red is considered a protection against witchcraft, and the cross a protection against various forms of evil.

7. *charges*: the instructions given by a bishop or archdeacon to his clergy.

8. *pice*: an Indian coin to the value of a quarter of an anna.

9. *station to station*: military posts.

10. *a little picture . . . of the Virgin and the little Saviour*: Raphael's 'Madonna della Sedia'. There is a tradition that it is circular in form because Raphael made the original sketch rapidly on the top of a cask.

11. *Aga*: Turkish for Lord, often used as a courtesy title for the English in India.

CHAPTER XII

1. *As somebody says, that was the question*: Hamlet, III, i, 56.
2. *pièce de résistance*: originally the main dish of a meal, the sense in which Mrs Gaskell uses the phrase here.
3. *a passage in Dickens*: Pickwick Papers, Chapter XXXII.
4. *the veiled prophet in Lalla Rookh*: the Great Mokanna, the veiled Prophet-chief of Thomas Moore's *Lalla Rookh* (1817).
5. *Rowlands' Kalydor*: a popular and much advertised cosmetic, used as a face wash.
6. *Peruvian bonds*: vouchers for money lent to the Peruvian government.
7. *Wombwell*: See Chapter IX, note 3.
8. *'surveying mankind from China to Peru'*: from the opening of Dr Johnson's 'The Vanity of Human Wishes'.
9. *chintz*: a cotton cloth printed with bright-coloured patterns.
10. *Tibbie Fowler*: a traditional Scottish song adapted by Robert Burns. Tintock Tap, in the line quoted, is Tinto Hill in the Central Lowlands.
11. *I put in my wonder*: a curious usage, 'my query' (i.e. something wondered about).
12. *mésalliance*: misalliance, to marry beneath one.
13. *her Order*: her place in the aristocracy.
14. *merinoes and beavers*: merino is a fine silky wool, originally from a Spanish breed of sheep; beavers means beaver fur.
15. *our liege lady*: the use of this feudal term, to denote homage given to someone of superior position, is characteristic of the narrator's gentle mockery of Cranford's outmoded social forms.
16. *the Queen of Spain's legs*: referring to the extravagant rules of etiquette observed at the Spanish royal court. The source is the Countess d'Aulnoy's *Mémoires de la Cour d'Espagne* (1692).

CHAPTER XIII

1. *welly stawed*: very nearly brought to a standstill.
2. *green tea*: green tea is roasted almost immediately after being gathered, unlike black tea in which fermentation is produced by exposure to the air. It is also sometimes artificially coloured.
3. *joint-stock bank*: see Chapter V, note 1.
4. *her being without teeth*: false teeth made of porcelain were introduced in England in the late eighteenth century.

CHAPTER XIV

1. *the Rubric*: any direction or heading, originally in red lettering, especially, as here, a liturgical direction in the Book of Common Prayer.

2. *Mammon*: the god of riches.

3. *I've money in the Savings Bank*: the first Savings Bank in Britain was founded by Henry Duncan in Dumfriesshire, 1810, and the practice soon spread to England. They were non-profit-making and were regarded as an important means of working-class self-improvement.

4. *'Ah! vous dirai-je, maman?*: a French song first published in Francis Sands, *Les Amours de Silvano* (1780).

5. *the loyal wool-work now fashionable in Cranford*: Mary Smith is again being ironic. The making of pictures in the fashion described by Mrs Gaskell was popular in the late eighteenth and early nineteenth centuries, and unfashionable by this date.

6. *filthy lucre*: money. A striking example of the slang terms sometimes used by Mary Smith.

7. *lion couchant*: a heraldic term meaning a crouching or resting lion. Elaborate moulds of this kind were popular throughout the Victorian period.

8. *I have seen uglier things under a glass shade before now*: glass shades or domes were one of the commonest forms of ornamentation in a Victorian drawing room. They might contain almost anything; a flower or shell arrangement; dolls; even locks of hair of dead loved ones.

9. *the East India Tea Company*: the East India Company was founded in 1600 and its monopolistic powers restricted in 1834. The expansion of the tea trade dates from the middle of the eighteenth century.

10. *quality*: people of high birth or position.

11. *chiffonier*: a piece of furniture like a small sideboard, with a marble top over a small cupboard and sometimes shelves.

12. *ladies'-finger biscuits*: see Chapter VII, note 10.

13. *another account-book that I have heard of*: beyond the obvious meaning here, there is also possibly a reference to the widow's mite, Mark xii, 42–4.

14. *lion*: E. P. Watson points out that in earlier editions this word is often given as loin. Lion does seem to be the more sensible reading and has been adopted here.

CHAPTER XV

1. *boxes of tea, with cabalistic inscriptions all over them*: see Chapter VIII, note 8.

2. *Congou . . . Souchong . . . Gunpowder . . Pekoe*: various kinds of china tea; Gunpowder is green, the rest black.

3 *train oil*: whale oil, from the old Dutch word 'traen'.

4. *the Old Hundredth*: a hymn tune, 'Praise God from whom all blessings flow,' composed originally for Psalm 134, but later used for Psalm 100, hence its name.

5. *stories . . . like Baron Munchausen's*: the hero of *Baron Munchausen's Narrative of his Marvellous Travels* (1758) by Rudolph Eric Raspe, who is notorious for the exaggerated accounts of his adventures.

6. *the siege of Rangoon*: see Chapter VI, note 8.

7. *Nabob*: the name given in the eighteenth and early nineteenth centuries to Anglo-Indians who returned home wealthy from India.

CHAPTER XVI

1. *quite as good as an Arabian Night any evening*: a reference to Scheherazade, who preserved her life by telling to the Sultan every night the stories that make up the *Arabian Nights*. The story of Sinbad the Sailor is one of these.

2. *the Father of the Faithful*: this would normally mean Abraham, but Miss Pole probably means Mohammed.

3. *negus*: made of wine, usually port or sherry, hot water and spices.

4. *Miss Betty (formerly her maid)*: E. P. Watson points out that this is inconsistent with an earlier reference (p. 106) where Mrs Jamieson is described as the former mistress of Miss Betty Barker's elder sister.

5. *the Preston Guild*: a guild of merchants, granted a Charter by Henry II, which has held festivals every five years since 1329.

6. *downright Dissenters*: nonconformists, who refused to subscribe to the doctrines and authority of the Church of England. See *Cousin Phillis*, Part I, note 2. Peter's ironic tone, here and elsewhere, is similar to that of Mary Smith, though he can of course be more open with his jokes, being both older than her and a man.

NOTES

Cousin Phillis

PART I

1. *Eltham to Hornby*: Eltham, like Cranford, Duncombe (in 'Mr Harrison's Confessions'), and Hollingford (in *Wives and Daughters*) is traditionally assumed to be based on Knutsford, the Cheshire town where Mrs Gaskell grew up. A railway was constructed at Knutsford in 1862, and this may well have led Mrs Gaskell to consider the kind of impact it could have on relatively isolated communities, though the actual setting of *Cousin Phillis* is some twenty years earlier.

2. *sturdy Independent*: the Independents were one of the older nonconformist sects, founded in the seventeenth century. They emphasised the autonomy of local congregations, and because of this were less highly organised and hierarchical than many other branches of nonconformity. Mrs Gaskell herself was a Unitarian.

3. *'Spare the rod, and spoil the child'*: Samuel Butler, *Hudibras*, I, 844. Considered as an appropriate motto for Nonconformists who were often regarded as imposing severe restraints on their children, sometimes to the point of cruelty. Mrs Gaskell is very careful to point out that while Paul's childhood was strict, it was in no sense cruel.

4. *wallowing in the mire*: 2 Peter ii, 22.

5. *vaulted into France*: see *Cranford*, Chapter IV, note 12.

6. *we call the Church clergyman here 'parson'*: Mrs Gaskell really explains this point herself, but it is significant that Holdsworth needs to have pointed out the difference between the Anglican 'parson' and Nonconformist 'minister'. It is an early indication of his view of life being far removed from that of Hope Farm.

7. *stone-crop . . . yellow fumitory*: stone-crop is a herb with bright yellow flowers which grows in masses on rocks or walls, in this case on the stone horse-mount: fumitory is also a plant that grows abundantly, hence its name, which means smoke of the earth.

8. *'the curate' . . . 'the rector'*: the joke is a fairly obvious one, but

neatly characteristic of Holman. By derivation a rector is someone who directs, a curate someone who cares.

9. *May-day*: celebrating the coming of Spring and disliked by Holman because of its pagan associations.

10. *handmaiden*: Luke i, 48.

11. *Abraham's steward . . . well*: Genesis xxiv.

12. *fraxinella*: a perennial plant with white flowers and leaves similar to those of the ash.

13. *traces*: the straps or chains of a horses' harness.

14. *whip-cord the plough-whips*: to furnish with new whipcord the whips used for driving the plough-horse.

15. *dauby*: wet and sticky.

16. *'Come all harmonious tongues'*: composed by Benjamin Milgrove (1731–1810) and published 1769. It was contained in the old *Union Hymn Book*, and is to be found in *The English Hymnal*, 1906, no. 196.

17. *the little petticoated lad*: it was common practice throughout the nineteenth century for boys up to the age of five or six to be dressed in smocks, skirts or petticoats.

18. *a line or two of Latin*: the reference is to Virgil's *Georgics* (29 B.C.) which are mentioned several times in *Cousin Phillis*. While clearly appreciating the beauty of the poetry, the *Georgics* appeal especially to Holman because of the close knowledge of rural and agricultural life they contain (see p. 296). The allusion here referring to the colours of an evening landscape could be to several passages in the *Georgics*, but probably to Book I, 453–5, which reads, in C. Day Lewis's translation:

The dark-green stands for rain, flame colour foretells an east wind;
But, should stains begin to be mixed with a ruddy fire,
Both wind and rain are brewing and you'll see them boil over.

19. *catechism*: a summary of religious doctrine taught on a question and answer basis, which children from a very early age were expected to learn by heart.

20. *I try to keep the parish rod as well as the parish bull*: to act, in effect, as the farmer-minister he is described as being at the beginning of the story.

21. *beau-pot*: a large ornamental vase for cut flowers.

22. *Matthew Henry's Bible*: Matthew Henry (1662–1714), Nonconformist minister and biblical commentator. His *Exposition of the Old and New Testament* (1710) provided the annotation for many

editions of the Bible. Perhaps referred to here is *The Christian's Complete Family Bible* (1817).

23. *shovel-board*: a wooden board used in the game of shove halfpenny.

24. *shunting*: the shifting of a train from one line to another.

25. *farriery*: the art of shoeing horses.

26. *all's fish that comes to my net*: proverbial: the phrase exists in many different forms; for example, 'What was his father's could not escape his fingers, all was fish that came to his net' (John Bunyan, *Mr Badman*, 1680, Chapter 1).

27. *'Whether we eat or drink . . . the glory of God'*: 1 Corinthians x, 31.

28. *tempus fugit*: time flies, a hackneyed cliché being all Paul can remember of his Latin.

PART II

1. *gauds*: trinkets.

2. *the Old Adam*: unregenerate man.

3. *a migration from the blue bed to the brown*: Goldsmith, *The Vicar of Wakefield*, Chapter 1. The phrase indicates a narrow but happy existence.

4. *George Stephenson*: (1781–1848) civil engineer and pioneer of steam locomotion.

5. *tillage*: the process of tilling or cultivating land.

6. *barrel*: the trunk of a horse or cow.

7. *as if they had been St Peter and St Paul*: whose views on the nature and upbringing of children were particularly severe. See, for example, Romans i, 28–30, where, as Samuel Butler was later to point out, 'St Paul had placed disobedience to parents in very ugly company'. (*The Way of All Flesh*, 1903, Chapter 5.)

8. *he drives his carriage*: indicating high social status within the community.

9. *the clown's definition*: Voltaire, *Philosophical Dictionary* (1764).

10. *cranching*: a variation of 'craunching' or 'crunching'.

11. *Baretti*: Guiseppe Baretti, editor of numerous handbooks and dictionaries, including A *Dictionary of the English and Italian Language*, 2 vols, 1778.

12. *theodolite*: instrument used by surveyors for measuring angles.

13. *fidging fain*: eager to the point of restlessness.

14. *Manzoni, I Promessi Sposi*: Alessandro Manzoni (1785–1873).

His historical novel *I Promessi Sposi* (1827), translated as *The Be-trothed*, was very popular with Victorian readers. The central story tells of two peasant lovers who eventually survive heavy social and religious pressures and marry.

15. *a novel to read*: many Nonconformists believed that the read-ing of novels was sinful. As in certain earlier moments, Paul under-stands this, Holdsworth does not. The comparison with Virgil a few lines later shows just how deep is Holdsworth's lack of understand-ing. See Part I, note 18.

16. *bugbear*: an object of terror or dislike.

17. *dram-drinking*: drinking spirits.

18. *stone-pines*: umbrella-shaped pine trees with edible seeds.

PART III

1. *she would have called them navvies*: the way of life of the navvies working on the railways during this early period was notorious for its drunkenness and immorality.

2. *agait*: going about with.

3. *Ceres*: the Roman goddess of agriculture.

4. *like the sleeping beauty*: who in Perrault's famous story slept for a hundred years and was awakened by a Prince's kiss. The irony of Holdsworth's comparison is obvious, but also important here is the irony of Phillis's 'seclusion'.

5. *'Servants, obey in all things your masters according to the flesh'*: Colossians iii, 22.

6. *all of them went down in ships*: Psalms cvii, 23, 'They that go down to the sea in ships, That do business in great waters.'

7. *I supose he went in a steamer?*: Holdsworth would, at this time, have been more likely to travel by sailing ship: but there were steamers crossing the Atlantic: Brunel's *Great Western* had made the trip in fifteen days in 1838.

PART IV

1. *De Lolme on the British Constitution (or some such title)*: Jean Louis de Lolme, *The Constitution of England*, published in Amsterdam, 1771, and in an English translation four years later. It was reprinted as a standard work throughout the nineteenth cen-tury.

2. *in some book of poetry*: the lines quoted are from Wordsworth's

'She dwelt among the untrodden ways', one of his 'Lucy' poems. The woman Holdsworth eventually marries is called Lucille – 'that's our English Lucy, I suppose?' (p. 295).

3. *Georgics*: see Part I, note 18.

4. *Tower of Babel*: Genesis xi, 1–9.

5. '*Whatsoever thy hand findeth to do, do it with all thy might*': Ecclesiastes ix, 10.

6. *that's our English Lucy, I suppose*: see above, note 2.

7. '*harvest of the first fruits*': probably Exodus xxiii, 29.

8. *in the first Georgic*: see Part I, note 18.

9. *sniggled*: snickered, laughed at.

10. *farred*: an unusual usage: to wish someone to be far, i.e. at a distance.

11. *need to be a deaf adder*: Psalms lviii, 4–5.

12. *gaupus*: simpleton.

13. *cut out my tongue . . . for a caution to magpies*: 'magpie' is a common dialect word for a gossip or scold, and the bird itself is a traditional symbol of ill-omen.

14. *penny-post reform*: from 10 January 1840 a letter of up to half an ounce in weight could be sent anywhere within Britain for one penny, postage being pre-paid and indicated by the use of adhesive stamps. The reform, always associated with its architect, Rowland Hill, was extremely controversial and accepted grudgingly by the Post Office.

15. *hoo*: her, she.

16. *Measter*: master.

17. '*Behold, thou hast instructed many . . . thou art troubled*': Job iv, 3–5.

18. *as a light set on a hill*: Matthew v, 14.

19. '*The Lord giveth and the Lord taketh away, Blessed be the name of the Lord*': Job i, 21.

20. '*My sins I confess to God*: Isaiah i, 18.

21. *welly*: very nearly.

NOTES

Appendix A

THE LAST GENERATION IN ENGLAND

1. *Southey . . . a history of English domestic life*: Edinburgh *Review*, 1848, volume 87, p. 390.

2. *the 'Doctor, &c.'*: The *Doctor* is a miscellany by Southey published between the years 1834 and 1847. The connecting link between the articles on a wide variety of subjects is provided by Dr Daniel Dove of Doncaster.

3. *ton*: style, fashion.

4. *cadets*: the younger or junior members of a family.

5. *ci-devant*: former.

6. *the Mohawks*. sometimes spelled Mohocks, the name given, after the tribe of Red Indians, to street gangs in the eighteenth century.

7. *basted up*: soaking in, covered by.

8. *calash and pattens*: see Cranford, p. 75, and Chapter I, note 8.

9. *'Jack' . . . Pref*: see Cranford, Chapter XI, note 2.

10. *squibs and crackers*: sharp or satirical remarks.

11. *comme il faut*: correct, proper.

12. *haute volée*: the leading members of society.

13. *broughams, droskys*: a brougham is a light, four-wheeled closed carriage; a drosky, a light two-wheeled open carriage.

14. *Adam and Eve in the weather-glass*: figures mounted on a weather-glass or barometer, appearing alternately to indicate fine or wet weather.

15. *dram-shop*: a bar selling spirits.

16. *brobdignagian*: huge. From Swift's *Gulliver's Travels*.

NOTES

Appendix B

THE CAGE AT CRANFORD

1. *since the year 1856*: probably a mistake. It should be 1853.

2. *a cross between a turban and a cap*: see *Cranford*, Chapter IX, note 2.

3. *servant-maiden Fanny*: another possible mistake. In *Cranford* Miss Pole's maidservant is called Betty at one point (p. 130) and Lizzy at another (p. 190).

4. *calico*: a fine cotton cloth originally from India.

5. *all of a piece with French things*: see *Cranford*, Chapter IV, note 12.

6. *go-cart*: a frame on wheels used originally to teach children to walk.

MORE ABOUT PENGUINS
AND PELICANS

Penguinews, which appears every month, contains details of all the new books issued by Penguins as they are published. From time to time it is supplemented by *Penguins in Print*, which is a complete list of all titles available. (There are some five thousand of these.)

A specimen copy of Penguinews will be sent to you free on request. For a year's issues (including the complete lists) please send £1 if you live in the British Isles, or elsewhere. Just write to Dept EP, Penguin Books Ltd, Harmondsworth, Middlesex, enclosing a cheque or postal order, and your name will be added to the mailing list.

In the U.S.A.: For a complete list of books available from Penguin in the United States write to Dept CS, Penguin Books Inc., 7110 Ambassador Road, Baltimore, Maryland 21207.

In Canada: For a complete list of books available from Penguin in Canada write to Penguin Books Canada Ltd, 41 Steelcase Road West, Markham, Ontario.

Jane Austen

SENSE AND SENSIBILITY

EDITED BY TONY TANNER

Jane Austen's tale of two sisters carries its subject in its title: good sense on the one hand and an excess of romantic 'sensibility' on the other. But this, as Tony Tanner makes clear in his introduction, is only a beginning. Far from being crudely schematic, *Sense and Sensibility* subtly probes, through the trials of its very real heroines, perennial questions about civilization and its discontents that have been more solemnly analysed in our own times. It is high drama, though acted out in sighs and glances and unspoken thoughts, of the kind to be found in 'a society which forced people to be at once very sociable – and very private'.

Also published by Penguins:

PERSUASION
Edited by D. W. Harding

PRIDE AND PREJUDICE
Edited by Tony Tanner

NORTHANGER ABBEY
Edited by Anne Ehrenpreis

MANSFIELD PARK
Edited by Tony Tanner

EMMA
Edited by Ronald Blythe

LADY SUSAN/THE WATSONS/SANDITON
Edited by Margaret Drabble

George Eliot

MIDDLEMARCH

EDITED BY W. J. HARVEY

Middlemarch (1871-2) is perhaps the masterpiece of a writer who is now recognized as a major literary figure of the nineteenth century. Virginia Woolf hailed as 'one of the few English novels written for adult people' this magnificent work in which George Eliot paints a luminous and spacious landscape of life in a provincial town. Indeed, in her analysis of human nature George Eliot achieved what Dr Leavis has called 'a Tolstoyan depth and reality'.

DANIEL DERONDA

EDITED BY BARBARA HARDY

In *Daniel Deronda*, her last work, the author of *Middlemarch* left behind the comfortable world of the Victorian middle classes to venture into areas of human experience that were completely new to the English novel. Like her hero, Deronda, she set out to come to terms with the English Jews, a society-within-a-society of which her contemporaries seemed to be oblivious. Like her remarkable heroine, Gwendolen Harleth, she discovered a vein in human relations that could lead, through the best intentions, only to despair.

Also published by Penguins:

SILAS MARNER
Edited by Q. D. Leavis

FELIX HOLT
Edited by Peter Coveney

SCENES OF CLERICAL LIFE
Edited by David Lodge

Elizabeth Gaskell

WIVES AND DAUGHTERS

WITH AN INTRODUCTION BY
LAURENCE LERNER

'The most underrated novel in English' is how Laurence
Lerner describes *Wives and Daughters*, Mrs Gaskell's last
work; and certainly the story of Mr Gibson's new marriage
and its influence on the lives of those closest to him is a
work of rare charm, combining pathos with wit, intelligence, and a perceptiveness about people and their relationships equalled only by Jane Austen and George Eliot. As
in *Cranford* she surrounds her fiction with a fragrant
evocation of English village life, but in *Wives and Daughters* this is underpinned by a sense of social change and of
the more basic realities of birth and death.

Also published by Penguins:

THE LIFE OF CHARLOTTE BRONTË

MARY BARTON

NORTH AND SOUTH

THE PENGUIN ENGLISH LIBRARY

Some Recent and Forthcoming Volumes